QUIET VILLAGE

Praise for Eden Darry

Z-Town

"The premise of the story is brilliant…The characters are well-developed and the good guys, at least, are easy to connect with. The bad guys (and there are more than one) are also well done…This is a wonderfully horrific, campy, gory, and romantic tale that I thoroughly enjoyed reading."—*Rainbow Reflections*

"Darry has a fantastic knack for spinning tales. The world building, character motivations and clear writing style kept me excited to read this book."—*Lesbian Review*

The House

"Eden Darry is on my to-watch list. I am eagerly anticipating her new release because I adored this one so much. The pacing was excellent; combining the thriller stalker with the haunted house was a stroke of genius causing threats from both sides and really putting the pressure on…If you have loved *The Shining*, *The Haunting of Hill House* (TV show), or *The Amityville Horror* then you should absolutely get this book. Eden Darry wrote a wonderful horror. It was exciting, captivating and had me on the edge of my seat with anticipation."—*Lesbian Review*

"For a debut novel, Eden Darry did really well. This book had everything a modern-day horror novel needed. A modern couple, a haunted house, and a talented author to combine the two. The atmosphere was eerie and the plot held a lot of suspense. The couple went between love and hate, and if only they had talked to one another! And the reader just kept turning those pages."—*Kat Loves Books*

"A solid debut that is creepy and intense."—*Lez Review Books*

Vanished

"*Vanished* by Eden Darry is a postapocalyptic horror that I thoroughly enjoyed. If you love stories where people have to survive against huge odds, postapocalyptic, end of the world kind of stories, then this is a must-read. If you love stories where something bad is lurking in the background being just sinister enough to make your skin crawl, then this is an awesome read."—*Lesbian Review*

"I really do like Darry's writing—she creates a great ominous atmosphere in her narrative. The initial chapters with the storm perfectly set the stage for what is to come. There's also a suitably unnerving and creepy feel as Loveday begins to realize that there is no one else in the village and a nice bit of tension while she and Ellery are searching houses."—*C-Spot Reviews*

By the Author

The House

Vanished

Z-Town

Quiet Village

QUIET VILLAGE

by
Eden Darry

2021

QUIET VILLAGE

ISBN 13: 978-1-63555-898-2

This Trade Paperback Original Is Published By
Bold Strokes Books, Inc.
P.O. Box 249
Valley Falls, NY 12185

First Edition: August 2021

CREDITS
EDITOR: RUTH STERNGLANTZ
PRODUCTION DESIGN: STACIA SEAMAN
COVER DESIGN: TAMMY SEIDICK

Acknowledgments

Thanks to Ruth again for endless patience and great advice. I'm very lucky. Radclyffe and Sandy, for publishing the stuff that comes out of my strange brain. And to anyone who reads it, I hope you like it. And lastly to Catherine. Always.

For Catherine

PROLOGUE

A t the sound of the horn he ran into the woods. The ground was spongy beneath his feet, and he felt like he was flying. He would have enjoyed the run under other circumstances but not tonight. Tonight he was running for his life.

He vaulted over a fallen tree, then pumped his legs to put on more speed. He was losing ground. He could hear it behind him, getting closer all the time. He knew he couldn't outrun it, but he had to try.

His lungs burned and so did his legs. He couldn't keep this up for much longer. He prayed for a miracle. If only he'd kept his nose out. If only he'd never come here.

He ran onto a well-used path where the ground went from soft and spongy to hard and compacted, and the force of his pounding feet reverberated up his exhausted legs. He did not stop. He would not stop running.

He should have known. When they came for him, he should have known. But how could he? That vacuous idiot in the village shop, how could he have guessed that? And not just her, but the—

Suddenly, he was hit hard from behind, and he went down. He put his hands out to break his fall and felt his palms burn as they tore on the small stones. The pain was nothing compared to what he felt when the thing tearing strips off his back bit down on his neck. Bright, burning fire. Blinding agony.

He screamed once before it turned him over and tore out his throat.

CHAPTER ONE

Collie Noonan opened her eyes. She reached without looking for her phone, knocking something off the crowded bedside table and onto the floor, and saw it was after two in the afternoon. Shit. She was supposed to call her sister Sasha at twelve.

Collie had been up most of the night working on characters for the new video game. Collie thought she had the best job in the world, and it took up most of her time, but she loved her sister. Sasha was probably the one person other than Tony she actually saw with any regularity.

She should have set her alarm. Since their grandparents died a few years ago, Sasha and Sasha's daughter Lana were the only family Collie had left.

Their grandparents had raised them and died within three months of each other. It was a huge blow for them both, and Collie missed them badly. She knew Sasha did too.

Collie hit the Skype app on her phone. Sasha had tried to call twice. Collie felt a stab of guilt. She pressed redial and winced against the loud bleeps that signalled the call was trying to connect.

Sasha picked up on the second cacophony of bleeps.

"You're a dick," were the first words out of her mouth.

"I know, I know. I'm really sorry," Collie said.

Sasha rolled her eyes. "You missed Lana. She had to go back to school."

"I still can't believe they let her come home for lunch. Remember how the dinner ladies used to patrol the playground with their walkie-talkies like prison guards?"

"Don't change the subject," Sasha said. "You're right, they were formidable."

"Is she really mad?" Collie asked. "Are you?"

Sasha rolled her eyes again. "Of course not. We're used to you. And you send great birthday gifts, which makes up for your unreliability. And the fact you're such a funny onion."

"I am unreliable," Collie said and smiled at Sasha's old nickname for her.

"You aren't. Not really. Not about the things that matter," Sasha said.

Collie heard a crash. "Is that your end?"

Sasha turned from the camera for a second. "Probably the bloody cat knocking something over. Hang on a sec while I check."

Collie waited. She could hear muffled thumping, and then Sasha was back.

"Sorry about that."

"No worries. That cat is a menace," Collie said.

"Tell me about it. Lana loves him, though," Sasha said.

"Well I—" Collie cut off as Sasha's head swivelled around and away from the camera. "Sasha?" Collie said.

"Yeah? Sorry, something else just crashed."

"The cat again?"

"I don't think so. It wasn't Tufty before either. I think it's outside," Sasha said.

"One of your lovely neighbours," Collie said.

Sasha gave a half smile and looked behind her again. She didn't seem right. She seemed…jumpy.

"Sash?"

"Yeah?"

"Are you okay? You seem a bit…I don't know, not yourself," Collie said.

Sasha sighed, and the screen stuttered, froze as she rubbed a hand across her eyes. "It's Damian."

At the mention of her sister's ex, Collie felt the familiar anger rise. "If he's bothering you again—"

"It was just a letter. He sent me a letter," Sasha said.

"He's not allowed to do that."

"It wasn't threatening or abusive," Sasha said, and Collie remembered how Sasha had always made excuses for him, always covered up for him. Even now. Collie guessed some habits were hard to break.

"What did the letter say?" Collie asked and tried to keep her voice even. Sasha didn't need judgement. It had cost her a lot to break free of that piece of shit.

"Just how sorry he was. He regrets everything, and he knows he made mistakes."

"Made mistakes? He battered you." Collie wished she hadn't said it. Sasha knew—she'd been there. She didn't need Collie to remind her.

"I know, Colleen," Sasha said.

"I hate it when you call me that."

"I hate it when you get all judgemental," Sasha shot back.

"I'm not judging you, Sash. I hate him," Collie said.

"I know you do. And you don't have to worry—one letter isn't going to send me running back to him. He beat me up once, and I'm not risking him doing it again. I know what he is," Sasha said.

"Okay, good. What did you do with the letter?"

"I threw it away."

"You didn't give it to the police?" Collie asked.

"No. I don't want it all dredged up again. He went to prison for what he did, and this is the first time I've heard from him in two years."

"He only got out four months ago," Collie said.

"I know. If he sends another, maybe I'll go to the police. The letter seemed to be an apology. He didn't mention getting back together or anything like that," Sasha said.

Not yet, Collie thought. "Okay, then. Just please, if he sends anything else—does anything else—let me know."

"I will, I—"

Another crash and the connection stuttered and juddered as Sasha turned around.

"Sasha?" Collie said. "Sasha, what's going on?"

"What the hell are you doing here? Get out," Sasha said to someone Collie couldn't see.

"Sasha? Sasha? Who's there?" Collie gripped the phone hard enough to crack it. "Sasha?"

The screen went blank. A little message popped up: *connection lost.*

Collie dialled 999. Something was wrong. Someone was in Sasha's house, someone she didn't want there. Collie's stomach turned because she knew who it was. Fucking Damian. Just like before when he beat the shit out of her. She jumped out of bed and dragged on jeans and a T-shirt while she spoke to the operator, the phone sandwiched between her shoulder and ear.

Bypassing the assortment of jumbled shoes, Collie picked up her car keys and ran out of her flat. Barefoot, she sprinted up the hallway with a sinking feeling that she was too late, much too late.

CHAPTER TWO

Collie loaded up the last box and slammed the boot closed.

"You'll crack the rear windshield," Lana said from behind her.

Collie turned to look at her niece. She was slight and fragile looking, even though Collie knew that was the last thing she was. Like Sasha, Lana had a spine of steel.

Sasha fought him. Damian. The police told her Sasha had fought like a hero. Collie knew she would have. There was no way Sasha would have left her daughter easily.

They said she fought in the ambulance too. To live. Damian had needed an ambulance as well. Collie took some comfort from that. She'd hurt him, and Damian was only just out of hospital.

When Collie arrived at her house that day—that awful fucking day—the police were already there. They'd stopped her going inside, so she knew it was bad. Collie didn't believe all that psychic-twin bullshit, but she swore she knew the moment Sasha died. She felt it, like someone ripping out her heart.

And now, he was going to prison for a long, long time, but it didn't matter how long he got. Sasha wasn't coming back. And Collie had a broken ten-year-old child to raise now, and her sister was fucking dead.

Collie rubbed her hands across her eyes. "How are you doing, Lana?"

Lana reached out and hugged Collie, squeezed her waist. "It's weird. I want to leave because of the memories, but I also don't want to. This is where I lived with Mum. You know?"

Collie squeezed her back. Christ, did she know. For a second, it was all too much. A sob fought its way up from her chest and into her throat, making it ache. Heroically, she pushed it down. Lana needed her to be strong, so she would be strong. She could cry at night, when she was in her bed and Lana was asleep and unaware.

"I know, sweetheart. I know exactly what you mean. We don't have to go, you know? We can stay here," Collie said.

"We sold the house."

"We can buy one close by. Or anywhere you want. You tell me. Whatever you need, sweetheart." Collie squeezed her again and kissed the top of her blond head.

"I love you, Collie. I'm glad you got me," Lana said.

"Me too." Collie didn't say that the only other option was Lana's father's parents, who were knocking on for eighty. Collie would make sure they kept in touch with them, though. They'd already lost their son when Lana was a baby. They didn't deserve to lose a granddaughter as well.

Suddenly, someone grabbed them both from behind. "Group hug." Tony.

"Get off, you weirdo," Collie said but didn't move. Tony was her best friend and had been amazing throughout everything. Lana loved him.

"Don't be mean to Tony." Lana laughed. Tony was one of the few people who could make her laugh at the moment.

"Yeah, don't be mean, Colleen." Tony gave them both a final squeeze and released them.

He stood at over six feet and had tattoos all the way up both arms. When Lana was a baby, she'd been fascinated by them. Today he wore a Chelsea FC shirt and Bermuda shorts.

"You look like a thug. Where's your hair?" Collie asked.

"I shaved it off. Summer vibes," he said.

"It's April," Lana said.

"Well, little La, you've got to be prepared. Summer comes up fast, and I want to be ready." Tony ran his huge hand over his freshly balded head. "Plus, the chicks love it."

"Oh yeah. Football hooligan chic." Collie rolled her eyes. "Since you're here, you can make yourself useful. We've just got the furniture to go, and then we're done."

Collie told Lana she could take whatever she wanted from the house to bring with them. Lana decided to keep her bedroom furniture and a chest of drawers that her parents were given as a wedding present. She chose a few pictures, some candles, and a houseplant. The rest they sold to the new owners of the house. It was their first home, and they were grateful for anything Collie wanted to leave.

Collie was surprised the house sold at all, let alone so quickly. She worried no one would want to buy a house a woman was murdered in. But it was in a good location close to the Tube and parks and decent schools. It sold quicker than her flat in Vauxhall had been rented out.

Collie was still in two minds about selling or renting it. She'd decided to rent it out for now, but who knew? Maybe they'd love country life and buy a farm or something.

Collie still wasn't sure why Lana wanted to move to Suffolk—she'd literally pointed at a random house for rent on the internet and said, "That one." And maybe letting a ten-year-old decide something so big was a bit stupid, but Collie was prepared to do whatever it took to help her get through this fucking nightmare. If Lana wanted to move to the moon, Collie would bust a gut trying to make that happen too.

With Tony's help, they loaded the furniture into his van pretty quickly. The plan was he'd follow them down and help unload at the other end. Collie knew it was a workday for him, and he was losing money by helping them, but when she tried to pay him, he refused. The only payment he would take was beer and pizza at the other end.

Collie and Tony's friendship was a strange thing. They'd met at a video game convention five years ago. Collie was there with work, and Tony because he loved gaming. He'd asked her what it was like being a woman in a totally male-dominated industry. Collie braced herself for a moronic conversation with a meathead, but Tony proved to be the opposite.

They'd exchanged numbers and gone for a drink after the event. Collie had a brief panic wondering if he'd thought it was a date. Tony laughed and poked her with one of his sausage fingers. He'd told her she was a bit butch for him, but he was flattered, and then he told her he was trans. They stayed in the pub until closing that night, talking about everything and laughing so much Collie's belly hurt. There was something about Tony that made her feel like she'd known him her whole life. Other than Sasha, Collie didn't remember ever being so comfortable around another person.

They'd been tight ever since, and the last couple of months Tony turned out to be the best friend she'd ever had. A rock. Collie loved him. And he was amazing with Lana too.

But one of the best things about him was he could move furniture like nobody's business.

CHAPTER THREE

"Why you'd want to move to the middle of nowhere is bloody beyond me," Tony muttered as he put the last box down on the living room floor.

"You know why," Collie said, opening Tufty the cat's carry box. He stuck his fluffy black head out, seemed to consider a moment, then bolted up the stairs. "It was all over the news when my sister died. And that fucking internet journalist plastered Lana's face all over their website. Everyone at her school knew what happened."

"London's a big place. You could have just moved north of the river," Tony said.

"We wanted somewhere quiet where people didn't automatically know who Lana was. Besides, me and Sasha grew up around here."

"You lived somewhere in Southwold for the first four years of your life. Not Hymen," Tony said.

"Hyam, you div." Collie elbowed him. "This is Hyam. Besides, it's only half an hour to Southwold."

"You plan on visiting Southwold a lot? Because God knows there's bugger all to do around here," Tony said.

Collie had got that sinking feeling as they drove through the village. If you could even call it that. One mini-roundabout, a co-op, and a pub did not a village make. Well, when you let ten-year-olds make decisions, this was what happened.

Maybe she wasn't being totally fair—there was a hairdresser's, and a bakery. Collie sighed. Had she made a big mistake moving her and Lana here? Collie felt like she was feeling her way through mud as far as Lana was concerned.

Collie had never given any thoughts to children. They hadn't really figured in her life plan. Now, here she was, raising her dead sister's child. Lana, who had lost both her parents, seemed to be dealing much better with it than Collie, or at least that's how it seemed. Collie was out of her depth. All she could feel was this overwhelming, crippling grief that lay on her chest like a concrete pillow. Sometimes it hurt to breathe.

Lana had seen the house online, on one of those property websites. She'd tapped the screen and said, "There. That's where I want to live."

"Why?" Collie asked.

"I googled the village—"

"Of course you did. I didn't know how to google at ten," Collie said and had immediately been given one of *those* looks. The ones all kids gave to hopelessly useless adults.

"Aunt Collie, you didn't even *have* computers. Weren't you still writing on stone tablets?"

"Cheeky little git." Collie had laughed and thrown a pillow at the kid. "But seriously, what did Google say?"

Lana looked up and wrinkled her little brow. Collie wanted to eat her up. Lana recited, "Steeped in Anglo-Saxon history, the county of Woden is home to quaint farming villages and unspoiled walking trails through forest and farmland, along with beautiful walks along the River Woden. The village of Hyam is still full of medieval structures, including a group of ancient standing stones known locally as a miniature Stonehenge."

"You memorized a tourist website? Wow, what a loser," Collie joked, though Lana knew she was in awe of her ability to memorize things.

"Jealously is an ugly trait, Aunt Collie." Lana grinned and laughed.

"Yeah, yeah. So you like the Anglo-Saxon history and the hiking?"

"I just think it looks like a really nice place where nothing bad happens. You know? And it's a nowhere place. No one will know who I am there, or what happened to Mum," Lana said quietly.

Collie swallowed the lump in her throat. She knew exactly what Lana meant. Even if she wasn't sure before, she was now. She wanted Lana to feel safe, and if a sleepy little village in the middle of nowhere did that for her, well, that's where they were going.

Collie sighed when Lana said that and pulled her into a hug. When she thought about the shitbag journalist who found Lana's school picture and posted it online, she wanted to track him down and kill him. *The London Eye* was what the online rag was called. Collie had emailed and begged them to take the picture down, but by then it was too late.

So, here they were. Luckily it was only a rental, and they could move any time after this initial twelve months. Collie could do her work from anywhere, so that wasn't a problem. They'd make the best of it. And Collie would do her utmost not to damage an already broken child even further.

❖

Lana felt the satisfying crunch of gravel under her feet as she walked up the long drive. Their house sat at the end, completely by itself and surrounded by high hedges. It was what Collie called *secluded*.

Tall, thick trees lined each side of the drive, and bushes and brambles squatted next to them.

There was another drive, but that one narrow, off to the left, which Collie assumed led to another house. Other than that, it was just Lana and Aunt Collie here.

The only downside was their bins were located right at the bottom of the drive, near the road, and it was going to be a pain to have to walk all the way down there every time they needed to put them out. And Collie said it was going to be Lana's job like it was at home.

Lana stopped and listened to the birds who called each other from the trees. The only birds she ever saw in London were pigeons, so it was nice to see the little brown and yellow ones that hopped from branch to branch above her.

Lana wasn't sure how to feel about her mother's death. Whenever she tried to think about it, it all just felt too huge, too horrible. She knew she'd have to deal with it at some point. Aunt Collie got her a counsellor down here, and Lana liked him well enough. She wasn't sure if she trusted him with this yet, though.

Lana looked up at the blazing blue sky and thought about how her mother would never see this again. Would never feel the sun warm her face. Lana's eyes prickled. Her stomach went watery, and she tried her best to swallow down the sob before it got past her chest.

It didn't work. She let out a sob, and the tears ran hot down her face. Then big arms were lifting her, and she turned her face into the solid shoulder. Tony. She loved Tony. He always made everything feel better—like Aunt Collie. Lana couldn't think of two better people to have if she couldn't have her mother.

"Come on, let's get you inside. It's all right, Lana. It's all right."

CHAPTER FOUR

Emily Lassiter sat back and rubbed her eyes. In front of her was a stack of workbooks she still had to mark. It was already past eight, and she wanted to follow up on a few leads she'd been emailed. Plus, she hadn't eaten yet.

Emily sighed and wondered, not for the first time, why she was doing this. Putting herself through this. Then she looked at the photo on her desk. It was taken about two years ago at her mum and stepdad's anniversary party. The picture was of all of them. Her sister had flown over from Spain, and both her brothers came down too. In the picture they all smiled for the camera.

All of her parents' children looking happy and healthy in the last photo that would ever be taken of them all together. The last time any of them would be happy. All of them completely unaware that in twelve months, her youngest brother Charlie would have gone missing.

Emily and her brother Chris were five and three when their parents divorced. Three years later, Emily's mum met her stepdad, Carl. Emily loved him to bits and thought of him as her dad too. Not that she didn't love her own father, but Carl was just as involved, and perhaps weirdly, both her natural father and her stepdad got on pretty well.

Emily was almost ten when Charlie was born, and from the moment she saw him, she loved him best—they all had.

Emily could never remember him crying, though he must have. He was a kind and sweet and loving baby and hadn't changed when he grew up.

Her mother liked to tell stories about how, when Emily was eleven, she'd taken him out in her doll's pram and pretended he was hers. She'd gone up and down the street talking to neighbours about the weather and other things she'd heard her mother talk to them about.

She really thought they'd believed her, as well. Of course, as a woman of now thirty-three, she saw how ridiculous she must have seemed. But Charlie was special. Everyone saw it. He'd been everyone's favourite, and his disappearance left a huge yawning crater in their lives.

Emily refused to believe he'd just decided one day to disappear. Charlie was a free spirit, but he loved his family. He doted on his nieces and nephews and was close to their parents. Emily knew the general consensus was he'd killed himself, and the body just hadn't been recovered yet. None of his cards had been used, and there was no trace of him anywhere.

Emily wondered, as she'd done so many times, if she was just kidding herself. If she just refused to believe the terrible truth and had put her life on hold to find him for no reason. Was she wasting her time? Some nights, like tonight, she thought maybe that's exactly what she was doing.

But something inside her—the journalist she'd been before she decided to do this—couldn't stop. Couldn't accept it. She had to keep looking, and her gut told her the answers were in Hyam. She just had to ask the right questions.

Emily pushed away from her desk and stood. She stretched out her back and felt a satisfying pop. First, dinner. She thought she had some frozen thing or another in the compartment that pitifully passed for a freezer in her twenty-year-old fridge.

Once upon a time, Emily loved to cook. She'd had a little flat in North London with a sliver of balcony overlooking the park. She'd often fired up the tiny barbecue she'd managed to fit on it and had friends over.

Friends. They seemed like a foreign concept as well now. She still got the occasional text or Facebook message, but to all intents and purposes, she'd cut them off. She'd had to. When she moved to Hyam and took the job as a teacher—dusting off her old qualification that she never thought she'd use again—she cut herself off from most people. No one in the village knew who she really was or why she was here. For reasons she couldn't explain, she wanted it kept that way.

Well, she could explain it. From the research she'd done so far, she'd found three people had been reported as missing in or close to Hyam in the last five years. For a population of a few hundred, that was strange. They were all outsiders too—either recently moved here or to a neighbouring town. One was just passing through.

Admittedly, it wasn't much and probably could be explained away, but to Emily, it was a lead worth following.

Emily found it hard to organize her thoughts when it came to the village. On the surface, everyone seemed nice enough and polite, if not friendly. But Emily couldn't help thinking there was something going on beneath the surface. It was almost like when you saw a house with thick paper lining the walls—you knew the plaster underneath was probably rotten.

That was why she'd started her search here—that and the emails Charlie sent her. He'd found out something and was worried about something. They were due to meet up. Charlie had something he wanted to tell her, but he'd disappeared before he could. This was the last place Charlie was seen alive. He'd been a teacher too. In the same school but teaching very little ones. Luckily, he hadn't been here long enough for her to come down and visit, so no one knew who she really was. Plus, they had different surnames, so that was useful as well.

Emily went into the kitchen and looked in the fridge. She pulled out a container of unidentifiable brown stuff and had a vague idea it might be leftovers from a shepherd's pie she'd made. She chucked it in the microwave and looked out the kitchen window.

It was pitch black with just a sliver of moon visible in the sky. That had taken some getting used to. How dark it got in the country. So dark you could barely see your hand in front of your face.

The microwave pinged to signal it was done, and Emily took out the brown stuff. She decided she'd eat it while she marked a few more workbooks, then have an early night. The leads she wanted to follow up could wait until tomorrow.

Emily looked out into the pitch black one more time before she pulled down the kitchen blind.

CHAPTER FIVE

Collie woke to the sound of birds, and the buggers were *loud*. "What is your problem?" she muttered as she lifted the blind behind her bed and looked out. The tree outside her window was full of them.

Collie squinted against the sunlight. It was going to be another beautiful day. The sun was just rising, and Collie realized she usually saw a sunrise just as she was going to bed. She liked to work through the night. Everything had changed in such a short space of time. She supposed she should get used to these early mornings. Her days of working through the night were gone.

She lay back down, hoping to get another couple of hours, but heard the creaking floorboards as someone walked past her bedroom. Lana, had to be. Tony would be stomping.

Sighing, she rolled out of bed and pulled on a T-shirt and old pair of joggers. Sleeping naked would probably have to change as well. If Lana came into the bedroom unexpectedly, the last thing she'd want to see was her old aunt laid out in all her glory.

She'd pick up some pyjamas today. Maybe they'd go for a drive and find the closest real town. She'd see what Lana wanted to do.

By the time Collie got to the kitchen door, music was blaring out of someone's phone, and she could hear the clanging of pots and pans.

"Everything all right in here?" she asked.

Tony and Lana both spun around with guilty looks on their faces. "We didn't mean to wake you. We were going to do breakfast," Lana said.

Collie walked fully into the room and ruffled Lana's hair. "You didn't wake me. Those bloody birds did."

"Noisy, aren't they?" Tony said, wielding a spatula. "You really need to upgrade your kitchen appliances, Collie. I swear this spatula is older than you."

Collie looked at the partially melted implement. "I think I had it at university."

"Aunt Collie." Lana laughed. "It must be *years* old."

"Hey, not *that* old, thank you very much," Collie said.

"Well, however long, it's too long. And your pans are grim," Tony said.

"They're clean."

"There's barely any pan left you scrubbed them so hard," Tony said.

"Fine, fine. Why don't we drive into Southwold today? I'm sure they have pans and spatulas you two would find acceptable," Collie said, holding up her hands in surrender.

Lana laughed when Tony bumped her hip. "Sometimes shaming people into doing what you want works." He winked to let Lana know he was joking. "Don't you want to try the village first? Introduce yourself to the neighbours and support local business?"

"Do they even have any shops that would sell kitchen stuff?" Collie asked. It wasn't a bad idea, though. Maybe they could head to Southwold after.

Tony nodded. "I saw a sort of general stuff store on the way in. It's on the edge of the…What would you call it, high street?"

Collie shrugged. "I don't know what you'd call it. But we can stop in there first if you want."

Collie accepted the mug of tea that was set down in front of her and watched the two of them. Tony was good with Lana. He knew how to bring her out of herself. Collie knew she was grieving, and a laugh wasn't going to cure her of that, but Tony had the ability to make Lana forget for a little while.

He was leaving later today, and Collie was kind of scared. She'd always been Lana's fun aunt. The one who bought her junk food and let her stay up late. Collie wouldn't be that aunt any more. Now, Collie was the one who had to make sure she ate three meals a day and went to bed at a reasonable time. And that terrified her.

❖

Tony was right about the general store selling everything. It literally sold *everything*. Pots, pans, and spatulas as well as buckets, fishing rods, ironing boards, hammers, screws, light bulbs, and paddling pools.

It was bigger than it looked from the outside too. It went all the way back and was stuffed with shelves from floor to ceiling, that were also stuffed with all kinds of dusty junk.

"Help you?"

Collie turned at the sound of the voice behind her. It belonged to an older woman with short grey hair and eyes so brown they were almost black. The word *intense* came to mind.

"Oh, well, I was looking to update my kitchen utensils," Collie said. "You know, some pans and a spatula."

The woman nodded twice, short, economical nods that told Collie she was all about efficiency. "Over here. We've a set of pans and a set of utensils." The woman walked off without checking to see if Collie was following her.

Collie narrowly avoided knocking into a manky and decidedly creepy mannequin dressed in waders, a sparkly pink T-shirt, and a floppy sunhat. Weird.

"Your shop is very, um, interesting," Collie said.

The woman cut her eyes at Collie. "We've been here a long time. The shop's been in my family since the sixteenth century. We'll still be here a long time to come."

Collie wasn't sure about that. Wasn't village life dying out? People moving to cities and huge super malls being built—not to mention the internet. "You do good business then?" Collie asked.

"We do just fine." The woman was looking at her with open suspicion now.

"Sorry, that was nosy. I'm new here—moved in yesterday, actually," Collie said.

"Yes, I know. You moved into the old Roper place."

"Roper place? That's who lived there before us?" Collie asked.

"No. Wilf Roper lived there about fifteen years ago. Died in that house, he did. Worked up at the Highmore house for the Cobb family for years. Nice man. His kids rent the place out now to outsiders. Not that they last long."

"Outsiders don't last long?" Collie asked. This woman was all kinds of fun.

"Get bored. This life isn't for everyone. Those soft city people come here looking to get away, have a change of pace. Until they realize it isn't all bucolic or a Turner painting. Then they get bored and leave."

The woman didn't have to say out loud that she thought Collie was one of those soft city people. It was on the tip of her tongue to remind the woman that this soft city person was currently in her shop and about to spend money, but she changed her mind. She didn't want to alienate everyone on her first proper day here. There would be plenty of time to alienate everyone later.

"Well, I'm Collie, and over there is my niece, Lana," Collie said.

"Denise Cutmore. Pleased to meet you." Though the woman looked anything but. "And him?" She motioned to Tony, who was currently modelling a fake—or at least Collie hoped it was fake—stole, much to Lana's delight.

"That's Tony. He's just a friend. He's leaving today," Collie said.

Denise Cutmore looked Collie up and down, and she wondered if the woman was trying to decide whether they were a couple.

Whatever she decided, she'd clearly had enough of the small talk and turned back to the assorted pots and pans hanging off a wall. "There they are. Prices are on them."

The woman walked off and left Collie hoping not everyone in the village was like Denise Cutmore. Collie quickly chose what she wanted, paid and left.

Chapter Six

Emily walked into the tiny village shop and almost laughed at the woman standing at the counter.

"It's like mince, but made out of…soya, I think. It looks like mince beef." The woman was speaking to Margaret, who Emily knew had worked in the shop since she was seventeen.

"I know what it is—I'm saying we don't sell it," Margaret replied as if she was speaking to someone stupid. Who knew, maybe the woman was.

"But what I mean is, can you, you know, order it in? Vegetarian stuff? For my niece." The woman was persistent—Emily would give her that. Unfortunately, what the woman didn't know was, if it wasn't dripping with blood, the village shop didn't stock it.

"No. I can't just order whatever everybody wants. What if you stop buying it? No one in the village is a vegetarian, so I'd be stuck with something I couldn't sell. There's a co-op in the next town."

"Fifteen miles away," the woman said.

"So? It comes frozen, doesn't it? Stock up," Margaret said and turned to Emily. "Ms. Lassiter."

She never called her Emily despite Emily asking her to. She was a funny old bird.

"Hi, Margaret. How are you?"

"Could be better," she replied with a pointed look at the woman.

When the woman turned to face Emily too, Emily's breath caught in her throat. She was gorgeous. Emily's stomach did a little flip. She was average height with dark eyes and dark hair. Thick dark hair. Yum.

"I'm just here for my papers," Emily said. She subscribed to a few national newspapers the shop didn't sell. Although she wasn't a journalist for the time being and maybe wouldn't be again, Emily loved newspapers. Online just didn't cut it. She liked the crisp paper in her hands, and the smell, ink and chemicals. Yeah, online wasn't even close.

"Got them here." Margaret reached beneath the counter and laid them on top.

"You order in newspapers." The woman just wouldn't give up.

"Yes. They are paid for in advance, by subscription," Margaret said.

"I'll pay in advance."

Margaret eyed her coldly, and Emily braced herself.

"You are new to this village, and I have to say, you aren't making a very good impression so far. It's a small village, and word gets around about new people," Margaret said.

"Is that supposed to scare me?"

"Look, I've got some meat-free mince in my freezer. I'll give you some," Emily said, trying to defuse the situation. Margaret was right—the woman really wasn't doing herself any favours with her attitude.

"Don't bother. I can see how it's going to be. You all stick together, and fuck the outsiders. Well, don't worry, I won't bother either of you any more."

With that, the woman stomped out of the shop.

Emily watched her go and thought what a pity it was that someone so attractive was such a spoiled little shit.

Collie marched up the road, feeling tears prickling her eyes. She wouldn't cry—she wouldn't. And what the fuck was wrong with her?

She must be losing her mind. She'd been so rude to that woman—to both women. It bothered her more that she'd been rude to the one who was trying to help her. The pretty one. The *really* pretty one. Collie always had been a sucker for a brunette with big blue eyes.

Why had she made such a big deal about fucking vegetarian mince? She wasn't normally like that. Something about the shopkeeper woman pissed her off and got her back up straight away, but that still wasn't it.

Usually, when faced with someone unpleasant, Collie had a knack for charming them and bringing them round. She wasn't a dick. Not normally, anyway.

Today had been hard, though. Life was hard at the moment. Too hard. *Get yourself together. You lost a sister, but your niece lost her mother, and she's not being a dick to everyone.* Collie booted a stone along the road. And it was a road because there wasn't a bloody pavement to be had.

She walked over the level crossing—which she hadn't seen a single train go past—and turned onto an even rougher road that would take her home.

Maybe they'd drive into the town fifteen miles away tomorrow. They could stock up on vegetarian food for Lana. God knew the only thing that weird little village shop seemed to sell was meat, and most of it red meat. Clearly the people here hadn't heard of vegetables because there wasn't one in sight in that shop.

"Well, that was a right shitshow." Collie plonked down onto the kitchen chair.

"No veggie mince?" Tony asked.

"No. And I managed to mortally offend the second two locals I've met so far." Collie folded her arms on the table and rested her head on them.

"What did you do?" Tony asked.

"Basically kicked off."

"Because they had no veggie mince?"

"No. Well, yes. Oh, I don't know. It wasn't about the mince," Collie mumbled into her arms. "Where's Lana?"

"In her room. Why did you kick off?" Tony sat down next to her.

"Do you have to leave?" Collie asked. "I mean, can't you just stay here with us?"

"I actually wish I could. I love you both. But furniture won't move itself. I'll come down all the time, though. I'm coming back Friday, anyway."

Collie sighed. "I'm sorry. I shouldn't do that, make you feel guilty. You've been amazing. I'm just...I don't know."

"You're grieving. And you're now responsible for a little girl who's also grieving. And you've upped sticks and moved to the middle of nowhere. Give yourself a break, Collie," Tony said and squeezed her shoulder.

"I don't know what I would have done without you these last few weeks. You've been more than a friend to me, Tony. You're my brother. Even if we aren't related by blood."

"Collie, you know as well as I do—especially in our community— family is often the people you choose. You're my sister, and Lana is my niece. And that's the end of it. You've been there for me more times than I can count. If not for you, I wouldn't have got my business off the ground."

"That was an investment I made. I never doubted you'd make a success of it," Collie said.

"That's beside the point. You've been there for me, and I'll be there for you. I'll come up whenever I can. You'll end up sick of me," Tony said.

"Never. I'll never be sick of you." Collie reached out and hugged him. Then the tears came. She couldn't stop them.

CHAPTER SEVEN

Dinner was a sad affair. Lana didn't want Tony to go, and nor did Collie. Collie's eyes were red, and Lana guessed she'd been crying. Tony was coming back on Friday, but it still seemed like an age until then.

Probably because now Collie would be left alone with her and Lana knew she was nervous about that. Lana was nervous too. It wasn't like before where they were aunt and niece, and Collie spoiled her and let her stay up late and eat junk. And they had her mother's death between them. And they were in a new place.

Lana stopped on the drive. She was carrying the rubbish up to the bins, and it was heavy. She offered to do it after dinner. All part of her plan to be helpful, so Collie wouldn't get rid of her. Grown-ups liked it when you did your chores. The sun was just starting to go down, but the weather was still nice. She stopped and breathed in the smell of warm grass and warm earth. It smelled so much nicer than London.

Beside her, on the right, the bushes rustled. Probably a bird. Or maybe it was a cat. Not Tufty because he had to stay in for another week. At least Collie hadn't made cleaning out his litter tray one of Lana's chores.

Lana picked up the bag and hefted it a few more feet before the sound came again, and she stopped. For reasons she didn't understand, the hair on her arms stood up, and her skin prickled. She was spooked. Which was stupid, because it was broad daylight.

All the same, Lana picked up the rubbish bag and moved a little faster.

She dumped the bag in the big green plastic bin. A swarm of flies rose up and scattered. "Gross," she muttered. Something smelled bad in there. Probably just old rubbish or a dead rat.

Lana started back up the drive. The bushes rustled again, and it felt strange. Like something was marking her progress up the drive, like something was watching her. She tried to make the kissing sound she made when she wanted Tufty to come to her, but her mouth was dry. Also, she wasn't sure she wanted what was in the bushes to come out.

A twig snapped, and whatever was in there seemed to be coming closer.

Lana panicked. On pure instinct, she started to run. She pumped her legs and flew over the gravel. The bolt on the gate was sticky, and she skinned her knuckle when she wrenched it back, her hand greasy with sweat, slipped, then found purchase again.

Lana swung the gate back on its hinges and charged up the garden path. Inside, she slammed the door shut and dropped the latch.

"Everything okay?" Collie called to her from the living room.

Lana strained to keep the panting out of her voice. "Fine. I'll be there in a minute."

Her heartbeat was slowing down now, and she was feeling more herself. Feeling a bit stupid, in fact. The thing in the bushes was a bird or maybe a fox. Lana looked up and saw Tufty on the stairs, staring past her, his tail puffed up and his ears pinned forward like he was straining to hear. He didn't blink. After a moment, his tail swished once, and he let out a hiss.

He was freaking Lana out more. She turned away from him and squeezed her eyes shut. There were no monsters, there were no monsters. She knew that, had known that since she was small.

She looked down at her hand. The fleshy part at the base of her finger was bleeding and the knuckle raw from where she caught it in the bolt. "I just need to get a plaster. I cut my hand on the gate."

"What?" Collie's voice coming closer. "Are you okay?" Then Collie was in front of her, face filled with concern. "Let me see?"

Lana held out her hand.

"Ouch. That bolt is stiff. I'll get some oil on it tomorrow," Collie said. Then her aunt was looking at her. "Are you sure you're okay, Lana?"

"Yes, I promise. It doesn't really hurt," Lana said.

"No, I mean…are you okay? You look worried—scared. Did something happen outside?" Collie asked.

"No," Lana said and dropped her eyes. She wasn't very good at lying.

"Lana."

"It's nothing. I just spooked myself. The bushes," Lana said.

"Ah. Yeah, they're pretty thick. You heard something rustling around in them?" Collie asked.

"It was probably a bird." But it hadn't felt like a harmless bird.

"Probably. Or a fox. It's the countryside. We'll get used to it," Collie said.

Lana nodded.

"Okay. Well, why don't we sort out your finger and then watch a film. I got popcorn," Collie said.

Lana nodded again. She liked watching films with Aunt Collie on the sofa. It reminded her of how things used to be. Before her mum died. Maybe Collie would let her stay up late as well. Lana felt lighter. By the time they sat down to watch their movie, Lana had almost forgotten about the thing in the bushes.

❖

The thing in the bushes hadn't forgotten about Lana. It sat and waited and watched. It moved up closer to the house. Initially, all it wanted was to see the new inhabitants. But then it caught the little one's scent and decided to stick around.

When she'd come out of the house alone and unprotected, it used all its willpower not to leap out of the bushes. There was time. All the time in the world. It wanted to know them first. Stalk them first. Make them afraid. People always tasted so much better when they were afraid. When the time was right, when everything was as it should be, it would take them. This was the way of things. The way things had *always* been, and they would be no different this time. The ritual must be completed, and this year's was one of the most important in a long time. It was the time of change, of handing over. It had been this way *always* too.

It waited until darkness fell before it left them. Waited until it saw lights go on upstairs and waited until the lights went off again. It sat just a little longer. And then it left. Melted into the night and joined the other things that moved around in the dark.

CHAPTER EIGHT

Emily watched the mole on Frances Cobb's lip as she spoke. It was large, with three hairs that poked out. They looked sharp. Frances couldn't help the mole, but Emily thought she might pluck the hairs. She must see them when she looked in the mirror, must feel them when she washed her face or moisturized.

As Frances droned on, Emily fantasized about holding her down and plucking the hairs out. Imagined the ridiculous scene as Frances struggled beneath her, Emily squinting and closing in with the tweezers.

Frances was an imposing woman. Tall and broad with a mane of steel grey hair that she must spray like crazy every morning to get it like that. The bloody thing was like a helmet and didn't move an inch even when she shook her head.

"So, in summary, I trust you will help to settle in the student and support her as she adjusts to life at Highmore," Frances said.

Emily realized she'd zoned out of most of the conversation. "Sorry?"

"The new student, Lana Franklin. I trust you'll help to settle her into the school," Frances repeated with a frown.

Ah, yes, Lana Franklin. Frances called Emily into her office last week to tell her about her new student. Poor kid's mother had been murdered by her psychotic ex-boyfriend. Unfortunately, not an uncommon story. Emily covered a similar one about two years ago.

Apparently Lana and her aunt had decided to make Hyam their new home. Frances told her Lana didn't have any behavioural issues, but due to *the circumstances*—that's how Frances put it—she wanted Emily to keep a close eye on her, just in case. Knowing Frances, she probably didn't trust Lana Franklin not to have a huge meltdown or something. For someone who'd worked with children her whole life, Emily got the impression Frances Cobb didn't like them very much.

When Emily interviewed with Frances for the job four months ago, she'd been struck by how much she resembled Miss Trunchbull from the Roald Dahl book. The woman had a sense of humour transplant somewhere along the way and was a solid proponent of the adage *Why use four words when you can use fourteen?*

From what Emily knew, she lived in a huge house on the edge of the village by herself. She'd never been married and had no children. Not that marriage and kids defined you—it better not or Emily was screwed—but what could one woman possibly want with a house the size of a museum?

But back to the question of whether Emily could settle Lana in. Could she in any way help a child who'd been through such a horrible trauma? That was part of her job, after all. Unfortunately for Lana, Emily wasn't such a great teacher. At least, she didn't feel like she was.

Emily sighed. "Yes, of course I'll make her feel welcome and give any support she needs."

Emily was not a natural teacher, and after two years of it, before she'd left to pursue a career in journalism, she'd never felt such relief to be able to shut her classroom door for the last time and hand in her pass at reception.

Somehow, she was back again and teaching a class of year sixes. Ten to eleven year olds, five days a week, from eight forty to three twenty. There were twenty in her class, which was a good number for a village school.

"Miss Franklin starts with us on Monday. I trust you'll have everything in place to assist in a smooth transition, Ms. Lassiter."

Emily resisted rolling her eyes just barely. "Of course."

"Good." Frances folded her hands on the desk and looked expectantly at Emily. Emily thought it was the shortest sentence the woman had ever uttered.

Back outside the dark-wood-panelled office, a throwback to the Victorian age, Emily breathed in the fresh air. Why did schools always smell that way? Bleach, over cooked cabbage and something she couldn't quite put her finger on.

Emily looked out over the green playing field. A group of little girls and boys in baggy rugby shirts and baggy shorts were kicking around a football, while Dennis Smythe, the PE teacher, chased around after them blowing his whistle and waving his arms.

Emily tried her best—she owed it to her students—but she really hated teaching. She'd known it six months into the training programme seven years ago, but she'd stuck with it. Two years later she'd left it behind with a vow never to return. Now here she was, back again in a job she shouldn't be doing. The kids she taught deserved better than her. She did her best, and she guessed they learned, but they should have a teacher who wanted to teach them.

A teacher like Charlie. He'd been born to it. She'd seen the way her little nieces and nephews hovered around him. How patient he was with them. Patient and kind. He'd spend hours showing them something, and he loved to teach.

Emily sighed again and reminded herself she was doing this for him. To find out what happened to him. He'd taken a job here and seemed to love it. He'd often had her in stitches with tales about Frances Cobb and some of the students.

Charlie taught the little ones, in the infants section of the school. Emily imagined they'd loved him. Fuck, she missed him. She and Charlie had still been best friends. They spoke at least once a week and emailed and texted constantly.

Emily swallowed the lump which sat aching in her throat and made her sinuses pulse and tingle. She needed to know what happened to him, had to find out. It was a living, breathing thing inside her that ached to know. A blinking eye that watched her every move and always whispered, *What happened to Charlie? Where is Charlie?*

"Emily."

Emily jumped.

"Sorry, didn't mean to scare you."

"Don't worry, Hamish. I was in my own world." Emily turned to face one of the year five teachers.

"Easily done. I wanted to talk to you about the end of term summer play," he said.

Emily couldn't have given less of a shit about the end of term summer play. "Okay." She'd completely forgotten they were in charge of it this year.

"I thought *Oliver* might be a good one. What do you think?"

"Sure. Sounds good." Emily tried to put some enthusiasm into her voice and failed.

"Of course, if you have any ideas, maybe we could go for a drink after school one evening?"

There it was. Hamish had asked her out in a similarly vague way when she first got here, and she'd gently rebuffed him. Obviously not firmly enough.

"No, I think *Oliver* is a good one to do. Let's go with that," she said, cursing herself for not just being straight with him.

"Well, we'll need to discuss casting and everything anyway. The Anchor and Hope has some live music Friday. Maybe we could have a meeting there and then just enjoy ourselves afterwards."

Emily nodded. "Okay, Hamish...look, I think you're a really nice guy." She had no idea if he was nice or not. "I don't date. And if I did, it wouldn't be anyone at school." Also, she was a lesbian but didn't generally share that information at work.

Hamish went red, and she felt bad. "I just thought we could get to know each other, that's all." He leaned in close and for a horrible minute, she thought he might try to kiss her. "I'm gay, Emily. I just thought, as we're both relatively new here, it would be nice to, you know, have a friend. I assure you, I'm not interested in dating you, pretty as you are."

Emily wanted to shrivel up and die right there. "I see." She didn't know what to say. Her face burned, and she felt arrogant and conceited and, basically, like a complete arsehole.

Then Hamish grinned. "Don't worry about it. I can see you want to climb under that bush over there."

"I'm so embarrassed," she managed.

"Don't be. You are pretty, and I did ask you out for a drink." Hamish laughed.

"I know, but I just assumed...I must seem so arrogant." Emily covered her burning face with her hands.

"Honestly, it's fine. Look, are we on for Friday night? I promise not to propose."

"Yes. Okay, yes, that would be nice." Emily was breaking her first rule—don't get friendly with anyone here—but how could she say no now? Plus, it might be nice to get out for once. She didn't have to make a habit of it.

❖

Never exactly hopping, the Anchor and Hope was at least fairly busy this Friday night. A few people—Emily guessed the band—were tuning their instruments up on the stage. The Hope and Anchor was actually a nice pub. During the day, it was bright and airy, and a blond wood bar ran the length of it. The brass pumps were polished, and the bar shone tonight.

It still had that pub smell, though, stale beer and grubby carpet. Emily wasn't sure any pub, no matter how fancy, could ever quite escape that smell.

She looked up as Hamish made his way over to her with what could only be cocktails in his hands. Cocktails? In Hyam?

"Thanks, I think," she said as he put them down on the table.

"Hope I wasn't overstepping by choosing your drink for you, but it's happy hour, and apparently they're trying out these new cocktails for the outsiders," Hamish said.

"Outsiders? You mean us?" Emily asked.

Hamish laughed. "No—well, yes—but this band is quite popular. I actually saw them down in Ipswich, and they are good. People have come from all over tonight to hear them."

"Have they? Will the pub fill up much more, then?" Emily asked.

Hamish shrugged. "I hope so. This place is usually dead, and it would be nice to see it busy for a change, have some new faces."

"How long have you been here?" Emily asked. "In Hyam?"

"Too long. Eighteen months. I followed my ex down to Suffolk. Highmore had an opening within a decent commute to where we lived. Not sure why I stayed after we split, really, except I always think it looks a bit dodgy on your CV when you leave jobs quickly. I decided to do three years here. Not sure if I'll stick to it, though," he said.

"Doesn't seem to be a lot going on," Emily said carefully. She didn't want to get too personal with him.

So why are you asking questions? Why did you agree to come out tonight? Because it was in her nature to ask questions, she supposed. She'd always been like that. She liked people, and she liked knowing about them. As to the other, well, she was bored rigid.

When she left London she left her friends too. And family. Sitting at her computer every night eating microwave meals and leftovers was fucking depressing.

"What about you? What on earth are you doing here?" Hamish asked.

There it was. The dreaded question. She must have taken a bit too long to answer because Hamish quickly said, "Sorry. That was rude. For all I know, you're from here."

"Hyam? Not likely," Emily said. "This is an odd place. I come from a village further south, but it's nice there. Friendly. I guess I moved here because I always missed a quieter pace," Emily lied.

"Really? You don't strike me as the country-life type. No offence—you seem more...I don't know, suited to the city perhaps," Hamish said.

"Because I'm unfriendly and stuck up?" Emily joked.

"Exactly." Hamish grinned. "No, but I haven't seen you participating in any country pursuits—or joining the Women's Institute."

"I only just got here," Emily said.

"Sorry, I'm being all judgemental. I just didn't have you down as a countryside lover. But if you are, there's a couple of really good walks I've been on recently. One through the woods to this weird little mini-Stonehenge place. Fancy going with me one day?" Hamish asked.

Emily couldn't think of anything she'd rather do less. Cold, damp, and covered in mud? No thank you. "Sure, that sounds great," she said, injecting some enthusiasm into her voice.

"Okay, how about Sunday? Around two? We can come here for lunch first. We can pick up the River Woden, which runs along outside the pub, and follow it down to the stones."

"Perfect," Emily said. "Let me get the next round. Same again?" she asked, hoping to move the conversation on before she agreed to camping or something equally awful.

It was true she was a country girl, but unlike the rest of her family, she'd never really taken to it. The family all stayed in and around the village they'd grown up in, and she could see the appeal, especially when you had children. Even Charlie had stayed in the country when he got his teaching job.

But Emily always wanted to live in a city—any city. She wasn't remotely outdoorsy, and the thought of knowing her neighbours didn't appeal either.

She pushed her way to the bar. The pub was filling up quickly, and she found herself waiting next to the stroppy good-looking woman from the other day in the shop.

Emily made eye contact with her, and the woman quickly looked away. *Fine, carry on being an ignorant cow*, Emily thought. She just hoped her niece wasn't as rude as she was. She'd noticed her new student was here.

Emily ordered her drinks and carried them back to the table. Out of the corner of her eye, she could see Lana Franklin's aunt doing the same. At her table was her niece and a tall man with a shaved head.

"Who's pissed you off?" Hamish asked her as she set down the drinks.

"What?"

"You're burning holes in someone with your eyes. Who is it?" Hamish craned his neck round to see where Emily was looking.

"It's no one. Don't worry about it," Emily said.

"Come on, tell me," Hamish said.

"It's nothing, really. Just that woman over there at the table with the little girl," Emily said.

"Kids are allowed in here until about nine thirty, I think," Hamish said.

"No, I don't care about that. The woman the girl is with. She's utterly rude," Emily said.

"She's very good-looking."

"That doesn't mean she can't be a pig. She is good-looking, though, isn't she?" Emily said.

Hamish looked at her then. His eyes narrowed, then flew wide open. "Are you…"

"Yes. And don't look so surprised. And keep it to yourself," Emily said.

"Of course. This is the first time in my life I've gone back in the closet, but I get the impression Miss Cobb isn't a fan of our kind," Hamish said.

"I couldn't give a shit if she is or she isn't. I just don't feel comfortable in Hyam at all. And I don't want people knowing my business."

"Fair enough. So, back to the sexy pig," Hamish said. "What happened there?"

Emily rolled her eyes but couldn't help laughing at Hamish's description of her. "Nothing happened. I met her in the village shop, and she was having a meltdown about veggie mince."

"Who was serving?" Hamish asked.

"Margaret," Emily said.

Hamish winced. "That won't have gone down well."

"No. Not at all. I offered her some of my veggie mince, and she bit my head off. Up at the bar just now, she totally ignored me. She's ignorant."

"Sounds like."

"Hamish, stop looking over at her," Emily said.

"Sorry, sorry," Hamish said. But he looked again. "Pity. She really is very nice looking."

"I know," said Emily. Not that she would have done anything about it even if Lana Franklin's aunt was the nicest woman on the planet. Emily was here for one reason. To find out what happened to Charlie. And tonight aside, she wasn't going to allow herself to get sidetracked.

Hamish started to say something else, but the band started up and drowned him out. Emily turned her attention to the stage and allowed herself to get carried away on the heavy beat of drums and the electric guitar as the band played a well-known rock song.

She didn't think about the sexy pig at all. Until the sexy pig— obviously with a bit of Dutch courage—weaved her way through the tables and over to Emily's table.

"Hi." The sexy pig hovered by Emily's chair awkwardly. "Um, may I sit down a second?"

Emily stayed quiet, watching her squirm. It was Hamish who saved her. "Of course," he said, and Emily felt his kick under the table.

"Look, I just wanted to apologize for my behaviour the other day. I'm Collie, by the way."

Emily looked at Collie. She was hot, and she probably knew it, but right now she looked genuinely sorry. "It's fine," Emily said.

"No, no, it's not. I was rude. I'm not normally rude. I just…well, it doesn't matter, but I wanted to apologize to you. I should have done it before, but I was nervous. I've been watching you all night—shit, that came out wrong."

Hamish snorted, and now Emily kicked him under the table.

"What I meant was I've been waiting for an opportunity to come over. I've had a few beers and, well—"

"It's fine. Really. Apology accepted," Emily cut in to save Collie, who was tying herself up in knots. Interesting that she had been watching Emily all night. Emily felt warm at the thought of this woman watching her, then quickly squashed it.

"Okay, well, thanks for accepting my strange and slightly creepy apology," Collie said and smiled.

"You're welcome. I'm Emily, by the way. And this is Hamish," Emily said.

"Nice to meet you both—properly, I mean. See you around probably," Collie said.

"Probably," Emily said and smiled. Despite her best intentions, she couldn't help but watch Collie walk away. Shit, she really was hot.

❖

On Sunday, as promised, Emily dutifully followed Hamish through Woden Wood. He'd kept his end of the bargain, and they'd had a nice lunch and a big gin each before setting off.

The weather continued to hold, and Emily thought at least she might get a bit of a tan—if they ever got out of the wood, that was. The trees in here were thick, and it was lucky they had the river to follow, otherwise Emily was sure even Hamish would get lost.

"How often do you come here?" Emily asked.

"Most weekends. It's a lovely walk. You can follow the river all the way to Five Elms, so you won't get lost. Be careful up ahead, though, because the bank starts to slide away, and the water gets choppy."

"And this river goes all the way to the mini-Stonehenge you're so excited to show me?" Emily asked.

"Sort of. We have to veer off a bit, but not far, don't worry," Hamish said.

Emily breathed in the fresh, warm air and enjoyed how pretty the wood was. Bluebells were sprouting between the trees, and the birds were chirping away.

"This is lovely," she said.

"I know. Neil and I—my ex—used to come here all the time. It's so romantic. Speaking of which, have you seen the sexy pig again?" Hamish asked.

Emily laughed. "No, I have not, and I don't really care to. Her niece, Lana, is lovely, though."

"How's she getting on?"

"Well, I think. She's tough. Frances Cobb has taken a keen interest in her," Emily said.

Hamish turned to her and rolled his eyes. "Of course she has. Until she gets bored and moves on to something else."

"Is that how she operates?" Emily asked.

"Afraid so. And the Spring Fair is coming up, so she'll be pretty consumed with preparations for that," Hamish said.

"Oh yes, the famous Spring Fair. It's all I hear about in the staff room."

"It's a very big deal around these parts. Speaking of which, have you got your scarecrow ready yet?" Hamish asked.

"My what?" Emily said.

"You don't know about the scarecrows?" Hamish asked. He slowed down and came alongside her. The river was wild here and so loud she could barely hear him. He hadn't been joking about how rough it got. Emily moved away from the bank. She wasn't sure of her chances if she fell in.

"Tell me about these scarecrows then," Emily said.

"It's a big part of the Spring Fair. Everyone puts one in their garden, and some people dress up as scarecrows. Don't ask me why because I don't know. It's all very strange, but they love it. You'll have to make one, or they'll give you one, and they're fucking creepy, so I advise you to make your own," Hamish said.

Emily laughed. "Noted. Not that I've ever made a scarecrow, but I suppose that's what YouTube is for."

Hamish turned off towards the left, and after a few minutes, they reached a clearing. It was still surrounded by trees, but in the centre was a group of stones, purposefully arranged.

"You're right. It does look like a mini-Stonehenge," Emily said.

"If you keep walking up that way, you reach Frances Cobb's stately mansion. That's also worth a look but from a distance. She's got signs up everywhere to keep off her land, and it wouldn't surprise me if she shot trespassers," Hamish said.

It wouldn't surprise Emily either. In fact, something told her Frances Cobb would probably enjoy nothing more than a good headshot on some poor bugger that wandered onto her land.

Emily focused again on the stones. "Can we take a closer look, or is Cobb likely to start shooting?" Emily asked, only half joking.

"We're quite safe. Come on," Hamish said.

As they got closer, Emily saw it wasn't quite as similar to Stonehenge as she first thought. For one thing, there were metal rings bolted to some of the stones.

"Looks like kids hang out here a bit," Emily said.

"Why do you say that?" Hamish asked.

"Fires. We used to do it when I was a kid. Find a quiet spot, start a campfire, and drink alcohol we'd stolen from our parents."

On the way over to the stones, Emily noticed a number of scorched patches dotted about. Definitely campfires. The sight of them brought a smile to her face. She remembered what it was like to be a teenager with nowhere to go.

"I suppose we're lucky they haven't burned the place down," Hamish said.

"Not likely. There's no trees nearby. And they've left the stones alone, so they can't be all bad," Emily said.

"True. It's cool, isn't it? Mini-Stonehenge?"

It was. Emily was pleasantly surprised. She'd been dreading this walk through the woods, but actually, she'd had a good time. "Thanks for bringing me, Hamish. I've enjoyed it. You're officially my local guide."

Hamish laughed. "I'm glad you had a good time. I've been all over the village and the woods. Stick with me, and I'll show you all the sights." He winked.

Emily laughed. "Come on, let's go back. I'll buy you a drink."

"Can't argue with that," Hamish said.

They linked arms and headed back into the woods.

❖

Collie rifled through the picnic bag and pulled out the sandwiches, half squashed. "Peanut butter or cheese?" she asked Lana. Lana screwed up her nose and looked between the pathetic offerings in Collie's hands. "Come on, Lana, it's not like I'm asking you to choose between death by bee stings or death by tickling."

Lana laughed. "But what did you *do* to them?"

Collie shrugged. "I think the drinks cans fell on them."

Collie and Lana both turned their heads at the same time at the sound of voices getting closer.

"That sounds like Miss Lassiter," Lana said and stood up.

Great, Collie thought. Another chance for her to make a fool out of herself in front of a pretty woman.

"Miss Lassiter," Lana called out.

Just then, Emily and Hamish came out of the woods and into the clearing. Collie watched as Emily frowned slightly. After Collie's comments the last time she saw her, Emily probably thought she was following her.

Collie stood up and did her best to smile. "Hi. Looks like we had the same idea today."

Emily's eyes moved over her, and Collie wondered if Emily knew she was checking Collie out. Collie hid her smile. Looked like she wasn't the only one with an interest.

"It is a lovely day," Hamish said. "And you brought sandwiches. We didn't think to do that."

"Do you want some?" Lana asked.

Collie shot her a look. She knew exactly what Lana was doing— trying to palm off the dodgy sandwiches, so she wouldn't have to eat them.

"What have you got?" Emily asked.

"Cheese or peanut butter," Collie said. "But the drinks squashed them, so they aren't my greatest work."

"Well, I'm *starving*," Hamish said, and Collie didn't miss the look Emily shot him.

"Oh, well, there's plenty. Emily? Cheese or peanut butter?" Collie asked.

Emily looked from one squashed sandwich to the next, and Collie saw the ghost of a smile on her face. She really was very pretty.

"Cheese, please. It looks less…duffed up."

"So rude," Collie said and laughed. "Plenty of room on the picnic blanket."

Hamish and Emily came over and sat down. Collie passed them the sandwiches. "Hey, Lana, don't think you're getting out of eating them. Peanut butter or cheese?"

Lana did an exaggerated eye roll. "Can't I just have crisps? I'm too young to die."

"Hey, these were lovingly made," Collie said.

"Yeah, that's why you chucked the drinks cans on them," Lana said. But Lana did come and sat down and took a sandwich.

They sat in a comfortable silence. The day was warm, and it was peaceful in the forest. Collie did her best not to look at Emily even though all she wanted to do was sit and stare at her.

You're so pathetic. Mooning over her like a schoolkid.

"So, what brings you to the woods?" Collie asked.

"I wanted to show Emily the mini-Stonehenge in the clearing," Hamish said.

"It's cool. You two should go and have a look," Emily said. "I was thinking I might plan a lesson around them this term. Maybe set a project."

"There you go, Lana. Bit of inside information," Collie said.

Emily smiled and winked, and Collie's heart skipped a beat.

Under other circumstances she'd be making a play for Emily. But she was Lana's teacher, and Collie still felt the black abyss of grief trying to drag her down into it, and Lana was the only thing keeping her head above water.

The touch of Emily's hand on her arm brought her back. It was warm and soft.

"You okay?" Emily asked quietly so the others—who'd started talking amongst themselves—couldn't hear.

Collie looked into the warmth of Emily's eyes and forced a smile. "Yeah, sure. Sorry."

Emily gave her arm a final squeeze, then took it away. "Nothing to be sorry for."

Collie gave her another smile, this one stronger and genuine. "I am okay. Thanks." Collie wasn't sure what she was thanking Emily for. Bringing her back?

"We'd better get going. I've got a ton of homework to mark before tomorrow," Emily said and stood up. She brushed down her jeans.

Hamish gave a dramatic groan. "No rest for the wicked," he said.

"See you soon then," Collie said.

"Yes. And you in school tomorrow, Lana," Emily said.

Collie watched Emily leave with a sense of loss she didn't quite understand.

"We'd better get going too, Lana Banana," Collie said. With Hamish and Emily gone, the woods were quieter. "It's getting cold."

Goosebumps rose up on her arms, and she felt a chill in the air for the first time all day. Suddenly, she couldn't wait to get out of the woods. Lana seemed to feel the same. Without a word she helped Collie gather up their things, and the two of them walked quickly back to the car. Collie resisted the childish urge to run.

CHAPTER NINE

Collie fought the cling film. It twisted up and stuck itself together, and in the end she gave up. Nothing was worth this much trouble. Instead she got a shopping bag from under the sink and carefully placed the sandwich in it. She chucked in a packet of crisps and a satsuma.

There. School lunches weren't so hard. Getting up at seven in the morning was. She'd ironed Lana's new uniform—blue tie, blue sweater, grey shirt, and grey trousers—and believed she hadn't done a half-bad job. She hadn't burned them or ironed in any extra creases. So far, so good.

She checked her watch and decided it was time to wake Lana up. She wasn't entirely sure how this was going to go. Collie had never woken anyone up for school before. When Lana stayed with her previously, she woke up when she woke up. And since Sasha's death, Collie followed the same rule.

But now there was school and probably after-school clubs and homework and all sorts of other shit Collie hadn't even begun to fully comprehend. Sasha had been a natural mother, one of those women born to it. Whenever Collie spoke to her, she was off here, there, and everywhere with Lana. Dance class and piano, swimming and drama club.

Lana hadn't mentioned any after-school stuff she wanted to keep up yet, and Collie thought she'd give her a chance to settle in first before she brought it up.

Cereal. Sasha always put out cereal and a glass for orange juice. Collie should do that. Would that mean she had to eat breakfast too? Like, set a good example? Collie couldn't remember the last time she ate breakfast, and she wasn't sure she could stomach cereal and orange juice. Then she remembered Sasha always had tea and toast, and Collie thought she could at least manage that.

Just then, something hit the kitchen door hard enough to rattle the frame.

"What the bloody hell," Collie muttered.

There it was again, followed by a scrape like nails down a blackboard. Collie went to the kitchen window and tried to look out, but her view was obscured by an overgrown bush.

She took a knife out of the rack, feeling a bit dramatic but unable to stop the fear that had lodged itself in her belly.

"Aunt Collie, what's going on?" Lana was standing behind her in the doorway.

"I don't know. Lana, do me a favour and wait upstairs," Collie said as calmly as she could.

Silently, Lana left, and Collie heard the creak of the stairs as she went up. That sorted, Collie went to the back door and gripped the handle. The glass panel was obscured, so there was no way she'd be able to see outside. The blurry shapes of the bushes and shrubs were indistinguishable from anything else.

"Who's out there?" Collie asked, feeling stupid.

No one answered, unsurprisingly.

Collie took a deep breath and quickly pulled open the door. She raised the knife, ready to confront whatever was outside.

The back garden was empty. Birds hopped about in the trees and called to each other. The sun was already warming the day and sat high and bright in the sky. It was a beautiful late spring morning, and if Collie hadn't turned just then and seen what was done to the door, she would have thought it a perfect day.

Instead, what she saw chilled her to the bone. Deep, long claw marks gouged into the wood panels at the base of the door. The wood had splintered from the force of it, in places.

Collie spun around wildly, half expecting some drooling, snarling monster to be standing there.

The garden was empty. She looked again at the marks on the door. They looked dramatic and almost contrived—almost as if whatever did it wanted to scare her. She wasn't sure why she felt that way, but it made sense in her gut. What animal battered your door and scratched it like that?

Even so, *something* had done it. And it *could* be an animal. What animal, Collie didn't know. The claw marks were almost a foot in length and about half that in width.

Collie looked around one more time. She couldn't see anything, but all the same, she felt like she was being watched. She squinted, half expecting to see a pair of demonic eyes staring out of the bushes.

Grandma, what big eyes you have.

She shivered and bolted inside and locked the door.

❖

It stayed well-back and out of sight, but it could see the woman clearly. It lifted its nose to the air and sniffed. Afraid. She was afraid, and that was good. Before it was done with her, she would be terrified.

This was just the start. If she was scared now, she had no idea what was coming, no idea how bad things would get. And just when she thought things couldn't get worse, it would show itself to her, and she would lose her mind before it killed her.

It wanted to stay longer. It wanted to leap from the bushes and tear her apart, but it wouldn't. The game was too much fun for it to be over so quickly. And it didn't get to play as often as it once had. Times were changing, and even though it was as old as time itself—older, probably—it had to be careful. It had to adapt.

And things needed to be done in the ancient way, the way they'd always been done. The rituals and rites must be carried out as they'd been carried out for all time. Except things were different this time, weren't they? And not just because this was the changing over.

It sensed another in a way it hadn't done before. It was used to having things its own way and couldn't remember a time when that had not been the way of things. Now, it felt the other's interest in the women and the girl and understood the other had its own plans for them. It sensed this other *knew* them, knew them and loved them. So who was it? It was unaware there was anything special about them. The only thing that made them special was that *it* had chosen them for the ancient ritual.

Part of it was interested to know what this other was, and part of it was unnerved. It understood that the other was working against it. Not that the other would win. How could it? It sensed this other as something new, while it was almost as old as time itself. Nevertheless, this change might make things more interesting. A game it might enjoy.

It waited a little longer and listened to the woman's telephone call to her friend. Enjoyed the fear in her voice. Then it slunk further back into the bushes and melted away into the morning, a dark shadow against the bright sun that caused birds to fall silent as it passed them.

CHAPTER TEN

Collie sat back and shut down her laptop. It was official. Nowhere in the United Kingdom was there an animal that could make those size claw marks on the back door.

Maybe a person did it—creepy, and also…why?—or someone in the area had bought a non-native animal as a pet, and it escaped and was now roaming around Hyam scratching up people's doors.

Neither was a particularly comforting thought. If it was an animal, why come up to her door, batter against it, then claw at it? It didn't make sense. But then, she didn't really know enough about animals.

She'd read about bears in North America coming up to people's homes looking for food, but she was pretty sure she would have seen a bear even in the overgrown bushes.

Plus, she didn't think bears were really a part of countryside living. She'd heard something about wolves being introduced back into Scotland, hadn't she? She thought so, but it had been a news story on in the background while she'd been doing whatever it was she'd been doing at the time, and she hadn't paid much attention.

Scotland was a long way from Suffolk, and she doubted wolves would just be allowed to roam about the country as they pleased.

Chances were it was someone playing silly buggers. Even so, animal or human, it was disturbing, and Collie didn't like it.

She'd tried to keep it from Lana and pushed her out the front door when the school bus arrived. She'd given her some weak excuse about thinking she'd seen a massive spider and that's why she'd sent her upstairs. But something in Lana's eyes said she knew Collie was full of shit. Of course she did—she was smart, and even though she was only ten, she wasn't easy to fool.

Collie remembered two years ago when Lana sat her down with

an adorably serious look on her little face and told Collie she knew
Father Christmas wasn't real because she'd figured it out. But Lana
made Collie promise not to tell her mum because Sasha would be
disappointed Lana no longer believed.

Yeah, Lana was too smart for her own good, and Collie knew she
hadn't got anything past her. She'd have to make sure she sanded down
and filled the gouges in the door before Lana came home from school.

Collie called the RSPCA—they dealt with animal stuff, right?—
but the woman on the phone told her they were more into cats, dogs,
and small furries than they were into bears and lions and such and
wouldn't be able to help her. Next she tried the council. At first they'd
wanted her to phone pest control.

Collie explained if it was a pest who'd gouged her door, she was
in big trouble. Eventually, she managed to find a small children's zoo
who said they'd come and take a look. The bloke on the phone clearly
thought she was batshit, but the description of the claw marks swung
it for her.

Other than that, Collie wasn't sure who else to call. It didn't seem
wise for them to be walking around with the chance of something that
big loose in her garden.

And if it *was* a person trying to scare her, well, that opened up a
whole load of questions, didn't it?

Primarily, why? She hadn't exactly got off to a good start with the
locals, but she couldn't see them taking such offence they'd do this.

Tony had a mate—he always seemed to have a mate—who worked
in a zoo. Tony said he'd try to get her to come down and take a look if
Collie had no joy with anyone else. Knowing Tony, the woman worked
in the gift shop.

Collie leaned back in her chair and tapped her fingers on the desk.
She needed to get on with some work, but she was restless. She checked
her watch. She wouldn't normally be up this early. She looked out the
window. It was nice, seeing the morning. Living in the countryside.

Collie leaned back in her chair again and picked up her sketchbook.
She flicked through the pages and studied the pencil drawings of the
characters for the new video game she was working on.

She stopped at one picture and shivered. The creature was hunched
with a grossly exaggerated upper body and head. Wicked sharp uneven
teeth were crammed in its mouth, and it looked deadly.

But what made her shiver was its hands. Gnarled bony fingers with long curled claws on the end. Claws that dripped with blood. *That* was the kind of creature who would leave those marks on the door.

Collie suddenly had an image of the great, hulking beast from her sketchbook climbing off the page and into the real world. Her fault. She brought it here.

Don't be so stupid.

Of course she hadn't brought a monster here. She drew them, created them in 3D on her computer, then sent them off to Sooba Games to be coded. All the same, Collie couldn't shake the image of the monster from her mind.

Outside, the sound of gravel crunching beneath tyres came up the drive.

Collie looked out the window and saw a white van with black and white zebra print on its side pull into the drive. She sighed and stood up, not holding out much hope that whoever this was would have the answer either.

Collie met her halfway up the garden path and led her round the back. Her name was Fiona Walker. She was pretty. In another life, Collie would have flirted with her, maybe taken her on a date if she was receptive to it. Now, things were different.

It dawned on Collie that dating was probably a thing of the past for her—not that she was close to ready. Anyone she met now would have a big part in Lana's life too. That was a scary thought.

Fiona was speaking to her, and Collie totally missed it.

"Sorry, what?"

Fiona smiled. "I said, I'm not exactly an expert. We tend to deal with your more domesticated animals—cats, dogs, guinea pigs. And we have a lovely line in donkeys if you're ever inclined to visit us."

Was Fiona flirting with her? Collie thought she was. At least she still had it, she supposed, but she didn't feel the familiar tingle. She wasn't sure if she would again for a long time.

That's a lie. You felt it the other night in the pub. And in the woods when Emily touched your arm.

Yeah, well that was probably just nerves and embarrassment.

Sure.

Collie focused on the woman in front of her. "Oh, well, yeah. I wasn't holding out much hope you'd be able to help. I wasn't sure who else to call. I've not had this sort of thing happen to me before," Collie said.

Fiona nodded, all business. "Show me the marks."

Collie led her a little further and stopped, then pointed at the back door. "There."

"Bloody hell," Fiona said and crouched down. "And you say it happened this morning?"

Collie nodded. "Yeah, about seven. I was sorting out my niece's breakfast, and something banged against the door—something big. It did it a couple more times, and when I went out to look, I saw those."

But did it happen this morning? If it was a wind-up, they could have done it last night.

"Well, I can tell you it's nothing native to this part of the world. Probably nothing native to the UK," Fiona said.

"I thought so. Do you know of anyone in the area with an exotic pet?" Collie asked.

Fiona shook her head. "No. For one thing, it's illegal over here. There's no zoos or animal sanctuaries close by, either—well, not the sort that would have animals this size."

"Something did it," Collie said.

Fiona brushed off her knees and stood. "Look, don't take this the wrong way, but have you pissed anyone off lately?"

"We only moved in a few days ago."

"I see." Fiona frowned.

"What?" Collie asked.

"What?" Fiona said.

"You look like you wanted to say something," Collie said.

"It's just…look, I grew up around here. Not this village, but Five Elms, eight miles away. Hyam is, well, I suppose it's kind of weird," Fiona said.

"What do you mean *weird*?" Collie asked.

"It's always had a reputation as being insular and closed off. People don't really move here, and they don't really leave. It's weird because most of the other villages are deserted. It's all townies buying holiday homes and young people leaving for cities to find jobs. Hyam seems to stay just like it is. Multiple generations live here, and it really isn't at all friendly."

"You think someone from the village did it? To what, make me leave? Wind me up?" Collie asked.

"A couple of years ago, a friend of a friend moved near here. Not technically *in* the village but close enough. And right next to Cobb land. He bought a house with a few acres and wanted to do a bunch of work to it. The locals opposed the plans—well, one local in particular—and they made his life hell. He had to leave in the end."

"Shit. Made his life hell in what way? And which local?" Collie asked, slightly afraid of the answer.

"He got hang-up calls, and none of the local businesses would serve him. A few other things he couldn't prove. Point is, they wanted him gone, and in the end, they got their way. If I can give you any advice, it would be not to piss off Frances Cobb. She practically owns the whole village, and if she says jump, the locals say how high."

"You think that's what this is?" Collie asked. "I haven't done anything to this Cobb woman. My niece starts at her school today."

Fiona shrugged. "Maybe. What I do know is no animal I've ever seen left those marks. And maybe it isn't Frances Cobb. I don't really know the woman beyond going to school at Highmore. But I didn't have much to do with her even then."

"She was running the school back then?" Collie asked and immediately realized how that sounded. "Sorry, I didn't mean you're old. I just—that's a long time to be a headmistress."

"Thanks a lot." Fiona laughed.

"Shit, I didn't mean that either." Collie could feel her face burning. *Way to go, you idiot.*

"It's okay—I know what you meant. That old battleaxe has been around forever. And I'm not saying she's got anything to do with it, or the locals want you gone—seems a bit extreme even for them—just that my friend's friend got pushed out, so watch your back."

"What happened to him?" Collie asked.

"What?"

"The bloke they ran out of town. What happened to him?"

"Oh. I don't know. He dropped off the radar. I think my friend said he moved abroad."

Collie sighed. "So now they're going to do the same to me."

"I don't think so. If it is them, it's probably more of a warning. Maybe just to scare you, or wind you up. I don't know—I'm guessing really. All I do know is that those marks weren't made by any animal I've ever seen."

Collie nodded. It made more sense that it was someone playing games. "I did wind up two women in the local shop. I was being a bit of an arsehole, going on about wanting vegetarian mince. We argued."

Fiona laughed. "Yeah, that might do it. Look, I'm not saying anyone here is evil, or they'll be coming with pitchforks for you. But probably whoever was in the shop told someone about it, and they thought it would be funny to scare you."

"Pretend there's some beast loose and trying to get into the townie vegetarian's house?" Collie said.

"Yeah, exactly that. Or maybe idiot kids. Who knows? Point is, I'm almost positive no animal did it."

Collie had to admit it made sense. Far more sense than a monster trying to break down her door. She took a breath, felt some of the fear leave.

"Well, that sounds more likely. I guess I have some apologizing to do if I want into the good books," Collie said.

"I don't know as you'll ever get in their good books. I live eight miles away, and I'm considered an outsider by them," Fiona said and rolled her eyes. "I would suggest building bridges, though. Plus, it was probably kids who did it anyway. I can't imagine an adult doing something as juvenile as that. My advice—if you want it?"

Collie did. She nodded.

"Mention what happened in the village," Fiona said. "They won't say anything to you, but you can bet they'll know which kids did it, and they'll deal with it—if it was kids. And if it's an adult, maybe they got what they wanted out of it already."

That sounded like a good idea. "Thanks, you've been really helpful."

"Of course. We're neighbours now," Fiona said and winked in a friendly way.

"You live eight miles away."

"That's neighbours, round these parts."

Collie laughed. "In that case, hello, neighbour."

Fiona laughed. "I have to go—got a few appointments today. If you're ever looking to visit the zoo, you should come by on Saturdays. It's when we do a little show with the birds of prey. You'd like it."

Was Fiona flirting again or just being friendly? Collie wasn't sure. The way she was looking at Collie suggested she might be flirting. Collie still felt nothing.

Because you can't get Emily out of your mind.

And that was ridiculous. She'd seen the woman three times.

If Collie was looking to start something up, Fiona was a much better bet anyway. Emily was Lana's teacher, and that would make things way messy. She looked at Fiona now. Depressingly, Collie just couldn't get up any enthusiasm to flirt back, so she didn't.

"Sure. My niece and my mate are animal lovers, so maybe I'll bring them by sometime," Collie said.

Fiona nodded. "Okay, then. Well, bye."

"I'll walk you out," Collie said and sensed Fiona's disappointment. Collie felt bad, but she just wasn't interested.

She watched Fiona drive off and felt relieved. She had the house to herself now until three thirty when the school bus would drop Lana at the end of the drive. Time to do some work. And fix those marks on the back door.

❖

Lana sat outside Miss Cobb's office. She knew she hadn't done anything wrong, but she felt a funny quiver in her belly all the same.

She was good at school and hadn't been in trouble before, so this was new for her. She waited for Miss Cobb to call her in and wondered what she wanted.

She didn't have to wait long. The big door opened, and Miss Cobb stepped out. Lana watched the huge woman look around the reception before her eyes landed on Lana, and she smiled. Lana felt the urge to pee. The story of Little Red Riding Hood came into her head, and she didn't know why.

Grandma, what big teeth you have.

"Lana Franklin," Miss Cobb said.

"Yes, miss," Lana replied in a small voice.

"Come in, come in."

Miss Cobb moved aside and beckoned Lana over. Lana went reluctantly. Part of her—the scared baby part—wondered if she'd ever come back out.

The office was full of dark wood, books, photos, and ornaments. Lana thought her mum would have hated a room like this. She liked clean and tidy and hated any knick-knacks.

"Sit down, dear." Miss Cobb motioned to an uncomfortable looking chair in front of her massive desk.

Lana sat.

"The reason I've asked to see you today, Lana, is that I'm aware of your situation, and I've taken a special interest in you. Settling in is going to be much, much harder for you than it would be for another student. I certainly don't give this much attention to everyone, you know."

Lana wanted to say something like, *Yay for me*. But she held her tongue. She'd been well-brought-up and wouldn't dream of talking to an adult like that. Especially not a headmistress. Instead, she smiled as best she could and nodded.

"My dear, I want you to feel free to come to me whenever you want. I'll be asking Miss Lassiter to keep me updated on your progress. We do things a lot differently than you're probably used to in London. Our standard of education is much higher, and you may find yourself, at times, struggling to keep up. If that happens, I want you to say something."

Lana nodded again. So far she hadn't any trouble keeping up with the lessons.

"Miss Lassiter is an excellent teacher, but like you, she's new here in Hyam. You'll find many things are done differently here, not just in school. My door is always open, dear."

"Thank you," Lana said, the first words she'd uttered since walking in.

"Usually for the Spring Fair the oldest year in the school—that's your year—walk in the parade. However, with what's gone on with your mother, I'd understand if you didn't want to do it. No one will think any less of you, dear."

The longer the conversation went on—if you could call it a conversation—the more Lana felt like a bug under a microscope. Miss Cobb was talking *at* her instead of *to* her, but all the same, she was staring. To listen to her, Lana might as well not be there, but Miss Cobb's eyes were like lasers boring into her.

Grandma, what big eyes you have.

It was stupid, but Lana thought Miss Cobb was maybe trying to see something like hurt or pain in her. Every time Miss Cobb mentioned Lana's mother, that's when she stared the most.

She wants your pain, and you'd better not give it to her, or she'll keep calling you back here to get more.

Simultaneously Lana decided the thought was both stupid and spot on. Whatever she wanted, Lana thought, she was not going to give it to her. Miss Cobb was not a nice person, not at all.

"I'd like to be in the fair if I'm allowed, please," Lana said.

Miss Cobb's laser eyes bored into Lana again, and Lana steeled herself against them.

"Well, I think I can say we'd all be delighted if you were. In fact, in honour of your starting at the school and beginning a new chapter in your life after your terrible tragedy, I think you should have the starring role," Miss Cobb said, and her mouth turned up in what Lana thought passed for a smile, except Lana knew the starring role was another push for a reaction.

"Okay, thank you," Lana said and watched the smile falter for a moment.

"Don't you want to know what it is?" Miss Cobb asked.

"Yes, please," Lana said.

A sly look came over Miss Cobb's face, the kind of look a girl called Marie at Lana's old school got just as she was getting ready to pinch you.

"Oh, why don't we let it be a surprise, Lana? It'll be more fun that way. You'll be part of a very, very ancient tradition, going all the way back to the Anglo-Saxons, my dear."

"But how will I know what to do?" Lana asked.

"It won't be difficult, dear, so don't worry about that," Miss Cobb said. "Now, I believe I can hear your friends getting ready to go outside for break. You should join them."

"Yes, Miss Cobb. Thank you," Lana said obediently.

"One more thing, dear."

Lana stopped, caught somewhere between standing and sitting. "Yes, miss."

"There's a funfair coming to Hyam at the weekend. Perhaps your new friends have mentioned it."

Lana didn't have any friends. She was hoping that would change. "No, no one's mentioned it."

"Well, it would be a good opportunity for you and your aunt to meet people. Perhaps get involved in the village," Miss Cobb said.

"I'll ask her," Lana said.

"For a small village, we have a lot going on. It's important to me to create a sense of community. I think your aunt in particular would benefit from adopting a similar mindset. If you get my drift."

Lana didn't, but she nodded anyway.

Miss Cobb put her hands on the desk and pushed herself up. Lana looked at those large hands and strong arms—

Grandma, what big arms you have.

And imagined Miss Cobb picking her up and throwing her—

Why won't this stuff get out of my head?

Then watched as Miss Cobb went to the office door and easily shoved it open. "I'll see you soon, Lana."

Lana felt like she was finishing a long prison sentence. She half expected Miss Cobb to slam the door shut again just as Lana got to it.

She didn't, though, and Lana didn't think she'd ever been as relieved to get out of a room.

CHAPTER ELEVEN

Emily watched Lana in the playground. She was playground monitor today, which meant cramming a sandwich down her neck at lunch and rushing out here to make sure none of the kids killed themselves or each other.

Highmore School served about five local villages, including Hyam, which was where the new girl, Lana, lived. Currently, Lana was sitting on a low wall, watching some kids kick around a football.

Emily had introduced her to the class this morning and since then hadn't heard a peep out of her. Understandable when you considered what happened to her. Mother murdered by an ex-boyfriend. Horrible.

Because she was still a journalist at heart, even if she was currently masquerading as a year six teacher, Emily looked the story up online. It was particularly brutal and made worse by some unscrupulous journalist from one of those internet rags full of misinformation publishing a picture of Lana. That kind of thing disgusted Emily. She firmly believed people had a right to know what was happening in the world and to know the whole story, but throwing a ten-year-old girl under the bus to get clicks was despicable.

Emily sighed. Lana was in her class, so she supposed she should go over and talk to her, make sure she was okay. Charlie would have been so much better at this.

"Hi, Lana," Emily said softly.

Lana's head swung round, and her eyes widened in alarm before she realized it was just Emily.

"Hi, Miss Lassiter," Lana said.

It was on the tip of Emily's tongue to say *Call me Emily* before she realized they were at school and Lana most definitely had to call her Miss Lassiter.

"I noticed you were sitting by yourself. Would you like me to ask if you can join in the football game?" Emily asked.

"Oh no. Please don't do that," Lana said as if Emily asked her whether she'd like to set light to the school instead.

"I'm sure they wouldn't mind," Emily said.

"No. No, it would make me look really pathetic," Lana said, and Emily realized she was right. She already knew she wasn't a great teacher, but she had been a little girl once, so there was no excuse.

"You're right. I'm sorry. I know these things are delicate. You will fit in, though. It just takes time," Emily said and hoped that was true.

She thought it probably was with most of the kids. Well, all except the Hyam ones, who seemed to stay in their own little cliques and rarely mixed with children from other villages. They were truly strange. Except, Lana lived in Hyam, and those were the children she needed to be friends with.

"Yeah," Lana replied without much enthusiasm.

Emily racked her brain, trying to think of what to do. It hurt her heart to see this little girl sitting completely alone in the playground. Then she had an idea. Kitty Wilson. She was a Hyam kid, but she was slightly more friendly than the others, and she was always on her bloody phone, which Emily could use to her advantage.

Emily scanned the playground and saw her over by the water fountain with Daisy Atkinson.

"Hi, girls," Emily said, approaching them. They both looked at her warily.

"We're allowed our phones at break time," Kitty said, hiding the phone behind her back anyway.

"I mean, you aren't really, are you?" Emily said. "You're allowed to check messages at break. You've been on that phone for about ten minutes."

"Are you going to confiscate it?" Kitty asked.

"No, but I want you to do me a favour in return," Emily said.

"Okay." Kitty looked so relieved she'd probably do anything to keep her phone. Emily didn't understand these kids.

"You know the new girl, Lana?"

"Yeah," both girls said in unison.

"I want you to go over and ask if she'd like to join you in whatever it is you're looking at on that phone," Emily said.

"Oh, miss. Do we have to?" Kitty's face scrunched up like she'd smelled something bad, and Emily wanted to laugh.

"No, you don't. But instead you'll have to give me your phone."

"Miss, that's blackmail," Daisy said. She looked outraged.

"I mean, yeah, it is. But those are my terms. Take them or leave them, girls," Emily said.

"Fine. But what if she doesn't want to hang out with us?" Kitty asked.

"If you fail in your mission, I'm going to have to take that phone. And I'll keep it until the end of the week," Emily said.

"Miss!" Kitty was shocked and outraged. Emily didn't blame her.

"We'll do it," Daisy said quickly.

Emily nodded and walked away.

About fifteen minutes later, she saw Lana, Kitty, and Daisy by the water fountain hunched over the phone. Emily thought they looked like they were getting on. Maybe she wasn't such a bad teacher after all.

Emily's own phone buzzed in her pocket. She took it out and read the message. *May have some info re the thing you asked me to check. Will email you tonight. Trish x*

Emily felt sweeping relief. She'd come to a bit of a dead end as far as her brother was concerned. Now, maybe, there was some news.

Emily checked her watch. Three more hours until school finished. She had a ton of marking to do, but if Trish wasn't emailing until tonight, she reckoned she could get the marking done in time.

❖

"Sorry she made you hang out with me," Lana said to the other two girls.

Kitty shrugged, barely looking up from her phone. "Don't worry. It's not your fault Miss Lassiter blackmailed us."

"I'm going to tell my dad," Daisy said.

"As if he'll believe you. Anyway, better not. She'll definitely take my phone then," Kitty said.

"Do you like TikTok videos, Lana?" Kitty asked.

"Sure. I watch them sometimes," Lana said.

"Where did you go before? When you left class?" Daisy asked.

"Oh, I had to go and see Miss Cobb. To make sure I'm *settling in*," Lana said and rolled her eyes.

Kitty scrunched up her face. "Yuck. She's so *weird*. Don't you think?"

"Totally. I wasn't sure I was going to get out of there alive," Lana said, relieved to have something to talk to the two girls about.

"You live in Hyam, don't you? The old Roper place near the woods," Kitty asked.

"Yes."

"She lives on the other side of the woods. In a huge old house all by herself. My mum said she's loaded and not even married. She's like, a hundred years old," Daisy said.

"She creeps me out," Kitty added. "My parents say I have a lot to thank her for, and I should be grateful. I don't know what for, though, except she owns everything in the village, and my dad said everyone works for her."

Lana thought about Miss Cobb living in her big house all alone. It sounded lonely. Although her mum and her dad were dead, Lana still had Collie and Tony.

"Doesn't she have any family?" Lana asked.

"She has a niece. Anthea. You've probably seen her at the shop. She's eighteen this year, and they're having a big party for her after the Spring Fair," Kitty said.

"I haven't been in the shop. And what is this Spring Fair? It's all anyone talks about," Lana said.

Lana noticed a look passing between Kitty and Daisy. "It's just an old fair thing we do. It's ancient," Daisy said.

"Miss Cobb told me I was going to have the starring role in it. But she wouldn't tell me what it was doing. She made it seem like a really big deal," Lana said.

Kitty rolled her eyes. "Don't worry. She acts like it's this huge thing, but basically you just walk in front with some flowers in your hair or something. It's so boring."

There was that look again. Lana knew they were keeping a secret, but that was okay. They were best friends, and Lana only met them today.

"Yeah, you'll be fine. She only ever picks Hyam kids to do it, so you should be honoured she chose you," Daisy said.

Lana had a lot more questions about Miss Cobb and the Spring Fair, but she decided to wait. She looked behind her at Miss Lassiter pretending not to see them on Kitty's phone. Lana liked her. And she was an outsider too, so maybe she could talk to her. Although didn't all the teachers stick together?

"Oh, hey, Lana look at this. It's hilarious," Kitty said, holding up her phone.

Lana looked at the stupid video and pretended to find it funny as well. But all she could think about was Miss Cobb, and why she might want to hurt Lana and make her upset. And at the same time give her the starring role in what was clearly a big deal in Hyam.

CHAPTER TWELVE

There. Collie looked at the door and thought it would do. The wood filler covered the marks, and she wouldn't sand the door until she was ready to paint. Otherwise, because the marks were so deep, they would still be visible and would scare the shit out of Lana—and if she was being truthful, herself.

Collie spent most of the day trying to convince herself it was a wind-up by locals. But the thought kept creeping in that maybe it wasn't. Maybe it was some kind of monster like the one she'd drawn, come to life and escaped off the page.

It was a stupid thought, but she couldn't get it out of her head. She hadn't been able to work either. Her job at the moment was working on the monster for the new Sooba video game, she couldn't bring herself to look at the thing she'd created.

Stupid, stupid, stupid. It was just a video game, and the door was just a wind-up.

What if it's not?

That voice inside her head just wouldn't be quiet. It had always been there, but lately it was starting to sound more like Sasha. Maybe she was going crazy? She hoped not. For one thing, she was pretty much all Lana had left. What would happen to the kid if Collie lost it?

She took a deep breath and felt her knees pop as she stood. Not as young as she used to be.

Collie collected up her tools and went back in the house. She'd have to do some work today whether she liked it or not. The company had been really good about the delays so far, but their goodwill wouldn't last forever.

Collie took several deep breaths and worked on thinking happy thoughts. Tony swore by meditation, and maybe he was on to something.

Collie was prepared to try anything to get her out of this weird mindset she'd found herself in.

❖

Lana stepped off the bus. Today hadn't been a bad day at all. She'd been dreading it at first. Especially after what happened this morning. Collie tried to hide it from her, but she'd heard the bangs and seen the look on Collie's face.

Lana knew it wasn't a spider that had Collie so spooked. She had an idea she knew what it was, though. That thing who watched her from the bushes. But that was stupid, wasn't it? Her mum always said she had a vivid imagination.

Lana spooked herself easily, and sometimes her imagination ran wild before she could rein it in.

How likely was it that something was lurking in the bushes watching her? Pretty unlikely. All the same, Lana was afraid. She tried not to be, but that small kernel of fear had taken residence in her belly and was always ready to blossom like popcorn at the slightest provocation.

She decided not to think about it as she approached the drive. Why psych herself out before she'd even started walking down? She turned her attention instead to her new school.

Lana had been terrified when she'd first walked into the classroom. She'd never started a new school before where she didn't know *anyone*. But Kitty and Daisy were nice. Even if Miss Lassiter made them be friends with her, they'd been nice about it. By the end of break the three of them were getting on well. Mostly it was their shared interest in TikTok videos—especially the dance ones, which they tried to copy without much success. Lana guessed she'd see tomorrow whether they dropped her or not.

Lana adjusted the rucksack on her shoulders and started off down the drive. She hadn't been up here alone since the day she'd taken the rubbish out and spooked herself.

Like before, the sun was shining, and bees buzzed nearby. It was a beautiful afternoon, and Lana thought she'd do her homework on the grass under the big tree in the back garden if Collie let her.

Something moved in the bush to her left. Fear blossomed and popped in her chest, and Lana broke into a run. She'd tried to be brave, but this drive was creepy. Her feet slapped the gravel, and she jumped a pothole before she could twist her ankle. The gate screeched in protest as she shoulder-barged it open and shoved it closed again.

Lana threw open the front door and winced as it banged the wall behind.

"Lana?" Collie's voice came from the kitchen. "Is that you?"

And then her aunt appeared in the doorway looking all worried and confused.

"Sorry, I swung it too hard," Lana said.

"Why are you panting? Did you run? Is everything all right?" Collie had come completely out of the kitchen.

"I'm fine. Honest. I wanted to see how long it would take me to run up the drive," Lana lied and felt bad.

"What? Why?" Collie asked.

Lana shrugged. "To see."

Collie scrunched her forehead. "Fair enough," she said. "If you're sure you're all right?"

"I am," Lana replied, more chirpily than she felt. She couldn't tell Collie the truth because she would seem like a baby. And the good thing about Collie was she didn't push. If Lana told her something, she accepted it. Which made Lana feel even worse. Collie trusted her to tell the truth.

"Can I get a snack to take upstairs while I do my homework?" Lana asked. The garden seemed less appealing now.

"Sure. There's crisps or chocolate. Oh, and I bought ice cream," Collie said.

Lana almost laughed. Her mum would be horrified. Usually she got a sandwich or cereal or a yoghurt for her snack. Collie was clueless.

"That's fine, I'll get a banana," Lana said. She couldn't dupe Collie a second time.

"Right. Oh. You aren't allowed crisps and stuff?" Collie asked. "My bad."

The way she said it made Lana's heart hurt. It was as if her mum was coming back, and Collie would be in trouble if Sasha found out what Lana had eaten.

"It's okay, Aunt Collie, you didn't know. I promise I'll tell you if you're spoiling me too much. I won't take advantage of you like other kids would," Lana said.

"Thanks, Lana Banana. I appreciate that." Collie laughed. "Are you sure you're all right?"

"Yeah, fine," Lana said and went into the kitchen.

"It's a lovely day—do you want to do your homework outside? There's a table and chairs out there," Collie said. "I cleaned them all up earlier."

It *was* a beautiful day. "Will you stay out there with me?" Lana asked.

Collie looked confused. "Sure, if you want. I can get my book."

Lana nodded. She did want to be outside but not alone. It might have been her imagination just now on the drive, but the other day there was definitely something lurking out there. Even though she tried to tell herself she was wrong, she knew it.

She should tell Collie. Especially after what happened this morning, but she was afraid. She didn't want to cause trouble, and Collie would probably make them move. Maybe even back to London. Lana would keep quiet for now. After all, it was only rustling in bushes. It could be anything. A fox or a cat. They were in the countryside, after all. Maybe, if she did end up becoming friends with Kitty and Daisy, she could tell them. They might know what it was.

Lana walked out the french doors and sat at the table. Collie sat down next to her and picked up her book.

Lana got out her homework and started on her maths.

CHAPTER THIRTEEN

Emily opened the last email her brother sent before he went missing. She must have read it a million times, looking for clues, looking for something that might tell her what happened to him.

They'd always emailed each other regularly, since their university days. Emily guessed it was their version of letter writing. She'd kept them all. They were all pretty much the same stuff—what they were up to, work, friends. Nothing big, nothing earth-shattering.

When Charlie moved to Hyam, the emails were the same until a few months before his disappearance. Something was wrong, he'd written. He'd felt as though he was being watched. Emily had a vague recollection of him mentioning it early on when he moved here, just a couple of times, and then the emails went back to normal. Four months later, he wrote to tell her something was very wrong in Hyam.

He wouldn't go into detail, not until right at the end. At the end, he wrote he was coming to see her, that he had something to tell her, something mad, something she might not believe. They'd arranged to meet in London, near her work, but he'd never shown up.

When he disappeared, she'd printed off the emails, but no one was interested. If anything, they said, it possibly showed a deterioration of his mental health, which might explain his disappearance. It wasn't, though. Something here genuinely scared him.

Emily sighed and leaned back from her desk. So much she still didn't know, so much he hadn't told her, and now she was here. She'd left her job and moved halfway across the country to figure out what happened, what had gone wrong. And Charlie, God love him, hadn't given her much to go on.

Her computer pinged with a new message. Trish. Emily opened the email.

Hey Em, as promised I got the information on the Head of your school that you wanted. I'm not sure it means much, but it's a place to start. Took a bit of digging for as well, which makes you wonder what she's hiding...Anyway, let me know if you need anything else. Trish x

Trish was great. Emily met her a couple of years ago for a story she was working on. Trish was a researcher, and she could find out anything. They'd got pretty close during that story and understandably thought that would translate into a relationship. They'd been very wrong.

Aside from the fact they were both completely obsessed by their work and hardly saw each other, when they did, they had very different ideas about what to do with their time. Emily loved nothing more than having friends and family over to her place for food and drinks. Trish, on the other hand, loved to go clubbing and bar-hopping.

Emily smiled at the memory of them both sitting on a low wall outside some club or other one cold and rainy Saturday night, deciding this really wasn't going to work out. They ended the relationship but kept the friendship, and Emily was glad.

She hadn't told Trish exactly what she was up to, and Trish hadn't asked. The woman knew how to mind her own business when someone didn't want to talk about something—great for friendship, and not so great for a girlfriend.

Emily double-clicked on the email attachment and sat back to read. It didn't take long for her to become engrossed. She read as the sky outside turned dark.

When she finished, Emily had a plan, a place to start. Like Trish said, the information might not mean anything, but it was a start. Frances Cobb.

Emily was working her way through people Charlie had known when he was here. She'd picked up a few names—Hamish was one of them, but he'd checked out.

He hadn't really spoken of many people, so a lot of it was guesswork on Emily's part, people she knew he would have come into contact with. She wasn't sure what she was hoping to find, but there had to be something here. People didn't just vanish.

Unless they kill themselves.

Even then, there was usually a body.

Maybe there is. In the woods or the river. They just haven't found it yet.

Emily sighed. All very plausible. He could have drowned—they were close to water. The forests were huge and probably largely unwalked.

Emily brought up Charlie's last email again.

Ems, sorry I haven't been in touch. Stuff's been happening here, stuff you probably won't believe, but I'll tell you anyway. Not on here, in case they can see it—hack my emails or something. I wouldn't put anything past these people. I'll come to you. Next week is half-term, and I was planning to come up and see the parents anyway. Do not come here. I may not be coming back. This place is not what it seems. I thought it was a quiet village, but it's not at all. I am being watched, just like I thought. And now it's all of them watching me, not just the thing in the bushes.

It's fucked up is what it is. Anyway, I'll text you when I get to London, and we'll meet somewhere. I'll tell you what I know. You're a journalist, so I'm guessing you'll have ways of digging into this better than I ever could.

Love you. See you soon.
Charlie

Emily still had no idea what he'd been talking about. He hadn't said much when she'd phoned him either. They'd just arranged a time and day to meet. Charlie hadn't wanted to talk on the phone for long—he'd never been one for telephone conversations anyway.

All Emily knew was he'd found something out. Something that had to do with whatever was watching him. Whatever was in Hyam. Emily didn't want to believe he was delusional like the rest of her family did. She knew him better than anybody, and she would have known if he was unwell.

Would she, though? He sent those emails which laid out pretty clearly how unwell he was. Being watched, everyone out to get him.

No. *No.* Charlie was not unwell. She would have known. He didn't kill himself either.

Outside, a dog barked. It made Emily jump, and for the first time she realized it had grown fully dark, and her curtains were still open. She got up now to close them. The dog was still barking.

Emily looked outside onto her back garden, heavy with shadow and dark places where the security lights didn't reach. She really needed to do something about it. The weeds had almost completely overtaken it. Not that she was a gardener, but everyone else around here had nice, neat English looking gardens. She was already a massive outsider, and leaving her garden looking like that wasn't going to help.

Just then, something darted out of the undergrowth and around the side of the house. Emily jumped back and let out a little shout of surprise. Her heart rate picked up.

She told herself it was probably a fox. But it looked too big to be a fox. A coldness settled in Emily's belly, and her skin prickled. Stupid. She was spooked because of the emails from Charlie. That was all.

Emily decided to lock the doors anyway. Since moving here, she'd become a bit lax about it. Hardly anyone around here locked up. Tonight she would. She started with the french doors in the living room where she was now.

Emily looked outside briefly, wanting to see if the thing was there and also not wanting to know. She started to draw the curtains. Suddenly, something hit the glass. Hard.

Emily jumped back in surprise and screamed.

Glass cracked and shattered.

CHAPTER FOURTEEN

Collie put the DVD back in its case and switched off the TV. Lana had taken herself off to bed. Collie said she'd look in on her, not knowing if Lana was too old for that now or not. Either way, she hadn't said anything—not that she would. Collie got the impression Lana was on her best behaviour. Aside from the grief, there was a stiffness and formality that hadn't been there before.

Collie hoped it would go away. The last thing Lana needed was the stress of being on her best behaviour on top of everything else she was going through. Collie thought she'd call Tony in the morning and see what he thought.

As she switched the light out in the living room, she heard a scream, then the sound of a dog barking ferociously.

What the bloody hell was that?

It sounded like it came from the front of the house. Collie remembered there was one other house on their drive, positioned up a small drive of its own. Should she go check or just call the police?

Ordinarily, she wouldn't hesitate to go and look, but she had Lana to worry about now.

"Collie, what was that noise?"

Collie turned to see Lana standing on the stairs, looking worried.

"I don't know. Listen, I'm going to go and see. Keep the door locked, and don't come out, all right?" Collie said.

Lana nodded.

Collie was very aware of the thing that marked her door earlier. Was this part two of that? Or was someone genuinely in trouble? Of course, it might be nothing at all. The number of times in London she'd been ready to dial the police when she heard screaming, and it turned out to be drunk people walking home…This wasn't London, though.

Collie stepped outside into the night. She breathed in deep and started walking up the path.

You couldn't see the other house from this angle—it was totally obscured by trees. Collie strained her ears to listen for any other sounds. Nothing. Somewhere in the distance an owl hooted.

Collie used the light from her phone to guide her way. There were no lights down here at all, and the moon was still just a sliver in the sky.

She started up her neighbour's small drive, and as she came around the bend, she saw lights blazing in the downstairs window and the front door wide open.

Collie started to call out when something hit her from behind.

❖

Lana peeked through the curtains in her bedroom. Her window looked out onto the driveway, and she saw Collie and her torch bobbing their way up the path before she disappeared up the neighbour's drive.

Was this to do with whatever banged into their door this morning? Lana thought the thing in the bushes on the drive was just her imagination, but what if it was real? What if there really was something lurking in there?

But that wasn't possible, was it? How many times had her mum told her there was no such thing as monsters? So many times that Lana believed it. What if her mum was wrong?

Lana had been getting into bed when she heard the scream. She was used to hearing things like that in London. Idiots being noisy because they were drunk or just messing about. But out here it was strange. Everything was so quiet, and at night all you could hear were owls and foxes—night animals.

Lana waited for the light from Collie's phone to reappear. Why did she go and look? Why didn't she just call the police?

After Mum died, when Lana found out someone put her picture online as the dead woman's daughter, she'd been desperate to get away. Go somewhere nobody knew her. Collie suggested the country, and she'd jumped at it. Now she was beginning to wonder if she'd made the right decision. She missed her house, she missed her friends, and she missed her life. Who let a ten-year-old make decisions anyway?

Collie did. Lana could have asked for a pony, and Collie would have got her one.

Lana carried on staring out the window. Where was Collie?

Out of the corner of her eye, Lana saw something move. She cried out and jumped back from the window.

Collie. Collie's out there with it.

Lana ran downstairs and grabbed a knife from the kitchen cupboard. It was as long as her arm, but it still felt useless and weak— she might as well have been holding a banana.

Only silver will stop that thing.

And that was a ridiculous thought. It wasn't a werewolf. Those things were make-believe.

All the same, Lana reached back in the drawer and pulled out an ornate cake knife Collie only used for special occasions, like cutting birthday cake. She said it belonged to Collie's mother and was made out of pure silver. Lana wasn't sure if Collie was just winding her up as usual, but it wouldn't hurt to take it, just in case.

Lana stepped out onto the garden path. She'd forgotten to put on shoes, but at least she had two knives. She felt stupid and small and useless. But she wasn't going to let that thing get Collie. She hadn't been able to help her mother, but she wasn't going to lose her aunt as well without at least trying to help her.

Lana made her way cautiously up the path. The gravel chips were rough beneath her feet, but at least the ground was dry.

Her attention was fixed on the bushes and on trying not to run back into the house. Her heart hammered in her chest, and the cold night air made her cheeks sting.

Nevertheless, she kept on. She got to the gate. Suddenly, from her left came a loud rustling.

Something was coming.

Lana widened her stance and held the knives up, ready for whatever came out, and tried desperately not to be afraid. She felt something move up behind her and almost bolted but just as quickly realized whatever was behind her wasn't *it*. Was it Collie? She didn't dare turn to look, but Collie would have said something. Whatever it was, it gave Lana confidence and made her feel almost protected. It was *good*.

She planted her feet and prepared to face the thing in the bushes.

CHAPTER FIFTEEN

Emily screamed again.

She drew back her fist ready to hit whatever she'd run in to, and then she saw it was Collie.

"What the bloody hell are you doing?" Collie asked.

Emily was momentarily blinded by Collie's phone torch, which shone in her face. "Can you point that somewhere else, please?" Emily asked.

"What? Oh, sorry." Collie turned it off, and they were left in mostly darkness. "Whoops," she said, and then it came back on, but the light was pointed downward.

"Thanks," Emily said.

"I heard a scream. Was it you? Are you okay?" Collie asked.

"Yes, I'm okay. Something smashed the glass in my living room doors," Emily said.

"Shit. What? I didn't call the police yet. Probably should have. Why didn't I?" The woman was talking to herself. "Sorry, I'm not very good at this."

"It's okay," Emily said.

"It was stupid really," Collie said. "And every time I see you, I seem to be apologizing."

"You came to my rescue armed with nothing but your phone torch. Nothing says sorry like a half-arsed rescue attempt." Emily tried to lighten the mood, and it seemed to work.

"Well, I thought if anything would save you, it would be this smartphone," Collie said.

"You're right—it's a formidable weapon. Thank you for coming to check on me. It was just a shock, that's all. I was right there when it happened."

"They smashed the whole door, you say?" Collie asked.

"Yes. The glass."

"A small village full of vandals," Collie said.

Emily wanted to tell her it wasn't a vandal that smashed her doors, but how could she? Emily didn't even see it, not properly. It was so fast all she'd been able to make out was a shape, large and hulking. Animal.

"We had someone damage our back door today. It might be the same person," Collie said.

"Really? Not that I've been here very long, but that seems strange. Before tonight I'd never heard of anything like that."

"I have a feeling that whole incident in the shop the other day might be why my door got done. Maybe yours too. Maybe they got a taste for it?" Collie said.

"Who did?" Emily asked.

"The vandals. I should have called the police when I heard you scream, but…well. I didn't exactly get off on the right foot, and I didn't want to be known as a nut as well as the vegetarian townie. You know, in case it was nothing."

Emily opened her mouth to speak, but Collie's eyes widened and she held up her hands. "Not that what happened to you was nothing. I mean, someone breaking your door, that's criminal damage. It must have been scary."

Emily couldn't help but laugh at the attractive, flustered woman in front of her. Even if at the back of her mind she couldn't shake the image of that hulking shadow moving, smooth as water, through her garden.

"It's fine, Collie. Really. I didn't see what smashed my door. Just that it was big."

"Like an adult?" Collie asked.

Like a monster out of a storybook, Emily thought. "Maybe. Maybe not. I will call the police to file a report, but I don't imagine there's anything they can do."

Emily remembered one of her brother's emails when he first got to Hyam.

Em, do you remember that book Dad used to read to us when we were kids? The one about the purple monster? Well I thought I saw one in my garden last night. Except it wasn't purple, and it wasn't friendly. Don't worry, I'm not going

mad. I did have a lot to drink, though, so it was probably just
a fox. Scared the life out of me—haha.

"Are you all right? Besides someone smashing your doors, I
mean?" Collie asked.

Was she all right? Emily wasn't sure. All she could think about
was the thing at her door and her brother's email. *Do you remember the*
one about the purple monster? Emily shivered.

"Here." To Emily's surprise and, she had to admit, pleasure, Collie
took off her zip-up hoodie and draped it over Emily's shoulders. "You
looked cold."

"Thanks," Emily said and pulled it around her. It smelled of
washing powder.

"Do you want me to come up to the house with you? While you
call the police?" Collie asked.

"No, that's okay," Emily said. She'd decided she wouldn't be
calling the police. For one thing, it would draw too much attention to
her. But also, she was starting to wonder about her brother's emails and
the things he'd alluded to in them. She needed to get back home and
reread them. After she'd sorted the door.

"Are you sure? I mean, someone smashed your door. They meant
to do that. Whether it's a prank connected with what happened to me or
not..." Collie said.

"Honestly, I'm fine. I promise. You've been great, but I need to
get back and sort the door out," Emily said, aware that she sounded
impatient. Under other circumstances, she'd like to stay and talk with
Collie more, maybe flirt a little bit. But finding Charlie came before
everything else.

"Please. I really would feel much better. Do it for me?"

Emily rolled her eyes, even though she was sort of touched by
the gesture. "Fine, but keep your phone handy in case we run into
trouble."

Collie laughed, and the sound pleased Emily. She liked making
her laugh.

Okay. Enough of that.

They walked back up to Emily's house in silence. Emily because
she was listening for any noises that were out of place, and she guessed
Collie was doing the same.

"Well, looks like everything's okay," Emily said.

"Let me just check round the outside. Where were the doors that got smashed?" Collie asked.

Emily pointed around the other side of the house. "You don't have to, you know." But part of her wanted Collie to check. Maybe it would make her feel better.

"You go inside, and meet me by the doors," Collie said. Emily went into the house. She walked into the living room just in time to hear Collie whistle. "Blimey. They *really* smashed your doors in."

Emily snort-laughed, then quickly covered her mouth with her hand. "Sorry. Juvenile," she said.

Collie grinned. "I'm glad you can laugh about it. Are you sure you're okay? You can stay with us tonight."

"No, honestly. I'm fine. I'm going to call an emergency locksmith now and get the doors boarded up."

"Well, I guess you know where I am if you need me," Collie said.

"I do. And thanks again for, you know, coming to investigate," Emily said.

Collie laughed. "Yeah, in a film I'd be the first one killed off, wouldn't I?"

Emily grinned. "Lucky we aren't in a film."

Collie looked like she would say something else, but instead she nodded, ducked her head, and walked away. Emily watched her go, which didn't take long in the dark.

Emily went back into the hallway and locked the door. She took her laptop up into the bathroom—the only door that locked—and booted it up. She dialled an emergency locksmith to come and board up the door until tomorrow when she'd organize a proper repair.

Normally, the landlord should pay, but Emily didn't want to draw attention to herself or what had happened tonight.

She scrolled through her emails and found the one she was looking for.

Hey, sis, how's it going? So, here's something weird for you. I think I'm being watched. Like, from the bushes outside my house watched...

❖

Lana thought she might have peed herself a little. The thing that darted out of the bushes wasn't a huge, slathering monster. It was a badger. A short little fat-bummed badger that had taken one look at her and waddled straight back into the bushes.

Lana laughed out loud. Was that what was watching her earlier? And the other day? She was so relieved that she felt like she might float away.

Her mum always said she had a vivid imagination, and Lana guessed that was true. The monster she'd drawn in her mind was nothing but a chunky little badger. It was so loud in the bushes, though—it sounded much bigger that it actually was.

She supposed that's what scared her. Well, she didn't need to be afraid any more, though she'd heard they could be vicious. Best stay away from it.

And best get the knives back in the kitchen before Collie saw her and thought she'd lost her mind. And as for the other thing, the one standing behind her when she'd faced the bushes...best not to speak of that at all. Lana breathed deeply, the smell of it still in the air, lavender. It smelled like her mum.

Lana hurried back into the house, put away the knives, and went back to bed.

CHAPTER SIXTEEN

Collie waited with Lana for the school bus. Maybe she was being overprotective, but she didn't care. After yesterday, she didn't want Lana walking around by herself, even up the drive.

Collie decided she'd head into the local shop today and mention about the damage. If anything else happened, she'd be calling the police. Who cared if no one in the village ever spoke to her again?

Vandalizing people's doors went beyond a prank as far as Collie was concerned. And there was something about it, something that didn't seem like kids. Did kids smash a woman's door? Collie didn't think so.

Once Lana was on the bus, she walked down into Hyam. The shop was open, and the same woman who'd served her the other day was there.

Collie picked up a basket and put a couple of things in—bread, milk, biscuits, and margarine.

"Hi," she said, approaching the cashier.

The woman scowled at her and started ringing up her purchases.

"Look, I'm sorry about the other day. I was rude." Collie tried again.

"Yes, you were."

"It's no excuse, but I'm a bit stressed at everything at the moment, with the move and all."

The woman nodded. "Seven pounds sixty-three." She held out her hand and gave Collie a snotty look.

Collie sighed. "Look, you don't have to accept my apology. You don't have to like me, but damaging my door and my neighbour's is going too far."

"What are you talking about?" The woman looked confused.

"Yesterday. Someone damaged my back door and smashed the

glass out of my neighbour's. I assume it's local kids or whatever, but it's out of order."

"You think one of the villagers did that?" the woman asked.

"Well, who else? A burglar wouldn't make big bloody claw marks in someone's door, then leave. I almost called the police."

"Claw marks?"

"Yes. And smashed my neighbour's door. I don't want to have to call the police," Collie repeated.

The woman sighed. "Look, I'm not sure what you think we're about in this village, but if you honestly believe someone came and damaged your property—"

"And my neighbour's."

"And your neighbour's, well, I can assure you that you're barking up the wrong tree. I can't think of one person who'd do it. Now outsiders, maybe. Have you thought about that? Or did you just assume it was someone from here?"

Collie was slightly taken aback. "Well, I..."

"You just assumed that someone from here—maybe me, seeing as it was me you were so rude to—decided to get up in the night and come and damage your door. And your neighbour's. Let me give you some advice—if you're going to go round accusing people, you should get some proof first."

"What makes you think I don't have proof?" Collie asked.

"Do you?" the woman asked.

"Well, no."

"There you go, then. Even so, despite your rudeness, I'll ask around. If it was one of our kids that done it, I'll find out, and I can promise you—it'll stop."

Collie hadn't expected that. She didn't know what to say. She'd come here expecting a confrontation, not a dressing-down. "Thank you."

"And a little advice?" the woman said.

"Okay."

"This is a small village, and getting off on the right foot will make your life here a lot easier. We may be country people, but we aren't stupid or inferior or any of that. Your superior attitude isn't going to get you far."

Collie nodded. "I'll take it on board."

"See that you do."

Now, fully dressed down, Collie took her purchases and left the shop. Just as she stepped onto the pavement, the woman called her back.

"There's the Spring Fair in a couple of weeks. It's a big deal around here, and they're always looking for volunteers. Maybe you could offer your services. I hear you're an artist."

Collie didn't ask how the woman knew that. She supposed the letting agent had filled everyone in on exactly who Collie was.

"I'm a graphic artist, but yes, that sounds like something I could do. Thank you."

The woman nodded, then disappeared out to what Collie assumed was the back of the shop.

Collie walked back along the street, thinking about what the woman said to her. She'd just assumed it was someone from the village, but what if it wasn't? What if it was just some random vandal?

Collie shook her head. None of it made sense, and she was sick of thinking about it. She'd wait and see if anything else happened and deal with it then. She knew thinking like that was a cop-out, but what alternative did she have? She'd pretty much ruled out an animal or her video game monster. So what did that leave? A person. Who, though?

She kept coming back to kids. That was really the only explanation. Both she and Emily had been in their homes when it happened, and no one had tried to steal anything.

Still, it was unnerving. The damage done to her door wasn't bad, but smashing a glass door? That was pretty serious stuff.

Collie would wait and see whether anything else happened. If it didn't, she guessed she could leave it alone. But if it did, she was going straight to the police.

Fiona's friend might have turned tail and run, but Collie wasn't going to. One thing she knew about bullies was that you had to stand up to them.

Collie turned up the drive, taking care to avoid the potholes. Maybe she could get one of those camera systems installed, the ones that linked up with your phone. They weren't too expensive, and the footage was good quality. Maybe she should tell Lana's teacher Emily about it as well.

It would be an excuse to see her again. And while she was at it, she should find out more about this Spring Fair. It might even be fun. And there was a chance that if the damage was being done by local kids, getting more involved in the village might put a stop to it.

❖

Lana liked Miss Lassiter. She was pretty. She was also their neighbour, which was a bit weird. Lana had never thought of her teachers outside of school before. It hadn't occurred to her they had houses they lived in and stuff.

But now Miss Lassiter was her neighbour, and that meant she might see her out of school. Aunt Collie helped her when someone smashed her doors. Maybe they'd be friends, and that meant Lana would have to see Miss Lassiter all the time. Weird.

Kitty and Daisy were officially her friends now. They'd asked yesterday, and Lana was excited. Having friends meant no more sitting on her own at lunch or dreading break time. Although they both lived in Hyam, they weren't strange like the other Hyam kids who played together and didn't hang with anyone else. Mostly, they just hung out with each other.

Kitty was having a camping birthday party the week after the Spring Fair, and Lana was invited. They also wanted her to go to the funfair this weekend. She hoped Collie would let her go.

Now that she was sure the thing in the bushes was just a badger, she felt much better about the countryside. Before, she wasn't sure if she would have gone camping.

Lana hadn't spoken to Kitty or Daisy about the stuff going on at her house yet. They were best friends now, but that didn't mean she was ready to tell them everything just yet. Besides, Collie said it was kids, so maybe it was. Lana wouldn't be surprised, if the kids at Highmore were anything to go by.

She had a meeting with Miss Cobb later as well. Lana had never spoken with the headmistress at her old school, and here she was seeing Miss Cobb twice in two weeks.

Lana had half thought the first meeting with Miss Cobb was going to be the last. Miss Cobb made her feel strange in her belly in a way she couldn't explain or properly understand herself. All she kept thinking about was the Little Red Riding Hood story.

Grandma, what big teeth you have.

Anyway, she had to see her after lunch, so she had ages yet. She'd say she liked it here and it was a nice school and hopefully get to leave pretty quick. She knew it would be weird, though. Miss Cobb—while maybe not actually the wolf from the story—was creepy. Kitty and Daisy telling her about how Miss Cobb lived in a massive house all by herself didn't help. Lana tried to stop her imagination from taking that information and running away with itself.

She wished she didn't do it, but she couldn't stop. For example, every time she thought about Miss Cobb, she pictured her sitting up in a big bed in her big house wrapped in a shawl, just like the wolf in the Red Riding Hood story. It was stupid and made Lana feel hot and embarrassed.

It made her feel like a baby. Miss Cobb had done nothing to make Lana think she was a bad person.

Except she has. She kept bringing up Mum because she wanted to see you upset. Nice people don't do that.

Fine. Well, some adults were mean. Lana already knew that. Her old neighbour Mr. Wright used to shout at her if she was playing in the garden and her ball went over the fence. He *never* gave them back. Like her mum said, some people were just shits. It's how it was. And maybe Miss Cobb was a shit, but that didn't make her a monster.

Well, either way, she hoped the meeting was quick. She'd nod her head and say yes to whatever Miss Cobb said, so she could get out fast.

She wanted to be back in time for afternoon break when Kitty was going to tell them more about her camping birthday and the Spring Fair.

Lana would have to get Collie to drive her to a shop for Kitty's present. She had some money in her piggy bank. It would be enough for a decent present in London, but she wasn't sure about Suffolk. One time, Lana had gone to France on holiday, and they used completely different money that Lana didn't understand, and stuff cost different amounts there.

Lana knew they used pounds in Suffolk, but maybe presents cost more? She'd ask Collie later.

It was Friday, so Tony was coming down—he was really excited about the funfair—and they were having movie night. Lana loved Tony. He always made her feel better about stuff. And he was so funny. Lana thought Kitty and Daisy would love him. Maybe they could have a sleepover at her house, one time when Tony was visiting.

Lana would remember to ask Collie about that as well. She doubted Collie would mind. Collie was easy-going. She hadn't said no to anything so far. But Lana would still be careful not to annoy Collie or ask for too much.

Losing her mum like that—here one minute and gone the next—

had taught Lana that things changed, and they changed quickly. You couldn't rely on people sticking around.

It was like keeping the thing in the bushes from Collie. Lana didn't want to be any trouble or make Collie think she was going nuts. She wanted Collie to keep her, and that meant being as little trouble as possible. Plus, the thing in the bushes turned out to be a badger. Imagine if she'd told Collie how scared she was when it was only a badger? Majorly embarrassing.

Maybe she'd leave asking about the sleepover this week as well. She had Tony and the funfair and movie night to look forward to. Not to mention Kitty's birthday camping trip.

Things weren't so bad. Once she got the meeting with Miss Cobb out of the way, the weekend would be great.

CHAPTER SEVENTEEN

Collie looked up at the sound of the garden gate screeching open. She really needed to oil those hinges.

The soft crunch of gravel got louder as someone came up the path. Collie sat up in her garden chair and braced herself. Whoever it was wasn't in a hurry and wasn't trying to conceal their arrival. Plus, it sounded human, which was a bonus.

Collie rolled her eyes. She really needed to get a grip on herself and her imagination.

"Hello?" Collie called out.

Emily appeared from around the corner, holding Collie's hoodie in her hand.

"Hi." Emily held up the hoodie. "This belongs to you. I thought I'd return it."

Collie stood and dusted off her shorts. Not because they were dusty but because she was nervous, and when she got nervous, she never knew what to do with her hands. "Thanks."

"I washed it."

"You didn't have to." Collie was uncharacteristically lost for words. Emily looked amazing. She only wore a fairly plain summer dress and her hair was down, but she took Collie's breath away and left her tongue-tied.

"Right, well. I guess I'll leave it here," Emily said, hanging it over one of the chairs.

Collie remembered her manners. "Can I get you a drink? We have lemonade." Tony had made it that morning. The unusually fine weather had inspired him.

"Well, I don't know…" Emily said.

"It's homemade. Not by me. Which means it tastes good," Collie said.

Emily laughed, and Collie realized she liked the sound. "Okay then, yes. How can I refuse?"

Collie grinned. "Have a seat—I'll be right back."

❖

"Where's your niece today?" Emily asked as Collie put a cold glass down in front of her. It looked good. Almost as good as the woman who brought it to her.

"She went out with my friend Tony. They're getting snacks for movie night."

"Tony of the lemonade?" Emily asked.

"The very one. He's amazing round the house," Collie said.

"I see. And you and Tony are…" Emily wasn't sure how to finish and wished she could shut herself up. It was none of her business, and yet she wanted to know if Collie was single.

"What? Oh. No, no, we're just friends—well, more like family. Did you get your smashed doors sorted out?" Collie asked.

Emily noted the change of subject. "Yes, I did. Hopefully that'll be the last of it."

"Hopefully," Collie said.

"The other night, you said you had some trouble. Someone vandalized your door?" Emily tried to ask carefully. She didn't want it to seem like she was questioning Collie, but since that night, she'd started to think she might have a better idea of what was going on in the village—or at least a starting point.

"Yeah, scratched it up. I think it was village kids trying to wind us up. You know, after the incident at the shop," Collie said.

"So you've had no more bother from them?" Emily asked.

"No, none. I'm hoping they got bored and moved on. I really didn't want to have to call the police. What about you? Any more trouble?" Collie asked.

"No, none," Emily said and sipped the lemonade. "Wow, you weren't lying. That's really good."

"Isn't it? He won't give me the recipe. He reckons it's a family secret passed down through generations." Collie rolled her eyes.

Emily laughed. "Maybe it is."

"Bollocks it is. I've met his family, and they can just about boil an egg between them," Collie said and was pleased when Emily laughed again. It was a great sound. She liked being the one to make Emily laugh.

What was she doing? She needed to get a grip. For one thing, she wasn't dating at the moment, and for another, Emily was Lana's teacher. How weird would that be? Not to mention she didn't even know if Emily was interested in her.

"How are you finding it here so far?" Emily asked.

"Hyam? It's a strange place," Collie said. "Claw marks and door breaking aside."

Emily nodded. "Yeah, I think so too. I've never lived in the country before, so maybe it's that. Everyone here is just so…"

"Weird," Collie said. And then immediately, "Sorry, that was rude. I'm sure some of them are lovely. You, for example."

"Don't apologize—I feel the same way. And I'm not actually from here. I lived in London before," Emily said.

"We're from London too. Whereabouts did you used to live?" Collie asked and regretted it. She saw Emily's face shutter closed. Strange. It wasn't exactly a personal question.

"I've lived all over. But originally I'm from Somerset," Emily said.

Collie thought the words sounded stilted. She searched about for a safer topic because she didn't want Emily to make her excuses and leave. Collie was having a nice time.

"I'm hoping I might yet win over the locals. I've volunteered for the Spring Fair."

"Really? Doing what?"

Collie was relieved when Emily relaxed again. "I think decorating floats. Drawing stuff on them, you know."

"Oh yes, you're an artist," Emily said.

"I design characters for video games," Collie said.

"That's still an artist. You went to art school?"

"I did. It was that or a plumbing course," Collie joked.

Emily smiled. "So they're having floats. I've been roped in as well, but I'm not sure what I'm doing yet. I've not seen one of their fairs before."

"Me either. I am intrigued, though. They take it very seriously," Collie said.

"They do. And Lana has a starring role, I'm told," Emily said.

"Yes, she's some sort of spring maiden. I've been given very strict instructions about her costume."

"From Frances Cobb?"

"No, I haven't had the pleasure of meeting her yet. I spoke to her on the phone a couple of times when we were moving down. She sounds…fierce."

Emily laughed and nearly choked on her lemonade. "That's one word for her. I probably shouldn't bitch about my boss, but she's something of a caricature. Big, stern headmistress. Everyone seems terrified of her—even the teachers."

"Is she that bad? Lana says she's a bit weird," Collie asked.

"No, not really. She's just very strait-laced. She told me when I started that she liked the female teachers to wear skirts and blouses and the men to wear suits."

"Blimey," Collie said. "What did you say to that?"

"Oh, I nodded and smiled. I wear trousers if I want to, though. She's not said anything to me about it."

"Can she? Legally, I mean?"

"No. But I get the feeling she's one of those who still thinks men should get paid more, and a woman's place is in the home," Emily said.

"And yet she's a head teacher."

Emily shrugged. "It's just a feeling I have. I've nothing to base it on, and I could be wrong."

Except the look in Emily's eyes told Collie she didn't think she was wrong.

Emily looked at her watch. "I'd better go. Lots of marking to do."

"Are you sure? Tony and Lana should be back soon. We were going to barbecue—you're welcome to join us," Collie said, trying to prolong the afternoon. She liked Emily and didn't want her to go.

"I'd better not. But I will have another lemonade if there's any going?"

Collie practically jumped out of her chair. "Yes, of course. Hang on, I'll be right back."

Collie tripped over her chair in her haste, and the sound of Emily's laugh followed her into the kitchen.

She came back and handed Emily the lemonade. "It's nice having another grown-up to talk to."

"Your friend Tony seems to be here a lot," Emily said.

"You've seen him?" Collie asked and then watched, fascinated, as Emily's face flushed. *So you've been paying just as much attention to me as I have to you. Interesting.*

"Only, you know, we share a drive, and I, well, my bins are down here…" Emily stuttered. Collie hadn't heard her sounding so unsure before.

"Oh yeah, can't miss his massive truck." Collie decided to save Emily's dignity.

"Exactly. It's distinctive," Emily said, clearly relieved. "But I know what you mean. It can get lonely in the village. It's so insular. It's nice to have a friendly neighbour."

"It is. When you aren't so busy marking homework, you should come for a barbecue sometime," Collie said.

"Maybe I will. It might be nice to have a friend here," Emily replied.

Collie noted her emphasis on the word *friend*. Being friends and only friends would definitely make sense and would definitely be the sensible thing to do. The thing was, Collie couldn't help herself from wanting…something. Each time she spoke with Emily, she liked her more.

But it was a bad idea for a load of reasons. You weren't meant to fancy your friends.

"I'd better go," Emily said and drained her lemonade. "That really is great lemonade."

"It is." Collie stood up. "So, you'll find a date in your diary and come over for a barbecue?" Collie knew she was pushing, but she couldn't help herself.

"I'll see you before then," Emily said.

Collie couldn't keep the dopey smile off her face. "Oh yeah?"

"Yes. At the funfair tomorrow, I imagine. I thought I might have a go on the dodgems."

"You're going to the funfair?" Collie asked.

"I am indeed. I love a funfair. Apparently this one is a lot of fun with a very Hyam flavour, according to my friend."

"Well, I'll see you on the dodgems, I guess," Collie said.

"Plus don't we have the Spring Fair volunteers' meeting in a couple of days? I assumed you were going," Emily said.

"Right. Yes, I am. I suppose I'll see you there. Want to walk over together?"

"I would, but I have a school thing just before, and I'll be heading straight from Highmore," Emily replied.

"Ah. See you tomorrow then," Collie said.

"Thanks for the lemonade. If you ever get the recipe, you have to let me have it," Emily said.

"Will do. Let me walk you out."

Emily nodded and Collie followed her down the path. Collie walked Emily to the garden gate and watched her walk away. She couldn't keep what was probably a slightly stupid smile off her face. She'd better wipe that off soon, or Tony would tease her mercilessly.

Collie looked at her watch and decided it was probably time to get the barbecue going. Lana and Tony wouldn't be much longer.

CHAPTER EIGHTEEN

Emily closed her eyes and breathed in deep. Summer night air mixed with hot fried doughnuts, greasy grilled meat, and spicy onions. The smell of the funfair. The sound of delighted shrieks, the wheeze of accordion music, and the hum whoosh of the rides all transported her back to her childhood.

"I haven't been to a funfair in years," she said as she linked arms with Hamish and walked in. "I forgot how much I loved them."

"Don't say I don't know how to show a girl a good time," Hamish said and pulled Emily over to the Waltzer. "Come on, let's do the sick-making ones before we eat."

Emily laughed. "Sounds like a plan."

They got in the queue. Right behind Collie, Collie's friend, and Lana. Emily shot Hamish a look. In return he gave her a look of pure innocence and mouthed, *What?*

"Hi," Emily said when Collie and Lana turned to look at her.

"How's it going?" Collie said. "Erm…Tony, this is Lana's teacher, Miss Lassiter."

"Nice to meet you. Collie's told me about you," Tony said with a slight smile on his face.

What did that mean? What had Collie said? Why did she care? She didn't.

"This is Hamish—Mr. Ford. He also teaches at Highmore," Emily said.

"Nice to meet you. Emily's told me about you as well," Hamish said to Collie, and Emily felt her face flame. Great.

The look that passed between Tony and Hamish didn't go unnoticed by Emily, and she resigned herself to an evening with Collie,

Tony, and Lana. Well, not *resigned* exactly. Emily actually found Collie's company quite pleasant.

Pleasant, is it?

Collie was funny and interesting—

And hot.

And hot. Fine, Collie was hot, and Emily was attracted to her. There. Her inner voice won, and she'd admitted it. But she wasn't an animal, and she didn't have to act on her feelings. She could enjoy the woman's company and not want to date her.

"Shall we all go in the one car?" Hamish asked as they got on the ride.

"Great idea," Tony replied before anyone else had a chance to.

Emily sighed and tried to avoid eye contact with Collie. She got in the car obediently and sat down and wasn't at all surprised when Collie ended up sitting next to her, her leg pressed tight against Emily's.

"So, um, are you enjoying the funfair?" Collie asked.

"I am. You?" Emily replied.

"I am. I'm finding all the people dressed as scarecrows a bit weird, though," Collie said.

"There are people dressed as scarecrows? At the funfair?" Emily said.

"Yes. You haven't seen them?"

"No. We just got here. Hamish was saying something the other day about them being a big thing in Hyam. They dress up and put them in their gardens for the Spring Fair."

Before Collie could say anything else, the ride started up, and Emily grabbed the handrail. The ride started slowly at first, but soon it was spinning and diving and climbing, and she was laughing and screaming along with everyone else.

Emily forgot she was annoyed at Hamish and squeezed his hand on one particularly brutal spin. She didn't think at all about how she would have liked to take Collie's hand instead.

For the rest of the evening—thanks to the designs of Tony and Hamish—they stayed as one party. Emily thought maybe the night was the most fun she'd had in a long time. She didn't want to think about whether Collie being there had something to do with it.

They rode the dodgems, something called Sky Drop where you literally dropped out of the sky, the scaled-down roller coaster, and even the carousel. Lana had refused to go on the carousel at first, saying it was a baby ride, but when the rest clambered on, she couldn't resist.

Collie didn't think she'd had so much fun in ages, and Hamish was hilarious. Despite his and Tony's painful attempts to set her up with Emily, she liked him. Tony would be getting a mouthful later, though.

As if you don't like it.

She wasn't saying she didn't like it exactly—Emily was gorgeous, and under different circumstances, Collie would have flirted and seen what happened. But things *were* different. She had Lana and a new village and all the other stuff. Now wasn't the time to start anything up. Even if Emily was funny and interesting and beautiful.

"Who wants a burger?" Collie said to get away from her own annoying thoughts.

"Burger, then ghost train," Lana said.

"Everyone okay with that?" Collie asked. They seemed to have become a group somewhere along the way.

"Sounds good to me," Tony said.

They got questionable burgers dripping in grease, onions, and melting cheese and found a free picnic bench on the edge of the funfair.

Collie doused hers in cheap ketchup—the kind that was pure vinegar and salt.

"Have some burger with your sauce," Emily said and smiled.

"This is the best kind of junk food," Collie said. "There's no buggering about. It's bad for you, and it wants you to know it."

Emily laughed again. "I know what you mean. Those fancy places that serve them with truffle mayo and Stilton are just kidding themselves."

"Exactly. With a burger van burger, you can't hide from the fact that you're eating pure shit," Collie said.

"You look delighted."

"Oh, I am." Collie couldn't keep the grin off her face. Damn it, she really liked Emily.

Before, she could tell herself Emily was aloof—which she was— and strait-laced. Most definitely not Collie's type. But after tonight, Collie saw she was fun and quick to laugh, and she was great with Lana. She talked to her like she was a person and not just a little kid. Tony clearly loved her, and the whole night he'd been throwing meaningful looks Collie's way.

Collie could feel his eyes on her now. She turned to him. "Yes, Tony?"

"What?" Tony asked innocently around a mouthful of burger.

"You were staring at me, so I assumed you wanted to say something," Collie said.

"You've got ketchup all over your chin," Tony said and laughed.

"You do, Aunt Collie," Lana said before she burst into laughter.

"Damn." Collie furiously wiped at her chin. She looked down and saw it was all over her T-shirt as well. Shit. The T-shirt was new.

Emily leaned over and dabbed at Collie's face and then her T-shirt. Collie completely forgot about the ketchup. All she could think about was Emily touching her, about Emily being so close Collie could smell her shampoo.

Their eyes met, inches apart, and Emily suddenly pulled back, her eyes going wide. "Here," she said and handed Collie the napkin. "You can probably do it just as well yourself."

Collie continued to hold Emily's eyes. She knew it was a cliché, but the air around them felt charged, heavy and full of promise.

Someone cleared their throat.

"Well," Tony said. "How about we have a quick go on the coconut shy before we hit the ghost train?"

Emily broke the stare first. "I'm up for that."

Decided, they all made their way over to the coconut shy. Tony went first and made a respectable show of it. Hamish went up next and wasn't awful.

Now it was Collie's turn, and all she could think about was Emily, the smell of her shampoo and the way their eyes had held across the table.

"You couldn't hit a barn door," Tony said, incredulous. "You're a total embarrassment, mate."

Collie hadn't managed to hit anything. Even Lana did better than her, and she needed both hands to throw the ball.

"Wow, I had no idea you were so bad," Emily joined in.

"Yeah, yeah. Sticks and stones," Collie said. "The lot of you can do one. I think my balls were off."

Hamish burst out laughing. "A bad workman always blames his— or her—tools."

Collie took the ribbing in good fun. She deserved it—her aim was terrible.

"I think we should go on the ghost train before you embarrass yourself any more, Aunt Collie," Lana said.

"Don't you start as well, Lana Banana," Collie said and pulled Lana into a hug.

❖

On the way to the ghost train, Emily saw her first scarecrow. It jumped out from behind one of the stalls and she nearly screamed.

"Bloody hell," Hamish shrieked. "What's wrong with you?" he said to the scarecrow.

Instead of answering, it did a cartwheel and ran off.

"That thing scared the life out of me. What is it with this village and scarecrows?" Tony said.

"I've no idea, but it suits Hyam. Bloody weird," Hamish said.

The queue for the ghost train was short. Again, Emily and Collie ended up in the same car—all part of operation matchmake.

But actually, she didn't mind at all. Back at the picnic bench Emily had felt something pass between her and Collie. There was definitely attraction there, had been from the beginning, but Emily was finding out she actually liked Collie. Collie was funny and didn't mind laughing at herself. She was easy-going and great with Lana. Plus, she picked great friends. Tony was hilarious and very kind.

"You okay?" Collie asked.

"Yes, fine. Just in my own world. Sorry."

"Don't apologize. I just wondered if you were scared of the ghost train," Collie said and grinned.

"I think I'll be fine. The scarecrows are more creepy than this thing looks like it's going to be," Emily said.

Their car lurched forward on its tracks and slowly made its way through the doors painted to look like wood. A plastic skeleton with wispy white hair was glued above it. Definitely not scary.

Emily turned back to the car behind, where Lana sat sandwiched between Tony and Hamish. "You all right?"

"Fine. These don't scare me at all," Lana said.

"Me either," Emily said and turned back around.

They rumbled down the track a few feet before they lurched to a stop.

"I'm very sorry." A nasal, tinny voice came over the tannoy.

"We're having a few technical difficulties. Please bear with us, and we'll get you moving again shortly."

Emily rolled her eyes and leaned towards Collie. "Sure they are. What's the bet something's going to jump out any minute?"

"As long as it's not one of those creepy scarecrows," Collie said.

Collie smelled good. Really good, and Emily concentrated on not leaning in further and nuzzling her neck.

What is wrong with you?

"No, we wouldn't want to see those again," Emily said, and her voice sounded strange in her own ears, slightly breathless. Her chest felt tight and her mouth dry. What was the matter with her? It wasn't as if she was a teenager out on her first date.

The car lurched forward again and then started to go up on its track. A door to the left of them opened, and a skeleton on a spring flew out, accompanied by the obligatory canned scream from a speaker buried in the wall.

Emily did jump, and Collie put her hand on Emily's knee and gave it a pat. "At least it wasn't a scarecrow."

Emily laughed. "No, at least it wasn't that."

The car sped up again as it went down on the track, and the ceiling opened above. Hundreds of plastic spiders on strings fell down on them, and Emily couldn't help but wonder if these things were ever cleaned and how many faces they'd landed in.

Lana gave out a yell behind them, and Collie turned to make sure she was okay.

So far, the ghost train was just as dull as Emily suspected it would be. The feelings she got being so close to Collie were not dull at all—or expected.

They trundled along for a few minutes more, with the usual scares. Lana seemed to be enjoying herself, though, and that was the main thing. She'd seemed excited to do the ghost train.

The car stopped again, moved forward a couple of feet, shuddered, stopped, and the ever-present low-pitched whine died. All the lights went out. Once again the nasal tannoy voice was back.

"Sorry, folks, this time we do have some difficulties. We've lost power. We'll try to get it back up in just a minute."

"Lana?" Collie twisted around beside her. "You okay?"

"Yeah," Lana said.

"Don't worry, we'll be out soon," Tony said.

Emily turned to Collie. "You think it's really lost power?"

"I think so. Did you hear the electricity die?" Collie said.

"Yes."

"We might have to walk out," Collie said.

Emily looked around. Although dark in here, it wasn't completely pitch-black, and Emily thought they could all probably find their way out easily enough. She'd turned to Collie to tell her that when she caught something out of the corner of her eye.

A shadow darted past and out of sight. Probably one of the workers trying to get things going again. Emily moved a little closer to Collie.

"Are you okay?" Collie asked.

"Yes. I just thought I saw something," Emily said quietly so Lana wouldn't hear.

"What?" Collie asked and looked around.

"I think it was just a worker," Emily said.

Something moved again, this time to the right. It stopped for a second this time, but it was far back in the shadows, and Emily couldn't make out what it was. She could make out the arm it extended towards her, and she shrank back from it. It stepped forward, further into the light but still deep enough in the shadows she couldn't quite make it out.

"Collie," she whispered. "Look."

Collie turned her head to look. "What? Who is that?"

Emily could now make out the figure wore a wide-brimmed hat—like a cowboy hat or a fedora, maybe. The figure raised its head—*It's grinning. I don't know how I know that, but it's grinning*—brought its arm back, and made a motion across where its throat should be.

Emily heard Collie suck in a breath. "I'm not having that," she said and got out of the car.

"Collie, no," Emily said and reached out for her but only managed to snag the edge of her jacket.

Behind her, Emily saw Tony get out of his car and follow Collie. Emily sighed and got out herself.

"Where are you going?" Lana asked.

"Just over there, just for a minute," Emily said.

"They told us to stay in the cars," Lana said.

"I know, but I'll just be a second. Hamish, can you stay with Lana?" Emily asked.

"Sure."

They way Hamish said it made Emily think he'd seen what the figure did too.

Emily got out of the car and went the way she'd seen the other two go.

❖

Collie was mad. There she was, having a perfectly nice evening, and some local twat decided to take advantage of the situation and scare them. What if Lana saw that? It was the last thing she needed.

Collie didn't think—she got up and went straight after the pillock who'd stood there in the shadows trying to scare them.

Collie was dimly aware of Emily trying to stop her, just as she was dimly aware of Tony following her.

"Did you see that?" she said as she followed the tracks in the direction she'd seen the idiot go.

"Yeah. Lana didn't, though."

"Good. Wait until I get hold of that prat," Collie said.

She turned left and saw the exit doors up ahead. Where the bloody hell did he go? Definitely not through those doors. She looked around. It was so bloody dark in here that he could have gone anywhere.

"Shit," Collie said.

"Yeah, I haven't got a clue either," Tony said.

Collie took another look around. There was no way she could say with any certainty which direction he'd gone. He could still be in here, standing in the shadows and watching them. That thought gave Collie a chill.

Suddenly, the lights came back on, and she saw movement to her left. There. There he was.

"Oi," she shouted out. "Oi, you little prick." Collie started after him.

He turned once to look at her, and she saw he was one of those bloody annoying scarecrows. He did a sort of weird jig, made the cutting motion across his throat again, and then disappeared through a door cut into the wall.

Collie was furious. She didn't think she'd been this angry in a long time. She gave chase.

"Come back, you shit. You coward."

Collie pushed the door open and followed it down a narrow

corridor. She stepped carefully over the machinery that ran the ride, and that slowed her down. She could hear Tony following close behind her.

"Hey, you can't be in here," someone shouted as Collie ran past. She ignored him and carried on.

She followed the scarecrow through another door and out into the night. The crowds were heavier now, and Collie had to push her way through them. It was getting harder to keep sight of the scarecrow.

"Collie." Tony puffed behind her. "Slow down."

Collie ignored him and pushed on. Fury pulsed white hot through her and heated her blood. She wouldn't stop until she got hold of the little shit. Maybe the same little shit who vandalized her back door and smashed the glass in Emily's.

Soon, though, it became impossible to keep up. More and more scarecrows were appearing. What the local obsession with them was, Collie didn't know. They were creepy and strange, and it seemed an odd thing to do.

"Shit." Collie stopped, breathing hard. "I lost him."

"Bloody hell, you're like Mo Farah. I had no idea you could run so long." Tony hyperventilated beside her.

She turned to look at him, sweaty and red. "I'm surprised you can run at all with all those cooked breakfasts you eat."

"Shut up," he said and grinned. "You were so mad."

"I still am," Collie said, but she wasn't. The fury was dissipating now. What would Emily think of her? Running off like that? Swearing.

Why do you care? Thought you weren't looking to getting into anything with her.

She wasn't. But she was Lana's teacher, and she didn't want to make a bad impression.

Sure, that's it. She's Lana's teacher.

Collie and Tony made their way back to the ghost train entrance where Hamish, Emily, and Lana waited.

Feeling slightly sheepish, Collie sketched a small wave. "Sorry about that," she said.

"Are you okay now, Collie?" Lana asked.

Collie looked at Lana. "Okay? Wha—?"

"I told her you needed the toilet. Urgently," Hamish said.

"The burger didn't agree with you," Lana said.

Collie felt her face heat. From the corner of her eye she saw Emily shaking with the laughter she was trying to contain.

Collie rolled her eyes. She deserved it for acting like an idiot, she supposed.

"She's fine now, Lana. Not sure the porta-potty is, though. And there was a queue," Tony said.

Emily burst out laughing, and Hamish started to snigger.

"Yeah, thanks, Tony. I'm sure they don't all want to know," Collie said and gave him a sneaky elbow in the ribs.

"But you're okay now?" Lana asked.

The concern on her face dried up the laughter. "Yeah," Collie said and pulled her into a hug. "I'm fine now. Come on, I reckon it's time to go. Either of you need a lift back?"

"No, we came in my car," Hamish said. "It was very nice to see you all. I guess we'll see you at the town hall next for the Spring Fair meeting."

"I suppose you will," Collie said.

"Well," Emily said.

"Well," Collie said.

She wanted to ask Emily if she could see her again, try to engineer some sort of get-together, but she wouldn't in front of the others. Besides, Emily made it clear yesterday she wasn't interested in going to the meeting with Collie. And Collie should be thinking about Lana, not dating Lana's teacher.

Collie sighed. "See you then."

"Bye," Emily said.

Collie, Tony and Lana walked back to the car with Lana slightly ahead of them eating a candy floss they'd got her.

"You should have asked her out on a date," Tony said quietly so Lana couldn't hear.

"Don't be stupid. The last thing I need right now is a girlfriend. Besides, I don't think she's interested."

Tony scoffed. "Oh come on. Even you aren't that dumb. Of course she's interested. I saw the way she was looking at you."

"Really?"

"Really."

"I asked her if she wanted to walk down to the meeting together yesterday, and she turned me down," Collie said.

"So?"

"So, she's not interested. And nor am I."

Tony scoffed. "Yeah, okay then. Of course you aren't."

"I'm serious. I've got Lana to think about now. Not dating. Besides, I don't think I'm in the right headspace for it. Not with Sasha..." Collie trailed off.

Tony put his arm around her shoulder. "Yeah, all right. I get it. But look, all I'm saying is she's definitely into you. Who knows, maybe you could be friends, and when the time is right..."

"Let's wait and see," Collie said, which was her way of ending the conversation. Tony took the hint and obliged.

On the way back to the car, Collie couldn't help herself looking for the scarecrow from the ghost train. The memory of him running his hand across his throat wouldn't leave her head, and later that night, when they were all going to bed, she double-checked the windows and doors even though she told herself she was being an idiot.

CHAPTER NINETEEN

The function room at the back of the church smelled dusty and musty, and Emily tried not to sneeze. It reminded her of Sunday school when she was a kid. She half expected her old Sunday school teacher to come in and start handing out children's Bibles.

Plastic chairs were lined up in rows and facing the tables, which were pushed together at the end of the room. Emily guessed that's where the Spring Fair committee were going to sit and hand out jobs to the volunteers.

She'd taken a chair about halfway down the rows and was one of the first to arrive with Hamish and another teacher who kept sniffing but refused to blow his nose. He'd done it all the way over here in the car too, producing that awful phlegmy noise at the back of his throat that had Emily on the verge of throttling him.

The church was cold as churches always seemed to be, and Emily was chilly. She was surprised, then, when she felt sudden warmth along her left leg.

She turned and saw Collie had sat down beside her. All sorts of emotions ran through Emily. She remembered the other night at the funfair, where she'd had the best time in ages. Until the ghost train, that was.

Emily also remembered how being with Collie made her feel and how Emily couldn't stop thinking about her. She was getting in too deep, and it had to stop. Maybe under different circumstances, she would have seen where things went with Collie. But she was here to find out what happened to Charlie, and once she did, she would go back to her old life in London. Emily didn't see how Collie would fit into that. Plus, she was a distraction—a very sexy, very funny, very kind distraction, but a distraction just the same.

After a full night tossing and turning, replaying every moment with Collie from the funfair, Emily decided enough was enough. She was going to distance herself. Obviously, she'd see Collie on parents' evenings and stuff like this, but there would be no more outings or lemonade in the garden. Emily was going to cut it off and make it clear to Collie where they stood.

"Bloody freezing in here. How are you doing?" Collie said and smiled at her.

Emily smiled back, but it was more reflex than genuine emotion. Why had Collie chosen to sit next to her when the place was still half empty?

Irritated, Emily kept the polite smile on her face. "I'm fine. You?"

"Not bad." Collie leaned in close, and Emily could smell her washing powder—fresh and clean. She was even more irritated now. Why couldn't Collie just leave her alone? And why did she have to smell so good? And why, why, why did she have to be so attractive?

It was annoying. Emily wished she'd chosen to sit somewhere else. Emily didn't want to be this close to her. Didn't want anything to do with her, really. She'd made sort of friends with Hamish, and she certainly didn't need any more. That would be enough because Emily knew she wouldn't stay friends with Collie for long.

But Collie was lovely, and maybe she could do the friends thing with her.

It's not friendship you want from her, is it, though?

Damn it, she was going mad, and this was exactly what she didn't want. Emily found her thoughts consumed by Collie, and now, sitting next to her for a matter of seconds, she was already wavering in her decision and thinking they could be friends. Emily needed to get a grip.

"Sorry, what?" She'd been so deep in her head that she'd missed all of what Collie had been saying to her.

"I said, do you know what time this thing is supposed to start?"

"Oh. Anytime now, I think. Looks like everyone's here." Emily saw that in the time she'd been daydreaming about Collie, the room had filled up quite a lot.

The heads of the committee had taken their seats and were waiting for the last stragglers to sit down.

Emily wasn't surprised to see Frances Cobb at the head of the table. Of course she'd be involved in this. She probably had her hand in everything.

And from the documents Trish emailed her, Frances Cobb had a lot of financial interest in the village as well. Emily was taken aback to see she either owned every business in Hyam or the building it was in. Emily's own rented house belonged to a company owned by Frances Cobb, although she didn't seem to have any direct involvement in it herself.

Emily supposed it wasn't the strangest thing—there were local families across the country who owned large parts of various villages and towns—but something about Frances Cobb had always struck an off note with Emily. Nothing she could put her finger on, but she'd keep digging until she connected all the dots, and an instinct inside Emily told her Frances Cobb played some part in all this.

The meeting droned on just as Emily expected, with people being asked to put up their hands for various jobs. Emily was holding out for some small and meaningless task that wouldn't take up too much time.

"Now, we have two floats this year." Frances Cobb's booming voice filled the room, and everyone seemed to sit up just a little bit straighter. Emily did the maths and realized with some surprise that Frances Cobb must have been the head teacher when a lot of people in the room were at school.

"We need them repaired and decorated. I think three people should be enough. Volunteers?" She waited barely a beat before she pointed in Emily's direction. "Miss Lassiter, a job for you and Mr. Ford, I think."

Emily looked at Hamish beside her and tried not to laugh at his face. He'd told her he was holding out for running the refreshment stall on the day.

"That sounds fine," she said to Frances Cobb. "Hamish and I would be happy to do the floats." She tried not to laugh out loud when Hamish kicked her ankle.

"Good. Miss Noonan, perhaps you can lend them your artistic talents for the decorating portion?"

The smile dropped off Emily's face. Great. She wanted to say they could manage on their own without Collie, but that would sound so rude.

"Great, happy to do it," said Collie.

Emily groaned inside. Great. Three days at least, working next to Collie Noonan. Just what she needed after she'd resolved to stay away from her.

No, you'll be fine. You aren't an animal. You don't have to act on all your instincts.

And that was true. She could be polite and friendly with Collie and not let it go any further. Yes, that's exactly what she'd do.

Emily needed to get out of here and get back to her research. Fortunately, the meeting wrapped up pretty quickly now the jobs were handed out. Emily made her excuses and left. She knew it probably looked rude, but she wanted to get away from Collie.

❖

"What are you talking about? It's a great idea," Tony said.

Collie popped him one on the arm. "You take her, then."

"Can't. Things to do, furniture to move." Tony flipped the omelette in the pan so it landed perfectly. Collie needed to get him to show her how to do that one of these days.

"Tony, I've never been camping in my life. Mainly because I can't think of anything more bloody boring." Collie sighed and leaned back in her chair.

Collie had hung around for a bit after the meeting, chatting with a couple of locals and Emily's teacher friend, Hamish.

Emily cut out of the meeting like her knickers were on fire. She'd been pretty off from the start, and Collie wondered if it was because of her, maybe the thing with the scarecrow.

She'd sat next to Emily at the meeting because she was the only person she knew. It was natural to gravitate to people you knew, wasn't it? Nothing strange or desperate about that. Oh God, had she looked desperate? Like a little puppy hovering round Emily?

Collie hoped not. *That* would be really embarrassing. She wasn't even interested in Emily like that.

Liar.

It made sense for them to be friendly. They lived next door, were both outsiders, and hadn't lived here long. Plus, they were about the same age and—

You fancy her.

Collie sighed. Lying to other people was one thing, but lying to yourself was stupid. She did fancy Emily—it was true. But Collie certainly wasn't in a position to start up any kind of relationship. Her focus at the moment was Lana and would be for some time. And she got the sense Emily would rather stick pins in her eyes than get involved with Collie. It was a bit insulting, but what could she do?

On the plus side, nothing weird had happened since the incident with the back door—unless you counted the scarecrow, which Collie didn't because that had just been a stupid kid—and Collie hoped getting involved in village stuff would help endear her a bit to the locals.

"Collie? Were you listening to a word I just said?" Tony asked.

"Sure," she lied. "Every precious syllable. And the answer is still no. We'll go abroad for half-term. Tenerife or something," Collie said.

"You weren't listening. I knew you weren't," Tony said and slid the omelette onto a plate. He sprinkled something over it and placed it in front of Collie with a flourish. "Ta-da."

"Looks great." Collie was starving. "And I wasn't listening—you were right."

"You're so bloody ignorant." Tony flicked her head with a tea towel.

"Ow, that was wet." Collie rubbed her head.

"You deserved it. I was saying you can't go abroad at half-term. You have to go camping."

"And why is that, O Great Oracle?"

"Lana said she wanted to go. Apparently a new friend at school is having a camping birthday party. But first, so she doesn't make a tit of herself, she wants to try it out."

"She said that? Tit?" Collie asked around a mouthful of food.

"No, I interpreted. Jesus, Collie, why bother with a knife and fork when you're just shoving it in."

"What? I'm hungry."

"You eat like a pig," Tony said.

"Sticks and stones may break my bones."

"Yeah, yeah, and whips and chains excite me," Tony said and took her empty plate away. "All I'm saying is, she wants to go camping, and I think you should take her. Only for a couple of nights. See how you get on."

Collie sighed. If Lana wanted to go that much, of course Collie would take her camping. It bothered her a bit that Lana told Tony but not her. Since Sasha's death, Collie felt like there was a wall between her and Lana that hadn't been there before.

When Sasha was alive, Collie had been Lana's confidant. Now, it seemed Lana rarely told Collie anything. She was quieter too. That was to be expected, but Collie thought they were close. Lana had always been able to tell her anything.

"She doesn't talk to me any more, Tony," Collie said quietly. "I don't know why."

Tony sat beside her and took her hand. "I think she's got it in her head not to piss you off or be any trouble."

"But why? What does she think I'll do? I'd never give her up. Not in a million years," Collie said.

Tony gripped her hand. "I know that. But she's ten. She's lost her father and now her mother. You're all she's got. That's why I'm saying this camping might be good. It'll give you a chance to talk. Tell her how it is."

"Fine. Okay, fine. We'll go camping. You need to make me a list of what to bring, though."

"I've got everything you'll need," Tony said. "I love camping."

"So why aren't you coming then?" Collie asked. "You could show us how to do it."

"Collie, it's camping not astrophysics. Seriously, you need to calm down."

Collie laughed. "Shut up and show me how to flip an omelette."

Chapter Twenty

The thing in the bushes watched and listened. It had been good. It had been patient. It had resisted doing anything to draw attention to itself for weeks. Instead, it waited silently in the shadows and watched them. It could have taken them at any point if it wanted to. And it wanted to so badly.

The other was still there, watching it watching them. The other wasn't part of that world, it had come to understand. But it was still new in the other world, so new it could be *here* and *there*. But not for much longer. This other—whoever it had once been—would have to leave soon. It wouldn't be able to help the woman or the girl. Even if the other was strong enough, whatever was left of the other would cross over fully soon, and *it* would take the woman and the girl, and the changing over would happen, and more would be taken as they had always been taken.

It glanced left now, hearing the sound of the school bus pulling up at the end of the drive. The little one would appear shortly. Big bag on her back and scuffed black shoes crunching the gravel.

She knew it was here. She sensed it just like it wanted her to, and it could smell her fear. Could taste it. They always tasted so much better when they were afraid.

The little girl would get within a metre of it and then start running, just as she always did. Every day was the same. Sometimes it would rustle the bushes to make her run faster, to make her more afraid.

She'd convinced herself it was a badger, but that was its doing too. It could call the animals to it, a useful trick.

Soon though, scaring her—scaring *them*—wouldn't be enough. Soon, it would come out of the bushes and show her why she'd been right to be afraid, why she'd been right to run. It would realize all her fears before it destroyed her. But not today.

It watched her, marked her progress, and when the little girl started to run, its lips pulled back in a parody of a smile, and it knew its smile was a terrible thing.

Suddenly, there was movement to its left. Someone coming down the drive. The schoolteacher, the man's sister. It wanted her too eventually. She was smug and self-righteous, and she thought no one knew who she was. The man's sister came here looking for answers, and she thought it didn't know.

It knew everything that went on here. It had eyes everywhere and heard every whisper through the wall. It was ancient and knew all the ways of people. It could not be outsmarted or out-thought.

It listened now to the little girl and the man's sister.

"Lana? Are you okay?"

"Yes, miss."

"Why were you running?"

It smiled again. *It* knew why she was running.

"I just…I'm practicing."

"For what?"

"Sports day."

"Right." It knew the man's sister didn't buy the excuse, but she was tired. It smelled the sickness on her. Nothing more than a common cold, but people were weak and easily brought down by all kinds of illness.

"Are you feeling okay, miss?"

"I've got a cold. Do I look terrible?"

Not as terrible as she would look when it was done with her.

"No, miss. You just look tired. And your nose is red."

It heard the man's sister laugh. "Thanks a lot."

"Sorry, miss. You did ask."

"That's true, I did."

It slunk further into the bushes and watched as they went their separate ways. It lifted its nose to capture their scents. That smell of lavender was there—the other's smell—but underneath it were their scents. The woman's scent was very much like the man's. It had taken others since him, but it never forgot any of them. It always remembered. Even though it was ancient, it remembered all the ones it had taken. And these were special because they were the last it would take.

Silently, it left the way it had come in.

CHAPTER TWENTY-ONE

Emily blew her nose and chucked the tissue in the bin with all the others. She'd have to empty it soon. She couldn't remember the last time she'd felt so unbelievably shit. As in couldn't get out of bed and felt like she'd run a marathon shit.

Emily called in sick to work all week. Hamish, who she'd actually started to build quite a nice friendship with, brought round soup, tissues, and medicine. He was a lifesaver. Emily wasn't sure she'd have been able to go herself.

And that made her miss her friends and family with an ache she hadn't felt before. It made her realize how isolated and cut off she was here. Had Charlie felt like that too?

It also meant she hadn't been able to help out with the Spring Fair—also a good thing, because it kept her away from Collie. The fact that she was disappointed as well was an annoying feeling that she was trying very hard to ignore. There was no reason for her to want to spend time with Collie Noonan, and it was frustrating that she couldn't make her brain get on board.

Emily tried to spend some time looking into Charlie's disappearance, but the truth was she'd felt too bloody awful. She hadn't got very far at all. She'd got nowhere, in fact.

All she currently had was information on Frances Cobb, the long-lived Daddy Warbucks of Hyam, and not much else. That and Charlie's emails, which didn't really tell her anything.

Maybe you haven't found anything because there's nothing to find. Maybe Charlie was ill.

No, she refused to believe it. Three others had gone missing from around the area as well—she had that information. Of course, it didn't really mean much without any leads. It seemed as though Charlie really had vanished into thin air.

She couldn't find anything on any of the people he came into contact with. In her tentative pushes on the topic of Charlie, she'd got no sense anyone knew anything.

Because there's nothing to know. He took himself off somewhere and killed himself. Just like everyone but you believes.

Emily sighed. She was tired, and she was still sick, and now wasn't the time to start questioning herself. She knew Charlie better than anyone. She'd *know* if he was depressed or ill or suicidal. She would *know*.

Emily pulled out her laptop and opened a new email from Trish. There were a bunch of attachments titled *F Cobb*. The email was titled *Frances Cobb/Dorian Gray.*

Emily frowned, unsure what that meant. Wasn't Dorian Gray the man in the Oscar Wilde story who didn't age?

She clicked on the attachments. They were old newspaper articles. Trish had scanned them in from the originals, it looked like, and pasted them onto a Word document. At the top, she'd written: *Exactly how old is Frances Cobb?*

The articles started in around 1954. Seemed reasonable enough— Cobb looked like she was in her mid-sixties. Then Emily looked closer. The article was about a new wing being built onto Highmore School, paid for by Frances Cobb. There was a grainy photograph of a woman standing next to what Emily recognized was now the library.

She squinted, trying to make out the face. It resembled Frances Cobb, but there was every chance it was her grandmother, and she had been given the same name. Emily shrugged. So far she wasn't seeing what Trish was seeing.

Then she clicked on the land registry documents, and her skin prickled with the old familiar feeling she got when she was on to something. When she'd found a story.

Emily jumped and nearly knocked the laptop to the floor. She'd been so engrossed that it took her a moment to realize someone was knocking at the door.

Don't answer it was her immediate thought. But that was stupid. Of course she should answer the door. Why wouldn't she answer the door? That little voice inside her, her lizard brain as she thought of it, persisted, and Emily was thoroughly freaked out.

Emily reached the end of the hallway and could just about make out the shadowy figure behind the obscured glass.

"Hello? Who's that?" she asked, her hand on the lock.

"It's me, Hamish."

Emily sighed, suddenly filled with relief from the unexplained fear that gripped her. "You're losing it, girl," she muttered to herself before she opened the door.

"Everything all right, Em?" he asked, pecking her on the cheek.

"Yeah, sorry. I was deeply engrossed in something, and it took me a while to hear the door," she said, following him to her kitchen.

"It's good you're feeling better, but maybe don't overdo it. You were really sick," Hamish said, putting down two carrier bags on the worktop.

"Yes, Mum." Emily nudged him in the side and smiled. It was nice having a friend. She'd missed that. And Hamish was an outsider like her, so it felt okay to open up to him a bit. "What did you bring me?"

"Soups, lots of vegetables, more tissues, and this." Hamish held up a bottle of wine. "What do you think? Too soon?"

Emily laughed. "Absolutely not. You're staying for dinner then?"

"Darling, I'm cooking dinner. Something fattening and delicious. This week has been total shit," Hamish said.

"Why? What's happened?" Emily asked. She took the wine from him and opened it.

"My year fives have got the eleven-plus in autumn, and Her Royal Highness Queen Cobb is cracking the whip. I've spent most of today trying to convince her that eight hours' worth of homework for the weekend isn't appropriate for a bunch of nine- and ten-year-olds."

"I forgot we do the grammar school exams at Highmore," Emily said.

"Because you teach year six, and by the time they're ten their academic fate is sealed." Hamish rolled his eyes and took the glass of wine she offered him.

"You don't agree with grammar schools?" Emily asked.

"It's not that. I don't agree with Frances Cobb's take-no-prisoners attitude. She actually said to me, *If they can't hack it, that's their problem.* They're children."

"She's pretty harsh," Emily said non-committally.

"She's an awful woman who has no business running a school. She's only the headmistress because her family basically built the school. And all the village treat her like some kind of God." Hamish took a healthy sip of his wine.

"You think? I haven't been here long enough to know." Emily felt herself slip back into her journalist persona. She felt bad that she was going to milk Hamish for information without him knowing, but he wanted to talk about it. She hadn't brought it up. And from what she'd read so far in the email Trish sent, it seemed there was a lot more to Frances Cobb than Miss Trunchbull wannabe. "Let's go in the living room. You can offload, and I can blow my nose," Emily said.

Hamish picked up the bottle of wine and followed Emily. "I swear I'll cook dinner after I've slagged off Cobb."

"I'll hold you to it."

They went into the living room, and Emily quickly closed her laptop before Hamish could see what was on it.

"So," she said. "Tell me about Frances Cobb."

CHAPTER TWENTY-TWO

Collie finished filling in the last flower on the side of the float and sat back. Overall, she was happy with her work. It wasn't exactly her usual style, but there was something quite relaxing about painting flowers and moons and stars.

"You look like you could use this." Stephanie Willis handed her a cup of tea.

Since Emily had been out of action with a cold—something which had left Collie bitterly disappointed and annoyed at herself for feeling that way—the committee gave them Stef to help. Collie found she liked her even if at first she'd barely spoken to her.

"You're a star—thanks for that," Collie said and took the mug gratefully.

"Charming, don't I get a tea?" Hamish called from up on the float where he was attaching huge amounts of material with the help of a staple gun and Dave Willis, Stef's husband.

"I've only got two hands, Hamish Ford. You'll get yours in a minute," Stef called up to him.

"Well, it's all finished," Collie said to Stef, who was looking at her work and nodding in approval.

"I'll be honest, I wasn't happy about the idea of an outsider doing such an important job, but I'm happy to say I was wrong," Stef said.

Collie didn't ask why painting a couple of floats was so important. Over the last few days, she'd seen the way people treated this fair as if it was the biggest thing to ever happen.

It was still weeks away, but nearly everyone in the village was running around like little ants making sure everything was perfect. Pretty much everyone had one of those creepy scarecrows in their front garden, and Stef had been on at Collie to make hers.

"Well, thanks. I appreciate it. I know the village is, er, close-knit," Collie said in an effort to be diplomatic.

Stef looked at her. "It is. In most villages, young people leave, businesses close, and the place just dies. Not here, though. We have Frances Cobb to thank for a lot of that."

"Really?" Collie asked.

"Yes. It's no secret she has a lot of financial involvement here. But she's done a lot for the young people too," Stef said. "Scholarships and grants so they can stay in the village or near by."

"Right," Collie said, unsure where they were going with this or what it had to do with the Spring Fair.

"What I'm saying is, it's easy to judge. There are some things that might not be as we wish they were, but we have to remember the bigger picture."

"Stef." Collie hadn't heard Dave come down off the float. He walked over to his wife.

"Sorry. Sometimes I start talking." Stef threaded her arm around her husband's waist and leaned in to him. "It'll be nice. Your niece leading the parade on a float you painted."

Collie nodded, not sure what was going on here. Stef looked sad, and Collie didn't understand why. "Yeah. I know she's looking forward to it—nervous, though. Lana isn't one for being the centre of attention."

"It's an important role she's got. She'll be fine. The village is counting on her," Dave said.

Collie nodded. They really did take this thing seriously. The village was counting on Lana? It was a parade to kick off a fair, not exactly the opening ceremony of the Olympics.

Hamish came down now too. "Looks like we're finished here. Collie, are you walking home?"

"I am," Collie said.

"I'll walk with you. I wanted to pop in and see Emily. I've got some bits for her," he said.

Collie felt a momentary stab of jealousy, then guilt. Hamish hadn't done anything wrong. Collie guessed she was jealous because she wanted to be able to pop in on Emily but didn't have those sort of privileges. Maybe if Emily had helped out on the fair, she would have done.

But, as she had to keep reminding herself, there was absolutely nothing good going to come out of pursuing Emily Lassiter. Apart from the fact she'd made it fairly obvious she wasn't interested in Collie, Collie wasn't looking for a relationship. Whether she wanted one or not, her priority was Lana. Not dating. On the night of the funfair, Collie wondered if something might happen between them, but since that night she hadn't heard a dicky bird out of Emily, so she guessed nothing was going to happen there.

And that was good. Wasn't it? Yes, it was good, even if it felt shit.

Collie packed up her stuff, said goodbye to Stef and Dave, and left with Hamish.

"Here," she said when they were outside. "All I've got is some paintbrushes—let me help you carry this stuff."

"Thanks, I appreciate it. I'm like a bloody mother hen. I'm sure she doesn't need most of this stuff, but you know. You can never have too many tissues and paracetamol."

Collie laughed. "Well, I think you *can* have too much paracetamol, but I know what you mean." The bag she'd taken off Hamish was pretty heavy. "What's even in here?"

"Oh, that one has soups and fruit. In case she gets hungry. You know what they say, feed a cold and starve a fever," Hamish said.

"I suppose."

"They're taking this all quite seriously, aren't they?" Hamish said as they walked along the road passing horrible scarecrow after horrible scarecrow.

Collie switched hands with the bag. "They do seem to be. I take it you've not experienced one before?" Collie asked.

"No, I haven't. From what I understand, there's a parade, then stalls and games and a dance thing in the evening with a barbecue. I hope they take these scarecrows down soon, though. They're giving me bloody nightmares."

"I know what you mean. I think the whole thing's weird," Collie said. "Probably it's some old tradition, and that's why it's so important to them."

"Yeah. I read up on it, and it's been going since the middle of the sixth century. If you go to the church, you can see it depicted in the stonework. There's a bloody weird bunch of stuff in the church, but some of the stonework and tapestries of the Spring Fair are pretty good. The tapestries, especially."

"I might check it out," Collie said, not with any real conviction. Hanging around a draughty old church wasn't her idea of a good time.

Lana might like it, though. Perhaps they'd have a look when they were back from camping.

"I heard you tell Stef you were off camping," Hamish said.

"We are, me and Lana. I've never been before, but my friend tells me it's easy and fun, so we're going to have a crack at it."

"Whereabout are you going?"

"Not too far, just up in the Woden Wood." They turned onto the drive. "I can help you carry this up to her house if you want," Collie said.

"Thanks, I'd be grateful," Hamish said.

Up at Emily's front door, Collie set the bag down, then started to walk away. "See you later, Hamish."

"Wait a minute. Why don't you stay? I'm sure she'll want you to come in for a coffee."

Doubt it. If her face at the church when they handed out assignments is anything to go by, I doubt she wants me hanging around.

"No, I've got to be getting on. Please tell her I hope she feels better," Collie said.

Just then, the front door opened. Collie hadn't realized Hamish had rung the bell.

"Hamish. Collie," Emily said.

Collie turned all the way around to look at Emily. Even sick she was beautiful.

"Hey. You're looking better. Collie helped me up with the bags," Hamish said.

"Hamish, you don't need to bring me more stuff. I've still not got through the last batch," Emily said. "And Collie, thanks for helping him up. I'm still not great, but would you like to come in for a tea or coffee?"

"That's kind of you, but no thanks. I need to get on," Collie said. "Bye."

She walked off before either of them could say anything else. When she got to her own garden gate, she stopped and took a deep breath.

Collie really didn't like the fact that she liked Emily. Even just then, with her red nose and watery eyes, Collie thought she looked gorgeous. She needed to get a grip. She was in no position to start anything up, and Emily wasn't interested, which sort of made the ache in her chest worse.

Maybe the camping trip would be good. It would mean some distance from Emily and a chance to hang out with Lana and to remember all the reasons she'd told herself she wasn't getting involved with anyone.

CHAPTER TWENTY-THREE

Collie pulled into a little clearing, bounced out of a pothole, swore, and turned the engine off.

"Here we are," she said, trying to put some excitement into her voice. But really, how excited could you get about a horizon of endless trees?

"It looks so *big*," Lana said from the back seat. "Do you have the map, Aunt Collie?"

Collie twisted round in her seat and patted her shirt pocket. "Right here, Lana Banana. Don't worry, we won't get lost."

Collie had picked a campsite about a fifteen minute drive from the house—just in case they needed to abort the trip at short notice. Neither of them had spent a lot of time in nature. She'd opted for an already pitched bell tent. They looked roomy in the brochure, and there was no way she was struggling about with the dodgy looking contraption Tony had passed off as a tent.

"Right, then, I suppose we'd better head in," Collie said, trying to sound enthusiastic. To be fair, Lana didn't look all that excited about their camping trip, but that might be more to do with her uncertainty about Collie's survival skills than anything else.

"They left wheelbarrows here," Lana said.

Collie had read about those in the instructions. "Yeah, we can take all our stuff to the pitch in them. Saves us going back and forth."

Collie loaded up a wheelbarrow, and they set off into what was basically a bunch of trees with a vaguely defined path in the middle.

Collie breathed in the fresh, crisp air. Crickets chirped lazily in the tall grass either side of the path. Fortunately for Collie and Lana, the fine weather had held, and the day was sunny and warm.

"Okay, this is it, I believe," Collie said. "Looks nice, actually." She wasn't sure what she was expecting, but the small clearing was tidily arranged. On the right beneath a large tree was their bell tent. It was yellowed with age but looked sturdy and there was an awning at the front, which she guessed they could sit under in their camping chairs if it rained.

On the left was a picnic bench and a cast iron fire bowl. The owners of the campsite kindly left them a stack of wood. Collie had looked up how to make a fire and reckoned it wouldn't be too hard.

Their small clearing was surrounded by dense trees on one side and a fence on the other with what looked like thick bushes and scrub. It was quiet and secluded and, Collie thought, probably creepy as fuck at night.

"What do you think?" she asked Lana.

"I like it. It's...nature-y," Lana said.

Collie laughed. "It is definitely that. Regrets? Wish we'd gone for a spa weekend instead?"

Lana grinned. "No. I think it's great."

"Sure you do, Lana Banana. Think you'll feel the same when you see our toilet?"

"Toilet?" Lana asked.

Collie pointed back near where they'd come in. "There."

"That's a tent," Lana said.

"No, it's our toilet. I read it in the brochure."

Together they walked over to the tall thin tent, and Collie unzipped it. Sitting on the bare earth floor was a small portable toilet with a warning not to put anything but toilet paper in it.

"Oh," Lana said.

"It'll be fine. We just aren't used to camping, that's all. I think we'll have fun," Collie said, not quite believing herself.

"We're used to the city. That's all," Lana said.

"Your mum would have hated this," Collie said and then cursed herself for bringing up Sasha.

"Would she?" Lana asked.

Collie looked down at Lana's earnest face and felt the familiar ache inside, the prickle of tears at her eyes. Not trusting herself to speak, she nodded. "Let's get the chairs out, and I'll tell you about the time Sasha joined the Brownies and had to be airlifted out of a camping site."

"No! Airlifted?" Lana asked.

"Oh yeah. Come on."

Maybe talking about Sasha wouldn't be so bad. It might even make her loss less painful if they talked about her. Who knew?

Lana brushed her teeth, dipping the toothbrush in a plastic cup of water. She wasn't sure yet if she liked camping. They'd spent the day talking about Mum and walking around the woods. It was nice. At first, talking about Mum hurt. A real, actual pain in her chest that made it hard to breathe.

The more Aunt Collie talked, the less it hurt, and Lana found herself laughing at the stories Collie told. Lana obviously hadn't known her mum as a child, but the way Collie described her, Lana could imagine it. It made her feel better. And when Collie said Lana was very much like her, Lana was so pleased that she thought her chest might burst.

The woods were fine but a bit creepy. Occasionally they heard other voices—she knew there was a main campsite a bit further up the road—but for the most part, they were completely alone.

Lana thought about the thing in the bushes at home. And how relieved she'd been when she saw it was only a badger.

Was it, though? *Are you sure, Lana Banana?*

She told herself not to be silly, not to be such a baby. Of course it was only a badger. What else would it be? Monsters were for little children, and she was going to be eleven in July. It was babyish to believe in monsters, especially when she'd seen with her own eyes that the thing in the bushes was a badger.

Lana turned her thoughts away from what might or might not be in the bushes at home and concentrated on enjoying the time with Collie. She liked it here and thought she'd probably enjoy Kitty's birthday party too. Collie seemed like she was enjoying it too and, to Lana's shock, found she was pretty good at camping.

Later, Collie made a fire, and Lana was surprised. She hadn't held out much hope her aunt would be able to manage it. But now they toasted marshmallows to put between chocolate biscuits.

"Do you think Damian will be let out of prison again?" Lana asked. She glanced quickly at Collie to see how she'd taken it. Lana had wanted to ask for ages but didn't dare. Today Collie talked a lot about Mum, so Lana thought maybe it was okay. The look on Collie's face said otherwise. "Sorry," Lana said.

"What? No, don't be sorry. You can ask me anything you like. I just wasn't expecting it, that's all."

Lana watched as Collie's marshmallow dripped into the fire and burned black.

"Shit," Collie exclaimed. "To answer your question, no. He won't ever get out."

"How do you know?" Lana asked.

"His sentence is very, very long. He'll be well into his eighties by the time he's eligible for parole."

"So he could get out," Lana said.

"Lana, come here." Collie put down her stick and held out her arms.

Lana climbed into them gratefully. Talking about *him* always made her feel scared and a little sick.

"I don't want you to worry about it. He's going to die in prison like he deserves to. He's never going to get anywhere near you. I promise."

Lana believed her. Something in Collie's voice made Lana feel like that was true. Like Collie wouldn't let *him* anywhere near her. Collie made her feel safe. Lana snuggled in and closed her eyes.

❖

Emily nearly snorted her tea out of her nose. Very ladylike. "Hamish," she said.

"What? I'm just relaying facts to you," Hamish said.

"They aren't facts, they're supposition. You've got no proof at all," Emily said but couldn't help the thrill she felt.

"Oh, come on, anyone with eyes can see she likes you. She couldn't stop staring at you in the church hall. And then when I told her you were sick and wouldn't be helping out after all…Well, she had to pick her face back up off the floor—she looked so miserable," Hamish said.

"Hamish, stop," Emily said but actually she didn't want him to stop at all. She liked hearing how Collie was disappointed not to see her. "You're making stuff up because you're bored."

"I'm not. I think she likes you," Hamish said.

"Really? Was she fed up the whole time you were volunteering then? Did she say anything?" Emily couldn't help herself.

Hamish leaned back on the sofa and grinned. "I *knew* you liked her too."

"I do not."

"Do too," Hamish countered, and Emily couldn't help laughing.

"You're so bloody childish."

"Hey, maybe I could take her a note asking if she wants to be your girlfriend? She can circle yes or no, and I'll bring it back to you."

Emily hit him with a pillow.

"Ow," he said, but he was laughing now.

"You're such a little shit. And I'm sick. You're supposed to be taking care of me, not winding me up."

"I'm not winding you up. I really think she likes you. And you like her, so I've decided I'm going to matchmake. I got Tony's number at the funfair, and he's on board," Hamish said and sat up again.

"Please don't do that," Emily said. It was true that Emily was attracted to Collie, but the idea of being set up with her left Emily feeling panicked.

"Why not?" Hamish asked.

"Because it isn't as simple as just being set up."

"Why not?"

Emily looked at Hamish. He really didn't seem to understand. "A number of reasons. Probably the biggest one is she has a niece whose mother's been murdered, and Collie is now effectively her parent."

"Right."

"And I'm the niece's teacher."

"Oh, that's no reason not to get together. I mean, I get it makes things more complicated—she basically has a kid—but that's no reason not to date her," Hamish said.

"Except I wouldn't just be dating Collie, would I? There's a traumatized little girl to consider. Not to mention Collie, who's probably also dealing with all kinds of things I can't even begin to understand," Emily said.

And that was true, wasn't it? Emily's brother was missing, assumed dead, but Collie's sister had been murdered. By an ex-partner, from what Emily understood. And she was left with a niece to raise. Emily hadn't really thought about it like that before. The attraction she felt for Collie became something else—a respect and admiration for a woman who had to be under all kinds of pressure.

No, Emily wasn't looking for a relationship with Collie for all the reasons she'd outlined but also because finding out what happened to

Charlie was the only thing she cared about. But she could be a friend. Collie had to be pretty lonely out here in the middle of nowhere.

She couldn't be her girlfriend, but she could be her friend. If Collie wanted her to be. As long as Emily could make sure it didn't go any further.

CHAPTER TWENTY-FOUR

By the time Hamish left, it was after eight. The sky had begun to darken, and the sun would disappear any moment now.

Emily sat on her sofa, thinking about the things Hamish told her. From the kitchen she could hear the idle plink, plink of the dripping tap, and she briefly thought she should probably replace the washer.

Unlike Emily, Hamish made it a point to make friends with the other teachers at school. It was ironic, really—Emily studiously avoided them, so she wouldn't give away the reason she was in Hyam, but in doing so had missed out on what could be important information. Information that Hamish *had* got. By being friendly.

On the surface, it didn't look like much at all. It didn't really look like anything, but that familiar buzz was in her head. The one she used as a reporter and had almost forgotten about. The one that said she was on to something.

Emily remembered now how Hamish had almost casually commented on the Spring Fair. "Has anyone told you about the scarecrow yet?"

"What are you going on about?" Emily had replied as they sat on her sofa.

"You didn't know? Doug who teaches year four says it's a big Hyam tradition. Everyone sticks a scarecrow up in their garden or whatever. If you'd been outside in the last week, you'd see—the horrible things are all over the place," he said.

"For this bloody fair, I assume?" Emily couldn't believe so much work went into one fairly low-key and very local event.

"Oh, don't be such a spoilsport. I think it's going to be great. They've done so much with it. Apparently, it hasn't deviated much from Anglo-Saxon times. I'm looking forward to it."

"So I have to put up a scarecrow?" Emily asked.

"You do. Don't be so miserable about it." Hamish laughed. "It's a bit of fun. Try not to make yours as creepy as the others, though."

Emily supposed she was being a bit of a misery. She remembered that Charlie emailed her about the Spring Fair last year. He was pretty excited and told her they'd given him quite a big part in the parade. Of course they had—everyone loved Charlie.

Maybe that was why she was being so grumpy about the whole thing. It was after the fair that Charlie went missing.

"Emily? Hello? Earth to Emily?" Hamish had said.

"Sorry. I was miles away. What did you say?"

"I said, if you want to see more about the fair or the scarecrows, you should go over to the church. I was telling Collie today—they have a beautiful tapestry and some weird but also fantastic stone carvings of it."

"I haven't been to the church yet. Except for the fair meeting," Emily said.

"Well, you should. It's great to see it all."

Hamish was still speaking, but Emily was far away. Something was niggling at her. There was a tickle at the back of her head and the prickles on her skin. She was on to something. There was a connection to be made here, but she couldn't put her finger on it.

What it was, she still didn't know. After Hamish left, she sat for ages trying to focus on it, trying to pull it out, but she couldn't. It was annoying, and she'd given herself a headache.

You didn't have to be a genius to work out Hyam was a strange place. Ordinary on the outside, to the casual observer. But when you were on the *inside*, that's when you noticed. People were polite but stand-offish. You felt like there was some big secret, and you were the only one not included in it.

Secret smiles and knowing looks that passed back and forth between them all. Something unspoken but known. And only by them.

At first, maybe you could pass it off as a community not keen on outsiders, but after a while…After a while when *no one* warmed up to you, when people still didn't know your name—or pretended they didn't, when you walked into the pub, and all talk stopped, and those knowing looks and secret smiles…Unfriendly eyes tracking your progress across the room.

There was something up here. Emily sensed it from the moment she arrived. She still sensed it, and not for the first time, she wondered if it had anything to do with her brother's disappearance.

Suddenly, she had an idea. Emily rooted in her drawer and came up with the photo from the newspaper article her friend had sent her. She'd printed them all off and added them to the file she kept hidden in the bottom of her wardrobe.

She came up with one, and it must have been taken from the Spring Fair. In it, a woman who could only be Frances Cobb's grandmother, judging from the date of it, stood next to several scarecrows. She was pinning a rosette on one. Next to her stood a young woman in a pretty lace dress with flowers in her hair.

The headline read: *Local philanthropist F. Cobb crowns winning scarecrow with her choice for Spring Ides beside her.*

Neither the print Emily held nor the attachment in the email were of very good quality. Added to that, F. Cobb's face was turned slightly away as she put the rosette on the scarecrow. Even so, the resemblance to Frances Cobb was unmistakable. Both women had the large, powerful build that obviously ran in their family.

Spring Ides? Wasn't Lana Franklin going to be Spring Ides this year? Emily knew the phrase from school, where people had mentioned it was what the person leading the procession was called.

And it seemed that Frances Cobb chose who that person would be each year. Emily pulled another sheet of paper from the pile. An email from her brother she'd printed off.

Well, Ems, turns out they love me here. I'm going to be Spring Ides. You won't know—and why would you—that is probably the biggest honour that can be bestowed on a person in Hyam.

I'm not sure exactly what it means beyond standing at the front of the float. I'm going to feel like a beauty pageant winner. I've said it before and I'll say it again. This place is weird!

Anyway, I'm off to practice my wave. Catch you later.

Charlie's disappearance, Spring Fair. Something there.

Emily pulled out the other articles she had about the three other people who'd gone missing. She checked the dates at the top. All of them in April. Charlie went missing in April too.

Was it ridiculous to think there was some kind of link? Maybe she was losing her mind entirely.

She looked at the picture of F. Cobb again. It was dated 1949. The F. Cobb in it was well into her fifties, by the look of her. There was no way this F. Cobb and the current head teacher at Highmore were the same person. Ridiculous.

But Charlie went missing just after this fair. The other three also went missing in April. There was a link—she wasn't mad.

Emily sighed in frustration and leaned back on the sofa. Every fibre in her being told her there was something here, something she was missing. Or maybe she just didn't have enough of the pieces yet.

Would she ever have enough of the pieces? Currently, all she had was a suspicion that the Spring Fair and people disappearing were linked. She had no facts and no proof. She didn't even have a decent hunch to maybe think this was something worth pursuing.

Even so, she couldn't shake it. They were linked. She just had to prove it. And work out how.

Emily rubbed her eyes. They were grainy, and her head was starting to ache. She still felt like crap, and it was time for bed. She gathered up all her papers and put them back in the box, ready to take upstairs with her.

Outside, something slammed against the glass doors, and Emily screamed.

CHAPTER TWENTY-FIVE

They'd walked for longer than they should have. The sun was almost set, and Collie cursed herself for being irresponsible. They'd been having a good time, chatting and laughing, and she hadn't realized the hour.

"We walked for too long," she said to Lana.

"I think I remember the way back," Lana said, and Collie could hear the unease in her voice.

"Let's go then. I have my phone torch if it gets too dark," Collie said.

At some point they'd taken a wrong turn because they walked into a clearing, and Collie was struck by the strangeness of the place. She would have remembered this.

In the centre of the clearing were about five stones in a circle. They reminded Collie of Stonehenge except these were smaller and had thick heavy metal rings bolted into them. She remembered reading something about this place when they were choosing a house.

The article she'd read didn't do it justice. Collie shivered and rubbed her arms. It must be getting colder, she thought, but didn't believe it. Unlike Stonehenge this place felt wrong and creepy.

"What is that?" Lana asked in a small voice. "There's old fires all over the ground. Do people have parties here?"

It was probably kids, Collie told herself. Probably not much else to do in the countryside at night. Even so, the place had a vibe Collie didn't like.

"Yeah, maybe," Collie said. "But we need to head back before it gets really dark. I think I know where we went wrong."

Collie took Lana's arm gently and pulled her away from the

clearing. She had a feeling this place wasn't meant for them and had an urge to get away from it as quickly as possible.

As they turned to leave, something cried out, long and low, tapering into a growl. It came from nearby.

"Come on," Collie said, barely able to keep the panic out of her voice. They started to run.

❖

Hamish hadn't meant to stay out so late. He had a ton of marking to do and all of it due Monday. He supposed it would be another late one.

He sighed and kicked at a loose stone, watched it skitter down what passed for a pavement in Hyam.

The road was deserted. It wasn't unusual for this time of night, but even the pub looked quiet. Hamish could see a couple of shadows inside moving around. The warm glow of the lights in the window were deceptively inviting, but the reality was, if Hamish went in everyone would stop talking and stare at him.

This place was strange. Hamish himself came from a small village, but it was welcoming where this one was cold. Lately he'd thought more and more about going back. And why not? There was nothing for him here in this weird little place.

Hamish glanced once more across the road to the pub. Should he pop in for one drink? Brave the stares? He sighed. Better not, those workbooks weren't going to mark themselves before Monday.

Hamish walked over the level crossing, felt the steel tracks beneath his feet. Level crossing. That was a joke. He could count on one hand the number of times he'd seen a train go past.

Something moved in the bush next to him. Probably a fox or badger getting ready for a night of hunting.

He walked on past the pub, and now the village flattened out into fields separated from the road by hedges. Hamish fumbled in his pocket for his tiny torch. Hyam felt the same way about street lights as it did about pavements.

Hamish pulled out the penlight and was instantly comforted by the glow. Until it dimmed, then went out.

Shit. He'd forgotten to replace the batteries the other day. No matter, he still had his phone.

He wasn't afraid of the dark, but out here it was pitch-black, and you could easily lose your footing. He'd stumbled home a number of times in the dark after forgetting to bring his torch, and the light on his phone was a godsend. It just wasn't as bright as the torch, and the light from the screen often bothered his eyes and made it harder to see.

Again, something moved on the other side of the hedge, making the branches rustle and snap. Probably the same animal, Hamish thought. But he felt uneasy, all the same. Stupid. What else was it other than a fox or a badger or some other night creature.

Hamish picked up his pace anyway. The hedge beside him moved again. *It's keeping pace with me*, he thought. Goosebumps had broken out across his skin, and panic was starting to build inside him. *Stupid, stupid*, he thought again. *It's just a fox, just a badger.*

Hamish turned around and started to run. The thing on the other side of the hedge sped up too.

❖

Remembering the last time something banged against her french doors, Emily went over to them with some trepidation. This time the bang hadn't been nearly as loud, and it hadn't repeated either.

She was relieved to see the door glass was intact. Outside, on the patio, a bird lay on its side. One wing pathetically flapped, its legs twitched, and then it was still.

Poor thing flew right into the glass. It looked like a great tit, Emily thought. There was a smudge on the glass where it hit. Why it was flying in the dark, Emily didn't know. Perhaps it got lost.

As Emily turned to go and fetch a dustpan and brush, suddenly there was another loud bang. Emily cried out and turned. Another bird hit the glass. What the fuck? she thought just as another one smashed its little body against her doors.

Then another and another and another. Emily stood dumbfounded as what seemed like all the birds in Hyam flew a suicide mission into her glass doors. It was a hailstorm of birds. Great tits and sparrows and blackbirds and starlings. All of them throwing themselves at her doors. And now the glass cracked.

The light was blocked out, and the noise of them squawking and thunking against the glass was deafening.

Emily stepped back. Her mouth hung open in disbelief. The glass finally gave way, and Emily ran behind the sofa and crouched down as what seemed like a thousand birds flew into the living room. Emily began to scream.

❖

Hamish kept telling himself not to be stupid, it was just a fox, just a badger, but his heart knew something his head did not. His feet wouldn't stop and kept time with the mantra going around in his head. *Just a fox. Just a badger.*

He felt a surge of relief when he saw the warm glow of the pub's lights. He'd get in the pub, get a pint, and cringe at how pathetic he'd been.

Behind him, something growled.

Hamish didn't dare turn around. He picked up his pace.

Just a fox.

It was gaining on him.

Just a badger.

Something snagged the back of his collar and pulled.

Christ, but it was strong. Hamish wasn't a small man, and he was taken off his feet. The phone fell from his hand, hit the ground, and skittered away.

He tried to turn, to push the thing away. His hands met with fur, thick and coarse. *Just a fox.*

Deep, red hot pain in his back, and he felt claws sink into his flesh like it was butter.

Just a badger.

Hamish began to crawl towards the pub. He could see the door open and two shadowy figures step out into the night. He opened his mouth to call out to them, but all he could manage was a whistling breath. The—*fox, badger*—monster on top of him must have punctured his lungs.

He couldn't get a breath, couldn't get enough air. Hamish dropped his head, too heavy now, onto the road. One arm reached out towards the strangers now headed away from him.

Hamish was still alive when the thing started to eat him.

CHAPTER TWENTY-SIX

Collie held Lana's hand. It was small in Collie's, small and sweaty. Collie gripped it tight enough to hurt, but Lana was glad of it. Something crashed along in the bushes beside them, keeping pace.

It's the thing from the bushes at home, Lana thought. *It's followed us here. I brought it here. Not a badger, not at all.*

A bright light burst from the trees. Lana cried out, and Collie veered off suddenly to the left away from it, almost pulling Lana's arm out of its socket, and at the same time something crashed out of the trees next to them. It would have had them too if not for Collie's manoeuvre.

How had Collie known it would do that? And that smell was there again, her mother's smell. Lavender.

Lana didn't have time to think about that right now. She knew she was slowing Collie down and prayed she wouldn't leave her behind.

"Come on," Collie said, panting. "Up there." Collie boosted Lana into a tree. "Climb, Lana," Collie said and followed her up.

Lana scrambled up as high as she dared. The tree wasn't yet full with leaves, but it was full enough to block Lana's view to the ground. Down there, something snarled and paced.

Before, in the clearing, they had started to run without talking. Lana sensed something and so did Collie. Something—the thing in the bushes—was bad, and they both felt it. Both heard the sudden silence that fell over the wood, and in that silence they knew something was watching them.

Collie had grabbed Lana's hand, and together they'd gone crashing through the woods, the thing on their heels. Lana leaned against a branch and shut her eyes. She tried to will her breathing to return to normal.

"How you doing, Lana Banana?" Collie asked her, but her voice sounded strange and not just because she was winded.

She's afraid. She's as scared as I am, and if that's true, then what is it down there waiting for us?

"Lana?"

She felt Collie squeeze her foot.

Lana looked down at her aunt, who was sitting between the curve of a branch and the trunk below her.

"I'm okay, I guess. I mean, except not really. You know?" Lana said.

"Yeah," Collie said. "I know."

Lana watched her aunt fumble around with her phone. "No signal, obviously. Perfect."

"What do we do now?" Lana asked.

"It's full dark. I suppose we wait. Probably until morning," Collie said.

Lana sighed. "That's what I thought you'd say. How long will it wait down there?"

"I don't know, sweetheart."

"What is it?"

Collie shifted on her branch, making the tree sway slightly and Lana's stomach with it.

"I don't know, Lana. A wolf? A big angry dog? Maybe a boar."

"You think it's an animal?" Lana asked.

"Don't you?"

"No. I think it's…never mind."

"Tell me," Collie said.

Should she? What if Collie thought she was crazy? Couldn't get much crazier than hiding up a tree in the dark. And Collie had run, hadn't she? She'd known, just like Lana had, that whatever was in the trees was bad, and she'd run. They hadn't even talked about it. Collie hadn't even tried to explain it away—she'd just grabbed Lana's hand and run. Even if Collie didn't know like Lana did, that the thing was some kind of monster, she knew it was bad and wanted to hurt them.

"Lana?" Collie asked again softly.

Lana could hear the thing below them moving around, and some part of her, some part—she didn't know what it was—told her to be quiet. To wait for the thing to leave. *You don't want it to know what you know.*

"Nothing. I guess you're right." Lana moved carefully so that her back was to the trunk of the tree. "We'd better not go to sleep."

"No. We'd fall out of the tree and crack our heads open," Collie agreed.

"What time is it?" Lana asked.

She saw the light from Collie's watch blink on, then off again.

"Quarter past eight. It's going to be a long night. I'll keep checking my phone to see if I can get a signal."

"Even if you do, we don't know where we are," Lana said.

"Another good point." Collie sighed. "Want to play I spy?"

❖

The thing down below hadn't wanted to get them. If it had, they'd already be dead. It followed them out here after it finished with the man and watched them go into its sacred place. It hadn't liked that.

At first, it just wanted to chase them out, but they ran, and it couldn't help but give chase. It was instinctual.

At some point, hadn't it meant to catch them, though? Hadn't it thought to sink its teeth into their flesh and tear them apart?

Maybe.

But the woman surprised it. It turned them off the path and herded them down, then crashed out of the trees like a novice and landed on its back. The light. It was the light that made the woman change direction. That meddling other.

The precious seconds gave them a chance to get up into the tree.

Good thing they did because it had a feeling it might not have been able to help itself, and then it really would have been in trouble.

It would wait here a little longer, until all the light had gone. Keep them up in that tree until morning. It would be gone by then, but they wouldn't know that. It snorted to clear the scent of lavender from its nostrils.

Tonight, it still had things to do. And things to think about. For instance, where its self-control had gone, back there in the clearing. It wasn't yet time to take them, but it would have anyway. It would have taken them and ruined everything.

It was that other. The one whose presence it constantly felt pushing against it. This other was strong and deeply invested in those two up the tree. Not much longer now, and the ancient ritual would be performed, and the other would go back to where it came from. Forever.

It had business back in Hyam now, and it slunk off into the trees and melted into the night.

❖

Emily watched Phil Lakeland scratch his head, scratch his straggly, patchy beard, and whistle.

"Never seen anything like this before in my life," he said slowly. "Just flew into the window, you said?"

Emily sighed and tried to keep the impatience out of her voice. "Yes. Like I told you on the phone, they just flew into the glass. It felt like *hundreds*."

Phil used the end of his scuffed boot to toe a few of them. They were piled up in front of the doors like firewood, highlighted macabrely in the harsh light blazing out from the living room.

"Never seen anything like it." He shook his head. "I don't think there's hundreds. Maybe sixty. Seventy," he said slowly. "Did a number on the glass, as well. Totally smashed it."

Emily didn't argue with him. Regardless of how many had or hadn't flown into the window, it was still a lot. And currently, her glass was smashed, and a bunch of tiny corpses littered her patio, some of them still twitching in their final death throes.

Unlike before, when she simply replaced the glass herself, this time she needed someone to see what happened. Needed *proof* that she wasn't going mad. Because she was beginning to feel that way.

Initially she'd called Hamish, but he didn't answer. The only other person she could think of was Phil Lakeland, the handyman. When she'd moved in, his number had been at the front of her welcome pack. She'd called him out a couple of times for the dishwasher and the boiler, and he seemed fine. Friendlier than most people in Hyam—not that that was saying a lot, but still.

"Sorry, what?" She realized he'd been speaking to her.

"I was saying could be they were migrating and got confused. Those are big doors," Phil said, pulling a tape measure from his baggy work jeans and using his foot to make a path in the bird bodies.

"Is that likely? They all just flew into the doors?" Emily asked.

"Birds aren't bright. Could be one went, so they all went. Can you hold this end for me?"

Emily took one end of the tape measure and moved behind Phil. No way she was moving dead birds with her foot. "They're different species. Do different species flock together?"

Phil pulled the tape measure down while she held it against the door.

"Don't know much about birds. They might. What other explanation could there be?"

And that was the crux of it, wasn't it? What kind of animal crashed through someone's glass doors in the middle of the night, and what birds threw themselves like kamikazes into the same doors?

"Should be able to get the glass put back sometime next week. I'll board them up for now," Phil said and put away his tape measure. "You know…"

Emily waited. Phil's mouth opened and then closed again.

"What, Phil?"

"Never mind. Doesn't matter. I'll get the glass ordered. My granddaughter's over tomorrow night, and she knows how to work my blasted computer. I'll clean up the birds too."

While Phil went to his van to get the wood to board up the doors, Emily texted Hamish. *Call me when you can. Weird stuff happening here.*

She put the phone back in her pocket and rubbed her arms. Even though the days were warm, it was still cold at night, and Emily felt the chill through her cardigan.

The bushes that divided her property from the drive rustled, and for no reason she could think of, Emily's heartbeat sped up. Her skin prickled, and she fought the urge to go inside.

It's the birds—they'd freaked her out, was all. There was nothing in the bushes. Except…except it felt like something was watching her.

There was the other night, her traitorous mind thought.

The bushes rustled again. *Just a fox, just a badger.* And that thought felt alien in her head. *That* thought made her want to scream.

What was wrong with her? She was losing it. And was it any wonder? Hyam was a creepy fucking place to live. What Charlie had seen in it she'd never know.

"Here we are," Phil said, and Emily nearly *did* scream. "Sorry, didn't mean to scare you."

"It's fine. It's just dark out, and the thing with the birds…"

Phil nodded as though he understood completely. It made her feel a little better. "I'll have this done in just a little while. You should go inside."

Emily nodded. "Can I bring you anything? Tea, coffee?"

Phil shook his head. "No, thank you. Just you go in, and lock up tight. Lock this door too—I don't need to come inside."

If Emily thought that was a strange thing for him to say, she didn't mention it. Maybe he felt that thing in the bushes too. Although she thought it was gone now. That it left when Phil came back.

Shit, she really was losing it. Things in the bushes and some conspiracy that made birds fly into her doors.

Except there *had* been something out there, hadn't there? And there wasn't any rational explanation for the birds.

Emily locked the doors as Phil told her. She went around the house, locking all the other doors and windows too. Not that that would keep it out. It hadn't kept it out before. Whatever *it* was. And why hadn't Hamish texted her back yet? He must be home by now.

CHAPTER TWENTY-SEVEN

Collie started to nod off and caught herself. She was freezing. She'd given her jacket to Lana about two hours ago. Poor kid must still be cold, though.

She couldn't believe it. Couldn't believe this was happening. The more she thought about it, the more it seemed like she might have overreacted. She hadn't actually *seen* the thing in the woods. She'd just started running and dragged Lana along with her.

It could have been anything. *Just a fox, just a badger*. She shivered. Where the fuck had *that* thought come from?

Above her, Lana let out a soft snore. Collie reached up and waggled her foot. "Hey, Lana. Wake up, sweetheart."

"Sorry," came Lana's sleepy voice.

"It's okay. Don't be sorry," Collie said.

So why *had* she run? Why had she panicked so badly? The more she thought about it, the more silly she felt. Maybe whatever was in the bushes spooked her? Sure, that was understandable. She wasn't exactly familiar with the countryside, and it was natural she'd be a bit nervous. Especially with it starting to get dark, and them being lost, and don't forget those creepy stones in the clearing.

Had all that culminated in her losing her shit and taking off up a tree? She wasn't sure. It didn't *sound* like her. She wasn't someone who typically overreacted.

She'd been through a lot lately. Sasha, moving here, it took its toll. And the stupid kids who'd put claw marks in her back door. Maybe that was it. The claw marks were still in her head, and that bloody scarecrow at the funfair, and then she'd heard the animal in the bushes and just panicked.

More certain now it was—

Just a fox, just a badger

What?

She was losing her fucking mind.

"Collie?" Lana's voice from above was soft and apprehensive.

"What's up, Lana?" Her voice sounded strained, sounded on the verge of hysteria.

"Are you okay?"

"Sure, why?"

"Your breathing is funny."

And her breathing was funny. Her chest felt tight, like a band was tightening around it.

She almost laughed out loud. *I'm about to have my first panic attack, stranded in a fucking tree.* And that helped. That calmed her a little. That and the thought that on the branch above her was her ten-year-old niece. Small and defenceless and motherless.

"I'm okay. Promise." Her voice was sounding better. "Lana?"

"Yes?"

"Do you think we might have overreacted? Down there, earlier?"

"You mean when we ran?"

"Yeah."

Lana was silent a moment. "Do *you* think we overreacted?"

"I'm starting to. I'm wondering if it was just—"

A fox, just a badger.

Christ, but that was stuck in her head like a jammed-up record.

"An animal," she finished.

"Maybe," Lana answered.

"You aren't sure?" Collie asked.

"I don't know."

And why would she? Lana was ten. Collie was the adult—she was supposed to know. And she was becoming more and more sure she'd overreacted. Tony would laugh his head off. He'd bring it up for evermore. Every night out, every night *in*.

Collie almost laughed. She was feeling better. Not altogether back to her old self—she was halfway up a fucking tree in the middle of the night—but getting there.

"Lana, I think maybe I overreacted. I think we should get down," Collie said.

"But it's dark. We don't know the way back to the tent," Lana said.

"Can you see over there?" Collie pointed beyond the trees to a spot where lights twinkled. "I'm pretty sure that's the main campsite. If we head that way, we can get back."

"But what if it's still down there?" Lana said.

This was Collie's fault. She'd put the fear of God into Lana, and now Lana was scared. Why wouldn't she be? The aunt she loved and trusted, the grown-up, had legged it through the woods and made her climb a tree.

"I told Tony I wasn't cut out for camping," Collie mumbled to herself. "I think I overreacted before. I got a bit spooked when we saw those stones, and when I thought we were lost, and I just…I don't know. I think I just panicked, sweetheart. I am sorry."

Lana didn't answer her.

"Lana?"

"Yeah. So we're getting down?" Her voice was dull and resigned. *No, she's afraid. She's terrified. And it's your fault, bellend.*

"Look, I'll go down first, and you come after me. That way you'll know it's safe. Okay?" Collie said, putting some brightness into her voice. Some *I'm a confident adult who has my shit together* into her voice.

"Okay." Still that monotone.

"Honestly, Lana, I think it's—"

"Just a fox. Just a badger. Yeah, I know."

Where the hell did she hear that from? Did I say it out loud before? Why won't it get out of my fucking head?

Collie looked down, and for a second—just a split second—she thought she saw eyes down there. Bright orange eyes. Not an animal's eyes precisely because they were too knowing, too *aware*, but some creature's eyes. And in the distance, that white light again. The one from before. The one that smelled of—Sasha. Lavender. It was lavender.

Don't be such an idiot.

"Exactly," Collie said, clearing the scream from her throat. "Just a f—just an animal."

Collie began to climb.

❖

Down there, it waited. Not quite a fox and not quite a badger. Something much bigger than either, though it stood on four legs. It moved further back into the trees, sure the woman had seen it lurking here. It left earlier, but it was drawn back here, drawn to *them*.

It watched as the woman stood on the forest floor and looked around with her unseeing eyes. It knew she had talked herself out of believing in it. But the girl hadn't. The girl knew it was still here because it could smell her awareness and her fear.

It watched them follow the weak torchlight from the woman's phone. Watched them walk away from it.

It waited.

CHAPTER TWENTY-EIGHT

Emily watched Collie and Lana unloading the car and debated whether to say hello or not.

The decision was made for her when Collie looked in Emily's direction and waved. With the mail she'd come down the drive for in one hand, Emily waved back. Then, feeling awkward, she walked over to them.

"Looks like you've been somewhere exciting," she said, stating the obvious.

She noticed Lana flinch.

"Just camping. Don't really think it's for us, is it, Lana?" Collie said.

Emily studied Collie for a moment. She looked tired and worn out and maybe scared, despite the smile she plastered on her face.

"No, don't blame you. I tried it once and never again," Emily said.

The bushes rustled, and Emily noticed all three of them jumped. Lana let out a little cry.

"It's just Tufty, look." Collie pointed to their fluffy black cat, which shot out of the bush and hurried up the drive and away.

Emily sighed. "Sorry, bit on edge."

She noticed Collie glance quickly at Lana before saying, "Yes, I think we all are."

The conversation stuttered to an awkward and heavy silence. *Something's going on here. Secrets*, Emily thought and then on the heels of that, *Just a fox, just a badger*. She shivered.

"Well—"

"How are—"

She and Collie spoke at the same time.

"Sorry, you go," Emily said.

"I was going to ask, how you are? You look a lot better. Not that you looked bad before."

"I'm fine, thanks. Just a bad cold," Emily answered.

"Right. Well..." Collie toed the gravel.

"I should go," Emily said.

"Okay."

"Bye, miss," Lana said and headed inside, loaded up with camping gear.

Emily turned to leave, feeling Collie's eyes still on her.

"Emily?"

"Yes." She stopped, turned around.

"Can I ask you something?" Collie said.

No. Don't you dare, Emily wanted to shout at her because she thought she knew what was coming. How she *could* know wasn't something she wanted to think about, but she did.

Instead she said, "Sure."

"Have you, I mean, since your window got smashed, have you seen anything else...I don't know...weird?"

Emily wanted to tell her no. She hadn't seen anything at all. Whatever she *thought* she'd seen was all in her head. She was just going slowly mad, that was all.

She remembered her brother's email. *Em, there's something strange in this village. I feel like I'm being watched.*

"Last night about a hundred birds committed suicide against my french doors. They just *flew* at them. Smashed all the glass. Again." Why did she have to tell Collie that?

Collie nodded and seemed unsurprised. "Last night, we were chased by something. I thought it was just my imagination, that I just freaked out because of being in the woods, but..." Collie took a deep breath and took something out of her pocket. She held it out to Emily. "This morning, when I got up, this was outside the tent."

Emily stepped closer even though her brain was telling her not to look, *screaming* at her to turn back around and walk away.

Lying in the centre of Collie's hand was a small circular disc about an inch in diameter. There was a picture on it, but Collie put it back in her pocket before Emily could properly look.

"Someone left that outside your tent?" Emily asked.

Collie nodded. Emily thought Collie looked like she might be sick. "I don't understand it. I only asked you because, well, something smashed your glass. We thought it was kids, stupid kids, but what if it's not?"

"What else would it be?" Emily asked.

"I don't know. But something chased me and Lana in the woods last night. I thought maybe it was my imagination—I've never camped before and I'm prone to being spooked. I'd pretty much convinced myself I was just being an idiot, and maybe I am. But something left this outside my tent. And something left claw marks in my back door. Maybe it is just kids, or one of these weird locals, but Emily, something isn't *right* here. Can't you feel it too?"

Emily wanted to tell Collie everything in that moment. She wanted to unburden herself from the weight she'd been carrying since Charlie's death. About the emails he sent before he disappeared, each one more frightened than the last. About the people who all disappeared in April. About the strange likeness between Frances Cobb and her relative.

Instead, she said, "It's probably someone winding you up."

"And the birds flying into your doors?" Collie asked. Emily watched her touch her pocket where the disc rested.

"I don't know. But I'm sure there's an explanation," Emily said.

Collie sighed and nodded. "Okay, then. Sorry to have bothered you with it. Have a good day, Emily."

Collie's abruptness took her back. "I'm not saying you're wrong, Collie. Just—"

"You don't want to talk to me about it. It's fine, Emily. If you want to tell yourself that there's nothing going on here, you go right ahead."

Emily watched Collie pick up some camping equipment and walk back to her house without another word.

Emily stood there a moment, thinking. The fact was, she didn't know Collie Noonan. If Emily shared what she knew with her, it could be a big mistake. But Collie had come here after Charlie's disappearance—after Emily arrived, even.

And if she did tell her, what then? What could Collie do about it? Maybe nothing. But maybe she deserved to know. Emily couldn't leave until she found out what happened to Charlie, but Collie didn't have to stick around, did she?

And why wasn't Hamish returning any of her calls or texts?

Too much to think about—*just a fox, just a badger.* And that was driving her mad too. That phrase running around in her head.

The bushes rustled again, and Emily hurried back up her drive, glancing behind her, expecting something to come rushing out at her any second.

Nothing did, thank God, but she couldn't shake the feeling she was being watched.

Just like Charlie.

Exactly like Charlie. Had his watcher now turned its attention to her?

Of course, that was ridiculous. There was nothing in the bushes and nothing watching her.

Emily turned onto her garden path and saw someone up ahead by her front door.

"Help you?" she called out.

The figure turned and she saw it was Stephanie Willis. "Miss Lassiter?"

"Only the kids at school call me that. It's Emily, and how can I help you?" Emily thought she'd done a reasonable job of sounding friendly there. Although looking at Stephanie Willis, it was wasted.

"I came to speak with you about the scarecrow for the Spring Fair," Stephanie said.

"Oh yes, Hamish told me about them. I'll make sure I put one out on the day," Emily said.

"Do you know how to make a Hyam scarecrow?" Stephanie asked.

Emily resisted the urge to roll her eyes. "Well, no, but I've made many a guy on bonfire night so I'm assuming it's not too dissimilar."

"Stuffing an effigy of Guy Fawkes full of straw is not the same thing at all." Stephanie eyed her coldly, and Emily wondered again why everyone in this village was so unfriendly.

"I can google it. Look, Stephanie, I have to get on if you don't mind," Emily said. She wanted this woman off her doorstep.

"I've left you one round the back. You won't be entered in the competition, but I'm sure you don't care about that anyway," Stephanie said.

"You've left me one round the back?" Emily repeated.

"Yes. Near your living room doors. I thought it might save you having to *google* it," Stephanie said.

"Right. Well, thank you. That's very kind." Emily wasn't sure kindness was what had motivated Stephanie Willis, but she was grateful all the same. If she had to have one of those godawful things up, at least she didn't have to waste time making it.

Then, another thought occurred to Emily. "How did you get up here? I didn't see you walk up the drive."

Stephanie looked taken aback by the change of topic. "I came the other way. Through the woods."

"That's a long way. Those woods stretch in the opposite direction of the village, so you would have had to walk all the way round." Emily didn't need to say coming up the drive would have been much quicker.

"I've dropped a few off already. I was coming through the woods from Lowfield Road," Stephanie said. "I won't take up any more of your time. I'm sure you've got things to be getting on with."

Emily watched Stephanie leave, this time down the drive. She thought back to when she'd turned back after speaking with Collie. Stephanie was standing at her front door with her back turned. What if she hadn't been arriving but leaving? The estate agent would have a key to the property—it wasn't a stretch to think they had given it to Stephanie.

The folder.

Emily darted into the house and ran up the stairs. She went to the wardrobe and lifted the bottom out. The folder was still there. She sat back on her heels and breathed deeply.

Stupid to think Stephanie had let herself in here. To what? Steal a bunch of photocopied newspaper articles and emails that meant nothing?

Emily stood up and went back downstairs. In the kitchen, the tap was dripping again.

The tap.

It only dripped for a few minutes after you'd used it, and Emily hadn't been in the kitchen for hours.

She was being ridiculous. So what, Stephanie Willis got a key from the estate agents, let herself into her house, and what? Rinsed her hands?

Put like that, it did sound stupid. Nevertheless, Emily went back upstairs and looked around. She opened her wardrobe, her chest of drawers, and her bedside table. Everything looked like it was supposed to. Next she went back downstairs and into the living room. Where she nearly had a heart attack.

Right outside the window, a bloody horrific scarecrow stared in at her. Stephanie had stuck it in the grass facing the house. She probably thought it would be funny. Well, it wasn't staying there. Sod the villagers, Emily was going to stick it further out by the woods, where it wouldn't creep her out.

The scarecrow had bundles of hazel for arms and legs and poked out of a sackcloth. It had been generously stuffed with straw, and the pork-pie hat was fixed at a jaunty angle, totally at odds with the horror-film look of the thing.

Feeling it staring at her, Emily decided to move it right away. She turned from the window and noticed her laptop sat open on the coffee table.

There was no question this time. She definitely hadn't left it like that. She *always* shut the lid, ever since an unfortunate accident with a glass of white wine and her previous laptop. There was no way she would have left it open like that.

Emily looked back outside at the scarecrow. It almost looked like it was smiling at her and not in a friendly way.

CHAPTER TWENTY-NINE

Collie turned the disc over in her hand again and studied it. There was something comforting about it, which was strange because it wasn't exactly pretty. She ran her finger along the edge, then hissed in pain and pulled her finger back. She looked at her finger.

There was a paper-thin cut, beaded with blood. The disc cut her. It was sharp. Really sharp. The cut was deep.

Collie sucked her finger and looked at the disc again. On one side was a circle within a circle, crudely carved. On the other, two crossed swords. At least Collie thought they were swords. They were mostly worn away like something—a thumb or finger, perhaps—had rubbed at them.

Last night, when they'd finally found their way back to the tent, and even though Collie had mostly convinced herself it was an animal in the bushes and nothing was *actually* chasing them, she decided they were definitely leaving. They would come back tomorrow and pack up the stuff, but right now, they were going home.

Then the car wouldn't start.

It wouldn't even turn over. She'd called the breakdown people who'd come out eventually at about five in the morning. She couldn't even find a cab out here in the middle of nowhere.

She'd sat huddled in the tent, with Lana dozing on the sleeping bag next to her. Collie had been vigilant. No way she was nodding off at all. Except she had. For ten minutes. And when her phone rang, and the breakdown man said he was here, she'd come out of the tent and trodden on this thing.

The disc had been lying right outside the flap, on the small piece of carpet carefully placed there by the campsite owners, so people didn't track mud into the tent.

When she'd been in the tree, she'd managed to convince herself it was all in her head. It had just been—*a fox, just a badger*—an animal, that she'd overreacted to in major proportions—blame it on her wild imagination and all those video games she helped design.

All the way back to the tent, she'd been terrified. She'd kept her gaze on those distant lights from the campground like a person dying of thirst keeps their eyes on the oasis up ahead.

Even when the car, which had always been reliable and was only three years old, had failed to start, she told herself these things happen. Cars break down all the time—wasn't that why she'd got the breakdown insurance in the first place?

But that disc. *This* disc she was holding in her hand and staring at now, finally decided it for her. Something was out there, and it was fucking with her. Fucking with them. Maybe it was a person. Someone from the village with a screw loose who hated outsiders, or maybe it was something else. Something darker and far more dangerous.

Either way, it didn't matter. They were going. She'd made the decision. Lana's next school term finished at the end of April, which was only a few weeks away and also meant she wouldn't miss the Spring Fair.

They'd lose money on this house because she'd signed for a year, but it didn't matter. Collie wasn't going to be like one of these idiots in a horror film, sticking around as everything around them turned into a nightmare. Whatever it was that was tormenting them, well, it had won. Congratulations and nice work, they were leaving.

And what about Emily? Whatever was messing with Collie and Lana was messing with Emily too. Outside just now Collie knew she'd been lying. She couldn't say how, but she did.

Plus, who had a ton of birds fly into their window and thought that was normal, thought that was *okay*?

Whatever was going on here, Collie wanted no part in it. Lana had been through enough already.

Chances were it was a person—or the whole village—ganging up to scare them. Collie doubted any kind of animal had left that disc outside their tent. But that made it worse, didn't it? That someone was actively trying to scare them, terrify them.

And Emily's birds, and the claw mark, and the absolute certainty she'd had for a few minutes last night that something was chasing them—probably something or someone had been chasing them. And before that, something was watching them. Had been watching them for a while now. Something sly and animal and—

"What's that?" Lana asked from the kitchen doorway.

"Nothing." Collie quickly put the disc back in her pocket. "All unpacked?"

"I didn't really get packed to begin with. I just put stuff back in their boxes." Lana went to the fridge.

"No, I guess not. I am sorry about the camping, and that whole thing last night," Collie said. She could feel the disc pressed against her thigh in her jeans. It felt heavy and hot and solid. Reliable. What a weird way to feel about a bit of junk.

Lana shrugged and sat down with a carton of juice. "It wasn't your fault. I thought something was after us too."

"You did?" Collie asked.

"Yep. Something chasing us."

And that's what happened, wasn't it? Something *had* chased them.

"Lana?" Collie asked gently. "What do *you* think it was? In the woods, I mean?"

Lana shrugged and fiddled with the straw on her carton. "Something really bad," she whispered.

Collie's arms prickled, and the thing in her pocket seemed to pulse. "Do you think it wanted to hurt us?"

Lana shook her head. "I think if it wanted to hurt us, it would have. I think it was messing with us. Like when my cat catches a bird. She won't kill it right away. She likes to play with it first."

Collie thought Lana had it exactly right. That was what it had felt like. "What if it wasn't an animal?" Collie asked.

"You mean if it was, like, a person?" Lana asked.

"Yeah. Someone trying to scare us," Collie said.

"Maybe. But why would they do that?"

"I don't know."

And the truth was, she didn't. Last night in the tree, she had managed to half convince herself it was all in her imagination. That nothing had chased them through the woods. That it was just an animal—*just a fox, just a badger*—and why wouldn't that fucking phrase just get out of her head?

"Aunt Collie?"

"Yes, sweetheart?"

"Are we going to move now?" Lana asked.

"I think so. Yeah."

"Good." Lana stood up from the table. "I don't think it's safe here."

❖

It had had a busy night and a busy morning, and there was still more to do. It was foolish last night—it shouldn't have taken the teacher and drawn attention to itself. It should have waited. Just a little while longer.

It was finding it harder and harder to keep control of itself. It heard that came with age. When you were as old as it was, it became harder and not easier to wait.

But it wouldn't have to wait much longer. The time was getting closer now. It would deal with the man's sister first, before she could dig any deeper. Not that it mattered much. She could dig as much as she wanted, and it would make no difference. Her fate was set. It had been, the moment she came to the village looking for answers.

All the same, it knew who she was and what she was. A journalist. It knew she had asked a friend for help. She wasn't anywhere close to the truth, but that didn't matter. She knew something wasn't right, and it didn't want anyone even looking at Hyam.

As for the other two, they wouldn't be going anywhere. They were destined for it as much as the man's sister was. As much as the teacher had been last night, and the teacher before him, and all the others it had taken over the years.

The little girl was special, though. She had been chosen to continue the ancient way of things. To mark the end and the beginning, the changing over. Its time was coming to an end, but another waited to take over the mantle and continue the ancient ways.

It didn't spend much time in the bushes today. It was tired and needed to rest. There was still much more it had to do and places it needed to go before it could sleep.

It moved slowly from its watching place and headed up towards the man's sister's house. How easy it would be to go there now and deal with her. The glass in her door was still not fixed after its little trick last night.

It had sent one of its people into her home. She'd nearly been caught too. But she'd got the information it wanted, and that was all that mattered.

It could take her now, if it wanted. The knowledge of its power made it feel strong, invincible, and it ached to cry out. To burst into her house and tear her limb from limb and taste her blood and fear.

It would wait, though. It was used to waiting. It could wait some more.

Chapter Thirty

"Moving? What do you mean you're *moving*?" Tony asked. Collie could hear him banging around his kitchen.

"What is all that racket?" Collie asked over the cacophony of pans.

"I'm making a gourmet breakfast, and don't change the subject."

"Sounds like a lot of trouble for—wait. Are you making breakfast for a *woman*?"

"Yes. And I said, don't change the subject."

"Who is she then?" Collie smiled despite her current predicament. Tony didn't have the easiest time getting girlfriends. Not because he wasn't a catch—if Collie was that way inclined, she would have snapped him up. But people could be small-minded and bigoted. And when they passed Tony up, they passed up someone amazing.

Tony sighed theatrically. "Instead of worrying about my love life, you should be concentrating on your own. That's why you're single."

"That is not why I'm single, and don't *you* change the subject," Collie said. The banging pots had stopped for the time being.

"You changed the subject first," Tony replied.

"Come on, dish. Who is she, where did you meet her, and when am I meeting her?" Collie asked.

"Karen. Work. Never," Tony said.

"That's not nice," Collie said. "I let you meet all my girlfriends."

Collie laughed when Tony snorted down the phone. "Oh yeah, all one of them."

"Hey! There were at least two," Collie said.

"That woman last year doesn't count. You forgot her bloody name when you were introducing me. Now, you've procrastinated enough, why are you moving? What happened?" Tony said.

"No, look, I didn't realize you had company. Let's talk later."

"Collie."

"It's just…it sounds stupid, but I think I'm being watched." Collie realized how paranoid it sounded as soon as it came out.

"Come again?" Tony said.

"Not, like, horror-film watched, but like, I think people in Hyam are trying to scare us."

"Okay. What makes you think that? The claw marks on the door?"

"That, and just a feeling. I don't know. It sounds stupid," Collie said.

"It's not stupid, Collie. If you really think you're being watched, you should call the police."

"And say what? They'll think I'm nuts. I've got no proof—it's just a feeling. Look, just forget I said anything. It doesn't matter. I'll talk to you about it tomorrow."

"Collie—"

"Honestly, it's not a big deal. Enjoy your gourmet breakfast and whatever else you get up to. I'll speak to you later."

She heard Tony sigh down the phone. "Fine. I'll call you tonight. But if anything else weird happens, please promise me you'll call the police."

"Okay." Suddenly, her throat felt tight and her chest ached. She would not start crying.

"Love you, mate," Tony said.

"Same," Collie replied and hung up the phone.

She scrubbed her face with her hands and forced back the tears that were gathering in her throat.

Everything was so fucked, and she had no idea how to make it right. She'd thought she was making things better by moving here, and now it was obvious how big a mistake that had been.

Collie felt lost and alone. Tony was amazing, but she couldn't keep relying on him for everything. At some point, she'd have to stand on her own two feet. She had Lana to think about now after all.

❖

Lana looked out her bedroom window. She could see the top of Miss Lassiter's house—mainly just the roof. It poked out above the trees.

In front of their house and all the way up the drive, which she could also partially see from her window, were thick, dense bushes. Trees that had been there since before even Collie was born lined the drive and blocked the view around their house.

Lana thought anything could be hiding in there. It wouldn't even have to make much of an effort to be totally concealed by the bushes and trees.

Last night was terrifying. More terrifying than going into her old head teacher's office and seeing Collie sitting there, eyes red and face crumpled in on itself. She'd known something had happened, something bad, and her tummy was sick and her skin itched.

But last night was more terrifying than that. Her mother's death hurt her in a way she didn't quite have the words for. When she thought about the pain of that, it was like a deep, black yawning chasm, and she worried if she looked into it too long, she would fall in and never hit the bottom of it.

But Last Night—that was how she thought of it—Last Night Lana knew, the way you just sometimes knew stuff, that the thing that chased them through the woods hadn't wanted to kill them—at least not then— but it *could*. If it wanted, they would be dead back in that wood right now.

The understanding she was only alive because that thing *wanted* it that way was the most terrifying thing Lana ever had to think about. She came so close to death that she could have reached out and touched it with her fingertips.

Lana knew Collie felt that way too. She was trying to hide it from Lana, but Lana *knew* Collie was just as scared as she was, and that made it worse. Because kids were used to being scared about stuff and having adults tell them it was fine. But when the adult was scared... well, that was something altogether different.

Lana wondered if she should tell Collie about the thing in the bushes. Before, she'd been worried about Collie not believing her or thinking she was way more messed up about Mum than she was letting on.

Now, though, Collie felt the thing herself. Collie had been stalked by it, *watched* by it. Maybe she'd believe Lana.

But then, what was the point? Collie already said they were leaving Hyam, so was there any point in telling her about the thing in the bushes now?

Lana wasn't sure. She'd think about it some more. She looked over at Miss Lassiter's roof and wondered about her. Lana knew she'd been waiting for Lana to go into the house this morning so she could talk to Collie.

Lana might be ten, but she wasn't deaf, and she heard Miss Lassiter tell Collie about the birds that flew into her window. And Lana was there when Miss Lassiter had jumped when something moved in the bushes.

Miss Lassiter definitely knew more than she was saying, and Lana had a feeling she was just as scared as they were.

As if thinking about her conjured her up, Lana saw Miss Lassiter come down the drive they shared. She was in a hurry, and she looked worried. Lana wondered what all that was about.

CHAPTER THIRTY-ONE

Emily couldn't stop her mind from thinking the worst. It was just like Charlie. Hamish still hadn't returned her calls, and though Emily didn't know him all that well, people generally returned calls when the message was *Please call me as soon as you can. I'm worried.*

It had been hours since Emily last saw Hamish, and he'd disappeared into thin air. Something wasn't right. But unlike Charlie, Hamish had only been out of contact for twenty-four hours. Something could have happened—a family emergency, lost his phone—

Or he's lying in a shallow grave somewhere, just like Charlie.

Emily told herself to stop with the morbid thoughts. Hamish wasn't dead, and maybe Charlie wasn't either.

She manoeuvred her tiny car down the tiny country lanes and over the level crossing. Hamish lived in a short row of neat houses just past the shops.

She pulled up outside his place, not bothering to park properly, and leaving a gap you could drive a bus through between the car and the pavement.

Emily got out and knocked on his front door.

No answer.

She peered through the window facing out into the street. Hamish's curtains were open, which meant he'd either done it this morning, or he hadn't made it home last night.

Emily cupped her hands around her face to cut down the reflection of the street. She could see a small sofa with a coffee table in front, and on it a couple of remote controls neatly lined up.

Towards the back of the room was a dining table, and there was a doorway which led to the kitchen.

She stepped back and looked up at the bedroom window.

Dark.

Emily could tell the curtains weren't drawn up there either, but nothing much beyond that.

"Help you?"

Emily nearly jumped out of her skin at the sound of the voice.

She turned to see an older woman standing near her with a carry box of cleaning products.

"Sorry. I'm looking for my friend who lives here. Hamish Ford?"

The woman nodded. "Yes, I'm his cleaning lady."

"Have you seen him at all today?" Emily asked. She didn't recognize the woman from the village.

"No, but I just got here. You're a friend, you say?"

Emily nodded. "I've been trying to reach him since last night, and he hasn't returned any of my calls or messages."

"Perhaps he stayed out last night," the woman said and fished in her pocket, bringing out a bunch of keys.

"No, he was with me until about eight or so. He said he was going straight home."

Emily saw the woman's face rearrange itself into something that resembled pity.

She thinks Hamish and I are in a relationship, and he's cheating on me.

"Well, miss, in my experience of men, they don't always do what they say. Perhaps he decided to pop into the pub after he left yours, and he's upstairs now, sleeping it off."

The thought had crossed Emily's mind, but then why wouldn't he have got back to her by now? It was after midday.

"Maybe you're right," Emily said.

"Why don't you come inside and check for yourself," the woman offered.

Emily almost laughed. In London, no one would ever do something like that, but out here, even in a village as unfriendly as Hyam, people trusted other people to be who they said they were. It was one of the things she'd missed about the country. People were much kinder here than in the cities. Plus, the woman clearly thought Hamish was giving her the runaround and felt sorry for her.

"If you don't mind? I'd be ever so grateful," Emily said. "I just don't understand why he can't at least text me." No harm in reinforcing what the woman already believed.

The woman sighed deeply and unlocked the door. "Some men just aren't worth the trouble, dear. Took me years to wade through a lot of rubbish before I found a good one."

Emily nodded as if contemplating doing the same, and then, she was in Hamish's house.

It felt strange, being in here without him. She'd only come over once, and that was a while ago now.

The house was neat and clean—no surprise, with a cleaner—without much clutter or the usual bits and bobs that personalized a place.

Emily dutifully went upstairs, where the cleaning lady expected her to go.

She's probably hoping I'll find him in bed with a woman and give her a show better than any soap, Emily thought, perhaps a little unkindly.

"He up there?" the woman called from downstairs, and Emily did detect a little excitement in her voice, so perhaps she hadn't been that uncharitable in her assessment of the woman after all.

"No," Emily called back down.

Hamish's bed was made, and the room was just as neat as the rest of the house. Floorboards squeaked under her feet as she walked over to the wardrobe.

Emily had never looked in Hamish's wardrobe, so she was really going on instinct. When she looked inside, it didn't seem as if anything was missing. The clothes hung in tidy order, suits on one end, going down to shirts, chinos, and jeans. There were no gaps or hangers fallen down.

The shoes were lined up along the floor, heel to heel and toe to toe, again with no discernible gaps as though several pairs had been removed.

If he looked inside my wardrobe, he'd have a fit.

Emily dropped down and looked under the bed, which was admirably free from dust. There was a travel bag pushed towards the end of the bed but no suitcase she could see.

"What are you doing?"

Emily nearly banged her head on the bed frame. She jumped up. "Just checking he hasn't done a moonlight flit." She grinned with no humour.

The woman gave her another sympathetic nod. "My ex-husband did that. I told him I was pregnant, and when I came home the next day, poof, gone. Took my Elton John LP with him as well."

Emily nodded, pretending to understand what the woman was going on about.

"You didn't tell him you were pregnant, did you? Might be the reason he's not calling you back," the woman asked.

Emily nearly burst out laughing. The lesbian and the gay man, sounded like the punchline to a joke. "No," Emily said. "Nothing like that."

"Well, I really need to be getting on."

Emily took the hint. "Sure, I'll get out of the way. I appreciate you letting me come in and check, though."

The woman nodded then narrowed her eyes. "You know, he normally leaves my money on the dining table."

"And he hasn't today?" Emily asked.

"Oh no, he has. But he's left it in the kitchen, by the kettle. What I mean is, at first, I thought maybe he'd done a runner as well, when I didn't see my money there. But what I'm saying is, he can't have done a runner. Because he left the money for me. So he must have been back last night or this morning."

"Yes, I suppose you're right," Emily said.

She went back out the way she came and got in her car. It took four manoeuvres and a lot of back and forth before Emily could pull out because the woman had parked so close to her bumper. Probably pissed off at Emily's terrible parking.

At least she knew Hamish was around. He had to have been to leave money out for his cleaner.

He could have done it yesterday before he came to see you. He could still be lying in a ditch somewhere. Probably next to your brother.

That nasty little voice again that wouldn't shut up.

Emily turned on the radio to drown it out. Hamish would call her back when he was ready.

CHAPTER THIRTY-TWO

Collie's new tenants hadn't been exactly over the moon when she called and told them she was exercising the six-month break clause, but they'd been understanding. All she had to do now was ask Tony if they could stay with him until her tenants left.

It was a relief, knowing that soon they'd be back in London and away from Hyam. Not that a flat in the middle of London was ideal for a ten-year-old, but Collie did the sums, and she definitely couldn't afford to pay rent on this place and another. Her mortgage was small enough that the rent she got for her Vauxhall flat covered the mortgage. But it didn't cover the building's service charge.

While it was true she and Lana could move to another small town—and maybe they would—rent in London was expensive. Plus she'd come to like a lot of aspects to the rural way of life. And she thought it might be a better way for Lana to grow up as well.

She'd obviously pay her way with Tony, but rent and bills twice over was a no-no.

The house in Hyam was a twelve-month let, and there was no way she could get out of it. Collie could probably have released some funds from the trust Sasha's money was held in, but that was for Lana when she got older, and Collie hated the idea of dipping in to it. They could stick it out a bit longer.

By now, Collie was convinced it was the locals who were scaring them and not some unnamed monster who lurked in the bushes. She was a grown woman, for God's sake, and the time for believing in things that went bump in the night was long gone for her.

"Hey, Lana," Collie called up the stairs.

"Yeah?" Lana stuck her head over the banister.

"Fancy going into Southwold for a bit?" Collie asked. Now that she'd made the decision to leave, she planned on them spending as little time in Hyam as possible.

"Yeah." Lana trotted down the stairs. "Can we get ice cream on the beach again?"

"We can get whatever you want, Lana Banana."

"Champagne and oysters?" Lana giggled, starting up the old game Collie had almost forgotten.

"Monks and cloisters," Collie agreed and grinned. She picked up her car keys.

"Lobster and thermidor?"

"Rat tail and cat paw." Collie closed the door behind them.

Lana giggled, "Aunt Collie, that's gross!"

"I disagree. It's a delicacy in France, you know."

"Is it?" Lana looked horrified.

Collie laughed. "Not at all."

They got in the car and carried on the silly rhyming game.

Collie backed out and heard a sickening crunch.

Fuck.

"I'm so, so sorry." She was speaking before she'd even got the car door all the way open.

From her own car, Emily looked at her but stayed seated.

"I don't know what I was thinking. Are you okay?" Collie said through the open window. She tried Emily's door handle but her car was locked.

Emily continued to stare at her with a dazed sort of look in her eyes.

"Emily? Are you hurt?"

Collie was starting to worry. She'd been doing about two miles an hour—surely that wasn't fast enough to injure Emily.

Emily looked at her then, really seeing her. "Collie. Shit, I'm so sorry."

Emily got out of the car and Collie held the door for her. "Are you okay?"

"Yes, yes, I'm fine. It was my fault. I was going too fast."

"No, no, I didn't look," Collie said, slightly bemused that they were both trying to take the blame. "Let's see the damage." Collie got back in the car and pulled forward again. She turned to Lana, who was still in the car. "You okay?"

"Fine." Lana nodded. "It was just a little bump."

Collie guessed they'd soon see about that.

Actually the damage wasn't too bad. Her car had a light scuff that she could probably polish out, and Emily had a slightly longer, deeper scuff that might also be easily repaired with some touch-up paint.

"I'm so sorry, Collie. It really was my fault. I came tearing down the drive," Emily said. "You didn't stand a chance."

Collie looked at her. She was close to tears. "Look, it's really okay. I think I can sort the damage on both vehicles easily enough. Don't worry."

Emily nodded and then the tears did come.

Shit. Collie had no idea what to do.

Do something, you idiot.

Collie reached out and patted Emily's shoulder.

Emily hastily wiped away the tears and tried to smile. "Sorry. Rough morning."

Collie nodded in sympathy. "Yeah, I know what you mean."

They stood there in the awkward silence that always seemed to surround them.

"Miss Lassiter, we're going to Southwold for the day," Lana said.

"Are you?" Emily rubbed at her eyes again. "That's nice."

"Why don't you come?" Lana said.

"Well—" Emily said.

"I don't—" Collie said at the same time.

They looked at each other. They looked at Lana.

"You should come because it means you won't be in Hyam," Lana said. "Sometimes it's nice to get away from here."

Emily nodded. "There is that. Well, if your aunt doesn't mind."

"I don't," Collie said and found that she didn't mind.

Because you fancy her. She doesn't fancy you back, Collie. You're just going to get hurt.

Collie ignored the killjoy voice. She was an adult. She could be friends with a woman she was attracted to. The idea of spending the day with Emily gave her a warm feeling in her belly. Little alarm bells were going off all over the place in her head, so she silenced them. She could be friends with Emily. Of course she could. "You'd be more than welcome. If you aren't doing anything. I'll even buy you lunch as a way of apologizing for crashing into your car."

Collie looked at Lana, who was grinning and looking back

and forth between them like she knew something they didn't. Collie frowned. Was she matchmaking?

Collie watched Emily's brow furrow, obviously trying to decide if this was a good idea. Then she nodded. "Let me just park my car," Emily said.

Collie had an idea that today was going to be a good day after all.

CHAPTER THIRTY-THREE

Emily looked across the table at Collie. The weather had stayed beautiful, and Emily didn't think she'd ever seen such a lovely spring. Memories of Charlie splashing about on his paddleboard at the holiday house they always rented tried to push their way in, but she forced them back out.

She was going to enjoy this day. She was out in the warm sunshine with a good-looking woman, and she was going to enjoy it. There was, of course, the small matter of the good-looking woman's motherless niece, but Emily found she was enjoying Lana's company too.

The voice inside, which had been screaming at her not to come today, that it was a terrible idea, finally quietened. Or rather, she'd shut it up. She guessed she probably should have said no when Lana asked her for a number of reasons.

But she'd been worried about Hamish, and after thinking Stephanie Willis broke into her house, she supposed she needed a friendly face. Collie was definitely a friendly face, and she wasn't from Hyam. Of course, Emily completely skated over the fact she was attracted to Collie and knew Collie was attracted to her, and nothing good was going to come out of spending an idyllic day with someone you liked and who liked you back.

What swayed it for her was Lana was coming along as well. They couldn't get into much trouble with a ten-year-old in tow. She didn't think. What surprised Emily was how much she actually *liked* having Lana around.

Lana wasn't loud or obnoxious, and she didn't demand attention. She alternated between following the grown-ups' conversation and playing on the brightly coloured handheld video game console she'd brought with her.

They'd found a pub on the seafront with picnic tables that looked out over the sea. Emily sipped her gin and tonic. She'd missed this. Just sitting in a pub with a friend and enjoying the day.

Yeah, that's what Collie is, a friend, the sarcastic little voice piped up again.

"So, you make video games?" Emily asked.

"Not really. I design the characters for video games. People far smarter than me make the actual video games," Collie replied.

"You're an artist then?"

"Aunt Collie is brilliant at drawing," Lana piped up. "When I was little, she'd draw whatever I wanted, *and* she could draw me into the picture as well."

Emily smiled and looked between the two. It was clear Lana adored her aunt. "Is that so?"

"It was fun. I thought about doing a comic, you know, Lana in different scenarios," Collie said.

"Why didn't you?" Emily asked.

"Time, commitment. Plus, I love my job and didn't want anything to get in the way of that. Not many people can say they love their job. I know how lucky I am."

I loved my job too once, Emily thought. Instead she nodded. "You're very lucky."

"I am. Do you like your job? I have to admit—I admire you. I don't think I could do it."

Emily thought of Charlie, how much he had loved teaching. "Sometimes I wonder if I'm doing the right thing," Emily said. She hadn't meant to, but it just came out.

"I think you're a really good teacher, miss." Lana glanced up from her video game.

"No, I'm not. I try my best, I really do, but my heart isn't in it." What was she doing? Telling Collie this stuff was one thing, but in front of Lana?

"Well, do something else then. You're what, thirty?" Collie asked.

"Thirty-three," Emily said.

"That's plenty young enough to start something else."

Emily nodded because she couldn't say, *Well, actually, I'm a journalist. I've taken this teaching gig because I think something terrible happened to my brother, and the longer I live in Hyam, the more certain I am it has something to do with the people living there.*

"Sorry, I've overstepped," Collie said.

"No, you haven't. Not at all. I shouldn't be saying all this stuff. Especially not in front of one of my students," Emily said.

"I won't tell—don't worry, miss." Lana glanced up and smiled.

Emily smiled back. She was a good kid. Emily liked her. "Thanks, Lana. I don't think Miss Cobb would be very happy."

The smile dropped off Lana's face. "She's scary. Sometimes in the playground, I can see her looking out her office window at us. I don't think she likes children."

Emily watched as Collie put an arm around Lana and pulled her close and said, "All head teachers are scary—it's part of the job. I'm sure she does like children."

Emily wasn't so sure. In fact, she thought Lana had it spot on. Frances Cobb didn't like children. Emily noticed how she avoided any sort of contact with them, the way she would flinch backwards if one came near. The few times she'd addressed Emily's class, Cobb hadn't made eye contact with any of them and seemed desperate to get away as soon as possible.

But Emily *had* noticed the way she watched Lana. Maybe it was because she'd taken a special interest in her because of the horrible thing that happened to her. Emily wasn't sure, but the look was possessive and…and something else she couldn't put her finger on.

"I think you're right, Lana. But I don't think she really likes anyone," Emily said.

"Why on earth would she become a teacher if she didn't like children?" Collie asked.

Emily wanted to tell Collie about the photograph she'd seen. The one of the woman who Emily would have bet money on was Frances Cobb if she hadn't seen the date. Of her suspicions that Stephanie Willis had been in her house, and of the people who had gone missing, all around this time of year. But she didn't.

Doing that would open up all sorts of further questions Emily didn't want to answer. She wanted to enjoy the day. The idea of actually *telling* Collie about what she was doing here didn't fill her with alarm any more. In fact, she almost wanted to. And *that* thought alarmed her. She needed to keep her distance. From the woman and the girl.

"Who knows? Maybe she did like kids once. Working with them for years, you probably end up hating them," Emily said and looked at Lana to see if she'd bite.

"Hey." Lana didn't disappoint. "Kids are great."

"Nah, they smell," Emily said.

"We do not smell." Lana laughed.

"You do. Really bad." Emily nodded solemnly.

Collie said, "You know, Emily, I have to spray lots of air freshener when Lana's about. *Buckets* of it."

Emily tried not to laugh. "Me too. In the classroom."

"Hey, you're so rude." Lana was really laughing now, which made Emily and Collie laugh too.

Emily reached out and ruffled Lana's hair. To her surprise, Lana leaned in to her and rested her head on Emily's shoulder.

The look Collie gave them didn't escape Emily. Slightly sad and amused at the same time. Emily wondered if she was thinking about her dead sister. Probably. Emily was thinking about her missing brother. When he was little, he used to rest his head on her shoulder the exact same way.

"Another drink?" Collie asked Emily after clearing her throat.

"I probably shouldn't."

"You can if you want—I'm driving, after all, and I'm on lemonade," Collie said.

Emily did fancy another. She wanted to feel that gentle numbness that came with being tipsy. And being a lightweight, one more would definitely make her tipsy.

"Okay then, thanks," Emily said.

Collie got up and took their empty glasses with her while Lana sat up and picked up her game again. Emily checked her phone. Still no Hamish.

"Are you waiting for someone to text you? Your boyfriend? Or girlfriend?" Lana asked.

Emily smiled. Christ, the kid was astute. Emily thought she'd been engrossed in her game, but evidently not.

Maybe it was the gin or maybe it was the sun, but Emily said, "No, I'm not. And if I was, it would be a girlfriend."

Great. She'd just outed herself to a student. What on earth was she thinking? Emily regretted it as soon as she said it.

"Interesting," Lana replied and raised one eyebrow.

Emily burst out laughing. She couldn't help it. "Lana, if you spread that around—"

"I won't," Lana said, sobering. "I would never. Aunt Collie says everyone should always mind their own business. Especially about stuff like that."

"Okay, right. Well—"

"My aunt's single as well. And she's gay too," Lana said and went back to her game.

Emily didn't know what to say. What did you say to such an obvious attempt at matchmaking?

And who was she kidding? She'd said what she had to Lana because she wanted it to get back to Collie.

Emily liked her. And apparently that was obvious to Lana as well. Great.

CHAPTER THIRTY-FOUR

Collie paid for the drinks. It was strange to be here with Emily and Lana, but also nice. Well, more than nice really, it was great.

Collie was surprised at how open Emily was. Usually their interactions were awkward, and Collie always got the sense Emily was hiding something. Not that she wasn't doing the same thing now, but she'd given a bit more.

Maybe it was the gin or maybe it was the sunshine—it really was a beautiful day. Either way, Collie was having a good time. The best time since Sasha died. It was good to be away from Hyam as well, and that thought only cemented what Collie already knew. They needed to leave.

What about Emily? If you leave, you probably won't see her again. That much was true. But really, it wasn't as if they were friends. Today was an anomaly. Plus, everything Collie did from now on had to be about Lana. It's what Sasha would have wanted.

What Collie wanted or needed came second, and she wouldn't have it any other way. Saying that, though, wasn't it Lana doing the matchmaking? She thought she was being subtle, but Collie knew her. She could be a right little shit about stuff like that.

Collie remembered the time Lana decided Collie would be perfect for her friend's mother. The fact the woman was completely straight didn't seem to deter Lana at all. At every opportunity she tried to get them in the same room. Finally, Collie had to tell her to pack it in. She was so obvious even the friend's mother was starting to cotton on, and Collie was feeling awkward and worried she'd think Collie had put Lana up to it.

Lana was disappointed but soon moved on to trying to set Collie up with a teacher. To be fair, that one was gay but not Collie's type at all.

Emily, though, Emily was very much her type. Lana had got it spot on this time—more luck than judgement, but Collie was pleased she'd got Emily to come with them today.

Collie looked up and noticed the barman staring at her.

"Everything all right with your drinks?" he asked.

"What?" Collie realized she'd been standing there staring at them. "Oh yes. Sorry. They look fine."

Face flaming, she picked them up and hurried back outside. What a knob. He must have wondered what was wrong with her, standing there staring into space.

Back at the table, Collie saw Emily and Lana laughing about something.

"Everything all right?" Collie asked.

Emily and Lana gave each other a secret smile, and Lana went back to her game.

"Yes, fine, thanks," Emily said and took the drink Collie offered. "Thanks."

"So, I was thinking. Unless you have something you need to get back for, maybe we could head down to the beach for a bit, then have dinner before we head home," Collie said.

Emily glanced down at her phone.

"If you have to get back, it's no problem," Collie said but felt disappointed anyway.

"No, I don't have to get back for anything. That sounds like a great idea," Emily said.

"Sure? No boyfriend or anything waiting for you back in Hyam?" Collie asked, then wanted to punch herself in the face for being so obvious. Emily and Lana burst out laughing. Something to do with that secret smile earlier. "What?" Collie asked, feeling her face heat.

"Nothing. And no, no boyfriend," Emily said.

"No *girlfriend* either," Lana said, and the two of them started laughing again.

Whatever was going on, it was clear they weren't going to share it with Collie. Didn't matter. She sipped her lemonade and watched them. For the first time since Sasha was murdered, she felt happy.

❖

Collie leaned back in the rented deck chair and sighed deeply. This was the life. The sun was warm on her face, and the sound of the waves coming in relaxed her and made her feel loose and sleepy.

She glanced across at Emily and Lana doing the same in their respective deck chairs. Lana was fast asleep, letting out soft little snores. And no wonder, after their night. Why hadn't she thought of this sooner? Why hadn't they come here instead of on that nightmare camping trip?

Emily opened her eyes and Collie found herself staring straight into them.

"Hi," Collie said.

"Hi," Emily replied. "This is nice, isn't it?"

Collie nodded. "The best. I was just thinking, we should have done this and not that awful camping trip."

"Why did you go camping? Doesn't really seem like your sort of thing," Emily said.

Collie sighed and sat up. "Kitty's birthday camping trip at school. Lana got invited, but she's never been before."

Emily nodded.

"Lana wanted to go on a sort of trial run first, to see if she liked it."

"And something chased you?"

Collie debated about how much to say. Something had passed between them this morning, and Collie knew there were things Emily wasn't saying.

"Yes. At least I thought so. I think daylight brings a kind of clarity that disappears at night. You know?" Collie worked a stone loose from the sand with her toe.

"Yes, I know. So nothing was actually chasing you?" Emily persisted.

Collie glanced at Lana, who still looked deeply asleep. "I don't know. I know there's something in Hyam that isn't right. And it's not just how unfriendly people are. There's something wrong with the place. We've decided to move. Back to London in the next school holidays. They don't want us here—I think they're trying to force us out, in fact—and we don't want to *be* here."

"Why did you come?" Emily asked.

"To escape London and everything that happened there. One of these fucking online newspapers did a big story about my sister's murder. They put a photo of Lana in their article. Bastards."

"I'm sorry. A reputable journalist wouldn't have done that," Emily said.

"You think so? They were at our door, wanting a comment, wanting an interview. They're all the bloody same, these jackals. We wanted to get away from it, and we wound up in Hyam. We thought the quiet and isolation would be good." Collie couldn't help the bitter laugh that came out. But Emily didn't need to hear all this. Collie asked her, "Why did you come here? No offence, but I can't really see the allure of Hyam to a young, attractive lesbian."

Something flickered in Emily's eyes, and Collie thought she wasn't going to answer. Then she did.

"My brother was a teacher in a small village. Last year, he went missing. No one's heard from him. His bank cards haven't been used. He just vanished. My whole family are devastated. I guess I wanted to feel close to him. I thought I could work in a village too, like he did. And it helped to be away from my family. Oh, I know that sounds terrible and selfish, but their grief was just like an avalanche. I felt as though I was lying trapped, underneath it all."

Collie felt something inside her reach out in understanding. Emily had it just right—the grief was like an avalanche, and all you could do was lie there with the crushing weight of it, hoping to be rescued.

She reached out and squeezed Emily's hand. It was soft and delicate in hers.

"We're both grieving then," Collie said.

Emily turned to her. "I'm so sorry about your sister. Frances Cobb called me into her office when I knew Lana would be in my class. To tell me what happened. I'm so, so sorry."

Collie felt tears prick the back of her eyes. She wouldn't cry. Not here and not in front of Emily. Not on this beautiful day.

She squeezed Emily's hand once more and let go. "Come on, no grieving today. We'll get ice cream and watch it melt all over our fingers instead."

Emily smiled at her and nodded. "That sounds good. I'm buying."

CHAPTER THIRTY-FIVE

Emily let herself into her house. It had been a lovely day. *Apart from all the lying you did.*

Emily pushed the nasty voice away. She had lied to an extent, she supposed. But she couldn't tell Collie the truth. She didn't know Collie well enough to trust her, and from what she'd said, she was no fan of journalists. Although, Emily *had* wanted to tell Collie, hadn't she? She'd wanted to offload all of it, didn't want secrets between them.

Get a grip. You barely know the woman. And she doesn't like journalists, which doesn't exactly bode well, does it?

Emily couldn't blame her for not being keen on journalists after her experience, she guessed. Collie had done what she'd needed to do. Besides, Collie said she and Lana were leaving at the end of term, so it wasn't as if they were going to strike up some great friendship...or anything else.

Emily was annoyed the thought of that stung so much. She barely knew the woman. Sure, they'd got on today and had a good time—

You had a great time.

Fine, a great time then. And maybe they were both single.

And attracted to each other.

Emily turned on some music to drown out the nasty little voice.

She went to the windows and drew the curtains. Phil had texted her to say he would fit the new glass tomorrow, which was a relief.

No texts from Hamish, though.

Emily tried not to think about it. It was like Charlie all over again. Hamish had just seemed to vanish.

But he'd left money for the cleaning lady, and his clothes were all there. Would she have known if he'd taken some with him? Probably not. Most likely he had a family emergency and hadn't got around to replying to her yet.

You know that's nonsense. He's missing, just like Charlie. And it's April too.

No, she didn't know that. She didn't know anything of the kind. If he wasn't in school tomorrow, she'd talk to Frances Cobb. There. Sorted.

Right, because Frances Cobb is the person to go to about it.

Who else would she tell? And Frances Cobb was the head teacher—if he'd told anyone where he was going, it would be her.

Emily went into the kitchen and poured herself a glass of wine. She probably shouldn't after the two gins, but that was future her's problem. Right now, she needed wine.

She carried the glass upstairs to the bathroom and ran herself a bubble bath. From here, she could see the top of Collie's house. Through the trees came the warm glow of lights. It soothed her to think of Collie over there, getting on with her evening.

Emily pulled down the blinds and got undressed.

She slid into the bath and couldn't help but sigh as the water warmed and relaxed her tired muscles. She leaned back and closed her eyes.

Bang, squeak, bang squeak.

What was that? It was coming from downstairs. Emily sat up and listened for the noise to come again. There it was, a soft bang and squeak. Was it the letter box?

She sat up, one hand clutching the side of the bath, the other still holding her wine, head cocked to the side, listening.

It came a third time. Now she was sure it was someone moving the flap on the letter box. What if Stephanie was back? Or someone else with a key?

If it was, they'd have let themselves in. They wouldn't be banging the letter box, would they?

Emily got out of the bath and put on a robe. She tiptoed to the top of the stairs and peeked round the corner.

Her front door was one of those uPVC things with obscured glass, but you could see vague shapes if someone was out there.

There was someone out there now. Emily could see the blurred outline of them filling the doorway. Her heart stuttered in her chest.

She saw the letter box flap pushed upward and someone's fingertips poke through the gap. What the fuck were they doing?

"Hello?" she called, trying to make her voice sound confident and strong. "Who's there?"

No answer. The door vibrated once in the frame as someone pushed against it.

"Emily." It was almost a whisper, and Emily was sure she'd imagined it. Then, it came again. "Emily."

Her mouth tasted metallic, and she absently understood that it was the taste of fear as she hurried down the stairs.

She picked up the godawful statue on the hall table, which came with the house. She was glad she hadn't shoved it in a cupboard now. The statue was cool and heavy in her hand.

"Who is it?" she called out, half hoping there would be no answer.

"It's me. It's Hamish." The voice was still quiet and weak sounding, but Emily recognized it now.

She put the statue down and threw back the deadlock. She opened the door.

"Jesus, what happened to you?" she cried.

Hamish stood just outside the doorway with his head down, on the porch, in the shadows. In the inky light Emily could see he was covered in some dark substance. His clothes—the clothes he was wearing the last time she saw him—were torn and dirty.

"Hamish, come inside. I'll call an ambulance."

But he just stood there, swaying slightly.

"Hamish?" she said again.

"It wasn't a fox or a badger, Emily. I saw what it was, and it wasn't from here. I think it's from *outside* but it came here somehow, and now it straddles *both* places."

"What are you talking about?" Emily asked.

Hamish looked up at her, and Emily saw his neck was a mess of gristle and tendons. She felt sick.

How could he still be talking to her?

"It lives in the shadows. It likes to watch you from there. Do you see? It knows who you are, and it's watching you, biding its time. It's watching them too." Hamish turned slightly and when he held up his hand to point in the direction of Collie's house, Emily saw most of his fingers were gone. "It likes to watch, and it likes to wait, and when it's ready, it'll take you. Just like it's always done. You can't stop it, Emily, but you can run. You must run."

"I can't." Her words came out a whisper. "I can't because of Charlie."

"It took him too. I'm sorry," Hamish said.

Emily shook her head. Hamish might have well as punched her in the kidneys because she found it impossible to breathe. She shook her head again. "No."

"You never did look in the church, did you? I told you to. Remember? If you won't run, then at least look in the church, Emily."

Before Emily could say anything else, a howl as terrible and as frightening as any in a horror film filled the night. It was all Emily could do not to let out a scream of her own. Her breath came rushing back, filling up her lungs and oxygenating her blood, preparing her for fight or flight.

The bushes to the left of her house shook violently, and then she saw two glowing red eyes.

"Shh," Hamish said. "It's here. We have to be quiet."

"Oh Jesus, oh God. Hamish, get inside. *Get inside now*," she screamed, but Hamish was gone.

Emily stepped back into the house and slammed the front door. She leaned against it, wondering what the fuck to do now.

Suddenly, it was hard to breathe. She felt like there was water

Water in

Water in her lungs

She couldn't

Can't breathe, can't breathe.

Emily sat up with a start. She coughed and spluttered. Water poured from her mouth and nose.

Shit, she'd fallen asleep in the bath and slid down and nearly drowned. Great. Brilliant.

Way to go, Em. Drowning in the bathtub.

The dream was still with her, though. She felt like she could reach out and touch it. It was so real, so *tangible*.

Emily got out of the bath and drained it. She pulled on a robe and went downstairs. She half expected to see the blurry shape of Hamish outside. She turned on the porch light, took a deep breath, and opened the door.

Nothing. No one was there.

Emily breathed a deep sigh of relief and let out a laugh that sounded more like a bark.

It was all that booze. She'd fallen asleep and dreamed about Hamish because he'd been on her mind all day. That was all. Just a dream.

Was it, though, Em? Look at the door.

Emily looked at the outside of the door. Near the letter box, just above, was a smear. It looked like blood.

CHAPTER THIRTY-SIX

When the loud banging started, Collie was in the middle of emptying the dishwasher. She ran for the front door before the inconsiderate arsehole could wake Lana.

She pulled open the door, ready to kick off at whatever delivery-man thought it appropriate to thump on the door and hold down the bell for what seemed like an eternity.

"Emily."

Not what Collie expected. Nor did she expect Emily to be standing there in nothing but a dressing gown with a wild look in her eyes—well, she'd imagined, sure, but not in this context.

"I'm so sorry, can I please come in?" Emily asked.

Her teeth were chattering and not from the cold. The fine spring weather held, and the evening was warm and fragrant.

"Of course." Collie stepped aside so Emily could come in. "What's happened? Do you need me to call the police? An ambulance?" Collie asked.

"No, no, none of them. Jesus, this is so embarrassing and so weird," Emily said.

Collie saw her hands were convulsively clutching at her dressing gown. She took Emily's hands in hers. They were freezing.

"Sounds like you've had some kind of shock. Come and sit down." Collie had an idea exactly what kind of shock too.

"Yes, I did." Emily sat on the couch.

"Can I get you a tea? Or something stronger?" Collie asked.

"I'll take a brandy if you've got one," Emily replied.

Collie thought she did. Somewhere at the back of a cupboard. She went into the kitchen and came back with a glass almost full to the top.

Emily smiled gratefully and then gave a small laugh. "I'm not sure I'll manage all of that. I must look terrible."

"Not at all. I don't really drink spirits, so I'm never really sure how much to put in a glass," Collie said.

Emily took a sip and winced. "Me either. But you always hear about people drinking brandy when they've had a shock, so I thought... Anyway, it's doing the trick."

"Emily, what happened?"

Emily took another big gulp of the brandy and told her.

When Emily was finished, Collie leaned back in her chair. "Well. I don't really know what to say."

"I don't actually think Hamish was there, if that's what you're worried about," Emily said.

"I didn't think you did," Collie said. But was that true? Something about the way Emily told the story made Collie wonder if part of Emily maybe *did* think her friend Hamish had really been there.

"The dream makes sense—you're worried about your friend. Have you reported him missing or anything?" Collie asked.

Emily shook her head. "No. What would I say? Someone I'm sort of friendly with from work hasn't returned my calls and texts since yesterday? Hardly think they'll send out a search party, do you?"

Collie saw her point. "No, I suppose not. But you're worried enough about him that he's on your mind. Presumably it's out of character for him not to respond to you?"

"Yes. We've only recently become what you'd call friends, I guess. But he's not one of those that waits days to reply to you."

"And he's not mentioned a sick relative or anything before? As in he might have had to leave in a hurry?"

"No," Emily said. "But then I guess he might not. Like I said, we're new friends."

"Maybe wait until tomorrow. If he's had a family emergency, he would have called the school so they can get a substitute teacher," Collie said.

"Yes, you're right. I won't take up any more of your time," Emily said and stood up to leave.

"You don't have to go. You're welcome to stay here the night," Collie said and immediately regretted it when she saw Emily blush and look awkward.

"I'd better not. Small village and all that," Emily said.

"Oh yes. Yes, of course. I didn't mean...what I meant to say was we have a spare room. But yes, you're right." Collie could feel her cheeks heat. Why did she feel like she'd made a pass at Emily when she hadn't? Or had she? She didn't think so. The offer was made in innocence.

"No, I know," Emily said. "I didn't think you were suggesting...I just mean Phil is coming to replace my door glass before work tomorrow, and if he sees me coming out of your place..."

Collie felt her face heat even more. And not just for the awkward situation she found herself in. She couldn't stop herself wondering what it would be like to kiss Emily, to touch her.

She forced the thought from her mind. "Let me walk you back, at least. You didn't even bring your phone to use as a torch."

Emily nodded. "Thanks."

They walked back to Emily's house in silence. The awkwardness was back in full force. They'd lost it earlier with their trip to the beach. Collie wasn't sure how to make it go away again. Well, she could think of one way, but that would be a terrible idea.

At Emily's front door, Emily turned to Collie. "Here we are then."

Collie nodded, feeling like she was at the end of a date and with no idea why it felt that way. "Okay. Any more bad dreams or smashed doors, you know where I am."

"I do. And thanks, Collie." Then Emily leaned forward and kissed Collie on the cheek. "You've been great."

Collie was speechless. It was only a peck on the cheek, for God's sake. What was she? Fourteen again? All she could manage was a nod, and then Emily was inside her house and closing the door.

"Great," Collie mumbled. "Must look like a right idiot. Couldn't even say bye."

Collie started back down the pitch-black drive. With Emily's kiss still burning away on her cheek, she found the dark didn't even bother her all that much.

She aimed the torch beam at her feet to avoid twisting her ankle in any potholes.

That was when she saw them.

Footprints in the wet, squelchy earth.

Collie shone the torch ahead to where they went across the grass, flattening it in the perfect print of a shoe.

Against her better judgement, she followed them. The grass was starting to spring back up in places, and if it hadn't been for the heavy rain tonight, they probably would be gone by now.

The prints circled Emily's house and led off into the woods behind. Collie stopped here, though, not prepared to go any further. She remembered the other night in the woods and thought better of it.

She looked back at Emily's house. One window glowed with the light beyond, probably Emily's bedroom. The curtains were drawn, though, so there was nothing to see, if that was the owner of the footsteps' intention.

Collie shone the torch back to the footprints on the ground. One set went towards the house, and the other way. So whoever was hanging around her house left the way he'd come.

And Collie was sure it was a he. The footprints were big and wide. Maybe that was part of why Emily had the bad dream. Perhaps she sensed whoever this was, watching her.

It gave Collie the creeps. She didn't know how close to the house he'd got. The drive was partially gravelled, which would have disguised his footprints if he'd gone right up to the front door.

Hadn't Emily said there was a small spot of blood on the door? Maybe it was him, rather than the dream Hamish, that sent her running to Collie's house in the middle of the night.

Collie wasn't sure, but now that she'd seen the footprints, Emily probably shouldn't stay in the house alone tonight. Collie couldn't take the couch because Lana was asleep in their house.

Emily would have to spend the night with them. Collie tried not to think about why that made her so happy.

CHAPTER THIRTY-SEVEN

When the doorbell rang, Emily felt a sense of dread—it was like her dream all over again. Dread quickly turned to pleasure when she saw Collie on the other side of the door.

"Well. Can't keep away, can you?" Emily said and caught a smile at the embarrassed look on Collie's face.

"No, but I'm not knocking about something pleasant, I'm afraid," Collie said.

The good feeling Emily got on seeing Collie again was quickly replaced by the return of dread. "What is it?" Emily asked.

"Someone was here, watching you, I think," Collie said.

Emily felt hot and cold all at once. Something like fear dropped into her belly and sat there like a lead weight. "What do you mean?"

"I saw footprints in the mud and in the grass. They led out of the woods and around your house up to the drive. I don't know how close he got, but it was close enough. That might explain the blood on the door. And the bad dream. Maybe you sensed him out here."

"Jesus, that's terrifying." Emily shivered. "We should call the police."

"I already did. They're coming round tonight. I said you'd be at my house. I know you didn't want gossip, but I don't think you should be here alone," Collie said.

"No, no you're right. But what about Lana? Won't all this scare her?" Emily asked.

"I told them to come quietly. She's a deep sleeper, so unless we make tons of noise, I don't think she'll wake up," Collie said. "Come on, grab some bits, and let's go. I don't want to leave Lana any longer."

Emily turned and went back into the house. Upstairs, she threw some underwear and a few toiletries into an overnight bag. She tried not to think about the person who'd been standing outside her house, walking around—looking for a way in, maybe?

And there was the dream. Hamish had come to her front door, hadn't he? Was it him who'd come out of the woods to warn her? His footsteps, his blood?

Don't be so bloody ridiculous. It was just a dream. Like Collie said, you probably sensed whoever was out there, and that's why you dreamed Hamish came to you.

To think otherwise was foolish and would put her in danger. Because she couldn't for the life of her think why someone would come creeping around another person's house for reasons that weren't, well, creepy as fuck.

The suspicion she'd had that Stephanie Willis was in her house didn't seem so stupid now. It could have been her, come back to let herself in again. But Collie said the footsteps belonged to a man. Dave Willis?

One of Charlie's emails came back to her.

> *I feel like I'm being watched all the time, Em. Like there's something out there that I can't quite see and don't want to see. Remember when we used to squeeze our eyes shut at night, so we wouldn't see the dressing gown on the back of the door we were convinced was a monster? Every time I think about the thing that's watching me, I want to squeeze my eyes shut, Em.*

And Hamish's warning in the dream, what was it? *It's watching you.*

Emily shuddered. She grabbed her bag and went back downstairs. Thank goodness for Collie. If she hadn't seen those footprints, Emily might have gone to sleep with no idea someone had been outside her house tonight.

The question was, what did they want?

"Ready?" Collie asked as Emily came down the stairs.

"Yeah. Let's go."

She pulled the front door shut behind her and followed Collie back up the pitch-black drive, half expecting someone—or some*thing*—to jump out at them.

"Show me the footprints," Emily said. She wanted to see them for herself.

"Emily—"

"I want to see them." She knew her tone was firm.

"Fine. This way," Collie said.

Emily followed Collie's torch and immediately saw the footprints. Large, like Collie said. Definitely men's, like Collie said.

Something's not right.

Aside from the footprints, that was. Something was…missing.

That godawful scarecrow.

It hit Emily. The scarecrow was gone. She quickly walked over to where it had been and saw a divot in the earth from its stand.

Okay, that's good. You didn't imagine it. The scarecrow was *there.*

"Emily?" Collie asked softly.

"There was a scarecrow here this morning. For the stupid Spring Fair."

"Here?" Collie came to stand beside her. "Oh yeah, I can see the mark. We've got one too. Spooky bloody thing."

"It's gone now," Emily said, and for reasons she couldn't really explain to herself, it terrified her. "Where the fuck is it?"

"I don't know, but I don't like it. Emily, let's go." And when Emily didn't move, "*Now.*"

Emily nodded. Yes, that was probably a good idea. She looked up into the dark, dense wood beyond her garden. A very good idea.

They made it back to Collie's house unscathed, and Collie went in the kitchen to make tea.

She came back a couple of minutes later with two steaming cups. "Here, this will help."

Emily took a sip. "Tea always makes everything better, doesn't it? Why is that?"

Collie shrugged. "It tastes good. Listen, the police said they'd be here within the hour. There isn't a force in Hyam—I think they come from one of the bigger towns."

"That's good. God only knows what a Hyam force would look like," Emily said.

Collie laughed. "Probably as weird as the rest of them."

"Right? They are a strange bunch. Do you remember the funfair a few weeks ago?" Emily asked.

She would have remembered it anyway. It was where she and Collie and the others had gone to war at the coconut shy.

"I knew you'd bring that up again," Collie joked. "I was off my game that day."

"I thrashed you, Collie. I'd say you've never been *on* your game."

"So rude," Collie said and laughed. "But probably true. Coconut shies are not my go-to game."

"What is, then?" Emily asked, relieved at the lightness of the conversation. She knew she'd have to face the creeper outside her house soon enough.

"Golf," Collie said.

"What? Collie, how on earth did you get into golf? Last time I checked, you weren't an old white guy looking to fill his retirement years."

"So, so rude," Collie said. "I'll have you know, golf is a game that requires skill and stamina. It's not chucking a little white ball at a hairy little coconut and hoping for the best."

"You couldn't hit a coconut if it was the size of a house. And also, coconut shies are not *my* chosen game either."

"No?" Collie asked, and Emily thought she seemed genuinely interested. "What is then?"

Emily tried not to laugh and give herself away. "Apple bobbing."

Collie burst out laughing. "You have the look of a bobber," she said.

Emily couldn't help laughing. She liked how silly Collie was. Not long ago she was terrified, and now, well, she was still scared, but here with Collie in her cosy living room, things seemed if not okay, then better.

There was something so appealing about Collie, Emily thought. A kindness that shone out of her. Emily could tell she was trustworthy and honest. After a career in journalism where people were not, Emily had got good at reading people and sizing them up quickly.

She debated telling Collie about why she was really here in Hyam. She opened her mouth to, and then the doorbell rang.

"Shit, I told them to text. They'll wake Lana." Collie jumped out of her seat and bolted for the door before they could ring the bell again.

Emily sighed. Maybe telling Collie wouldn't be the right thing anyway. It seemed journalists weren't her favourite people, and really, what good could she do anyway.

CHAPTER THIRTY-EIGHT

Collie looked at the clock above the mantelpiece and sighed. It was well after midnight, and her eyes felt grainy and dry. She yawned.

"Sorry," she said.

"No, *I'm* sorry for keeping you up so late," Emily said. "I didn't think they'd ever leave."

Collie was impressed by the police officers who'd come by. She wasn't sure what she was expecting, but they were professional, concerned, and thorough.

They'd asked Emily a number of questions while their colleagues took swabs of the blood on Emily's front door and photographed the footprints in the mud—the ones in the grass were long gone. They also took photos of the divot from the missing scarecrow.

Emily hadn't been able to give any reasons why someone might be lurking around her house at night, and Collie hadn't missed the worried looks the officers gave each other.

Collie hadn't allowed herself to think too much about who was watching Emily, or what they might want. She didn't know her very well after all, but how many enemies could a country school teacher have?

Collie guessed it could be an ex hanging around. Yes, the footprints looked like men's feet, and though Emily said she liked women, that didn't make her a lesbian. There could be a disturbed ex-boyfriend hanging about.

Collie liked her. A lot. But she had Lana to think about. Her first instinct was to help Emily, but she also needed to be careful. She didn't want to drag Lana into another situation like the one that had seen her mother murdered.

"Emily, can I ask you something?" Collie said.

"Yes, sure," Emily replied.

"Look, don't take this the wrong way, but were you completely truthful with the police back there?"

"Of course I was," Emily said.

But something flickered in her eyes. Collie saw it, saw the way her eyes darted off to the side. She was lying—Collie would have sworn it.

"Emily," she said.

"What? Look, Collie, I'm grateful for what you've done for me tonight, but I really don't appreciate being called a liar," Emily said.

And the indignant way she said it was just a little too perfect, a little too rehearsed. It sounded wrong to Collie's ear, like an instrument off-key in an orchestra.

But what could she say without pushing Emily into an argument and potentially going back to her house where not long ago, someone had stood outside watching her.

Collie sighed. "Okay, then. I think it's time we both got some sleep."

"I can go home. I've put you out enough already tonight," Emily said and stood.

"Don't be ridiculous. You can't go back there tonight," Collie said, annoyed now.

"How dare you call me ridiculous. And I can do what I bloody well like."

"Why are you being so stubborn? I told you you could stay here tonight."

"Yes, you did. Right before you accused me of lying and called me ridiculous. And stubborn."

"Because you *are*," Collie said and pushed her hand through her hair. God the woman was infuriating. "You are lying—"

"I'm not."

"You *are*. Look, I barely know you and it's your choice what you tell me and what you don't tell me. But I have Lana to think about. I can't have her put in danger, not again," Collie said.

She watched the fire go out of Emily's eyes. "I didn't realize… of course you'd think maybe I was lying about a crazy ex. Collie, I'm sorry."

"It's okay."

"No, it's not. You've been nothing but kind to me. I promise, that's not what I'm hiding," Emily said.

"So you are hiding something," Collie said. She knew it. She was disappointed, but not surprised. There was something about Emily that was closed off. And she didn't fully buy that she'd moved to the country to feel closer to her missing brother. Maybe she was running from something.

"This thing you aren't telling me. Is it going to put Lana in danger?" Collie asked.

"No. Absolutely not. And I hope you think more of me than to imagine I'd bring something like that into your house. I *honestly* have no idea who's hanging around outside my house or why anyone would even *want* to."

"Okay, I believe you. Though I can't say I know what it is you won't tell me. Are you in some kind of trouble?" Collie persisted.

"No. I'm not in any trouble. Look, Collie, it's nothing you need to worry about. Nothing that's going to hurt you or Lana or put you in any danger. Truly," Emily said.

Collie thought she was being sincere. There was something terribly tired but terribly honest in the way she spoke now. Collie wanted to go to her, wanted to hold her and find out what it was that was hurting Emily so badly.

Why shouldn't she?

Collie went to her now and put her arms around Emily. At first, Emily felt stiff. Then she relaxed and her arms came up around Collie's waist. They stood like that for a while. Emily's head rested under Collie's chin and her body felt soft. She smelled good, the shampoo she used or something. It reminded Collie of lazy summers and cut grass. It was fresh and clean and totally Emily.

Collie ran her hands up Emily's back. Emily felt strong and capable, and Collie didn't think she'd ever wanted to kiss someone so badly.

Emily's head shifted from beneath Collie's chin, and now Collie was looking down into her eyes—blue with flecks of gold—and their lips were inches apart, until they weren't.

Collie wasn't sure who moved first or if they both moved together, but now they were kissing, and it was wonderful.

Emily's lips were soft, and she explored Collie's mouth in a way that told Collie she knew what she was doing. Not to be outdone, Collie took control of the kiss, deepened it, and held Emily tighter against her.

Emily broke the kiss first and left Collie searching for her breath.

"Well, that was…" Emily said.

"I know," Collie replied.

"We should leave it there," Emily said.

"I know," Collie said and wondered if she'd forgotten all other words. It was a cliché, but that kiss had knocked her socks off.

Emily smiled and reached up to push back Collie's hair. "Want to show me to the spare room then?"

"Absolutely," Collie replied. She took Emily's hand and led her upstairs.

At the door to the spare room, Collie let go of Emily's hand. "Here it is." She pushed open the door, reached around, and flicked on the light.

"It's very nice," Emily said.

Collie shrugged. "Well, it's not all that, but the bed is comfortable, and the sheets are clean."

Collie's throat was dry, and her hands itched to take hold of Emily. Her lips still tingled from their kiss.

"Collie…" Emily said. Her eyes were half closed and dreamy looking, her mouth slightly reddened and her lips a little swollen.

Collie cleared her throat. "I hope you, you know, sleep well."

Emily took hold of Collie's hand, and that was all Collie needed. Something inside her snapped, and she pulled Emily to her.

Collie pushed Emily into the bedroom and kicked the door shut behind her. She was desperate to taste Emily's lips again, to feel Emily's body under her hands.

Collie guided Emily to the bed.

"Collie," Emily gasped, breaking away from the kiss, "is this a good idea?"

"Definitely not," Collie answered and kissed her again. It wasn't a good idea at all, but it was too late now. Collie wanted Emily in a way she didn't remember ever wanting a woman before.

She pushed Emily back on the bed and lay down on top of her. Emily's arms came up around Collie's shoulders and held her down, kept Collie locked in the kiss.

Soon, the kissing wasn't enough, and Collie pulled off her own T-shirt, then reached down and guided Emily's top over her head.

Collie moved Emily's bra strap aside and kissed her way along Emily's collarbone. Emily moaned softly, and Collie's brain popped and fizzed, all her senses filled with the taste and smell of Emily.

Soon, they were both naked. Emily reversed their positions, and she now sat astride Collie. Collie reached up and gripped her waist. She ran her hands over Emily's hips, thrilled by the softness of her skin and the curves of her beautiful body.

Emily lowered herself and tugged Collie's bottom lip between her teeth. Collie groaned when Emily bit down gently.

Collie guided Emily up and settled Emily on her face. Collie began to lick, her hands still on Emily's hips as they began to rock and Emily's breathing changed.

Sensing Emily was close to coming, Collie slid out from under her and pushed Emily onto her back. Collie kissed her way down Emily's body and gently pushed her legs apart. She started to lick her again. Emily's hips moved in rhythm at first, then became more and more erratic. Suddenly, Emily reached down and grabbed Collie's head. She pushed herself more firmly into Collie's mouth and came in a quiet moan ending on a sigh.

Collie rolled away and came up to lie beside her. Emily turned her arms so they were facing each other.

"Well," Emily said.

"Yeah. That was a good bad decision," Collie said.

Emily laughed and kissed her. "It really was. And since we're still in the middle of that good bad decision…"

"What do you mea—oh." Collie closed her eyes and rolled onto her back as Emily worked her way down Collie's body, alternating between nips and kisses. "Bloody hell," Collie said.

When Emily reached the junction of her thighs and began to lick, Collie sighed. This was one of the best bad decisions she'd ever made.

❖

It sniffed the ground and smelled all the scents of those who had walked out here. Underneath it though, it smelled *him*. He had been here, and it didn't know how that was possible.

It had torn his throat out with its own teeth. How could he be both *there* and *here*? The way it was *here* and also *there*. It hadn't known he was that strong, and usually it did know these things. Underneath the scent of the man was the other. That made more sense. The other had been at work here again, signalling its presence to the women. And it had had no idea.

That was worrying.

It was old—ancient—and sometimes complacency was to be expected at its time of life. But it was used to being alone, to doing what it did whenever it wanted to. It had had things its own way for so long now, and it wasn't used to any other way of being.

It lifted its head and sniffed the air. Yes, the other was there. Just out of sight beyond its reach. The other lived in the shadow of the shadows.

For the first time in its long life, it felt something like fear.

The man came to warn them. It didn't know what he said, but it knew they were all together now and aware *something* watched them. Maybe even aware it sent its minions to watch them too.

It should use the opportunity and take them all now while they slept under one roof. But it was too early, and if it took them too soon, it risked everything it had built. This thing must be done as all things had been done for all time. The rules and rituals must be observed.

It looked at the sky and saw the moon was not even close to ready for the ritual, which would see the changing over. Its long life would end, and its young would take over the mantle of the ancient ways. And it was so important the ritual was completed. Its time was over—it felt it in every fibre of its being. Felt it in the way it was becoming harder and harder to control itself and keep its form to the rest of the world. Felt it in the way it could barely keep from tearing these women limb from limb.

It had to hold on for a little longer. Long enough to perform the ritual and see a new dawn ushered in. To see its young take over and live another thousand years. But only if it did things the right way.

It must not allow the other to put it off course. It must not allow the other to rattle it and cause it to make an error. It sensed that was what the other wanted. It could feel the love the other had for the woman and girl and how much power there was in that. The other wanted to protect its young, just as it would protect *its* young too.

It followed the scent of *him* into the woods until it disappeared.

It noted with some discomfort that if the woman had followed those footprints all the way in here—as it was sure she was meant to— then she would have found its place. Because that's where the man had come. Right to its place, and now it felt something that could be considered fear. A new experience for it and one it wasn't keen on repeating.

It looked at the moon again and willed it to hurry on its course. Something was coming—it could feel it in the air. It shivered.

CHAPTER THIRTY-NINE

Emily dodged students who rushed past her like speeding bullets as they ran for the playground. Their coats flapped out behind them, and their little legs pumped.

As she walked down the corridor, she checked the open classroom doorways, hoping to catch a glimpse of Hamish.

The dream last night left her feeling strange and with a heavy lead weight of dread lodged firmly in her belly. She still hadn't heard from him.

Emily turned the corner, pushed through double doors, and walked down a short hallway off the main corridor and into reception. To get to Francis Cobb's office, she had to pass through here, and Harold Gardener was more guard dog than receptionist.

From what Emily understood, he'd been here for years and didn't look to be leaving any time soon.

"Miss Lassiter. How can I help you?" His pale faded blue eyes fixed on hers and then moved away again, making Emily feel judged and found wanting each time.

"I'd like to see Frances, please," she said, trying to sound assertive. Why did he always make her feel so off balance?

"Is *Miss Cobb* expecting you?" he asked with a look on his face that said he knew Miss Cobb was not. And that Emily should not be using the Great Headmistress's first name.

Sometimes Emily genuinely forgot she had stepped back in time at this school, and sometimes she used Frances Cobb's first name just to be bloody-minded.

"No, but I only need five minutes, and it's important," she said. Her palms were starting to sweat. Something about Cobb and Harold always made her feel like she was a pupil and not a teacher. True, she'd only worked in one school before this, but Highmore was a rigid, formal place.

"Let me see if she's available," he said.

Harold Gardener took an age to push back his chair and stand up. He had to be knocking on seventy at least. A state-of-the-art phone and computer sat on his desk, but he either refused or didn't know how to use either.

Rather than call Frances on the extension, Harold shuffled off to the office at the back of reception. He knocked once, obviously got a reply Emily couldn't hear, stepped inside, and shut the door behind him.

Emily rolled her eyes and sighed. Such a song and dance just to get five minutes with the woman. Most of the teachers were wary of her, but some seemed to treat her like she was some sort of god rather than the head teacher of a tiny village school.

Okay, that wasn't fair. The school wasn't all that small. It served most of the neighbouring towns as well as Hyam and was as well equipped as any Emily had seen—in fact, it was probably better equipped.

They had a state-of-the-art computer room, sports equipment coming out their ears, tennis courts—and Emily heard a rumour they were thinking of adding a swimming pool to stop the half-hour coach trips to the nearest council facility.

Emily frowned. Why had she not found that weird before? Where was a public school getting that sort of money from? Parents? As far as Emily knew, most were the regular mix of agricultural, factory, and general sort of workers that made up small towns everywhere.

The journalist in Emily woke up, turned over, and sat up. *Why* had she not found that strange? Because she was so caught up with Charlie and what happened to him. And then the odd things going on at her house. Where she was now the one being watched.

"She's not in at the moment. I'll tell her you came by."

Emily jumped at the sound of Harold's voice. She hadn't heard him come out of Frances Cobb's office.

"I can wait."

"There's no ne—"

"I can wait *all day*, Harold," Emily said.

Harold narrowed his eyes at her. "Fine. You can wait, but I don't know when she'll be back."

"Thanks," Emily said.

"Over there." Harold pointed at several chairs in the reception area.

Emily sat and waited. And waited.

Now that she had nothing to distract her, Emily couldn't stop herself thinking about last night. What a bad decision *that* was. But so good. It was a long time since Emily had been with anyone that way, and Collie was certainly a good way to break the dry spell.

They'd had sex most of the night, and Emily was sore almost everywhere. Not to mention tired beyond belief. But she couldn't deny it was worth it. Even if they'd opened up a huge can of worms. Emily sighed. A *really* huge can of worms.

The main problem, as far as Emily could see, was she was more attracted to Collie than she had been to anyone else. Probably ever. And it wasn't just a physical thing—though, that was ridiculously strong too. Emily liked everything about Collie. Collie was someone she could easily fall for.

Who are you kidding—you've already fallen for her.

What did she do about that? Collie was leaving. Emily was staying until she found out what happened to Charlie. Collie didn't even know what Emily was really doing in Hyam, and if she found out? Emily wasn't certain Collie would want anything to do with her.

Emily's thoughts were interrupted by the shrill ringing of the phone. Harold answered it, spoke into it very quietly, and then abruptly stood up.

"I have to leave for a few minutes," he said.

"Okay."

"You wait there." He pointed one gnarled finger at the chair she was currently sitting in.

"Of course." She graced him with her coldest smile.

Harold looked like he wanted to say something else, changed his mind, and hobbled off down the corridor.

Emily waited until he was just about round the corner before she got up and went to Frances Cobb's office. She pushed open the door and went inside.

It was empty.

Emily briefly wondered what she'd do if Cobb came back. And where was she?

Look out the window—maybe she's parking her broom.

Emily looked around the office and noticed a wall of shelves along the right-hand wall, stuffed with books and other objects. Emily went over.

It was mostly the usual stuff, photos of Cobb with various local movers and shakers. Certificates and awards, framed. Books on child psychology, manuals, some poetry and well-known literature.

As she looked, Emily's gaze landed on a small circular object. It sat partially behind a framed photo of Cobb and a bunch of old white men—probably school governors.

It had something carved into it—a symbol? No, an animal. It could have been a wolf, but its snout was too short and its legs too long. It looked like something out of a nightmare, and it gave Emily the creeps. On the other side were two crudely drawn swords, crossed in the middle.

Her fingers itched to reach out and touch it. She wanted to feel the smooth cold hardness of the thing and run her fingers over that ugly, snub snout and mouth full of fearsome teeth. Something about the horrible thing made her feel—

Protected.

Yes, protected.

Without meaning to and almost against her will, Emily picked it up and put it in her pocket. Almost immediately, her face heated with shame and embarrassment.

What the hell are you doing? You just stole *from your boss.*

"Emily."

For the second time today Emily jumped out of her skin.

"Christ," she said and turned to face Frances Cobb. "Sorry, you scared me."

Frances Cobb smiled, though it didn't reach her eyes, and there was a shadow of satisfaction on her face. "I wasn't expecting you. What can I do for you?"

Frances Cobb went behind her huge desk and sat in a chair that wouldn't look out of place in a palace somewhere. The first time Emily saw it she thought how ridiculously ostentatious it was.

"I wanted to speak with you about Hamish," Emily said. "I'm sorry I just walked in—I was, well—"

Frances Cobb waved Emily's excuses away and motioned with one hand to the seat in front of her desk, a straight-backed wooden affair that didn't encourage anyone to sit in it for long.

"Hamish Ford?"

"Yes." Emily sat.

"What about him?" Frances Cobb leaned back in her chair and looked at Emily over her nose.

Emily resisted rolling her eyes. "I haven't heard from him since Friday. He hasn't returned any of my calls or texts."

"The two of you are friends?"

"Yes." Emily wasn't prepared to say more. Let Cobb think what she wanted.

"I'm afraid he had a family emergency. He called here on Saturday morning. Usually I'm not in school on the weekends, but I had some paperwork to catch up on, so I spoke to him myself." She linked her hands together on the green leather that was so shiny, someone must polish it every day.

"Really?" That sort of made sense—it was what Emily thought. But then, why not return her messages?

"You think I'm lying?" Frances asked.

"What? No, no." Except she did, didn't she? Or at least, part of her did. That sleepy, slowly waking journalist inside her.

"I'm sure he'll be in touch with you when he's able."

"It's just strange he wouldn't have told me," Emily said.

"Maybe you aren't as close as you thought. From what I understand, a family member is quite ill. I'm sure it probably slipped his mind."

Emily ignored the jibe. "I'm sure he will. Did he say when he'd be back?"

"Who can say? I told him to take all the time he needed. I believe he'll be away for a few weeks, at least."

This just didn't seem right. Something about it was off. Emily looked around the room once more.

"Where did you come from? Just now?" Emily asked and was pleased her change of tack seemed to throw Cobb off balance for a moment.

"I have a bathroom off this office. I came from there." Frances Cobb shifted in her seat.

This is making her uncomfortable. Why?

Because if she was in the bathroom, she's been there ages, so she knows you know what she was doing in there.

"I can't see a door," Emily said.

"No, you can't. If that's all, Miss Lassiter, I have work to be getting on with, and I believe break is almost over."

Cobb stood, and Emily was once again reminded of what a large woman she was. At least six feet and strong looking, fit. Emily tried to place her age and found she couldn't. She could be anywhere from fifty to seventy.

Emily stood and headed for the door. "Well, thank you for your time."

"Of course. My door is always open."

Except that wasn't remotely true. Emily could count on one hand the number of times she'd been in this office, and two of those were for the interviews.

Emily nodded and left. She could feel the amulet in her pocket—that's what it was, wasn't it? something to protect her—pressed against her leg. It was hot, but Emily thought that was probably just her projecting the shame of what she'd done.

Another thought occurred to her. Cobb appeared out of nowhere. How long had she been standing behind Emily? Had she seen her steal the amulet?

No. Definitely not. If she'd seen her, Emily wouldn't be leaving her office.

All the same, she couldn't shake the low-level fear, that cold heaviness in her belly that wouldn't go away.

Chapter Forty

Collie generally avoided going into the village shops if she could help it. Despite her inroads with some of the locals, most were still pretty unfriendly. But they were out of milk and bread, and she didn't have time to go to the next town. It had completely slipped her mind this morning.

No surprise, really. Not after what she and Emily got up to last night. Collie couldn't help grinning at the memory. Not that she *should* be grinning. She and Emily just made their lives a whole lot more complicated. How many times had Collie told herself not to get involved with Emily? And there she was, sleeping with her at the first opportunity she got.

Brilliant. She wanted to call Tony and ask him what to do, but he was already worried about her after what she said the last time they spoke. She couldn't dump this on his doorstep. Plus, he'd been hounding her with texts all morning, wanting to talk about this being-watched thing.

Collie sighed. What a pickle. Last night was amazing, though. Collie wasn't so self-deluded that she couldn't admit to herself she was falling for Emily. Of course she was. How could she not? Emily was smart, interesting, funny, gorgeous, and after last night Collie knew she was great in bed. That didn't mean it had to go any further. Collie did have some self-control somewhere inside. She was leaving Hyam, Emily was staying, and at the moment, she wanted to be solid for Lana and make her a priority. Dating needed to wait.

She'd have to have a talk with Emily. Maybe later. Maybe Emily wanted to come over for dinner and they could talk then, when Lana was in bed.

Yeah, right.

Who was Collie kidding? She had no self-control when it came to Emily.

After Emily left and Lana went to school, she'd gone back to bed for a couple of hours. Now it was three thirty, and Lana would be home in ten minutes.

Collie hurried up the road and past the pub. As she got to the level crossing, something winking in the sun caught her eye. It was half caught beneath the brambles and bushes that lined the edges of the road.

Collie couldn't make out what it was. Obviously something shiny because it was catching the light, and it was fairly large.

As she got closer, she saw it was a phone. The screen was cracked, but it was still working by the looks of it because there was a flashing red light in the top corner. Collie was surprised it had any battery left even if it was about to die on its arse.

The phone was smeared with mud, and some other red-brown substance had left a small streak across its back cover. It almost looked like it was coming out of the cannon printed in white.

Obviously a Gunners fan. Collie pocketed it for now. She needed to get to the shop—she'd find the owner later.

The village shop was quiet as usual, but this time with the odour of fake lemons. Someone had been cleaning. But not dusting, Collie noted as she wiped a layer of dust off a packet of custard creams.

She wondered how the bloody place stayed afloat if that much dust was able to collect on things.

Collie grabbed a loaf of surprisingly fresh bread and milk that also looked in date. Since the incident where she'd had a meltdown, she hadn't been back in here. And because of the weird stuff that had been happening, she wasn't inclined to shop anywhere else in the village either.

Collie went up to the till which doubled as a post office. She didn't recognize the woman behind the counter, but her face was familiar.

"Two pound twenty, please," the woman said.

She was tall and broad and actually smiled at Collie. Collie dug around in her pocket, her fingers brushing over the little disc she'd found outside her tent, and handed over the exact money. She really needed to chuck the thing but seemed to keep forgetting to take it out of her pocket.

"I don't think I've seen you in here before," the woman said pleasantly.

"No, I've only been in once," Collie replied.

"You're in the place up on Drummers Road." It wasn't a question.

"That's right."

"Been there a few months now. Don't blame you for not coming in here, though." The woman gave a quick look round, then leaned forward. "It's a really *shit* shop."

Collie laughed. "Should you be saying that? You work here."

The woman shrugged and waved her hand. "My aunt owns it. Can't imagine she'd fire me. I mean, she probably should because I'm terrible at it."

Collie was starting to like this woman. She couldn't have been more than twenty, and she gave off an air like she really didn't give a fuck. "Why are you terrible?" Collie asked.

"Oh, you know. I *never* turn up on time. Sometimes I close early— that really winds my aunt up. My heart's just not in it," the woman said.

"What would you like to do?" Collie asked. "I'm Collie, by the way."

"Oh, I know that. I'm Anthea. Anthea Cobb. And well, I suppose I'd rather be doing nothing at all. I honestly don't think I'm cut out for work. My aunt says I should find a rich husband and live off him. I told her, why do I need a rich husband when I have you?"

Collie laughed again. "And what did she say?"

"She said, *Anthea, that is not the attitude.*" Anthea rolled her eyes. "She's the headmistress at Highmore. You probably know her."

Collie now realized why Anthea looked so familiar. She was Frances Cobb's niece. And it sounded like Frances had her fingers in a lot of pies. Headmistress of the school and owner of the local shop. Not that this place was exactly hopping.

"Didn't fancy getting into the family business?" Collie asked.

Anthea frowned. She looked confused.

"Teaching," Collie explained.

"Oh! God no, I couldn't bear it. Being surrounded by kids all day? No thanks. That's what being an only child does to you, you see. I told my parents they should have had more kids, but they wouldn't. I probably put them off. But now look at me. Spoiled and aimless."

Collie was finding the whole situation utterly bizarre. She'd met this girl five minutes ago, and now she was getting her life story.

"I don't suppose anyone's been in here saying they've lost a phone, have they?" Collie asked.

Anthea shook her head. "Not that I know of, but then I haven't been in since last week. First day back."

"I see. Well, I found a phone near the level crossing. It's got an Arsenal case. If anyone asks about it, can you tell them I've got it?" Collie asked.

"Oh, I know whose phone that is," Anthea said. "Why don't you give it to me, and I'll pass it on."

"Whose phone is it?" Collie asked, not making any move to hand it over.

"Hamish Ford's. He's the only Arsenal fan around here. Everyone else supports Norwich or Ipswich."

Hamish's phone. Hamish who was missing. Collie supposed it explained why Emily couldn't get hold of him. He'd lost his phone on the way home. All the same, it seemed odd it was sitting out there by the level crossing.

This didn't feel right at all.

"Don't worry, I know a friend of his, so I'll give it to her to pass on," Collie said.

Anthea shrugged. "Suit yourself. You know, my aunt also owns the hairdresser's. You think I'd make a good hair stylist?"

"What? I don't know. Yes?" Collie said.

She made her excuses and quickly left before Anthea revved up again. She was a funny girl, but it made a nice change from the last woman who'd served her. Collie headed back home with a bad feeling in the pit of her stomach.

CHAPTER FORTY-ONE

L ana only lived a fifteen minute walk from school, but Collie insisted she take the school bus.

Two buses left from Highmore, one which went south to the surrounding towns and villages, and one which went east, to where she lived. It mostly dropped home Hyam kids and some others who lived right out on the edge of the village, sort of straddling this one and the next.

Lana had watched these kids. Like the Hyam kids, they stuck together but were much more friendly. Weirdly, they didn't speak to the Hyam kids at all, and if they passed them in the corridors, they would move out of the way, like the Hyam kids were diseased or something.

Take now, for example. Lana was sitting by herself near the front of the bus because she was one of the first off. The Hyam kids were in the middle and the—what would you call them?—outer Hyam kids were at the back.

Lana would have put it down to being an outsider in the countryside, but her dad's parents lived in a village like Hyam, and that was a lovely place. People were friendly and helped you. If she was asked, Lana would have to say there was something really wrong with Hyam.

She felt bad because she was the one who'd wanted to move here. She'd decided they needed to get out of London, get away from journalists and the memory of her mother. She'd found this house online and told Collie this was the place she wanted to live.

Of course Collie had done what Lana wanted. Who wouldn't? Lana had lost her mother and basically hadn't stopped crying for a week. Collie probably would have painted herself blue and sung a Little Mix medley if Lana had asked her to.

The thought of that made Lana giggle into her hand. She quickly looked up to make sure no one had seen her laughing to herself.

It didn't look like anyone was paying her any attention. And that was another thing. Anytime she'd been on a bus in London that was full of schoolkids, it had been totally noisy, with people running around, laughing, shouting, and sometimes fighting.

No one hardly said a word on this bus. It was so weird.

Not everyone in Hyam was weird, of course. There was Miss Lassiter. Aunt Collie and Miss Lassiter seemed to be getting on very well. Lana fancied herself a bit of a matchmaker. Although she hadn't totally thought it through because they'd be leaving here soon. She guessed they could visit each other, or email or whatever.

She liked Miss Lassiter. Lana thought she could probably live with her. Plus, Lana didn't completely trust Collie to choose her own girlfriend.

She'd brought one round once, maybe last year? Aunt Collie had introduced her as a friend, but Lana knew what *that* meant. Plus, she'd caught them kissing when they thought she couldn't see them.

Adults could be so stupid sometimes, because they thought kids were stupid. Well, Lana saw a lot more than Aunt Collie knew. She knew, for example, that Miss Lassiter had stayed over last night.

The doorbell woke her up, and she'd heard them talking. She'd heard *everything*. Some creepy man had been walking around outside Miss Lassiter's house.

Yeah, Lana hated this place. She wished she'd never chosen it. But leaving here also meant going back to London. Lana wasn't sure if she was ready for that.

"Lana Franklin, isn't it?"

Lana looked up. A boy she vaguely recognized as one of the Hyam lot was standing with one arm on the top of her seat to steady himself on the weaving bus.

"Yes," she said.

"You can sit with us if you like." The boy motioned with his thumb to the small group near the back of the bus.

"Thanks, but I'm getting off in a minute," Lana said.

"Okay, well, if you change your mind." He started to make his way back and then stopped, turned around. "You should hang with us at break. I've seen you with those two town girls. You live here now, so you should hang with us."

He didn't wait for an answer before he went back to his seat.

Now, that was *really* weird. Those kids hadn't given her the time of day before. They didn't give *anyone* the time of day. Why now were they suddenly trying to be all friendly?

Lana wasn't sure. A paranoid part of her thought maybe it was to stop them leaving. But no one knew they were yet except Miss Lassiter, and Lana doubted she'd told anyone.

And she was being paranoid. There was something horrible here in the village, something dark and mean that watched them. But he was just a boy from school. Maybe they thought she was one of them now.

Lana looked out the window and saw she was nearly at her stop. She stood up and went to the doors.

The bus stopped and the doors hissed open. The warm afternoon air brushed against her face, removing the horrible air conditioning of the bus from her nostrils.

"Bye, Lana," the boy who'd spoken to her said from his seat.

"Bye," another of the Hyam kids piped up.

"Bye, Lana. See you tomorrow," another said.

Lana sketched them a wave and hurried off the bus. Now that really was weird. Wait until she told Aunt Collie she'd been accepted into the exclusive Hyam club.

CHAPTER FORTY-TWO

Emily sat back in her chair and held the strange little amulet up to the computer screen.

Well, they certainly looked similar. Oh, who was she kidding? They were exact replicas. She'd stolen a sixth century Anglo-Saxon protection amulet from her boss's office. One that was apparently worth a fair bit and probably of cultural significance to the county, if not the country.

So now she had two questions. One, what in the holy hell had possessed her to take it, and two, why was it in Frances Cobb's office, hidden behind a photo?

Emily clicked on the image to take her through to the website and read about her pilfered amulet.

> *Anglo-Saxons were superstitious. They believed in many gods, in monsters, trolls, magic, and potions. Charms, amulets, poems, and other methods were all used to ward off various monsters and mark-steppers. The above pictured amulet was made as part of a set of two. It was said to have been carved by a powerful Anglo-Saxon witch to ward off the Bargus, who was said to be a monstrous wolflike creature and mark-stepper—or boundary crosser—that prowls parts of Suffolk.*
>
> *Legends say that, like a werewolf, the Bargus is a shape-shifting monster who can take on the appearance of a human and will change into its true self at night to stalk unlucky travellers or those who get lost in the woods. Over the years, people have reported seeing the Bargus, a huge*

beast with red eyes and thick black fur and long, viciously sharp claws and teeth.

Emily looked up from what she was reading and glanced at the amulet. She reached out and touched it with one finger.

Mark-stepper.

What was a mark-stepper?

She typed the phrase into the search bar and came up with another web page showing this Bargus creature: *The Bargus is a mark-stepper. A creature who thinks like a human but chooses to behave like a monster.*

Emily shivered and didn't know why.

She almost jumped out of her skin when the doorbell rang.

After the other night, Emily ordered one of those doorbells that had a camera you could hook up to your phone. She checked her mobile now and smiled when she saw the familiar face of Collie.

Emily pushed the memory of last night out of her mind.

"Hey," Emily greeted Collie and winced. What she'd wanted to sound light and breezy sounded way too excited.

"Hi. You all right?" Collie asked.

The smile Emily only just realized was splitting her face in half faded slightly. Collie looked like she had something on her mind.

"I'm good. You look like something's bothering you, though," Emily said and wondered if it was to do with what happened last night. She braced herself for The Talk.

"I need to speak with you about something. Can I come in?" Collie asked.

"Sure." Emily stood back from the door and let Collie in. "Cup of tea, coffee?"

"No, thanks." Collie stepped into Emily's hallway and reached into her pocket.

At first, Emily wasn't sure what she was looking at. Something covered in mud and something else.

"What's that?" Emily asked.

"Apparently, it's Hamish's phone. I found it by the level crossing— in a bush," Collie said.

"What?" Emily looked down at the phone again. She took one step back as if everything would be better if she could get away from the thing.

"Have you heard from him yet?" Collie asked.

Emily shook her head. She tried to speak, but her mouth was so dry. Her tongue felt thick and stupid in her head.

"Emily, it might not mean anything. He may have just dropped it. You know what it's like out here. No bloody street lights. He probably couldn't find it," Collie said and took a step towards Emily.

"I...Jesus, Collie."

"Could be the reason he hasn't called you back."

Emily looked at Collie and saw she didn't believe her words either. Despite what Frances Cobb said, Hamish had vanished off the face of the earth. And now, here was his phone, abandoned in a bush and covered in mud and what looked a lot like blood.

Maybe the Bargus did it. Maybe it was alive and well and living in Hyam. Emily tried to shut down that hysterical little voice inside her.

Maybe that's what got Charlie too.

"Emily?" Collie reached out and put her hand on Emily's shoulder. It felt warm and steadying, and Emily came back to herself a little bit.

"Frances Cobb said he'd called her to say he had a family emergency," Emily said. Her voice still didn't sound quite right, but it was better.

"Oh, well, that's probably what happened. And if he doesn't have his phone, he can't call you," Collie said. "Who memorizes anyone's number these days?"

"True. But why is there blood on it?" Emily asked.

Collie held it up again. "Maybe it's something else?"

"No, it's blood. You can tell when it's blood," Emily said quietly.

"He cut himself?" Collie tried again.

God love her for trying.

Emily shook her head. "Collie, I need to show you something. Wait here."

Without waiting for a reply, Emily went upstairs and got the amulet. She came back down.

"Here. Look." She held it out, so small in the palm of her hand.

"Wow, that's really weird," Collie said and fumbled around in her pocket.

She pulled something up and held it out, in the palm of her hand. It was an amulet. And identical to the one Emily held.

"What are the chances? Where did you get yours?" Collie asked.

Emily's face heated. "I stole it."

"You what?" Collie started to smile, then looked confused, like Emily had told a joke she didn't get.

"I stole it."

"Why? From where?" Collie closed her hand over her amulet—probably thought Emily might try and steal that one too.

"I'm not sure. From Frances Cobb's office. This morning," Emily said, relieved to have got the truth about her crime off her chest. "Problem is, I think it's quite valuable. I googled it."

"I'm not sure if you're joking or not," Collie said.

"Oh, I'm not joking. It was hidden behind a photo in her office and I was just…just sort of *compelled* to take it," Emily said.

"Like a kleptomaniac?" Collie asked.

"Yeah, I suppose so," Emily agreed.

"Emily, what's going on?" Collie asked.

Emily sighed deeply. She guessed it was time. "Look, Collie, I haven't been completely honest with you, and even though I don't know you very well, I think I want to tell you. Something very weird is happening in Hyam—"

"You're telling me—"

"And I think I might have an idea it's pretty serious. People-going-missing serious," Emily said.

"Maybe I will stay for a tea then," Collie said. "You can tell me."

"There's something else," Emily said. When Collie didn't answer, Emily took her by the hand and led her into the living room. She turned her to face the french doors. "The scarecrow is back," Emily said.

"What?" Collie turned to look at her. "What do you mean it's back?"

"It's standing on the edge of the woods now. See?" Emily couldn't keep the wobble out of her voice.

"Yeah, I see. Someone put it back," Collie said quietly.

"Did they, Collie?" Emily asked.

"You think it walked there by itself?"

Emily remembered what Hamish said to her in the dream. *It's watching you.* And another thing she didn't properly register at first. *You have to go to the church.*

What was in the church? Emily wasn't sure she wanted to know.

CHAPTER FORTY-THREE

Y ou're a journalist," Collie said.
        She'd finished her tea ages ago, and she was mindful Lana was at home by herself. Sure it was only down the drive, but even so she didn't want to leave her alone for much longer.

Plus, Emily was a journalist. She'd lied. Taken a teaching job as a cover for trying to find out what happened to her missing brother. Great. Lana must be getting a fine education from this one.

"Why did you lie to me?" Collie asked.

"Because I didn't know you. How was I supposed to trust you?" Emily said, and she made a good point.

She didn't owe Collie anything, but even so Collie felt betrayed. She knew she was being unreasonable. But after they'd spent the night together...Collie couldn't help feeling betrayed.

"You hate me, don't you," Emily said.

"I don't hate you. You've done nothing that's earned my hate. But I let you stay at my house. We slept together. You looked me in the eye and said there was no reason anyone would be hanging around outside your house."

"There isn't."

"No? You said something weird is going on in this village. Your brother went missing here, and now you think Hamish has gone missing too. Come on Emily, wise up."

"Collie, I've been careful. No one knows Charlie was my brother. We had different fathers so different surnames."

"But you've been digging around," Collie said.

"Not really. Not as much as I should have. I think I've been barking up the wrong tree altogether," Emily said.

"What does that even mean?" Collie asked.

"Look, we agree that Hyam just isn't right?" Emily said.

"Yes."

"You were chased through the woods the other night."

"Yes."

"I had something crash through my french doors, and then a load of birds smash into them."

"Yes."

"You feel watched. *I* feel watched. There's something here and it's *stalking* us," Emily said.

"I know, Emily. I saw the footprints," Collie said.

"What if it's not a person."

"That doesn't make any sense," Collie said.

"What if it's a...well, a sort of animal." Emily ignored her.

Collie thought about the claw marks in her back door and how Fiona Walker told her they weren't made by any animal she knew about.

"An animal stalking us?" Collie asked.

"Why not? You hear about it all the time. The Loch Ness monster, the Beast of Bodmin Moor," Emily said.

"None founded. You think it's like Bigfoot in Hyam?" Collie asked and felt bad when Emily recoiled.

"You don't need to make fun of me," Emily said.

"Look, I'm sorry. That was mean. It's just...you've dropped a lot on me. You believe your brother didn't go missing, that something happened to him here. And it's clear you think the same happened to Hamish," Collie said.

"Does it sound completely outside the realms of possibility? How many people live here? Three hundred, max?"

"Yeah, probably about that," Collie agreed.

"My brother took a job here, and now he's missing. Hamish— granted, we don't know he's missing, but you found his phone by the side of the road, and I've not heard from him."

"Okay, I'll accept that it's looking dodgy for Hamish," Collie said.

"So in a village of three hundred people, two have gone missing. You've been chased through the woods, something left an amulet to ward off the Bargus—"

"The *what*?"

"Bargus—I'll explain later. You've had something leave great big bloody scratch marks on your door and I've—"

"Okay, okay. You're making a good case. This place is fucked. That's why I'm getting Lana out. Even without what you've just said," Collie said. "So what's a Bargus?"

"It's a sort of werewolf that picks off unwary travellers," Emily said. "A mark-stepper."

"A what?"

"Something that thinks like us but chooses to behave like a monster."

Collie nodded. Like Damien. Just like that sister-murdering piece of shit. A fucking monster. And something else that tickled the back of her mind, something…a memory. Something she'd seen? But where?

"Collie? You okay?" Emily asked.

"Yes, I just…something…I can't put my finger on it," Collie said. It was infuriating. Something she should know. "I have to get back to Lana."

Emily nodded. She looked disappointed, and Collie felt bad. Not that she should. Emily lied to her. About everything. Except, Collie couldn't help thinking she was letting her down, just leaving like this.

"Do you fancy coming for dinner?" Collie asked and wondered why she just did that.

"Are you sure?" Emily asked.

"It's nothing special. Just spaghetti bolognaise."

"Sounds nice."

"Out of a jar." Why couldn't she just shut up?

Emily laughed. "It sounds fine. But I don't have to come—you don't need to feel sorry for me."

"I don't. You'll be feeling sorry for me when you taste my cooking," Collie said.

"Well, thanks. Can I come in a few minutes? There's a couple of things I need to do here first," Emily said.

"Sure. We won't eat for about an hour yet. Come over anytime before then."

Collie stood up and Emily stood with her. She smiled and fought the urge to kiss Emily again. But now wasn't the time. And she was still mad at her for lying. And her theories about Hyam were mad.

But as Collie walked back down the drive and jumped when something in the bushes moved, she wondered if maybe Emily was on to something. And if she was, there was no way Lana was staying here any longer.

Something was clearly going on in Hyam. Whether it was a monstrous werewolf or not, she couldn't risk Lana.

The bush closest to her rustled again, and Collie picked up her pace.

CHAPTER FORTY-FOUR

Emily unplugged her laptop and slipped it into its case. She put the amulet into her pocket. When she looked up, she couldn't stop her scream.

The scarecrow who had previously been back near the woods was now about ten feet from her living room window. Her feet seemed to move independently of her body, and she found herself back out in the hall, facing the living room.

Emily tried to remember when she'd last seen the horrible thing. Surely she would have noticed if it moved between yesterday and today?

She definitely saw it this morning. She remembered opening the curtains and jumping when she caught sight of it. And now it had moved to ten feet from her house.

It moved? You mean someone moved it.

Who would have moved it? She'd been here all morning. She'd called into school to take a day off so she could wait in for Phil to fix her doors. Ordinarily, she'd have just let him get on with it, but after the other day, she didn't want to make it easy for these people to just waltz into her house.

So people are breaking into your house, and the scarecrow is moving around by itself. Are you sure you're okay, Em? Are you sure you aren't going mad just like Charlie?

Emily pushed away the nasty voice in her head. Charlie wasn't mad, and neither was she. She'd told Collie about what was happening, and Collie hadn't looked at her like she was a lunatic. Collie invited her to dinner. And you didn't do that if you thought someone was having a breakdown or whatever.

The other day, *someone* had been in her house. *Today* the scarecrow had moved again. Those were irrefutable facts, and she wouldn't allow any seeds of doubt to form in her mind. Yes, it sounded crazy, but it wasn't.

Emily went back into the living room and looked at the scarecrow through her window. It was a sinister looking thing. Had they made it that way on purpose? Or were scarecrows just one of those things that were naturally scary? Like clowns.

Its body was fat with straw, and the overstuffed head lolled forward and rested on its chest. The pork-pie hat mostly hid its face from view. Not that it had a proper face. They hadn't taken the time to draw eyes or a mouth. Instead it was a stretched and stuffed piece of canvas. The scarecrow's arms of bundled sticks were lashed to the wooden support and stuck out either side of it. Like a crucifixion.

Like a sacrifice.

Yes, just like a sacrifice.

And on the back of that...

Why was Hamish so keen for me to visit the church in my dream?

She vaguely remembered the non-dream Hamish mentioning the church and the stone carvings and a tapestry there. Something tickled the back of her mind and lodged itself there, just out of reach.

Emily checked her watch. She needed to get over to Collie's, but she didn't want to leave the house.

Scared of the scarecrow? Worried it might get you?

No, of course not. Maybe. Emily shivered. She could admit the thing had her spooked. But was she actually worried it would climb down off its wooden support and come after her?

No. That stuff was for horror movies, not quiet villages in the middle of nowhere. And yet...and yet she was afraid. She was terrified it would do just that. The childish, primitive part of her that never truly left any of us, but just sat and waited for an opportunity to surge forward and remind us of all the foolish things we were once afraid of. It made our hearts beat hard and made our hands sweat and made us turn on the light even though we knew there was nothing there. It was just a dressing gown on the back of the door, just the house pipes contracting or expanding.

Emily took some deep breaths like she'd learned in a yoga class somewhere in the past, in her other life, and looked at the scarecrow again.

It was starting to look like just a scarecrow again. Just a human effigy made of straw and sticks—

I'll huff and I'll puff and I'll blow your house down.

"The Three Little Pigs." Great. Maybe she really was losing her mind.

No, no more. It was a scarecrow, and she was a grown woman. And whatever was going on in Hyam, it wasn't a crazed scarecrow murdering people. That would be ridiculous. *That* would *not* fly. She was Emily Margaret Lassiter, and up until recently she had been a fairly successful journalist with her own flat and great friends, and there was *not* a scarecrow in her garden fucking stalking her and waiting for its moment to kill her.

I'll huff and I'll puff—

No. No.

Emily picked up her jacket, opened her front door, closed it again, locked it, and hurried down the path to Collie's house and a dinner of mediocre spaghetti bolognaise.

❖

Collie poured the gloopy jar of bright red sauce into the pan and stirred it into the lumpy, slightly burned veggie mince. Her phone was squashed between her shoulder and ear.

"The mince isn't looking too great," she said.

"Because I told you not to put it in first. I feel so bloody sorry for Lana and your new love interest," Tony said on the other end of the phone.

Collie ignored him. It was the best way because if you protested, he just did it more. He was like a dog with a bone.

"Speaking of which, how's your mysterious new lady friend?" Collie asked.

"She's good. I'm seeing her later," he said. "Things are, you know, getting more serious."

"What do you mean?" Collie tipped some chopped mushrooms into the pan, put the lid on, and called it good.

"Well, she's talking about introducing me to her parents," Tony said.

"Blimey. That *is* serious," Collie said.

"I know. The thing is, I mean, she hasn't told them about me," Tony said.

"Told them what? That you're a massive twat?" Collie asked.

She was pleased when Tony burst out laughing. She knew this was something he worried about. How the family would take it—take *him*. "Look, Tony, you're a catch. Any woman would be lucky to have you, and once her parents meet you, they'll see that too. No one is going to treat their daughter better than you will."

"Thanks, that means a lot," Tony said.

"It's true. I know I muck about, but you're easily the best person I know. Unless they're stupid, they'll see that too, and they'll love you. Everyone loves you," Collie said.

"No, they don't. Some people won't even accept that I exist, Collie. You know that," Tony said.

He was talking about his parents. And all the other people out there who thought they had a right to an opinion about who he was.

"Tony, I can't even begin to imagine what it's like for you with your family—with people in general who are ignorant and bigoted. I was lucky—my grandparents took it in their stride and let me be. But I do know that you have some great people around you who do love you and do support you. Sounds like this new girlfriend is one of them. Don't psych yourself out before you've even met her parents."

"I know, I know. I miss you. I wanted to get up to see you, but it's been mad down here. And the being-watched thing, have you told the police?" Tony said.

"Don't worry about it. I accept you have a life separate to me, mate. Plus, this new woman." Collie ignored his other question.

"Collie," he said.

Collie sighed. "Look, I have no proof, and I'd feel stupid going to the police about a *feeling*."

"Well, I thought I'd come up in half-term. Maybe bring Karen. I'd like you to meet her. Maybe we can talk about it then."

Collie still hadn't asked him if they could crash at his for a while. With his new girlfriend Karen, she wasn't sure it was even fair to ask. If things really were getting serious, Karen wasn't going to want Tony's mate and her ten-year-old niece hanging around.

Now was not the time to bring it up with him, though. Emily would be here any minute and the pasta sauce looked like it was done. Maybe. How could you even tell?

"Collie? Are you still there?" Tony asked.

"Yeah, yeah. Sorry. I think the food is done," Collie said.

"Look, if you don't want me bringing Karen up—"

"No, no. It's not that. I want to meet her—I really do. I'm just not sure if we'll still be here," Collie said.

The doorbell rang and Collie heard Lana's feet pounding down the stairs. "I'll get it, I'll get it," she shouted and Collie had to smile. Lana had really taken to Emily.

"Looks like Emily's here," Collie said. "Can I ring you tomorrow?"

"If I say yes, will you tell me what's going on?" Tony asked.

"Yeah, promise. And don't worry, it's nothing to stress about."

"I'm not worried."

"Tony, I can feel your worry rays coming through the phone. But please, don't. It's fine. I'll call you tomorrow. I'd better go."

"Okay, talk tomorrow," Tony said.

Collie ended the call and stuffed the phone in her pocket. She went out into the hall where Lana was busy talking Emily's ear off.

When she looked at Emily, Collie was struck by how much she fancied her.

Bit more than fancy, isn't it?

Collie wasn't going to go there. Now was not the time, and what was the point, anyway? She wouldn't be here much longer, and from what Emily said, she wasn't leaving until she knew what happened to her brother.

"Lana, at least let her get her coat off before you bend her ear beyond all recognition," Collie joked.

"Don't listen to her, Lana—she's just jealous she isn't Spring Ides," Emily said.

"Spring Ides?" Collie didn't understand.

"That's what they call me. Because I'm leading the parade at the Spring Fair. I'm Spring Ides," Lana said. "I saw my dress today. It's lovely."

"That's good," Collie said. "I'd better put the pasta on, so why don't you show Emily into the living room and get her a drink."

"Okay, and then I can tell you more about the Spring Fair," Lana said.

Collie smiled. It was nice to see her so excited. She'd dealt with her mother's death and everything that had been thrown at them amazingly well. But Collie hadn't seen this sparkle in her for a while.

Collie sorted out the pasta and laid the table for three. She got a loaf of bread out of the cupboard and put a few slices on a plate. She wished she'd gone to some posh bakery for some artisan bread, but all she had was this square cardboard stuff. Never mind, it wasn't like she was trying to impress Emily or anything.

She opened the wine she'd put in the fridge earlier and got out two mismatched wine glasses. She was starting to regret ignoring Tony's badgering that she needed proper tableware. The table looked shit. Everything was mismatched. She didn't even have fancy cheese, just a bit of cheddar she'd found knocking about at the back of the fridge and going hard at the edges.

Collie sighed. If she wasn't trying to impress Emily, why did she care so much what the dining table looked like?

But it wasn't just that, was it? She had Lana now. Time to grow up and get some fancy kitchen stuff. At some point Lana would want to bring friends back. Mismatched, chipped plates probably wouldn't cut it any longer.

At least she was on top of the food aspect of things. Except for the cheese. In the fridge were a ton of green vegetable things, and the freezer was full of the tasteless, nondescript vegetarian gear Lana insisted on eating. To be fair, some of it wasn't actually that bad.

"Hi."

Collie spun around at the sound of Emily's voice. She was standing in the doorway with a slight smile on her face.

"Hey. Nearly done," Collie said.

"Great, I'm starving. It smells good," Emily said and came fully into the kitchen. Collie was aware of the space reducing between them, and the air had become heavy. Or was that her imagination?

"I'm not sure it'll taste good, but we'll see. And I'm sorry about the plates and that. I need to buy new ones," Collie said.

"Ah, is that why you had that deep frown on your face when I walked in?" Emily asked.

Collie felt herself go red. She must have looked like a right idiot, standing there staring at her pathetically laid table. "I was just thinking, I needed to get some new stuff. Some nice stuff. I'm a bit embarrassed about this"—Collie gestured at the table—"to be honest."

Emily laughed. "Collie, I didn't come over because of your crockery."

"Good job."

"I came because you invited me. And I very much enjoy your and Lana's company," Emily said and moved closer.

"We enjoy yours too," Collie said. Her chest felt tight and light and tingly.

"I like you, Collie," Emily said and came even closer. She reached out, ran her hands over Collie's arms.

Collie nodded and swallowed. She liked Emily—it was obvious.

Anyone who looked could see. But it was a bad idea. Collie knew from experience that long-distance didn't work. But Emily was so good with Lana. Lana loved Emily. And Collie couldn't stop thinking about her.

She needed space before she kissed Emily again. Collie stepped back and scrubbed her face with her hands. "Emily, I don't think this is a good idea."

Collie watched Emily take a deep breath, close her eyes, and nod. "You're right. I'm sorry."

"Don't be sorry. You've nothing to be sorry for. It's just…"

"I know. Bad timing and way too complicated. If there wasn't Lana to think about…"

"We could give it a go, or at least, you know," Collie said.

Emily laughed and nodded. "I definitely know. But it'll confuse Lana, and she's been through enough."

"She's already attached to you," Collie said.

Emily held out her hand and smiled in a way that made Collie's heart hurt. "How about friends?"

"Can we?"

"We can try," Emily said.

Collie reached out and grasped Emily's hand in hers. Soft and warm. She pumped it twice. "Friends."

"*Good* friends," Emily said.

CHAPTER FORTY-FIVE

After the dishes were cleared, and Lana had gone to bed, Collie and Emily sat in the living room with a fire in the wood burner and a glass of wine each.

Emily was painfully aware how romantic the setting was, and after their conversation in the kitchen, Emily wondered if they could just be friends. She'd never been attracted to any of her friends, and Collie was becoming more attractive by the day. Every day, Emily learned something new about her—even the fact she could not cook at all was endearing and made some secret space in Emily's heart open just a little wider.

"I'm so sorry about dinner," Collie said.

"It wasn't *that* bad. I mean, it was edible."

"Barely."

"Barely," Emily agreed and they laughed. "Next time, you both should come to mine."

"You can cook?" Collie asked and leaned forward on the sofa, right into Emily's personal space, and it set off all kinds of warm skittering feelings.

"I can. In my old life, I cooked a lot. For friends and family," Emily said.

"But not here?" Collie asked.

"No, not here. When I came, I thought it best not to keep in touch with anyone. I didn't know what happened to Charlie, and I was convinced it was something to do with Hyam."

"The Bargus," Collie said.

Emily sighed. "I don't know. I'm aware how mad I sound, but something is watching me."

"You mean, someone," Collie said.

"I mean *something*. Maybe it's a person, I don't know. The scarecrow moved again today. After you left," Emily said.

"Moved? What do you mean?"

"I mean it *moved*, Collie. It was on the edge of the woods, and now it's about ten feet from my living room window," Emily said.

She watched as Collie sat back and sipped her wine. The look on her face wasn't one of disbelief, however, and Emily was relieved about that.

"Are you sure it's not the village again? Messing with you?" Collie asked.

"I have no proof it's not. And I don't believe the scarecrow got up and walked over, if that's what you're worried about."

"I'm not worried," Collie said.

"I keep thinking about the dream I had. Hamish telling me I should look in the church," Emily said.

"You think there's answers in there?"

"I don't know, but it's worth a look. I'm getting nowhere," Emily said.

"What do you actually have?" Collie asked.

"I know Charlie probably went missing in mid-April. That's when he stopped emailing me or replying to my emails. It was the Easter holidays, and he didn't show up at Highmore after the break."

"You reported him missing?" Collie asked.

"My parents came up. His house was untouched. Nothing missing. No one had seen him. I was on holiday in Italy at the time, or I would have come up too. They reported him missing at that point."

"The police investigated?" Collie asked.

"Yes. They listed him as a missing person—he still is, officially—but the consensus was he'd had some sort of breakdown and taken himself off to commit suicide. None of his bank cards or credit cards have been touched. His phone hasn't been used."

"Why did they think he had a breakdown? Was he depressed?" Collie asked.

Emily smiled. "You should be the journalist."

Collie pretended to shudder. "No thanks."

Emily laughed, and she was surprised to find she could talk about Charlie without the crushing weight of grief becoming too much. She wasn't sure if that was time or Collie or maybe a bit of both. "Before he went missing, his emails were mostly about feeling watched and followed. He was convinced there was something in the village out to get him."

Collie nodded. "I can see why they might have thought he was unwell."

"Me too. To an outsider. But I knew him. He wasn't just my brother—he was my best friend. I know it sounds arrogant, but I would have *known* if he was unwell. I genuinely think something was watching him," Emily said.

"I'm inclined to agree," Collie said.

It was simply put and only a few words, but it made Emily feel a sense of huge relief. Someone actually believed her, believed her brother wasn't ill or depressed or any of those things. She didn't realize she was crying until she felt the hot tears sliding down her face.

"Thank you," she managed to get out. And then she was in Collie's arms, and there was nothing sexual about it, but for the first time since she'd arrived in Hyam, she felt safe and not so alone.

Sometime later, Emily opened her eyes. Her cheek was pressed against Collie's T-shirt, and her neck ached. Shit. She sat up quickly.

"I'm so sorry. I can't believe I fell asleep on you." Emily felt her face heat.

"Don't be sorry. I enjoyed it. You're very nice to hold," Collie said.

Emily felt another heat then, but it wasn't in her face. "That isn't something friends say to each other."

Collie sighed. "I know. I'm working on it."

"How long was I out?" Emily asked.

"Only about ten minutes. Don't worry," Collie said.

Emily leaned back against the sofa and faced the fire. She didn't want to look at Collie any more. She thought if she did, she might do something stupid and not at all friendly. It was frustrating. If they'd met in London, Emily would have wanted to date her—they probably would be dating. But there was so much against them here. Not least, Collie was leaving. The thought of that made Emily feel lost and lonely. Hamish was gone—perhaps to a family emergency, but Emily didn't think so.

"I should probably go," Emily said.

"I'll walk you," Collie replied.

"You don't have to."

"I know. But in light of what's been going on, I think two are better than one," Collie said.

"You'll still have to walk back, though," Emily said.

"I'll be fine."

Emily should turn her offer down, but she'd didn't want to. The truth was, she was scared of walking back by herself. That bloody scarecrow had given her the creeps.

"Lana is going to a friend's house tomorrow," Collie said.

Emily waited. She wasn't sure where Collie was going with this.

"Well," Collie continued, "if you plan to go to the church, maybe I could go with you. Tomorrow. I have to drop Lana off first."

"That could work. I need to pop to Highmore to pick up some books I need to mark, so maybe we could meet at the church," Emily said.

"Okay, that sounds good," Collie said.

"Are you sure? I mean, I don't want to put you in any danger," Emily said.

"What danger could there be, going to a church?" Collie asked.

"Whatever's watching me might see you as well. I don't want to bring attention to you," Emily said.

"They're already watching me too, Emily. Don't worry. After the Spring Fair on Sunday, me and Lana will be packing up and leaving. I'm sure I'll be safe at the church."

"Okay then," Emily said. But it didn't feel okay, though she couldn't say why.

You're spooked, that's all. It's a church in daylight. What could happen?

They walked back in silence. Emily was listening for anything out of place, and she imagined Collie was doing the same. By unspoken agreement, they kept away from the bushes as much as possible.

Emily kept expecting the scarecrow to jump out at her, even though it was a stupid and childish thought. *It's not real, it's not real.* They turned up the drive and onto her garden path—

These woods aren't safe for a little girl to walk through alone.

What the hell? Where had she dredged up that line from? A fairy tale? Yes, "Little Red Riding Hood."

They got to her front door, and Emily gave Collie a quick hug. "Thanks for walking me back. Are you sure you're okay to go back by yourself?"

"Look, in the spirit of our new friendship, I'll be honest. I'm probably going to run all the way back," Collie said and laughed.

"Wow, you are such a big loser," Emily joked.

"I know. I'm an embarrassment to the Noonan name," Collie said. "Are you going to be all right?"

"I'll be fine. The rest of the house is all locked up, and I'll put the deadbolt on the front door when I get in."

"Okay, then. See you tomorrow," Collie said.

"Yes, see you tomorrow," Emily replied.

They stood awkwardly for a moment, Emily half hoping Collie would kiss her and half hoping she wouldn't. The look in Collie's eyes told Emily it could go either way.

In the end, Collie turned and left, sketching a little wave behind her as she went.

Emily sighed and watched her go. When she was out of sight, she went in the house and locked the door like she'd promised.

Bloody hell, it's cold in here.

She must have forgotten to turn the ancient heating system on.

She still felt unnerved and more than a little spooked, and she couldn't shake the feeling that going to the church was a bad idea.

"It's just a church," she muttered to herself and went into the living room. She flicked on the light and cried out.

"Jesus, fuck," she said on a rush of breath.

The scarecrow was now right up against her window—literally three feet away from the glass.

That settled it—tomorrow she was going to go out there and burn the fucking thing. Then she was going to the police. They might laugh at her, but someone was messing with her. Breaking into her house, watching her, following her. She'd bloody well report it. Sod trying to stay under the radar, and sod it if they found out who she was. This had to stop.

Emily decided to pack a bag. She was out of here. She'd stay in a hotel tonight and then deal with the rest tomorrow. She should probably tell Collie as well. She might not want Lana hanging around either.

Emily looked at the scarecrow again. Something about it was off. She stepped a little closer but still nowhere near it. What was it? A warning bell shrieked in her head, but she didn't know why. The scarecrow, what was it?

It doesn't have a wooden support behind it.

That's ridiculous. How could it be standing without—

It moved.

A twitch of the head, Emily was sure of it.

Then it looked up.

Its face. Where's its face.

It was still just a sackcloth with no eyes or mouth, and yet there were lumps beneath, in the shape of a nose and lips.

Emily backed out of the room. She fumbled her phone from her pocket, but she didn't dare look away from the scarecrow. It stepped forward now and put its gloved hands on the glass.

Emily dropped her phone.

Shit. She'd have to bend down.

She quickly looked down and saw the phone on the carpet. She picked it up and backed out into the hall.

When she looked up, just as she'd feared, the scarecrow was gone.

Emily whirled around and hurried into the kitchen to make her call and get a knife out of the drawer. What good it would do against a fucking scarecrow she didn't know, but it was something to defend herself.

You don't think it's actually a scarecrow, do you? It can't be. There's someone inside it.

Whatever it was, it wasn't getting indoors.

In the kitchen, Emily saw why the house was so cold. The back door was standing wide open. And in the doorway, framed against the night, stood the scarecrow.

CHAPTER FORTY-SIX

Collie parked her car in the narrow side road that ran behind the church. It was a pretty church, she supposed, and the plaque on the wall outside said it was built on the site of an Anglo-Saxon church by the Normans. The tower part of the building was the only feature of the original church remaining.

It looked typical of a lot of churches in Britain, Collie thought. Dark stone and blocky. The round tower with its tiny windows reminded Collie more of a castle than a church.

Still, the place was peaceful with old headstones still fairly well maintained out front—even if they did list like drunks.

Collie sat on a bench just outside the church. She turned up her face to the sun and felt herself relax. She thought about nodding off for a bit but decided against it. She didn't really want Emily to catch her snoring and drooling when she arrived.

Collie felt her eyelids go heavy, and her head dipped to her chest. In the distance, someone's lawnmower droned.

Maybe I'll just close my eyes for a minute.

She jolted awake with a start. Shit. She'd fallen asleep. She checked her watch and was relieved when she saw only five minutes had passed. She stood up and stretched out her back. It was another beautiful day, and Collie could feel her face starting to get hot. She was prone to burning, and the last thing she wanted to do was greet Emily with a sweaty red face.

Collie went into the church. It was cool and dark, the opposite to outside. She had only been in the church hall, which wasn't attached to the church, and she found she liked it in here. It reminded her of her childhood with her grandparents. How many hours had she sat on one of these hard wooden pews, her bum going numb? Too many to count.

Even the smell reminded her of her childhood church—did they do a line of diffusers that were only sold to old churches? Dusty Damp?

Like in the tower part of the church, the windows were small and high up. Collie walked down the centre aisle to the altar. A large dusty wooden cross sat on a platform about two steps up. A table was in front, draped with a cloth, and tapered candles sat on that. To the left was a wooden door, and Collie assumed that led to the tower.

She wandered up and down for a bit, not that there was all that much to see. Collie checked her watch and saw it was half past. Emily was late. Not rude late—not yet—but Collie was starting to wonder if she'd got the time wrong. She decided to give Emily another fifteen minutes, and then she'd text her.

Collie pushed on the tower door and was surprised when it opened. Half of her had been expecting it to be locked. Emily did say you could just walk in, but Collie wondered why when there was supposedly a tapestry in there from the Middle Ages. Weren't those things worth tons of money?

She guessed not because when she walked inside, the tapestry pieces were mounted to the walls behind Perspex on the ground floor. There were three of them in total.

Collie studied the first panel. She'd never say so for fear of sounding totally ignorant, but she'd always found medieval art a bit disappointing. The drawings were one rung up from stick figures in her opinion, and everyone had big, long noses and about three fingers on each hand. When Collie saw them she was reminded of the pictures Lana used to do for her at school when she was seven.

This first panel was no exception. In the top and bottom sections people were eating and drinking and playing instruments and generally looking like they were having a great old time. The banner was bordered with flowers in yellows and purples.

In the middle section were crudely drawn—to her mind—tents dotted about and people on horseback. There were a few banners with Latin words Collie didn't understand written on them. It looked like some sort of party or fair.

Probably a Spring Fair, which made sense as it seemed to be a big thing around here. Collie moved on to the next panel. This one was slightly stranger. It looked like the same event but later in the evening. Campfires burned, and while there were the same people drinking, eating, and playing music, there was also now a girl dressed in white with flowers in her hair. She was stroking some kind of dog. A huge dog with red eyes. No, not a dog, a wolf.

And when Collie looked closer, she saw the girl wasn't stroking it. Her hands were tied up, and the dog was...attacking her. It was bigger than the girl, and while medieval artists weren't all that keen on drawing things in perspective, you could see the dog was *meant* to be huge.

And was that...? Yes, Collie thought it was. In the centre of the scene, dotted about and partially hidden behind people and tents, were scarecrows. They were turned towards the dog, and Collie got the sense they were enjoying themselves. And the banner on here was not in Latin, and Collie had no trouble understanding it: *Bargus Feast.*

Collie stepped back a moment. The Spring Fair. The one where Lana was star of the show. But that was ridiculous. They weren't actually going to finish off the festivities by sacrificing Lana like in this tapestry.

Aren't they? How do you know*? This is a strange place and something is watching you.*

Right, but not a bloody great wolf from the fiery bowels of hell.

Collie moved on to the last panel. This one showed a ring of stones. Where had she seen them before? Somewhere, somewhere.

It looked like a mini-Stonehenge, and now all the scarecrows were out in the open, no longer hiding, and the girl in white was lying on one of those slabs and the dog—

The Bargus

Was standing over her.

Collie reared back. Her palms were sweating, her heart was triple-timing, and she was afraid. She was so afraid, and it was ridiculous because this was *just* a tapestry, and there were no monsters except the ones she made up in her head.

And hadn't they been through enough, her and Lana? Hadn't they lost too much already? Their lives were littered with losses, and Lana was not going to be sacrificed to this fucking monster, this—

Mark-stepper.

What?

Thinks like a human and chooses to act like a monster.

No. She wouldn't have it. She was losing her mind.

Are you, Collie? Those stones are familiar because you've seen them before. On the night of the camping trip, remember?

And now she did remember. She remembered walking through the woods and getting lost and coming upon some strangely arranged stones and thinking it looked like a mini-Stonehenge. And the way the stones were laid out was like some kind of—

Sacrificial altar.

No. No, not that. And now the thing that had been tickling the back of her brain, the thing she couldn't quite remember.

"The stones. Before we got chased away, the stones were splashed with something. I thought it was paint—"

Blood. It was blood. You knew it, but you didn't want to see it because it reminded you of Sasha's house. The front door handle was covered in—

"Blood. Jesus, I have to get Lana out of here," Collie said again and turned to leave the tower.

She pushed open the door, and at the same time felt a hard blow to the back of her head. It stunned her, and she felt her legs turn to jelly and give out. Something caught her before she could hit the stone floor, and she had a moment to think, *I must have really hit my head because I'm seeing scarecrows,* before the world blinked out.

Collie briefly came to again, but she couldn't move. She willed her legs, her arms, *something* to get going, but it was like the blow to the head had knocked out the link between her brain and her limbs. Thick, wet blood ran down her face and into her eyes.

"You hit her too hard."

That sounded like Stephanie Willis.

"Shut up. She's fine." Stephanie's husband, Dave. But that was ridiculous—why would they hit her in the head?

"She's not fine."

"She's alive. That's all that matters. We only need her alive. It doesn't matter what state she's in."

"Of course it matters. She needs to be able to use her legs."

Then Collie felt hands moving around her waist.

Oh no, oh no.

But they slid into her pocket instead. Her phone. They wanted her phone.

Collie tried to speak, tried to coordinate her lips and her tongue, but they weren't having any of it.

Collie couldn't see, and she worried they'd blinded her when they'd hit her. All she could see was a bright white light, and even though the thought of blindness terrified her, there was something comforting about the light. And the smell. Such a strong smell, was it perfume? Stephanie, maybe? The smell was lavender.

Sasha.

Collie could feel herself slipping away again, and that was okay. She fell into the light.

❖

Somewhere in the black, Emily woke up. She felt like she was floating. She knew she was lying on the ground because the floor was hard and cold beneath her.

She had no idea how long she had been here, but she did know the darkness was complete. The last time she woke, she waited for her eyes to adjust and shapes to appear, but they didn't.

Emily wondered if this was how it was for Charlie. Had he lain on this cold damp floor and thought the same things as her? Was she about to find out what happened to her brother?

Emily's head pounded, and she remembered being hit with something from behind in her kitchen. All her attention had been focused on the nightmare scarecrow, and she didn't notice someone creeping up on her from behind.

The next thing she knew, she was here. Wherever here was. No one had come, and she'd heard no one. She thought she might be in a basement, but she didn't really know. Was this how it was going to end? Starving to death in the dark? The thought of it filled Emily with utter terror.

But to die like that seemed pointless. Watching her, messing with her. They'd gone to a lot of trouble. Emily had a feeling there was more to come, and that maybe by the end she'd wish she had died starving in the dark.

And what about Collie? She'd be wondering where Emily had got to. They were supposed to meet at the church. Would Collie call her, text her? Would it be another situation like Hamish? Someone would find her phone by the side of the road, and Frances Cobb would tell Collie that Emily had a family emergency?

Probably. Probably that's exactly how it would go. Emily just hoped Collie was all right. She prayed Collie had waited for her in the church for a while, then left.

Emily couldn't help feeling like she'd put Collie and Lana in danger. Collie had even asked her, and Emily had said there was nothing to worry about, no one here knew who she was. Well, the joke was on her, wasn't it.

Maybe they don't know who you are. Maybe it's just bad luck that whoever got Charlie got you too.

Maybe. Emily adjusted her position on the hard floor and sat up, except she couldn't move far because of the handcuff on her wrist. She'd followed the chain and found it was bolted into the wall. No way out. She leaned back and ignored the chill and waited.

CHAPTER FORTY-SEVEN

Lana was sitting on Kitty's bed watching YouTube videos when her mum knocked and came in.

"Hi, girls, sorry to barge in," she said.

Lana liked Kitty's mum. She gave them their space and didn't bug them every five minutes like some mums did, insisting they go out and play or find an activity to do. She didn't care if they watched YouTube or TikTok videos all day.

"What's up, Mum?" Kitty said.

"Lana, your aunt had to go to London. Tony's had a bit of an accident at work."

Lana jumped up off the bed. "Tony? Is he okay?" She felt sick and hot, and her belly turned over.

"He's fine, he's fine. He's got a broken leg is all," Kitty's mum said and put a hand on Lana's shoulder. "She's just gone down to make sure he's all right. She asked if you could stay here the night, and we'll drop you at school tomorrow for the Spring Fair."

Lana had been looking forward to it all week, but now she didn't care. She wanted to see Tony, and she couldn't believe Collie hadn't stopped to pick her up first. She'd just left Lana behind.

"Can I call them?" Lana asked.

"She said she'd give you a ring in the morning. It'd be too difficult to call today, what with the drive down there and him being in hospital," Kitty's mum said.

"Right," Lana said.

"I'm sorry, I know tomorrow is a big day for you," Kitty's mum said.

"That's okay. I guess I'll speak to them tomorrow," Lana said.

"Yes, if they can. Your aunt said she couldn't promise anything, but she'd try."

"You spoke to her?" Lana asked as casually as she could.

"On the phone. She called me about ten minutes ago," Kitty's mum said. "Now, you girls shouldn't be on your phones all day. I thought we'd go out to Southwold, make the most of the weather."

Lana nodded and smiled while Kitty said, "Oh, Mum."

"Don't *oh, Mum* me, Kitty, give me your phone. You won't need it in Southwold," Kitty's mum said.

And that's when Lana knew. There was no way Collie would have left without her for London, and especially not when it was Tony who was hurt. She would have picked Lana up. She would have known Lana would want to come, and Lana couldn't ever remember a time when Collie left her out.

Second, Kitty's mum never cared if they were on their phones. And she *never* made them go out.

Something was wrong, really wrong. Lana had to get to a phone. She reckoned if she could call Collie or Tony, she would find out what it was. The sick feeling was gone, but now there was a cold, squirming feeling radiating out from her belly. It ran along her arms and legs and made her brain feel funny.

It's panic, came a voice far older than Lana and sounding very much like her mother. *It's panic because you know something's wrong. It's whatever is wrong with this village. And it's finally caught up with you.*

Her phone was in her bag downstairs. She had to get to it.

If it's still there.

But that was just her being paranoid. Of course it was there—where else would it be?

It might not be there, darling, so you need to think of something else just in case.

Why wouldn't it be there? Kitty's mum was certainly lying about something, but she wouldn't take Lana's phone. Would she?

Maybe, maybe not. The point is you need to be ready. You still remember Tony's phone number?

Yes, she did. Collie made her memorize Collie's and Tony's numbers when they moved up here—just in case, she said. Lana insisted it was on her phone if she needed it. Thank goodness she'd done what Collie asked. She repeated the number in her head now.

Downstairs, Lana looked through her bag.

"What are you looking for, Lana?" Kitty's mum asked.

"My purse," Lana lied.

"Don't worry about that. You won't need any money."

"In case I see a present for Tony. A get-well one." Lana was surprised how quickly she was thinking.

She rifled through her bag one more time. The phone was gone. Someone had taken it out of her bag.

Not someone, Kitty's mum. You need to be careful, Lana. Keep thinking—look for an opportunity.

Lana glanced longingly at the phone on the hall table. She wanted to use it, but she daren't ask. She didn't really know why, but she *did* know it would be a very, very bad idea. That voice inside her—

Mum

Or whatever it was, it felt like she was being guided by something much bigger than herself. She'd go to Southwold with Kitty and Kitty's mum, and as soon as she had the chance, she'd call Collie or Tony—

No, Tony. You'll call Tony.

She'd call Tony.

❖

Collie woke with the worst headache of her life. She turned on her side and vomited. She probably had concussion or something. Great. Just what she needed.

Collie tried to look around her, but it was pitch-black. Not even a sliver of light from anywhere. She retched again, and ropy tendrils of spit hung from her chin. Her face was tight and itchy from the blood which had run down it like a river.

Collie lifted one hand to feel the damage and found she was chained at the wrist. Even that slight movement made her head pound. It felt like someone was simultaneously driving spikes into her eyes and tightening an iron band around her forehead.

Who knew, maybe that was going to become a reality. She wouldn't panic. She *couldn't* panic. Collie swore to herself that if she possibly could, she'd get out of here and get back to Lana. But to do that, she had to be smart, and she mustn't panic. If she did, it would all be lost. She had to think. At the moment, however, she could barely breathe around the terrible pain in her head and the fear terrible damage had been done to her skull.

Collie brought to mind an image of Lana. Better. That was better. For Lana, she could—she *would*—do anything.

Collie lifted the other hand, the one that wasn't chained, and felt the back of her skull. She pushed beneath her matted hair and hissed at the sudden pain there. There was a lump the size of an egg and a cut that would probably need stitches. She probably had a mild concussion as well. Other than that, she seemed okay.

Collie tested her arms and legs, wriggled her fingers and toes. So far, so good. It didn't look like the blow she took had caused lasting damage.

She was sure if there was light right now, she would be able to see okay as well. Apart from the sickening pounding, Collie thought she'd got off light.

So the question was, why was she here, and why did Stephanie and Dave Willis do this to her? And why were they dressed as scarecrows? She wondered at first if it was a combination of the blow to the head and the tapestry that caused her to hallucinate the scarecrows, but she didn't think so.

Come on, Collie, you saw the tapestry. You know *why. Emily herself said the scarecrow was moving around her garden. You're being watched by something in the bushes. You got chased in the woods. So don't say you don't know, because you fucking well do, and if you don't get out of here, then Lana is going to end up just like the girl in the tapestry.*

She should have taken Lana away from here sooner. Got out straight after the camping trip and not waited. Maybe if she'd done that, none of this would have happened.

And where was Lana right now? Collie felt the panic bubble up again, and she forced it back down.

That's helping no one.

Lana was fine. She'd dropped her at her friend Kitty's house, and she would be there now. If the tapestry was right, nothing would happen until the Spring Fair.

How do you know it hasn't already happened. It might be happening right now—

Collie forced the nasty little voice in her head to shut up. Because the truth was, maybe it *had* already happened, and maybe it *was* too late, but if she believed that…She *couldn't* believe it. She wouldn't.

What she did have to do was find a way out of here. Someone

would come soon. What was the point of keeping her down here if not to bring her up at some point?

Maybe to get you out of the way so they can sacrifice Lana. Maybe they'll just leave you down here in the dark to die. To starve.

No. No, not true. She remembered something now, something Dave had said in the church. Stephanie was worried he'd hit Collie too hard and that she'd need to use her legs.

Fucking cheery thought. As long as she could use her legs. What did that mean? Collie guessed she wouldn't have to wait too long to find out, and she was certain it had something to do with the Spring Fair.

CHAPTER FORTY-EIGHT

Lana was convinced Kitty's mum was dragging this trip to Southwold out. They'd walked round the shops at least twice and were now sitting on the beach. Lana thought about the day she came here with Collie and Miss Lassiter. Miss Lassiter told Lana to call her Emily out of school, but Lana couldn't stop herself thinking of Emily as Miss Lassiter.

She guessed if Collie and Miss Lassiter got married, she'd have to call her Emily, otherwise it would be a bit weird.

Lana was tired. It was hard work pretending to have a nice time when really you were worried to death about something.

Lana looked over at Kitty's mum, who had fallen asleep on a deck chair. She looked over to Kitty and saw her friend watching her with a strange look in her eyes.

Lana debated, then decided she'd have to trust her. She leaned forward so she was close to Kitty. "I have to use the phone. I'm going to go up there." Lana pointed to the ice cream place. They'd let her use their phone, wouldn't they? If she said it was an emergency.

Kitty shook her head. "You aren't supposed to. I'm not supposed to let you out of my sight."

Lana's belly went cold again, and fear slithered in the pit of it. "Please, Kitty. I have to call them."

Lana watched a multitude of emotions cross Kitty's face—fear, sadness, anger—and finally, she gave Lana a small, sad smile. "I like you, Lana. And I'm sorry about how things turned out. You can't fight what's going to happen, you know."

"What do you mean? What's going to happen?"

Kitty mimed zipping her mouth shut. "Can't tell. It's a secret."

"*Please.* I'm begging you, Kitty. You're my friend. Please be my friend," Lana pleaded.

Kitty's brow furrowed and she looked across at her mother. "Okay. But you have to promise you won't call the police."

Lana nodded. "Okay. Promise."

Kitty held out her hand and extended her little finger. "Swear."

"Swear." Lana linked little fingers with Kitty.

She got up as quietly as she could and crept up the beach. When she reached the promenade, she sprinted.

Lana shoved the door to the ice cream place open a little too hard and just about managed to catch it before it swung into the wall. There was only a short queue, but Lana didn't want to wait. She had a feeling she only had a little time. Kitty agreed to let her come up here, but what if she got nervous and changed her mind?

Hurry up, darling. Hurry up now.

Lana skirted the queue, feeling some shame even though it was an emergency. She'd been taught never to push in.

"Excuse me," Lana said to the woman behind the counter.

"Queue's there." The woman frowned and pointed, and Lana felt her cheeks heat with shame.

"I'm not pushing in, honest. I really need to use your phone, please. It's an emergency," Lana said.

The woman's frown changed to a look of concern. "What's happened? Are you alone?"

"No. My mother is in the car park, the car broke down, and she wants me to call my dad and get him to pick us up. Her phone died," Lana lied and felt a stab of guilt.

"Okay, come behind here," the woman said and lifted the hinged part of the counter.

Lana felt a surge of relief. Maybe everything was going to be okay after all. She waited until the woman went to serve another customer, then dialled Tony's number from memory.

The phone rang and rang and rang. Lana almost started crying.

He's not going to answer, he's not going to answer.

Then, the line clicked, and Tony's voice filled her ear. "Hello?"

"Tony?"

"Lana? What's wrong?"

"Tony? Is Aunt Collie with you?"

"No. Lana—"

"Are you hurt? Did you have an accident?"

"What? No, I'm fine. Lana, what's going on?"

Lana forced her tears back. "I don't know. They said—" Lana looked out the window and saw Kitty and her mum hurrying along the pier. Kitty *had* told.

"Lana? *Lana?*"

Kitty's mum was opening the shop door.

"I think they have Aunt Collie. You have to come, please."

Now she was looking around. She spotted Lana.

"Who? What?" Tony asked but Lana put the phone back down and didn't answer him. She just hoped he came.

Lana knew now that Kitty's mum lied. Tony was fine, and Aunt Collie was missing.

"Lana," Kitty's mum said and lifted the counter flap. "Come out from behind there. Who were you calling?"

"Everything okay?" The woman who worked in the ice cream shop had come over now and was looking at all of them suspiciously.

Should Lana tell her no? That she'd basically been kidnapped?

No, don't do that. If you want to see Collie again, you won't do that.

That voice again, her mother's voice, and Lana wanted to believe it was her mother. It was kind. It wanted to help her. And she believed what it told her.

"Sorry, yes. I guess the car is working again," Lana said and forced a cheery smile.

"Thank you for letting her use the phone," Kitty's mum said.

The woman nodded but the suspicious look hadn't left her face.

Kitty's mum took Lana by the arm and squeezed. Lana swallowed the hiss of pain.

"Let's go," she said and marched Lana out. She bent close to her ear and whispered so only Lana could hear, "You'll pay for that."

❖

Emily woke with a start. She'd nodded off again. How long had passed this time? It was impossible to tell. She was still in complete darkness.

Somewhere above her, she heard a click as a door opened quietly. Someone was coming.

Emily couldn't stand up because of the way her wrist was shackled, but she got up on her knees. Maybe if whoever it was got close enough she could—

What? What can you do?

"Shut up," she whispered to that nasty voice. "Just fuck off, can't you?"

Someone was coming down the stairs. Their footsteps were soft and measured and sure.

How can they know where they're going? I can't see my hand in front of my face.

The footsteps stopped, and Emily could hear soft breathing. But whoever it was didn't come any closer. Emily refused to be the first to speak. She wouldn't play this game even though every nerve ending was screaming at her to panic.

No.

Emily waited.

Nothing. Even the breathing stopped.

"Hello, Emily." The voice was inches from her ear, and Emily couldn't help crying out.

She cut it off and willed her heart to stop hammering in her chest. Whoever it was laughed.

"I didn't mean to scare you. I sometimes forget your kind can't see well in the dark."

Still, Emily said nothing.

"You can't see a thing. Can you, Emily?" The voice was cloying and crooning, and Emily tried hard to pinpoint where it was coming from so she could punch whoever it was in their smug face. It kept moving.

Did she recognize the voice? She wasn't sure. It sounded familiar and alien at the same time. It was a deep, guttural voice. Barely human at all.

"Not going to speak to me, Emily?" It paused. "That's very rude. But then you are a rude bitch, aren't you?"

Emily breathed shallowly and tried to hear around the blood rushing in her ears.

"Don't worry—you'll be able to see again quite soon. Although I think you might wish you were back in the dark when you see what we've got in store for you."

There. To the left of her. Its breath tickled her ear. Emily held her breath, prayed, closed her eyes, and punched.

She connected with something solid. It couldn't have shaved for a while, it had bristles—it was fucking *hairy*. It moved its head back—she was sure she got its cheek—and her hand slid down and caught on something sharp. She did cry out then. Was it teeth? Christ, that *hurt*.

Grandma, what big teeth you have.

Something grabbed her hand, the one which had connected with it. "You'll pay for that," it growled. It squeezed, and Emily felt the bones in her hand creak.

It's going to snap my hand. Oh God, it's going to turn my bones to dust.

Mercifully, it let go. Emily's hand throbbed, and tears of pain stung her eyes. She pulled her hand back and cradled it in the other.

"Fuck you," Emily ground out and was pleased her voice sounded strong.

"I can smell your tears, you know. But those tears are nothing to how much you'll cry later. You shouldn't have come here. But you wanted to find out what happened to your brother, didn't you? Well, you'll find out later, Emily. He fought too, you know. Just like you. But he screamed and begged like all the others when I killed him."

Emily threw herself forward, then, blinded by rage and grief and pain and with no thought about what might happen to her. She fell into air, and her shackled arm pulled painfully at her shoulder. It was gone.

She screamed. She kept screaming. She couldn't stop.

❖

Collie stuck her fingers in her ears and pulled her knees up like the child she'd once been. She wished the screaming would stop. Every time her brain tried to think about what was happening to cause that screaming, she forced her mind away.

Panic fluttered in her chest like a leaf caught on the wind. She would *not* give in to it. She wouldn't. If she did, then all would be lost. She rocked back and forth.

Finally, after what felt like hours but was probably only minutes, the screaming stopped. Collie didn't think she'd been more grateful for anything in her life.

She made herself think about the screaming. Did she recognize the person doing it? Hard to tell. Definitely not a child, and that was good because it meant it wasn't Lana. Who, then? The likelihood was it was Emily. That thought hurt Collie more than she thought and started that terrible fluttering again in her chest.

Was this how it was going to end? Was she going to be tortured to death? Would that screaming start again, and when it stopped for good, would it be Collie's turn?

Stop thinking that shit. Just. Stop.

Those thoughts would help no one. At the moment, as far as Collie knew, Lana was alive. Lana was *fine*. The tapestry showed Collie what was probably going to happen, and she thought her fate and Emily's were probably tied up in it as well.

Collie took several deep breaths and shuffled back, following the chain that held her wrist to where it ended at the wall. It was attached with a bolt, and Collie was sure the bolt was drilled into the wall.

The wall itself was brick, and it was *old* brick. Collie went back to scratching at it with her fingers.

"Career as a hand model is probably over before it's begun," she mumbled to herself. Not that she was one for talking to herself, but she'd do anything to fill this utter blackness.

Another fingernail came off, and Collie hissed against the stinging pain. Fuck, that one hurt. She thought the whole thing was probably gone this time.

She sucked the empty nailbed for a moment, then went straight back to digging away at the brick around the bolt.

CHAPTER FORTY-NINE

L ana was in a basement. Kitty's basement. She'd been terrified in the car because of how angry Kitty's mum was. She wasn't sure what was going to happen, but she was actually pretty relieved to just be frog-marched into the house and down here.

Kitty's mum had told her it wouldn't have to be like this if only she'd been a good girl. Lana resisted rolling her eyes. *Good girl*? Kitty's mum had something to do with Aunt Collie going missing, but she was mad because rather than just going *oh well*, Lana tried to fix it.

But she'd managed to get hold of Tony, and Tony would make things all right. He'd call the police, and they'd bust in here and ask why Kitty's mum had a kid in the basement. Then Kitty's mum would tell them where Aunt Collie was.

At least Lana *hoped* that's what would happen. It might not, though. Maybe it wouldn't happen like that at all. Lana had lost her mum and her dad, and she knew better than anyone that life didn't always turn out the way you wanted. Only stories had happy endings—life was a lot different.

What if Tony came here, and they got him too? What if he sent the police, and they were in on it? The way Kitty's mum was in on it.

Collie would be mad at her, as well. Mad she didn't tell the woman in the ice cream shop what was happening.

But Collie was all she had left. Well, she had grandparents, but they were really old, and she didn't see them much. They spent a lot of time on cruises or in their caravan, and when Lana went to see them, it was always awkward and boring. Lana had a suspicion they didn't really like her at all. People thought kids couldn't tell things like that, but they could. Her grandparents didn't like children, and if anything happened to Aunt Collie and Lana had to live with them...

No point thinking like that, though. Besides, Lana wasn't stupid. She was being kept in a basement. Whatever had happened to Aunt Collie was probably going to happen to Lana as well.

Lana wondered where that voice in her head was now. The one who led her up to the pier and to the phone. Lana had tried several times to tentatively talk to it, but it hadn't replied.

She sighed. Maybe it hadn't been there at all, and Lana just imagined it.

She looked around the basement. Same as most others she'd ever seen. Piles of boxes, a washing machine, tiny window at the end, and weird damp sort of smell.

Lana looked at the window again. Way too small to crawl through. She would try anyway, but what if her head got stuck? She'd done that once in the banister when she was really small, and her mum had to cut them with a saw to get her head out.

Upstairs, Lana heard footsteps creak across the floor. They were coming closer. She heard the door to the basement open.

"Hello?" Lana called, hoping it was Collie come to get her, and this was all just a big, stupid mistake.

"Lana." Kitty's mum's voice. Lana's heart sank.

Kitty's mum came down the stairs and stopped a few steps from the bottom. "You lied to me, Lana. You *did* manage to make a call, didn't you."

Lana didn't say anything. Kitty's mum didn't look mad so much as worried. *Really* worried.

"You called that man, didn't you?" she said. "Tony. He called your aunt."

Lana swallowed.

"Luckily for you, he's no longer worried sick and ready to call the police."

"What do you mean?" Lana asked.

"What I mean is that we have your aunt's phone, and text is a wonderful thing. But you put him in harm's way, Lana. I *told* you not to do that."

"Why do you have Aunt Collie's phone? Where is she?" Lana asked, afraid of the answer.

Kitty's mum bent forward with her hands on her knees and twisted her face in a way that was meant to look like concern but really wasn't at all.

"Miss her, do you? Worried about her? Don't worry, you'll see her soon enough. And then you *and* her will be joining your mother. Bet you miss her too, don't you, Lana."

Lana stepped back and put her hands over her ears. She didn't want to hear any more, and she knew it was babyish, but she didn't know what else to do. She just wanted Kitty's mum to stop.

"Oh, you can cover your ears, you little madam, but it won't help you. You're a sneaky little liar. You'd better hope your friend Tony doesn't come here. You'd better *pray*, because if he does, he's going to end up—"

"Sara." A man's voice from the top of the stairs. "Enough."

Kitty's mum—Sara—stood up straight and smiled at Lana in a way that made her legs tingle and made her wonder if she might wet herself. "You're right. Let her find out for herself. Don't want to ruin the surprise."

With that, she turned and went back up the stairs. Half a second too late, Lana thought she should have followed, tried to dart round her and escape.

No, don't do that.

It was the voice again. Lana suddenly felt loads better even though she didn't understand why.

"What should I do, then?" she asked.

In your head, darling. You can speak to me in your head. Go over to the washing machine. Hurry.

Lana did as she was told.

Now what, Mum? she said in her head. And she was sure it was her mum. It sounded like her. She didn't know how, but her mum was here.

Reach underneath, at the front. There's something there for you, her mum said.

What is it? Did you put it there?

Just reach under. Yes, I put it there. I gave one to Collie and one to her friend. And now I'm giving one to you.

Lana reached under, and her fingers touched something hard and cold. She slid it out with her finger.

It was a coin—no, more like a tiddlywink.

It's an amulet. You need to hide it. Don't lose it, her mother said in Lana's head.

Why? Will it help me?

Yes. Yes it will. Now, Lana, you have to listen to me carefully, darling. Tomorrow night, they're going to come for you and you have to be ready.

Fear slid under Lana's skin and into her bones.

Will I run?

No. You'll go with them. Listen out for me, and I'll tell you what to do.

What's going to happen?

But the voice was gone. It left an ache in Lana's chest. People might say she was mad, but she knew that was her mum. *She knew it.* It was the voice she had heard every day for ten years and, up until recently, the most important voice in her life. Up until today, losing her mother was the worst thing that ever happened to Lana. And even though she was terrified now and sick with worry about Collie, part of her thought it was worth it, just to hear her mother's voice again.

CHAPTER FIFTY

Collie leaned her forehead against the wall. She was sweaty and dusty, and her hands were in agony. She'd barely managed to shift the bolt at all and thought maybe the tiny bit of give she felt had been there to start with.

Collie.

At the sound of her name, Collie jerked up and away from the wall. She looked around even though there was nothing to see in the pitch-black.

She listened. Distantly she could hear the whisper of voices, but they were far away and definitely not close enough for her to hear them call her name. Must be her tired brain making shit up.

Collie.

There it was again.

"Hello?" she whispered. "Is someone there?"

Truth was, there could be someone in here with her, she guessed. It was so dark that she would never see them. Unless they moved. Or spoke to her.

Collie, be quiet and listen to me.

Sasha. It sounded like Sasha, but it couldn't be.

It is. Now be quiet and listen.

It was certainly impatient like Sasha.

"Fine. Go ahead." At this point, Collie was too tired to argue, and her brain couldn't cope with another shock.

Talk to me in your head. They're always listening. They're always watching.

Who?

You know who, Collie.

The villagers.

Yes.

Are you really Sasha?

Yes, I really am.

Are you sure I haven't just lost my mind?

I don't know about that, Collie. You always were a bit of a funny onion.

A sob burst from her. She didn't know how this could be or what the fuck was going on, but she was speaking to Sasha. She was sure of it. Only Sasha called her a funny onion.

God, I've missed you. Even her mind voice was sobbing.

I've missed you too. I don't have much time, so you have to listen to me now.

Okay.

No interruptions.

Not even one.

Collie.

Sorry.

I can be here now, talking to you, because tonight is the night when the veil between this world and the other world is at its thinnest. They call it Spring Fair, but that's not what it is. It's when the Bargus comes into its full power because it can be fully in this world, and it needs to renew itself—

The Bargus is real then. Sorry, I know you said no interruptions.

Yes, the Bargus is real. It's an ancient thing. A monster who thinks like a human, and it's been picking people off for centuries. The people here serve it as they've always served it and will continue to serve it unless you stop it. Because tonight it's fully in this world, so it's vulnerable.

Collie rubbed her poor battered head with her poor battered hands.

This is a lot.

I know and I'm sorry. But it means to take Lana tonight as its sacrifice, and we can't let that happen.

No. I won't let that happen.

I know, Collie. I know how much you love her. It's been watching you since you came here, Collie. All of them have, the villagers. They chose Lana almost as soon as they saw her. The Bargus has been waiting, and now it can't wait any longer. It needs her to renew itself and it's very old and much weaker than it ever was. That's in our favour. It's a mark-stepper. That means it straddles this world and the next, and that takes a lot of effort. A lot of energy. If we deny it Lana, we deny it its renewal.

And then it dies?

I don't know.

What do you mean, you don't know?

I can't see the future, Collie, just the past. This is what it's always done, and this is what it will always do. And the villagers will always help it because that's the way it's always been. They have to help it.

Why?

Because it takes care of the village, and the village takes care of it. It only takes outsiders, never their own. They need each other.

It keeps their village from going the way of so many others. But how? Frances Cobb owns pretty much all...oh.

Yes.

Collie suddenly understood. *Mark-stepper. It thinks like a human and behaves like a monster. Like Damian. But it has a different face for living her monstrous truths, and Damian didn't.*

In a way, Damian did. His face for the world and his face for me. The Bargus has two faces. Its face for the world and its face for the ones like you.

Its sacrifices. Me and Lana and Emily. I saw it in the tapestries.

Yes.

It can't have Lana. It can't have Emily either, but it can't have Lana.

No.

Tell me what to do.

Collie listened to her sister, to the things she told her, and she understood what she had to do. When Sasha was finished, she just kind of disappeared from Collie's head, and Collie felt the loss almost like the first time. She wept. And then she went back to digging at the wall. Except this time, she took the amulet out of her pocket to do it. She'd forgotten about the amulet, and it seemed so had those who took her from the church, which seemed strange as they'd rifled through her pockets to get her phone.

Luckily for her, they hadn't found it for whatever reason—

Sasha—

Maybe. Either way, the amulet cut through the bolt like it was butter. Collie gathered up the chain by winding it around her other hand until she had about a foot of length in the middle. Then she waited.

❖

Emily sat with her head back against the wall and her knees drawn up. Her throat was raw and her face was hot and itchy from crying and sweating. The fear was gone and in its place was a terrible numbness. A big black emptiness.

She came here looking for answers, looking for her missing brother. Emily knew what happened to him, now. That *thing* murdered him. And in a twist of irony, she was about to find out exactly what that meant.

Her parents would have two missing children instead of one. Emily had a feeling that was a mistake on their part—on that *thing's* part. It would be too much of a coincidence that brother and sister had gone missing from the same village, no matter how they spun it. But that *thing* was arrogant. She'd sensed it when its face was inches from hers. The arrogance, the certainty in its own infallibility had come off it in waves. *That* would be its downfall.

Emily felt in her pocket for the amulet. She'd almost forgotten it was there, and then, suddenly in a flash, it seemed like, she'd remembered it.

She held it in her hand now and turned it over and over in her fingers. It was sharp on the edges, and Emily believed it could cut and probably quite deeply. She'd tested it on the brick behind her and it cut into it easily. Whoever came down here next was going to have a fight on their hands.

Emily had nothing to lose now, and that was the *thing's* other mistake. If you took away everything from a woman as it had done to her—her freedom, her expectation of living, and the most important person in her world, Charlie—then that woman was unpredictable. Emily didn't give a shit about her own life and she would take one of theirs if she got a chance.

Emily closed her eyes.

❖

Lana gripped the amulet in her hand for a moment and then slipped it into her pocket. She lay down on the floor on a couple of blankets she'd scavenged from a box. It was getting cold down here, and she could see out the window that it was dark. She didn't have long left. Tomorrow they would come for her.

Lana slipped her hand back in her pocket and held the amulet. She closed her eyes and tried to sleep.

CHAPTER FIFTY-ONE

It was time. The Bargus had waited patiently for this. It was weak and tired, and though it was still strong in this world, it worried.

It felt the other like a tickle in its throat—annoying and disconcerting. The other was getting stronger as it was getting weaker. It felt how thin the veil was. It wasn't supposed to be this way. The other should have left by now and passed fully over to the other side, but it hadn't. Instead it was still here, hanging around and imposing its will on proceedings. It was strong, stronger than it had first thought. Another mistake.

But it wouldn't be long now. It had sent its people to fetch the women and the girl and bring them to the stones. Then the ritual would begin. But before the ritual it would have its fun.

❖

Collie heard a door open, and then there was blinding light. She cried out and closed her eyes. She'd been in darkness so long now, but she'd have to just suck it up because someone was coming and she'd only get one chance.

❖

The lights went on and Emily squeezed her eyes shut. She gripped the amulet in her palm with the edge sticking up between her first and second fingers, then made a fist. She cowered against the wall and dropped her head on her arms, hiding the fist which held the amulet. She was ready.

❖

When the door above opened, Lana stood up. She listened for her mother, but there was nothing. That was okay. She would tell Lana what to do when the time was right. Until then, Lana would do whatever these people told her.

"Are you going to behave?" Kitty's mum asked from the top of the stairs.

"Yes," Lana said.

Kitty's mum walked down with something in her arms. A dress.

"It's pretty," Lana said.

"Yes, it is. You're Spring Ides, so of course it's pretty," Kitty's mum said.

Lana could tell she was still mad at her. It was kind of stupid, considering Lana wasn't the one who'd kidnapped somebody and held them in their basement all night.

Get ready, darling. Put both your hands in your pockets.

Lana did as her mum said. "Oh yes, that's today, isn't it?"

"This evening," Kitty's mum said.

"Is it evening, then?" Lana asked innocently.

"Almost. Now come on, put it on."

Kitty's mum stepped towards Lana and held out the dress.

Now, Lana, cut her with it. Now, darling.

Lana pulled the amulet out of her pocket and lunged at Kitty's mum.

❖

Collie waited until Stef Willis was at the bottom of the stairs and lunged at her. She pulled up the chain tight between her hands, and before Stef knew what was happening, Collie had it wrapped around her neck.

She gave a hard pull using all her strength, and Stef stumbled forward and into her. Collie took the impact and twisted behind Steph, pulling tight on the chain and looping it so it crossed at the back where Collie held it.

Stef reached up to try to pull the chain from around her neck, but Collie was much stronger, and Stef had no chance.

Collie barely registered the snarl coming from her own throat but she clenched her teeth and pulled the chain as hard as she could.

Soon, Stef stopped struggling. Collie held on for a little longer, then released her. Stef dropped to the ground. Collie saw she'd gouged her own neck trying to get the chain away. Collie couldn't drum up any sympathy for the woman she thought she'd made friends with.

Collie headed for the basement stairs.

❖

Emily pretended to cry—or maybe she really was crying, who knew? Either way, Phil the handyman came nice and close, which was the point.

"Come on, less of that. It'll be better if you just accept it," he said.

When Phil bent down, reached out, and gripped her shoulder, Emily looked up, smiled, and lashed out with the amulet right across his throat.

"Oh," Phil said and stumbled back, holding his throat. Blood poured between the fingers of both his hands. Emily got to her knees ready to cut him again, but he was finished. He dropped to the floor in front of her and died.

❖

Lana wasn't sure if she could do it, but when the amulet slashed across Kitty's mother's stomach, Lana realized that not only could she do it, but that she could do it again, if she needed to.

It turned out she didn't. Kitty's mum made a quiet sort of *oomph* sound, then fell to her knees, holding her stomach.

Lana didn't hang around. She legged it up the stairs and into the kitchen. Kitty sat at the dining table with a spoon of cereal halfway to her mouth. When she saw Lana, it plopped back into the bowl.

"What—"

Lana didn't wait to hear the end of Kitty's sentence. She ran out of the kitchen and went for the front door.

Lana turned the lock and threw it open. She sprinted out of the house and onto the street.

Head for home, darling.

Won't they look for me there?

Just run.

Lana tore off down the road and into the night.

"Hey, Lana. Come back."

Lana recognized the voice as Kitty's dad. She didn't stop, though. She kept pumping her arms and legs. It wasn't long before she heard the pounding of feet behind her—bigger, faster feet.

She reached the level crossing. For the first time she'd seen, the barriers were down, and the red lights were flashing to indicate a train was imminent.

She pulled up. *Now what?*

Jump the barrier, darling. Do it quickly.

Lana jumped over the level crossing barrier just as she felt a hand brush against her back.

"You little bitch. You murdering little bitch," Kitty's dad screamed from behind her, and he sounded close. He'd followed over.

Lana sprinted over the train tracks and reached the opposite barrier and almost at the same time, she heard a scream and the sound of rushing air as a train screeched past. A bright white light flared around her and behind her.

You did that.

Yes.

You killed him.

Yes. He would have hurt you. Time to go, darling.

She dared to look behind her but all she saw was the blur of the fast train. She wondered if the driver even knew he'd hit Kitty's dad.

No time for that, Lana. Time to go. Head for home.

Lana took off.

When Collie reached the top of the stairs, she was flying. She skidded to a stop almost immediately when she reached the top and looked around. Front door to the right, about three closed doors in the opposite direction.

She had to get out of here. She had to get to Lana. But those screams. What if they belonged to Emily?

Right or left?

Collie looked between the two, aware she was wasting time.

She tightened the chain in her hands and turned right. If they had been coming for her, that meant the Spring Fair hadn't started yet. She still had time.

Then she heard a scream coming from the door at the end, and that decided it for her. She ran towards it.

Collie pushed open the door and saw Emily grappling with a man. He had his back to her.

Without too much thought Collie took several long strides towards them. In the same way she had in the basement, Collie wrapped the chain around his neck, twisted it, and pulled. Her arms were aching terribly, but she found the strength.

This man was bigger than Stef had been, and he bucked and twisted, and Collie struggled to keep control.

Collie pulled the chain tighter, as tight as she could manage. Suddenly, he dropped, and Collie realized Emily had kicked his legs out from under him.

It took him a little longer to stop moving than it had taken Stef, but he did stop, and Collie released the chain.

"Hi," Collie said to Emily.

"Hi. Fancy seeing you here," Emily replied.

Collie smiled slightly. "We should get out of here."

Suddenly, Emily pulled Collie into a quick, hard hug. "Thank you. For not leaving without me."

Collie nodded. "No problem. We should go—I think they have Lana."

Emily nodded. "Let's go get her then."

Emily took Collie's hand and they left the kitchen. They crept towards the front door, past the doors lining the hallway, Collie half expecting one of them to fly open and an army of villagers to be waiting for them.

They managed to creep past, almost there, almost at the front door.

To the right, one of the doors opened. It was Dave Willis.

"What the fuck?" he asked.

Collie didn't answer him. She squeezed Emily's hand, and together they sprinted for the front door, praying it wasn't locked. It wasn't. She threw open the door, and they raced out. Her lungs were burning, and behind her she could hear Dave calling for others to help.

Collie vaguely registered the grand gravel drive and the mani-cured lawns—where the fuck were they?—as they legged it into the woods ahead of them. Maybe they could lose Dave and whoever else was bound to be coming after them there.

❖

Lana, guided by the voice of her mother, came through the woods that backed onto Miss Lassiter's house. She almost tripped over the weird scarecrow that lay half covered in leaves at her feet.

So far, she hadn't seen anyone on her journey over here. At times in the woods, she'd wondered if she'd ever get out, if her mother's voice was just Lana going mad and imagining it.

But every turn she was told to take she took, and now, here she was. The problem she had was that her house was hidden by the long drive, and she couldn't see if anyone was waiting for her.

Go now—you don't have much time.

Lana, as she had done since she was very small, listened to her mother and ran home.

As she turned onto the drive, she saw Tony's car parked up and nearly burst out crying there and then. Her legs, which were beyond tired, now got a new lease of life, and she sprinted all the way to the front door. She threw it open.

"Tony? Tony?" she shouted.

"Lana?" Tony came out of the living room and she ran at him.

He lifted her high into the air and held her tight against him. She buried her face in his neck.

"Thank God, thank God. Where have you been? Where's Collie?" he asked and put her down.

"We have to call the police. We have to. They've got Collie," Lana said.

"What do you mean? After you called, I drove up here. They said you'd gone camping. Collie texted me."

"They're liars," Lana said. "They took me. I think they've taken Collie too."

"Who?"

Lana didn't know exactly. "The people who live here. The villagers."

"Jesus. That text, I knew there was something wrong with it. That's why I hung around—that's why I came here. But you didn't come back this morning, and Collie's car is still parked out there."

"We didn't go camping," Lana said.

"I know that now. Collie thought someone was watching her—watching you both. She was right," Tony said.

Lana nodded. "We have to leave."

"We have to go to the police."

"Yes, but—" Lana broke off. She heard gravel crunching as a vehicle came up the drive.

Go. Now.

"Tony, we have to leave." Lana pulled on his hand.

"Someone's coming up the drive."

The back door. Circle round and back into the woods.

Lana nodded and pulled on his hand. "This way." She was relieved when he followed her without question. "We have to go back into the woods."

Tony pulled Lana up as they got to the back door. "Not so fast, Lana Banana. Get behind me."

Tony eased open the door, and Lana peeked around his waist. It was full dark now, and she could hear footsteps crunching in the gravel. More than one set. The garden gate squealed.

"Shut up," someone whispered.

"I can't help it."

"You go round that side. You—go round the other. I'll go through the front."

Lana felt Tony's arm reach round and pull her against his back. He shuffled forward slightly. He'd heard them too.

You have to go now.

"We have to go now," Lana whispered.

Tony turned and knelt. He held her shoulders. "Lana. Here." He reached into his pocket and pulled out his phone. He pressed it into her hand. "When I say so, you run into the woods. Keep running. Find somewhere with a signal, and call the police. Okay?"

Lana shook her head. Tears welled, and she could feel her bottom lip starting to tremble. "No. You have to come too."

Tony reached out and brushed Lana's hair behind her ear. "Lana, you need to do what I say now. We don't have time to argue."

Do what he says.

No.

Lana.

Lana always listened to her mum, and she wouldn't stop now. Not when it would mean going against Tony too.

Lana nodded.

"Good." Tony stood. He gently guided Lana out in front of him.

Lana looked to the path that led round to the front of the house. Someone was there. A scarecrow. At first, Lana didn't understand, her brain couldn't make the connection. Then it looked up at her and she screamed.

"Lana, run," Tony shouted and pushed her aside as he ran towards the scarecrow. "What the fuck have you come as?" she heard him say just before the scarecrow lifted something above its head. Something that shone and glittered in the moonlight.

Run, Lana. Run now.

Then Lana's brain engaged, and her feet got moving. She darted past Tony and the scarecrow and heard someone—one of them—cry out before she was back in the woods, back in the dark.

CHAPTER FIFTY-TWO

Everything was going wrong. Never in all its years had this happened before. It stalked through the woods, not even enjoying the sudden silence of the night animals who quivered and shook at its passing.

It was this other. Meddling in what wasn't its concern. And who was it? *What* was it? From the beginning it had sensed this other there, and it could do nothing to make it go away, to mind its business. And now, look. Its sacrifice, its fun—all gone.

Those fools couldn't do one simple thing, couldn't do one easy task. And now it was out here doing *their* job when it should be getting ready for the Spring Fair. But if it didn't do something, then there would *be* no Spring Fair.

Those stupid, useless villagers would pay after it was over, though—well, the ones who hadn't already paid.

Now it lowered itself closer to the ground and breathed in the dirt, searching. There. There they were. It felt a measure of relief that it found them. It stood back up and moved further into the woods where the moon didn't reach.

❖

"We're lost," Emily said and stopped. She sat down on a fallen tree. They'd been walking for what felt like hours.

Collie turned to face her. Not that Emily could make out much more than a vague shape. This deep in the woods there wasn't even moonlight to guide them.

"I'm not sure what to do now. Any ideas? I have to get to the stones," Collie said and came to sit next to Emily on the tree.

"I know you do. But I don't remember which way they are. I wish I had my bloody phone on me," Emily said.

Collie dropped her head and clasped her hands in front of her. Was she praying? Emily thought she was.

"How's that going to help?" Emily asked but Collie didn't answer her.

Great. Although, Emily guessed they didn't really have any other ideas, did they? They were well and truly lost, and time was not on their side.

Emily sat quietly and waited. Eventually, Collie shifted beside her and looked up.

"Well?" Emily asked.

"I know which way," Collie said.

"What?"

"I said I know the way," Collie said.

"And you got that from praying?"

Collie laughed. "Not exactly. Come on."

Collie held out her hand, and Emily took it. Emily could barely see Collie in this light, and yet she knew she was smiling. Since that *thing* had come to her yesterday, Emily found herself spending all her energy on trying not to think about anything except getting out of Hyam. Every time thoughts of her brother threatened to break into her thoughts, she pushed them away. And now here she was, thinking about how Collie had come for her instead of tearing out of that house at full speed. The way she felt about Collie—which was already more than she wanted to feel—bloomed, and Emily realized she might be falling in love. Shit. Great timing.

Emily grasped Collie's hand and allowed herself to be pulled to her feet. "You'd better actually know the way, Collie."

"Yes, I'd better," Collie mumbled and led Emily even further in the woods.

It waited in the dark. It could hear them coming. When it realized what direction they were headed, it had circled round and doubled back. Now it waited. Everything inside it wanted to tear them apart when they appeared, but it wouldn't. It would wait because it had to wait.

But when it was finally allowed to rip them apart, it would do it slowly and with more pleasure than it ever had before. It hated them. It had never hated anything more than those two.

It preyed on people because that was what it did, what it had always done, and would continue to always do. It took pleasure in it, in their fear and pain, but it had never hated any of them—not as individuals. It despised these weak, pathetic, short-lived humans, but until tonight it had never hated them. These two would die in agony and madness.

❖

Lana crashed through the woods with the sound of screams chasing her. She prayed it wasn't Tony, but she couldn't tell, and she mustn't think about it. Something's feet pounded the ground behind her, and it was getting closer.

Her lungs burned, and her heart pounded in her chest. She felt like she must have run miles today and would have given anything to just stop. Except she couldn't. Tony had sacrificed himself for her, and she had to keep running as long and as fast as she could.

Lana could barely see a metre in front of her, but she ran like she could see for miles. She jumped fallen branches and ditches and didn't stop, couldn't stop, even though her lungs were bursting.

The pounding feet behind her were close now, so close. Of course they were—she was small and they were much bigger—but she ran anyway. The voice of her mother was silent, and Lana wished it would come back. But there were lots of things she couldn't have, and so she ran.

A few moments later, he grabbed her.

❖

The feeling of being watched was back. Emily tugged the back of Collie's T-shirt to make her stop.

"What?" Collie asked.

Emily leaned in close to Collie's ear. "It's watching us."

"I know," Collie whispered back.

"What do we do?" Emily could feel the blood rushing in her ears as she remembered what it said to her back in the basement.

"It can't catch us both," Collie said. She pulled Emily close. "I shouldn't ask this, but I will. If you're the one who gets away, please help my niece. Please."

Emily nodded. "I will. I promise. This is the only way, isn't it? For us to split up and hope it can't catch both of us?"

Collie nodded and hugged her. "Keep running in the direction we were headed. It's not much further at all to the stones. But be careful—I think they're all assembling there."

"Collie, you know, if things were different, I think I might fall in love with you," Emily said.

Collie smiled. "I know what you mean. I feel the same. You'd be easy to love, Emily."

"Good luck, Collie."

"Good luck, Emily. Maybe see you again."

Emily smiled in the dark. "You never know. Ready?"

"Yes."

Emily ran left and was vaguely aware of Collie going right. She heard something come crashing out of the undergrowth and waited for it to bring her down.

She pumped her legs and her arms and prayed there was nothing out here to trip her because she couldn't see a thing.

Emily turned to the right and kept running. She couldn't afford to stray too far from the path. She hoped she might be able to go around in a circle or something.

Soon, her lungs gave out, and she slowed to a jog. She believed she'd doubled back around and was still on the right path.

Emily pushed through some trees, and there it was in front of her. It was huge, even standing on all fours. Its red eyes blazed out of the blackness.

Emily stumbled backwards and tripped. She fell down, and now the *thing* loomed over her, larger than ever. It smelled of dampness and rotting meat, and Emily gagged as it came closer.

Its front legs were thick and ropy with muscle, and its claws would tear her to pieces. Its mouth was crammed with teeth like razor blades, and the numbness Emily had been feeling disappeared and was replaced with utter terror.

She had never imagined anything so grotesque or so unhuman. That's how she thought of it, *unhuman*, as though it was from another planet. Another world.

"What now?" Emily managed to croak out.

Behind her twigs snapped and bushes rustled. She daren't look behind her. It was as if she was holding this *thing* off with her eyes, and if she looked away, it would fall on her and destroy her.

"Emily." Emily recognized the voice but couldn't immediately place it. "Don't be foolish. Just come with us."

"Or what?" Emily said.

The *thing* growled low in its throat. Its elongated snout rose up and into the air.

"Do you really need me to tell you?" the voice asked. Margaret. It was Margaret from the shop. "And if you think about doing what you did earlier, you'll find yourself quickly dealt with this time."

Emily sighed. She stood up. It was not over yet, but running wouldn't be the best decision right now. That *thing* would tear her limb from limb.

The *thing* backed away and melted into the night. At least that was gone, but Emily didn't imagine it had gone far.

She turned to face Margaret, who was flanked by two men Emily didn't recognize. One of them reached out and grabbed her arm, and she spat in his face.

"Get your fucking hands off me," she said.

He slapped her hard in the face, and she fell back down, her cheek on fire.

"Don't mark her up too much," Margaret told the man. "She's already in a bloody state that's going to be hard to fix up. Just take hold of her, and let's get going. We don't have long."

Emily allowed them to drag her off the ground and out of the woods. She watched and she waited for an opportunity to get away again. She held on to the fact that Collie must have got away. If that *thing* came for Emily, then Collie *must* have got away.

CHAPTER FIFTY-THREE

Lana shrank back against the stake behind her. All around her, people danced, drank, ate, and laughed. Lots of them were dressed as scarecrows—this village was obsessed with scarecrows.

Fires were lit in pits they'd dug in the ground, and a pig roasted on an open spit. Lana watched as villagers greeted each other, hugged each other, and their children chased each other around the stones.

Lana watched and wondered if she was the one who'd lost her mind. If not for the rope keeping her tied to this wood thing, she wouldn't have guessed anything was wrong. Lana pinched her own wrist just to make sure she wasn't dreaming.

The whole situation had the quality of a dream, and Lana felt her mind slipping the mooring of reality.

Lana hadn't seen Tony or Collie or Emily since she'd been here, and she was half expecting them to be tied to the stones over in the clearing. She was sort of hoping because that meant they were still alive somewhere.

Now she accepted that maybe they weren't. That she'd lost them just like she'd lost her mother and her father before she'd even formed a memory of him. Still, she might only be a kid, but she knew tonight wasn't going to end well for her, and although she was scared, she wondered if it might be better than living without any of the people she loved.

From somewhere, a drum started up. One of the people dressed as a scarecrow had it strapped around their neck and chest, and they banged it loudly. Lana thought something must be about to happen.

The other scarecrows began doing cartwheels, handstands, and backflips, and people clapped and cheered in time. Lana looked about for what had got them all excited, and then she saw it.

Lana was relieved and terrified at the same time. There were Tony and Emily. They were both tied by the neck on a long rope and being pulled into the fair, towards the circle and away from the edge of the woods where she was tied. But where was Collie?

Lana started to cry.

❖

Emily allowed herself to be led without a fight. She recognized the man tied to the rope with her.

"Hi, Tony. How's it going?" Emily said. The rope pulled and rubbed at her neck, but her hands were tied in front of her so she couldn't pull it away.

"Groovy. I feel like I'm in the fucking Twilight Zone. Have you seen Collie?" he asked.

He was limping heavily and the front of his shirt was dark with what Emily guessed was blood.

"About half an hour ago," Emily said. "We were separated in the woods. I'm praying she got away."

Except that wasn't looking likely, was it? If she had, wouldn't the police be here by now? Unless of course she got lost again. It was easy to do here.

"Do you know what's happening?" Tony asked.

"No." But Emily thought she had an idea. She thought if Tony really considered it, he'd have a good idea too.

"It looks like a fucking party. There's those scarecrows. One of them got me, back at the house," Tony said.

"Me too. At mine," Emily said.

"Why do you think they dress like that?" Tony asked. "What's the point?"

"To scare us, of course. They're scarecrows, remember?" Emily said.

The woman leading them on the rope pulled it harder. "Less talking, more moving."

The woman led them through the trees. Emily could hear the sound of drums and laughing and shouting. It was going to be a regular party then.

Whatever happens, you won't scream. You won't scream or show you're afraid. If you're going to die, you'll do it with dignity.

They walked into a field, the same field she'd visited with Hamish what seemed like a lifetime ago. This time the stones were lit by the fires that burned. Emily wondered if the weather had been dry enough to make the whole place catch light. But that would be too easy.

Emily and Tony were dragged into the centre of the stones, and each end was tied around one of the stones and pulled taut. Emily felt the rope push into her neck and resisted the urge to gag on it.

One of the scarecrows bounded into the centre and mimed tying a rope around his neck and choking. The gathering crowd laughed.

Emily looked around and recognized most of the faces assembled. Children from her class and their parents. Shopkeepers and other faces she couldn't put a name to. It looked like everyone was here. The whole shitting village. Bastards.

The drum started up again, furious and pounding. It made Emily's blood beat in time.

A loud cheer went up, and the crowd parted. Emily found she wasn't at all surprised when Frances Cobb walked into the circle with her niece, Anthea.

They treated her like a queen, and Anthea was a princess, bowing and scraping and fawning all over her.

"Emily," Frances Cobb said.

"Frances. Can't say I'm surprised to see you. I assume you're behind all this nonsense," Emily said.

"You can believe it's nonsense if you want to, Emily, but you'll soon see it has very real consequences for you."

"You. All of you are disgusting. You take care of this...this *monster*, this mark-stepper. Why?" Emily asked.

"The Bargus takes care of this village. All it asks in return is a little sacrifice." Frances Cobb smiled, and it was a cold and humourless thing.

"You're all sick. Sacrifice me if you want to, but you'll be found out," Emily said.

Frances Cobb laughed. "I don't think so, dear. We haven't yet, and it's been *centuries*. Besides, don't flatter yourself that you're the sacrifice. No, you and this chap beside you are the entertainment. The sacrifice is over there."

Emily craned her neck to look where Frances Cobb was pointing but couldn't see what she was pointing at. Then Tony cried out and pulled so hard on the rope that they both fell to the ground.

"No," he screamed over and over again. "No. Take me, have me, but let her go. I beg you. Please. She's just a child."

Lana. It was Lana. Emily knew it would be, but still. Knowing it and actually *knowing* it were two different things.

She closed her eyes. The one thing Collie asked her to do. And she'd failed. They would all die here like Charlie, and no one would know what happened to them. No one at all.

"Frances, she's just a baby. Let her go. Me and Tony will be enough for you. We'll scream and be terrified and do everything you want. Please," Emily said.

"You've changed your tune. But there's no point begging. It's done. This is how it's always been and how it will always be."

"Anthea," Emily tried. "Please, Anthea. Make her see sense. I'm begging you."

"Sorry, no can do, amigo. This is the way it's always been, just like she said. And it's my coming of age, so I really, really, really, *really* want it to happen. You're the entertainment, and that kid is the sacrifice."

"You bitch." Tony rocketed to his feet and lunged at Frances Cobb. Emily was dragged with him and flung back with him when the rope rebounded.

Emily thought her neck had probably lost most of the skin on it, but that was the least of her worries.

Frances Cobb laughed. "Oh, you're going to be so much fun. Now, the rules. We'll release you and give you a five-minute head start. After that, we all come for you. Not with pitchforks but definitely a lot of villagers."

Emily looked at her. "Like a hunting party."

"Exactly. And you two are the foxes. And I do hope you run. Your brother was excellent, but the other one he was with froze like a deer, and it was no sport at all," Frances Cobb said.

"You're a monster," Emily said.

"You only just realized?" Frances said and stepped back. She turned her face up to the moon and let out a howl that made every hair on Emily's body stand up.

Frances Cobb shook her head once, twice, and bent forward with her hands on her knees.

Emily watched as her body seemed to lengthen and grow. Her clothes ripped.

Beside her, Anthea clapped her hands and laughed with delight.

"What's happening?" Tony asked.

Emily looked at him and opened her mouth but couldn't make any words come out.

Frances Cobb let out another howl as her face stretched, her jaw appeared to dislocate, and her mouth filled with vicious, sharp teeth.

This couldn't be happening. It *couldn't* be. Werewolves or Barguses or whatever the fuck Frances Cobb was? Did. Not. Exist.

Emily couldn't look away from the transformation. Frances Cobb—or whatever she was now—turned her face—snout—up to the moon and howled long and loud, and Emily wanted to scream.

Then she turned and raced off into the darkness.

"Well, that *never* gets old," Anthea said, full of joy.

She's mad. She's completely mad. So is Frances, but she hides it well.

"Right. Best not to dilly-dally. You heard what she said. You get five minutes, and then we come for you. And *then* the sacrifice and I turn for the first time. So exciting. Release them." Anthea clapped her hands and stepped back.

Emily felt the rope slacken and then fall away as someone cut it. Her hands were next, and she rubbed the blood back into them. Tony was standing with his head down, breathing hard. He didn't appear to react to any of it. Emily wondered if he'd completely checked out. But when he looked up at her, she could see that wasn't it at all. His face was set, jaw tight, and his eyes blazed.

"When you hear the horn, that's your signal to start running. And you'd better run, because we've got some chasers who are pretty quick on their feet." Anthea grinned and winked at Emily.

A horn blasted out and split the air. Emily didn't wait, nor did Tony. They ran. It turned out they had the same idea because they both ran towards where Lana was tied. It didn't take long for them to both see she'd gone.

CHAPTER FIFTY-FOUR

Collie crept through the undergrowth towards the stake her niece was tied to.

Sasha guided her there, and by now Collie was used to her sister talking in her head, and talking back to her.

You're sure this is going to work? Collie said in her mind.

No. But it's all we've got left. Things haven't exactly gone to plan.

Well, excuse me. It's not like I had the whole fucking village and some monstrous werewolf from a horror film against me.

I wasn't having a go at you, Collie. You're still alive, aren't you? And so's my daughter for now, so get a bloody move on.

Collie continued to fight her way through the undergrowth while Sasha grumbled in her ear. Under other circumstances, it might even have been nice. As it was, it was pitch-black, and there was a monster on the loose.

In the distance, Collie heard the thumping, tuneless pounding of drums start up.

Hurry, Collie.

I am hurrying.

Now Collie could see fire, dancing and twinkling through the trees and bushes. She was almost there.

Lana should be right up ahead.

Collie reached the edge of the wood and could see the clearing beyond where people dressed as scarecrows cavorted. People danced and ate and drank in some horrible parody of a party.

Collie could just about make out Emily and—shit, was that Tony?—in the middle of the stones. She looked to the left and saw Lana, right on the edge of the clearing, like she was tempting the night creatures to go those few extra steps and take her.

Without pausing to think things through, Collie started to hurry out of the woods.

No, Collie, not yet.

What do you mean? I have to get her, Sasha.

Yes, but not yet. In a moment, when they aren't watching her.

Who's watching her? Those fuckers are all having a great time.

No. Look. To the left.

Collie looked, and sure enough, Sasha was right. Partially hidden by the shadows and a large tree, one person wasn't joining in with the revelry. They were watching the woods.

They're watching for me, aren't they?

You and anyone else who doesn't belong. Give it a moment, when things really get going, and then you can go.

Collie waited. She watched the watcher, who she was certain couldn't see her. *How about that, you psychopath. I'm watching you.*

Collie sat back on her heels and waited. She wondered if she'd be able to get to Emily and Tony too. No. That was too big a task. She'd get Lana to safety, and then she'd come back for them and pray it wasn't too late.

And if it was? Well, she would have to live with that choice, wouldn't she? The choice she'd made to let her best friend and a woman she was starting to love die. She chose Lana, and she thought Emily and Tony would understand that. If she could, she'd trade her own life for all three of them, and if the opportunity came to do just that, she would, without hesitation. Right now, there wasn't even a choice to be made.

Emily and Tony were surrounded by a whole village, while Lana was here, on the outskirts of the clearing, seemingly unguarded, though Collie knew better. She seemed like…bait. Bait for Collie? Probably. But this was also part of the ritual Collie had seen on the tapestry. Two birds, one stone she guessed.

Get ready, Collie. It's almost time.

Collie got into a loose runner's stance with one leg beneath her and the battered fingers of both hands resting on the mud.

Collie watched the watcher. Then it came. The villagers surged towards the stones. The watcher took two steps in that direction, then stopped.

He wants to go. He knows he can't, but he wants to go.

A huge cheer went up, and the watcher moved forward another few paces. He turned to watch whatever was going on in the crowd.

I think this is the best we're going to get, Collie said in her mind.

I agree. Go.

Collie was up and off on the word *go*. Keeping low to the ground, she reached the stake Lana was tied to.

"Don't look at me, Lana. Don't move. Act like everything's the same. I'm going to untie you."

For her part, Lana didn't look at Collie, and she didn't speak.

Collie used her teeth and her abused hands to untie the ropes from Lana's wrists. At last, they came free.

"Okay, let's go," Collie said.

"But Tony and Emily," Lana said.

"I'm sorry, baby, we have to go. I have to get you to safety," Collie said and took Lana's hand. She pulled her towards the woods.

"We can't leave them," Lana said, pulling away.

Collie turned and knelt then. She held Lana by her small shoulders. "You think I want to? You think I'm happy about it? I have no choice, Lana. None at all." Collie realized she was squeezing too hard. "Shit. I'm sorry. Shit."

Lana threw herself into Collie's arms. "I'm sorry. I know you don't. I know you're trying to save me. I just..."

"I know. We have to go, Lana," Collie said.

She stood and took Lana's hand again just as a horn sounded.

"What was that?" Lana asked and squeezed Collie's hand.

"I don't know. We need to go." Collie pulled on Lana's hand, and this time she came willingly.

❖

As soon as Emily saw that Lana was no longer there, she veered to the left and took off into the woods. Tony was right on her heels.

She had no idea where she was running to, and underneath the terror of what was happening, she also felt a huge sense of relief. Lana was gone and hopefully safe.

Behind her, she heard the sound of feet crashing through the woods. Every now and then she caught sight of one coming up alongside them but not getting close.

There must have been tons of them—it felt like the whole village had given chase, and Emily wouldn't be surprised if they were. But they were supposed to give them a five-minute head start.

They're liars. What a shock.

"This way," Tony gasped and took her hand. He pulled her into a thick group of trees and to an embankment.

"Where are we going?" Emily asked.

"Haven't you noticed? They're herding us—or trying to. Let's go this way instead," Tony replied.

Emily hadn't noticed, but now that Tony mentioned it, it seemed unlikely that they were the fastest people here, and no one had caught them yet. And the villagers came up almost to their flanks. Yes, they were being herded.

"Okay. Lead the way," Emily said.

She followed Tony down the embankment and along the gulley, breathing hard. Emily was exhausted. She thought she was coming near to the end of her endurance. Part of her wanted to lie down and let those monsters she could hear chasing them have her.

But Emily was a fighter. She was a survivor, and she wasn't going down without a scrap.

Suddenly, Tony pulled up short, and she almost crashed into his back.

He turned to face her. "Can you hear that?"

"What?" Her tired brain tried to process what he was saying.

"Can you *hear* it? It's water."

"Water?" she said stupidly.

"Water. Come on." Tony took her hand and pulled her further towards the sound, and now she could hear it. Running water.

The dense woods opened out onto a fast-moving river. Now Emily remembered. She remembered walking here with Hamish. They'd walked down from the clearing and come to the river. She remembered him saying something...

What did he say?

That you wouldn't want to fall in there. The current would drag you under and drown you.

"Well?" Tony asked.

Emily looked at him. Behind her, she could hear the villagers getting closer. She could hear them laughing and calling and see the bobbing lights of their torches.

"Fuck it," she said to Tony. "I'd rather die this way and spoil their fun."

Tony laughed. He held up his hand and she gave him a high five. "Take my hand."

Emily took his hand.

Maybe I'll see you soon, Charlie. And I've missed you.

Together, they jumped.

CHAPTER FIFTY-FIVE

Collie felt Lana slowing. Of course she was slowing—she was running flat out, on a ten-year-old's legs.

Behind them, they could hear shouting and calling and laughing. She guessed it had something to do with Emily and Tony, and didn't want to think about it. Jesus, she really didn't. Every time she got close to it, she felt a crippling guilt.

"Collie, I can't." Lana gasped. "I can't run any more."

"I'll carry you." Collie scooped her up.

Lana shook her head and pushed away. "You can't. Not for long. And that thing's coming. It'll be looking for us."

Collie nodded. "Yes, and that's why we have to keep moving."

"How far are we?" Lana asked.

Collie went into her head. *Well, Sasha? How far?*

But Sasha was quiet now—if she'd ever been there at all. Maybe Collie had a brush with madness in that basement and imagined her.

It didn't matter. They had to keep moving.

"Lana, come on. We need to keep going for as long as we can."

"And if it finds us anyway?" Lana asked and sounded more weary than a ten-year-old should.

"Then I'll fight it. I'll do whatever it takes to keep you safe," Collie said and knew her words were hollow. What chance did she have against the thing she'd caught the briefest glimpse of in the woods when she'd been running with Emily?

"Okay." Lana started moving again, and Collie understood Lana was doing it for her, that she didn't really believe they were going to come out of this.

After a short while, Collie heard the sound of running water.

❖

Lana hadn't heard her mother's voice for a while now. She wondered if it had been there at all or if she'd just imagined it. Either way, it was gone, and Lana was reminded again of everything she'd lost.

Her legs ached, and her lungs burned, and she didn't think she could keep running for much longer.

She couldn't stop thinking about Tony and Emily, back there in the clearing. She understood why Collie couldn't help them—she'd wanted to keep Lana safe. But that gave Lana a huge feeling of guilt. It was because of *her* they were still back there, having who knew what done to them.

Lana thought about Kitty's mum. She couldn't bring herself to feel bad about that—or about Kitty's dad. They'd *wanted* to hurt her or at least let someone else hurt her. She'd had no choice. She'd done what her mother told her to.

Suddenly, Collie stopped, and Lana crashed into the back of her. "Ow."

"Sorry, Lana. Can you hear that?" Collie asked.

"No, what?" Lana asked.

"Water. Running water. Isn't there a river somewhere in Hyam?" Collie was looking around, and she looked excited.

"Yeah, we learned it in school. It's the River Woden or something. It goes really far, and it's not in Hyam exactly. It's right on the edge, more in Five Elms—"

"Okay, Lana. I think it's over there," Collie said.

"You want to get in it?" Lana asked.

"No, not in it. But maybe we can walk alongside it. That…that *thing* probably won't be able to follow our scent in water. Will it?" Collie asked.

"Because of that film we watched the other week?" Lana asked.

It was about a fugitive being tracked by a man and his dog. Lana wasn't sure about how true to life films were.

"Well, yeah. I mean, at least it might make it harder," Collie said.

"I don't think so. Aren't there those dogs who can track anyone, anywhere?" Lana asked.

"Yeah but this isn't a dog. It's a…a…I don't know what it is, but it's all we've got, Lana. I can't think of anything else," Collie said.

Lana couldn't see her aunt's face fully because of the dark, but she could hear in her voice how tired she was.

"Let's try," Lana said and took Collie's hand. "I think the sound is coming from this way."

Lana led Collie through some trees and down a slight incline. At the bottom, she could see water flowing, inky black and moving fast.

"There's not much room, Lana. Get behind me and hold on to my jeans. We'll try and shuffle along without falling in."

Lana reached out and grabbed the top of Collie's jeans. They shuffled along a few paces before they heard the sound of something crashing through the bushes.

Then it appeared. The Bargus. It stood so tall that Lana had to tilt her head all the way back to see it.

Grandma, what red eyes you have.

It was panting, and ropy spit hung from its huge mouth.

It wants me. It only wants me.

Lana glanced behind her at the water. So black. So fast. Then she looked back at the Bargus.

Will you follow me in there?

"Lana, stay behind me," Collie said as she fumbled around in her pocket.

Mum, if you were with me before, please be with me now.

I'm here, darling.

I'm scared to do this.

I know, but it's the only way.

Lana nodded.

She turned.

She jumped into—

The water. It's so cold.

Distantly, she heard Collie's and the Bargus's cries mingle together. Then she was twisting and turning in the frigid water. She fought to keep her head up, but the current kept dragging her down. Soon, she knew, she wouldn't have the strength to come back up.

Mum!

I'm here. Fight, Lana. Fight to stay above the water.

I'm trying. But it's so cold.

I know. But try.

Lana wanted to. She wanted to do what her mother told her, but she couldn't. She'd been running for a long time, and she was very tired. She went under again, and this time, she didn't fight to come back up.

❖

Collie dived into the water. Christ, but it was cold. The current was so strong that she could barely keep her head up. She pistoned her legs and forced them to carry her along, carry her to Lana.

Behind her, she heard a loud, heavy splash, and she knew the Bargus was in the water with her.

She dared not turn around in case she lost sight of Lana, who was being dragged up the river. Lana kept being pulled down and coming back up. Collie wondered how much longer she could fight the current.

Collie thought she'd used all her strength running from the Bargus, but it turned out that she had a ton more. Her arms and legs burned with the effort, and she knew the river wanted nothing more than to drag her down.

Behind her, she heard splashing and knew the Bargus was closing in. Collie prepared to feel those claws like knives rake down her back or take her head off. Neither happened. The Bargus went right past her. Right past her to Lana.

❖

This was not the plan. All along it had felt a force working against it—the other. It should have dealt with it, should have paid closer attention. Maybe it had become arrogant in its old age, complacent. But if it had, then so had the villagers who were sworn to serve it, and they would pay for their mistakes too.

Without the girl, it could not renew itself, it could not help Anthea transform. It had never swum, though it had a vague notion it could. Not very well because its body wasn't designed for it. But what other choice did it have? And it *could* swim. Couldn't it?

The Bargus jumped into the river after the girl. The cold didn't bother it at all, but its thick fur quickly became weighed down with the water. It struggled to move its arms and legs. They were built to run and chase and tear and gouge, so its legs—much shorter than its arms—couldn't kick properly, and the talons on the ends of its arms couldn't scoop the water.

Nevertheless it was gaining on them. It would grab the girl, then swim to shore. As it reached the woman, it was tempted to reach out and rip her head off, but that would slow it down, and the girl was drowning, and she was no good to it dead.

The Bargus swam past the woman and left her alone. Let the current take care of what it didn't have time for.

❖

Collie saw the Bargus swim awkwardly past her. She knew exactly where it was headed, and she had to stop it. Even if that meant dying, she had to try. It couldn't get to Lana.

Lana's drowning. You have to get to Lana.

Yes, I know. But first I have to get past the Bargus.

Hurry, Collie.

I'm doing my best, Sasha. Any ideas on how to get past it?

Your amulet cut through metal before. Do you still have it?

The amulet, of course. Collie risked reaching down to her pocket. There, it was still there. With only one arm pushing against the current, she was dragged under. Collie pushed back up, gasped for air, and swam on.

The Bargus was getting away from her, getting closer to Lana, and no matter how hard she swam, Collie couldn't keep up.

You have to, Collie. You have to.

She was so tired. With one last mighty effort, Collie propelled herself forward in the water. She was nearly there.

Then Lana went under. And she didn't come back up.

No, no, no. Sasha, help me. Help me now.

No answer. Collie surged forward again. Then the Bargus went under too. Collie found herself praying it would bring Lana back up. Lana was no good to it if she was dead.

But the Bargus didn't come back up either.

Collie pumped her arms and legs and forced her body to move her onward. She ignored her screaming legs and arms. She reached the spot where she had last seen them and ducked under the water.

She saw the Bargus immediately—it was reaching for Lana. Lana was struggling to get away from it—

Thank God, she's still alive.

Collie kicked her legs and, as she got close, pulled the amulet out of her pocket. She slashed at the Bargus, who still had its back to her.

The amulet slid through the Bargus's fur and flesh easily. Blood poured from the wound. Collie struck again, this time slicing just under its neck. Skin flapped, revealing meaty muscle.

The Bargus turned in the water to face her. It reached for her, its wicked claws extending towards her.

Collie pushed at it with her legs and propelled herself to the surface. On her way up, she felt it sink its claws into her leg, and bright pain spots danced behind her eyes. She managed to gulp down some air before she was dragged back under.

Collie slashed out with the amulet as soon as she was pulled back down.

She caught the Bargus full in the face, bringing the amulet up and over its eye. The eye burst, and its long, wolflike ear was severed.

The Bargus howled and struck out at her again. Collie twisted away, but not before it caught her back. Collie wasn't sure how deep it got her, but the pain was immense. She needed to finish the Bargus now, before it tore her apart.

As Collie kicked her legs to bring herself back around to face it, the Bargus came towards her.

It's expecting you to swim away.

So I'll swim towards it.

Collie gave one final push, everything she had, and launched herself at the Bargus.

They met in a clatter of bodies that took the wind out of Collie. She brought the amulet up between their bodies.

The Bargus reared back and opened its mouth.

It means to bite my head off.

As it bore down, all teeth and flapping flesh, Collie reached up one final time and slashed the amulet across its throat.

Collie felt the Bargus bite down, somewhere near the side of her face, and a terrible, agonizing heat burst out.

Collie loosened her grip on the Bargus, unsure if she had got it or not—praying she had.

You did. You got it, Collie. It's dead, or as good as. You saved Lana. Thank you, Collie.

I love you, Sasha. I miss you so much, and I love you.

I love you, Collie.

Collie battled to stay conscious, but it was no good. She had done all she could, and she could do no more. She thought she was probably dying, and that was okay. Sasha said the Bargus was dead.

Collie closed her eyes and let the current pull her deeper.

Chapter Fifty-six

It was Tony who wanted to follow the river. And it was Tony who thought he heard someone calling. Emily thanked God he had because now Emily could hear it too.

When they'd jumped into the river, Emily was convinced they were dead. After the news about Charlie, she wasn't sure she minded all that much. But while she was in there, fighting to stay above water, Emily realized she did want to live. And not only that, she wanted to see Collie and Lana and even Tony again. She wanted to see her family again.

She'd put her life on hold to find out what happened to her brother, and now she knew. And it would be an affront to Charlie's memory if she just gave up and let herself drown.

Emily kicked her legs but rested and let the fast-moving river carry her along sometimes. It wasn't long before trees began to line the banks thickly, and some of those trees hung over the riverbank, gently dunking their branches in. Emily also noticed the river had started to slow. Instead of a raging, twisting, churning violence, it became slower and calmer and less inclined to drag her under.

Ahead of her, Tony grabbed a branch and reached out his hand for her to take. "Grab it, Emily. I'll pull us out."

She did and he did, and they sat on the soggy bank and caught their breath. Thank God, the weather was still mild enough not to totally freeze them. Emily's teeth still chattered, though.

"Well, that was quite a ride," Tony said and shook the water off his bald head.

"Wasn't it? I genuinely thought we might die," Emily said.

"Could have gone either way. At least—"

"What?" Emily asked.

"That. Can you hear it?"

"No."

"Splashing," Tony said. "I hear splashing."

Emily strained her ears. "I think I hear something."

"Maybe it's Collie and Lana? They escaped before us, but they probably ran through the woods for longer. Maybe they went into the water near to where we did."

Tony sounded hopeful. But honestly, what were the chances? Their best hope was that Collie and Lana had made it through the woods, because a ten-year-old in those waters…

Then Emily heard it. Someone shouting for help. Lana.

"Lana?" Emily shouted, not caring who heard.

"Lana?" Tony joined in, obviously deciding, like her, it was worth the risk of someone hearing. After all, protecting Lana had been the point.

The moon sat high in the night sky and reflected off the water in a way that gave some visibility. And Emily saw her. Lana. Bobbing up and down in the water, waving her arms. She kept going under.

"She must be exhausted, Ton—"

But Tony was gone with a splash. Emily slid further down the bank. She watched Tony swim out into the river and catch hold of Lana. But where was Collie?

Look to the right.

Emily did as the foreign, alien voice in her head instructed and made out a shape in the water. It wasn't moving except where it was being carried along by the current.

"Collie!" she screamed.

Emily dived into the river. Every muscle in her body was aching, but she barely noticed it. She had to get to Collie.

Emily pumped her arms and legs, and soon, she drew alongside Collie. She rolled her over in the water. Collie wasn't moving.

No. No.

It *wasn't* going to end like this.

Emily half swam, half dragged Collie back to shore. The burden in her arms was eased when Tony took over and pulled Collie from the water.

Emily climbed out after them.

"Is she breathing?" Emily asked, afraid of the answer.

"No." Tony bent down over her and began to perform CPR. Nearby, Lana wept softly.

"She saved me. She saved me," Lana whispered.

Emily crouched down beside Tony. "Tell me when you want me to take over," she said.

Tony nodded.

Breathe, Collie, please breathe.

Emily focused on Collie's face and tried to will the life back into her. She stroked back the hair from Collie's head and saw a nasty wound there. The Bargus had taken half of Collie's ear off. Lucky it wasn't her whole head.

"You go," Tony said, panting.

Without missing a beat, Emily quickly took over. She tried to force the life back into Collie.

"Please, Collie. Please breathe," Emily said as she pushed against her chest. After a moment, Collie took in a deep, shuddering breath and began to cough.

"Roll her over, roll her over," Tony shouted.

Between the two of them, they turned Collie onto her side and waited while she vomited the river water up.

Emily felt Lana press against her back and reached round to hold her. "She's okay, Lana. She's okay."

Collie heaved again, then rolled onto her back with her eyes closed.

"She's probably lost a lot of blood. We need to get an ambulance," Emily said.

Suddenly, there was a loud crashing. Something was coming through the trees.

Oh no, not again. I don't have the strength.

Tony got to his feet and assumed what looked like a boxer's stance. Emily pushed Lana behind her and tried to shield the child's body with her own.

"What the bloody hell is going on here?" The woman's voice reached them before she did. Then she stepped out of the woods. Except it wasn't a wood, not really. More a small copse of trees and behind it, up an incline, was a house.

"You woke me up with all your shouting and splashing around," the woman continued.

"My friend," Tony said, dropping his stance. "She went into the water. She needs an ambulance."

The woman looked down, and for the first time noticed Collie. She was breathing now, but that was about all.

"Shit. There's a phone up at the house. Come on," the woman said.

"Lana, Tony, you go. I'll wait here with her," Emily said.

Tony nodded and held out his hand for Lana.

"I don't want to leave her either," Lana said.

"You're freezing, and it's not safe out here. Go on. I promise I'll take care of her," Emily said.

Lana nodded and took Tony's hand. She looked back at Collie uncertainly before she disappeared into the woods with Tony and the woman.

Emily sat back on the cold, wet ground. She took off her hoodie and tried to make Collie a kind of pillow with it. There was no point draping it over Collie because it was soaked. Collie started to shiver.

Emily reached out and stroked her hair. "It's okay, Collie. Help's coming."

Collie's mouth twitched, and then her eyes slowly opened. Emily leaned over her and took her hand. "Lana?" Collie croaked.

"She's fine, she's safe," Emily said.

"You?"

"I'm fine, and Tony's fine. He's gone to call you an ambulance," Emily said.

"Don't need one," Collie said and struggled to sit.

Emily gently forced her back down. "No, you need to stay there. You need a hospital."

"I'm fine. What if…" Collie struggled to speak. "Villagers. What if they find us."

Emily glanced around, almost expecting them to come piling out of the woods. "No. I think they've got bigger things to worry about at the moment than finding us." At least, she hoped so.

"Hope you're right," Collie said.

"How are you feeling?" Emily asked.

Collie looked up at her, and they both started laughing.

"Sorry, stupid question," Emily said.

"You're all right. I'm feeling better than I did in the water," Collie said. "That Bargus got me pretty bad."

"Yeah. I can see. Did you…did you—"

"Kill it?" Collie asked. "I don't know. I think so. My sister said I did."

"Who?" Emily asked.

"Never mind," Collie said.

"Tell me."

"Back at the house. I think my sister spoke to me. Or maybe she didn't. Maybe it was all in my head, and I made it up to help me get through. God, I must sound mad."

"Collie, after what we've been through, I find myself able to believe your sister spoke to you and helped you. And even if it wasn't her, even if it was something you made up to get through, does it matter? You're alive. Lana's alive. We're all alive."

Collie nodded and closed her eyes. "Yeah. You're right. And I'm not hurting anyone by believing Sasha came back to me for a little while."

"No, you aren't." Emily wondered about the alien voice in her head that told her to look right when Lana was in the water. After everything that happened, she wasn't about to discount anything.

She looked down at Collie, who was slipping into sleep. "Collie? Collie, no, don't go to sleep."

"I'm tired…" came Collie's dreamy reply.

"I know, but you have to stay awake, just for a bit longer."

"Why? I don't have concussion," Collie said.

"We don't know what you have. Please, just stay awake for a bit longer."

But Collie was drifting off anyway. Emily did the only thing she could think of that might keep her awake. She leaned down and kissed her full on the mouth.

Collie's eyes flew open. Emily pulled back.

"What did you do that for?" Collie complained.

"I did it because you wouldn't stay awake," Emily said, feeling embarrassed.

"No, not why did you kiss me. Why did you stop?" Collie reached up and cupped the back of Emily's neck. She pulled Emily back down until their lips met.

This time, Emily pulled away. "We shouldn't. You're not well."

"I'm fine, I told you. Besides, it's the best way I know of to keep warm," Collie said and pulled Emily in for another kiss. This time, Emily didn't pull away. She sank into the warm, gentle kiss.

In the distance, she heard sirens, and they were getting closer. She deepened the kiss and smiled when Collie moaned.

They were alive. Somehow, they'd come through this. Charlie might be gone, but Emily wasn't. She was still very much alive, and Collie was still very much alive.

Emily did what she'd come here to do. Found out what happened to Charlie. Now she knew. What she hadn't expected was to find Collie and Lana. But she had, and she wasn't letting go. She was going to live her life exactly like Charlie would have wanted.

Emily heard more rustling in the bushes, but this time she wasn't afraid because the accompanying voices were Tony's and Lana's. They were talking to the ambulance crew.

Emily broke away from the kiss.

"Hey," Collie said.

"Don't worry. We can pick this up again later," Emily said.

"You'd better mean that," Collie grumbled.

"I do," Emily said. "We've got a lot of kissing ahead of us."

"Oh, good." Collie closed her eyes again, and this time Emily let her.

Epilogue

Collie didn't care if she looked like a desperate idiot. When she saw Emily's car swing onto the drive, she hobbled as fast as she could to the front door and threw it open.

Emily was barely out of the car when Collie shouted, "Well? Did they buy it?"

Emily laughed. "Get inside, Collie, before you freeze to death."

It was November and the first chill had started to fill the air and leave frost on the grass in the morning. Collie forgot how much colder it got in the country.

Collie stepped back and let Emily into the house. Her cheeks were red from the cold, and she had that pure, fresh outdoor night-time smell on her. Collie kissed her.

"Well? It's cruel to keep me in suspense," Collie said.

"Can I at least get in the door? It's a long drive from London," Emily said and brushed past.

"You're enjoying this. I'm an invalid, remember?" Collie said.

Emily laughed. "Yeah, right. I don't remember there being anything wrong with you the last time I was here."

Collie grinned. Emily was right. She was getting stronger every day. The Bargus had done some damage to her back which affected the nerves there, and her leg would never be the same, but it was healing. Now she could walk around indoors without her cane, and she hoped she'd be without it at all come spring. She was still without the top part of her right ear, but Emily didn't seem to mind, Lana thought she looked tough, and Tony said if she didn't already have a girl, it would definitely get her one.

All in all, Collie considered herself lucky to be here at all and even luckier to have come out of it with Lana and Emily and Tony.

"Right, so am I going to have to beg?" Collie asked.

"No, let's save that for the bedroom," Emily replied.

Collie laughed. "I swear, Emily, if you don't spill—"

"They bought it," Emily said.

"They did?"

"They did. They're sending the contracts by the end of the week," Emily said.

"Oh my God. That's brilliant!"

Collie wanted to pick Emily up and swing her around, but her leg wouldn't take it, so she settled for a hug and lingering kiss.

"Mmm," Emily said, breaking away. "That kiss promises things."

"It certainly does. But first, I want the blow-by-blow," Collie said and sat down on the sofa.

Emily huffed and rolled her eyes. "Tease." Then she smiled. "Fine. If you must know, they loved it. Obviously with all the legal stuff still ongoing, it can't be published until the trials are over, but they definitely want my book."

"That's brilliant. I'm so proud of you," Collie said.

"Thanks, that means a lot. Especially because it's so personal to you. Like I said before, if you change your mind about—"

"I won't," Collie said.

"But if you do—"

"I won't. Besides, you left out a lot of what happened."

"Yes. The book is more about how an entire village can be co-opted into ritualistic murder at the behest of one person."

"We know how."

"Yes, but in *my* book, Frances Cobb is just a woman. Not a Bargus."

"She's still someone who thinks like a human but chooses to act like a monster."

Emily nodded. "That's exactly who she was, regardless of what she was physically. She managed to convince a whole village to murder people, and for *years*."

"You don't say for centuries in your book, though."

"No."

"They found so many bodies. All around her house. I read they arrested another two villagers this morning," Collie said.

"There'll be more arrests as they find more bodies. The problem is, so many of the victims were homeless or rootless. It'll take a long time to identify them," Emily said.

"But now they have the chance. Because we stopped them." Collie took Emily's hand.

"Yes, we did. And they found Charlie," Emily said.

"Yes."

The last seven months had been tough for all of them. Lana still had nightmares, though those were slowly going away. For the first few months, Collie had been in hospital, and it seemed like the visits from police, lawyers, journalists, and psychiatrists didn't stop.

Tony and his girlfriend Karen had been amazing. They'd taken Lana for Collie until she was released. Lana loved Karen, and Collie could see why. She was exactly what Tony deserved—kind, thoughtful, and caring. Apparently her family loved Tony, so Collie thought they must be pretty sensible people. She'd joked with Tony the other day that there would be wedding bells, and Tony blushed, looked down, fumbled in his pocket, and showed Collie the ring.

It was beautiful. He planned to do it this weekend, and Collie was busy organizing the party for afterwards.

"Collie? Earth to Collie?" Emily said.

"Sorry, I was just thinking. Things have turned out okay, haven't they? In the end."

Emily nodded and leaned in to Collie. "They have. In the end. You know, I was thinking…"

"Oh yeah?"

"Yeah. I was thinking, it's silly for me to be going back and forth from London all the time. Especially now that I have the book to work on. That'll be a full-time job."

"It will. Lots of edits. Lots of stuff to write," Collie said. "And it's a long journey."

"It is a long journey. So maybe I should just, you know, move here," Emily said.

Collie felt her chest swell with happiness. She'd wanted to broach the subject with Emily, but she worried it was too soon—that, and the fact Emily said she wasn't ever living in the countryside again.

Strangely, when Collie was out of the hospital, and she and Lana were deciding what to do next, Lana had mentioned another village— except this one not filled with weirdos.

They'd done their research this time and found somewhere in Sussex. St John's Cross was about as different from Hyam as you could get. People were friendly and kind, and they'd both already made friends in the village. Collie loved it. But, more importantly, Lana loved it.

"Look, Collie, if you don't want to, or it's too soon, I understand." Emily sat up and was looking at her carefully.

Collie realized she'd let herself drift off again, and Emily must be thinking she'd moved too fast.

"No," Collie said and squeezed her hands. "I was just thinking how happy Lana and I are here. In fact, the only thing that could make us happier would be if you lived here with us."

"Really?" Emily asked.

"Really."

"Lana won't mind?"

"Lana's been badgering me to ask you for weeks. She only went to stay at Tony's overnight because I promised I'd ask you," Collie said.

"And because Tony probably promised her popcorn and a two a.m. bedtime."

"Oh God. He probably did. Karen will put the kibosh on that, though," Collie said.

"Are you sure it's not too soon?" Emily asked.

"It's not too soon. It's perfect. Today is a great day," Collie said and pulled Emily back into her arms.

"It is?" Emily rested her head on Collie's chest.

"It is. And this weekend when Tony proposes to Karen will top it all off," Collie said. "Now, we should go to bed, so I can make good on that promising kiss from earlier."

"Mmm," Emily said. "You do owe me."

"Come on."

They stood and went up to bed.

After they undressed, they slid beneath the sheets, and Collie pulled Emily to her. She never tired of the feel of Emily's body. Collie ran her hand down Emily's side and over her hip, so soft and smooth.

Emily raised her head and Collie kissed her. She stroked her hand over Emily's breasts and pulled gently on one nipple and then the other. Emily moaned into her mouth, and Collie rolled her onto her back, then covered Emily's body with hers.

Collie kissed her way down the silky column of Emily's neck and feathered kisses over her chest.

"Now, Collie," Emily whispered and pushed on Collie's shoulders.

Collie slid further down the bed until she rested between Emily's legs. She stroked Emily's thighs and parted her legs. Collie lowered her head to Emily's centre and kissed her there.

Emily moaned again and put her hand on the back of Collie's head. She pulled Collie against her. Collie took the hint and went to work. She licked and sucked and kissed until Emily's moans became breathy, and her hips bucked off the mattress as she drove herself into Collie's mouth over and over and then finally came.

Later, they lay side by side in the dark, and Collie thought how lucky she was. She still missed Sasha like crazy, but little by little the hurt was healing. She'd never stop missing her exactly, but it was becoming easier to think about her now.

Over the months, Collie had kept returning to that night in Hyam. At the time, she'd been convinced it was Sasha speaking to her, helping her. Now, more and more, Collie thought she'd imagined her. In her time of greatest need, she'd somehow managed to bring her sister back to her.

Either way, she'd kept Lana safe and, these days, didn't think she was doing such a horrible job of raising her. Not that it wasn't hard, and Collie didn't know what she'd do without Emily, Tony, and Karen helping her along the way.

She'd lost her sister, and Emily had lost her brother. But they'd found each other and made a new family with their friends. Collie didn't think she could ask for more.

She rolled towards Emily, and Emily, sensing Collie, reached out to her. Collie closed her eyes and slept.

About the Author

Eden Darry lives in London with her rescue cat. When she's not working or writing, she can be found among the weeds in her allotment, trying to make vegetables grow.

Books Available From Bold Strokes Books

Calumet by Ali Vali. Jaxon Lavigne and Iris Long had a forbidden small-town romance that didn't last, and the consequences of that love will be uncovered fifteen years later at their high school reunion. (978-1-63555-900-2)

Her Countess to Cherish by Jane Walsh. London Society's material girl realizes there is more to life than diamonds when she falls in love with a non-binary bluestocking. (978-1-63555-902-6)

Hot Days, Heated Nights by Renee Roman. When Cole and Lee meet, instant attraction quickly flares into uncontrollable passion, but their connection might be short-lived as Lee's identity is tied to her life in the city. (978-1-63555-888-3)

Never Be the Same by MA Binfield. Casey meets Olivia, and sparks fly in this opposites attract romance that proves love can be found in the unlikeliest places. (978-1-63555-938-5)

Quiet Village by Eden Darry. Something not quite human is stalking Collie and her niece, and she'll be forced to work with undercover reporter Emily Lassiter if they want to get out of Hyam alive. (978-1-63555-898-2)

Shaken or Stirred by Georgia Beers. Bar owner Julia Martini and home health aide Savannah McNally attempt to weather the storms brought on by a mysterious blogger trashing the bar, family feuds they knew nothing about, and way too much advice from way too many relatives. (978-1-63555-928-6)

The Fiend in the Fog by Jess Faraday. Can four people on different trajectories work together to save the vulnerable residents of East London from the terrifying fiend in the fog before it's too late? (978-1-63555-514-1)

The Marriage Masquerade by Toni Logan. A no-strings-attached marriage scheme to inherit a Maui B&B uncovers unexpected attractions and a dark family secret. (978-1-63555-914-9)

Flight SQA016 by Amanda Radley. Fastidious airline passenger Olivia Lewis is used to things being a certain way. When her routine is changed by a new, attractive member of the staff, sparks fly. (978-1-63679-045-9)

Home Is Where The Heart Is by Jenny Frame. Can Archie make the countryside her home and give Ash the fairytale romance she desires? Or will the countryside and small village life all be too much for her? (978-1-63555-922-4)

Moving Forward by PJ Trebelhorn. The last person Shelby Ryan expects to be attracted to is Iris Calhoun, the sister of the man who killed her wife four years and three thousand miles ago. (978-1-63555-953-8)

Poison Pen by Jean Copeland. Debut author Kendra Blake is finally living her best life until a nasty book review and exposed secrets threaten her promising new romance with aspiring journalist Alison Chatterley. (978-1-63555-849-4)

Seasons for Change by KC Richardson. Love, laughter, and trust develop for Shawn and Morgan throughout the changing seasons of Lake Tahoe. (978-1-63555-882-1)

Summer Lovin' by Julie Cannon. Three different women, three exotic locations, one unforgettable summer. What do you think will happen? (978-1-63555-920-0)

Unbridled by D. Jackson Leigh. A visit to a local stable turns into more than riding lessons between a novel writer and an equestrian with a taste for power play. (978-1-63555-847-0)

VIP by Jackie D. In a town where relationships are forged and shattered by perception, sometimes even love can't change who you really are. (978-1-63555-908-8)

Yearning by Gun Brooke. The sleepy town of Dennamore has an irresistible pull on those who've moved away. The mystery Darian Benson and Samantha Pike uncover will change them forever, but the love they find along the way just might be the key to saving themselves. (978-1-63555-757-2)

A Turn of Fate by Ronica Black. Will Nev and Kinsley finally face their painful past and relent to their powerful, forbidden attraction? Or will facing their past be too much to fight through? (978-1-63555-930-9)

Desires After Dark by MJ Williamz. When her human lover falls deathly ill, Alex, a vampire, must decide which is worse, letting her go or condemning her to everlasting life. (978-1-63555-940-8)

Her Consigliere by Carsen Taite. FBI agent Royal Scott swore an oath to uphold the law, and criminal defense attorney Siobhan Collins pledged her loyalty to the only family she's ever known, but will their love be stronger than the bonds they've vowed to others, or will their competing allegiances tear them apart? (978-1-63555-924-8)

In Our Words: Queer Stories from Black, Indigenous, and People of Color Writers. Stories Selected by Anne Shade and Edited by Victoria Villaseñor. Comprising both the renowned and emerging voices of Black, Indigenous, and People of Color authors, this thoughtfully curated collection of short stories explores the intersection of racial and queer identity. (978-1-63555-936-1)

Measure of Devotion by CF Frizzell. Disguised as her late twin brother, Catherine Samson enters the Civil War to defend the Constitution as a Union soldier, never expecting her life to be altered by a Gettysburg farmer's daughter. (978-1-63555-951-4)

Not Guilty by Brit Ryder. Claire Weaver and Emery Pearson's day jobs clash, even as their desire for each other burns, and a discreet sex-only arrangement is the only option. (978-1-63555-896-8)

Opposites Attract: Butch/Femme Romances by Meghan O'Brien, Aurora Rey & Angie Williams. Sometimes opposites really do attract. Fall in love with these butch/femme romance novellas. (978-1-63555-784-8)

Under Her Influence by Amanda Radley. On their path to #truelove, will Beth and Jemma discover that reality is even better than illusion? (978-1-63555-963-7)

Swift Vengeance by Jean Copeland, Jackie D & Erin Zak. A journalist becomes the subject of her own investigation when sudden strange, violent visions summon her to a summer retreat and into the arms of a killer's possible next victim. (978-1-63555-880-7)

Wasteland by Kristin Keppler & Allisa Bahney. Danielle Clark is fighting against the National Armed Forces and finds peace as a scavenger, until the NAF general's daughter, Katelyn Turner, shows up on her doorstep and brings the fight right back to her. (978-1-63555-935-4)

When In Doubt by VK Powell. Police officer Jeri Wylder thinks she committed a crime in the line of duty but can't remember, until details emerge pointing to a cover-up by those close to her. (978-1-63555-955-2)

A Woman to Treasure by Ali Vali. An ancient scroll isn't the only treasure Levi Montbard finds as she starts her hunt for the truth—all she has to do is prove to Yasmine Hassani that there's more to her than an adventurous soul. (978-1-63555-890-6)

Before. After. Always. by Morgan Lee Miller. Still reeling from her tragic past, Eliza Walsh has sworn off taking risks, until Blake Navarro turns her world right-side up, making her question if falling in love again is worth it. (978-1-63555-845-6)

Bet the Farm by Fiona Riley. Lauren Calloway's luxury real estate sale of the century comes to a screeching halt when dairy farm heiress, and one-night stand, Thea Boudreaux calls her bluff. (978-1-63555-731-2)

Cowgirl by Nance Sparks. The last thing Aren expects is to fall for Carol. Sharing her home is one thing, but sharing her heart means sharing the demons in her past and risking everything to keep Carol safe. (978-1-63555-877-7)

Give In to Me by Elle Spencer. Gabriela Talbot never expected to sleep with her favorite author—certainly not after the scathing review she'd given Whitney Ainsworth's latest book. (978-1-63555-910-1)